Rosie Hendry lives by the sea in Norfolk with her husband and two children. She is the author of the East End Angels series, an uplifting and heart-warming saga that follows the lives and loves of Winnie, Frankie and Bella, who all work for the London Auxiliary Ambulance Service (LAAS) during the Blitz. Listening to her father's tales of life during the Second World War sparked Rosie's interest in this period and she loves researching further, seeking out gems of real-life events which inspire her writing.

Keep up-to-date with Rosie by following her on Twitter, becoming her friend on Facebook or visiting her website:

@hendry_rosie
rosie.hendry.94
www.rosiehendry.com

Rosie HENDRY

The Mother's Day Victory

SPHERE

SPHERE

First published in Great Britain in 2022 by Sphere

1 3 5 7 9 10 8 6 4 2

A CIP catalogue record for this book
is available from the British Library.

ISBN 978-0-7515-7573-6

Typeset in Bembo by M Rules
Printed and bound in Great Britain by
Clays Ltd, Elcograf S.p.A.

Papers used by Sphere are from well-managed forests
and other responsible sources.

Sphere
An imprint of
Little, Brown Book Group
Carmelite House
50 Victoria Embankment
London EC4Y 0DZ

An Hachette UK Company
www.hachette.co.uk

www.littlebrown.co.uk

For Nanny Crimas,
who is always remembered

Chapter 1

Oxfordshire, March 1940

'I'm so sorry to have to tell you this, Anna.' Mr Jeffries rubbed the bridge of his nose, making his glasses shift up and down. 'But as of this Friday I won't have a job for you. You see, I'm being sent abroad for work . . . so I really have no choice but to send Thomas to boarding school. I'll be taking him there on Saturday morning.'

Anna stared at him for a few moments, not sure how to respond as the news settled heavily in her stomach. When he'd asked her to come to his study so that he might speak with her, she hadn't expected this – to be losing her job. And with it, her home.

'Of course I'll pay you to the end of the month, and I'll give you an extra month's salary in lieu of notice,' Mr Jeffries added. 'I really am very sorry about this. Thomas has adored having you as his governess and I know it will be a wrench for him to say goodbye, but I really have no option since I don't know how long I'll be away for. At least he'll be able to stay on at school during the holidays if I'm not back. I'm sure you'll be able to get another job easily.' He smiled reassuringly. 'I will write you an excellent reference, which of course you fully deserve.'

Anna nodded. What could she say? His reasons were sound: he was in an impossible situation – a widower with no family who could take his son in – so sending him to a boarding school was the only choice. She had no idea what Mr Jeffries' job was exactly, only that it had something to do with the War Office and was important.

'I understand.' She dredged up a smile. 'I will miss Thomas very much; he has been a delight to teach.'

'You've been an excellent teacher. He's really blossomed under your tutelage, Anna. I only wish you could carry on, but it appears the war has other plans for me, and unfortunately they affect Thomas and yourself too.' Mr Jeffries sighed. 'I'll speak to Thomas about it later.'

He picked up his pen ready to return his attention to the pile of papers on his desk, signalling that their meeting was over.

Leaving his study, Anna retreated into the hall and stood for a moment as she absorbed what had just happened. An urge to weep at the suddenness of losing the job she loved threatened to overwhelm her. She'd been very happy here, the happiest she'd been since she came to England, and now it was ending.

What would happen to her? Where would she go?

Anna sniffed back her tears, telling herself there was no

point in crying because it wouldn't change anything. She had no choice but to accept what was happening and carry on with her job while she still had one.

Turning to go upstairs to the schoolroom where she'd left Thomas working on a story, she caught sight of her reflection in the large mirror hanging on the wall and halted. Her brown eyes stared back at her, stunned and sad. Thomas mustn't see her like this, she didn't want him upset, so she pasted a smile on her face, smoothed her shoulder-length bobbed brown hair and firmly reminded herself that nothing in life lasted for ever.

At least she was *safe* here in England, unlike at home. Far worse things were happening to Jewish people like her under the scourge of Nazi rule back in Germany. Compared to that, losing her job was a minor problem. She'd find another, and a place to live; she would survive and carry on.

Her wages would buy her some much-needed time and she could write to her friend, Julia, who might have heard of suitable jobs she could apply for. She'd met Julia – who was a Quaker – soon after she'd arrived in England. They were helping refugees who'd fled their homes before the start of the war, and the two of them had become friends and kept in touch ever since.

She would be fine, this was just another bump in the road; something to tell her father about when they met again, Anna thought. She had four days left with Thomas and she was determined to make the most of them. They at least had to finish the book they were reading together.

Taking a deep breath, she lifted her chin and headed for

the schoolroom that she'd set up when she'd first come to work here last autumn. Her pupil was waiting for her and she had a job to do. For now.

As the train began to slow on its approach into Euston station, Anna stared out of the carriage window at the barrage balloons floating over London like great silver fish. She was trying to distract herself from the image in her mind of poor Thomas's distraught face when she'd left this morning. He'd been so stoic, seemingly accepting his fate, but when she'd bent down to hug him goodbye his face had crumpled and he'd sobbed in her arms. It had taken all her strength not to break down as well, but that wouldn't have helped matters.

Instead, she'd kissed his cheek and promised to write often, then picked up her suitcases and left without looking back. It was only when she'd reached the end of the road that she'd finally let her tears fall. It was all right to cry, to acknowledge her feelings, she'd reasoned, but vitally important that she carry on and keep going, moving on to whatever came next.

Arriving at the station, Anna gathered up her cases and followed the stream of passengers along the platform, many of them dressed in uniform.

'Anna!' Julia's voice rang loud and clear across the station concourse as the older woman hurried across to meet her, arms flung out for a hug.

Standing back to look at Anna, hands still resting on her arms after squeezing her tightly, Julia gave her a searching look, her eyes taking in every detail. 'You look well, dear, if a little sad, but that's to be expected after leaving a post you enjoyed so much. Come on, let's go and get some tea.'

'It is good to see you again,' Anna said as Julia took one of her suitcases and led her out of the station. On the street, the hustle and bustle of London hit her, the noise and busyness a shock after she'd become so used to the quiet of a small English town.

Looking around, she noticed that signs of a country at war were everywhere, from the strips of tape across windows to the sandbagged buildings and the white-painted edges of the pavements.

'I've had an idea of a job that might suit you,' Julia said, once they were settled at a table in a small cafe, a pot of tea between them and a small currant bun each. 'It's not something that you've done much of before, if at all, but the person you'd be working for is a good friend of mine, and would be both good to live with and work for.' She paused while she poured them both a cup of tea. 'There's no guarantee, of course, and I didn't want to write to her and enquire about the job without asking if you'd be interested.'

Anna was intrigued. 'What would I be doing?'

Julia's eyes met hers. 'Gardening.'

'*Gardening!*' Anna hadn't expected that. Julia was quite right – it wasn't something she had experience of, having lived in an apartment in Berlin with her father. They hadn't had a garden, so growing things hadn't been part of her life, although she'd always enjoyed walking in the city's parks and gardens when that was still allowed.

5

'Growing vegetables and fruit, to be more precise. Not the tending-roses sort of gardening. My friend, Thea, moved back to live in her home village in Norfolk last year, and she's started to grow fruit and veg, both to eat and to sell to earn money, but with her nephew going off to train for the Friends Ambulance Unit, she'll be losing her help,' Julia explained. 'I know it's not what you're used to, but I honestly think it would be good for you. Thea's a lovely person who'll welcome you with open arms and make you part of her extended family in no time!' Her eyes met Anna's. 'Of course, it's up to you. If you think that gardening is something you really don't want to do then we'll find something else. Though I'm afraid it might be domestic work rather than teaching.'

The thought of going back to domestic work and being a servant sent an uncomfortable shiver through Anna. She'd already experienced that and wasn't keen to repeat it.

When she'd first come to England in early 1939, it had been on a domestic permit, having found a job working as a servant for an old couple in Richmond, but the experience had been far worse than she'd ever expected. She'd been made to do the work of two servants *and* a cook, and if she struggled to get things done on time their refrain was always, *If it's too much for you, we could always send you back to Hitler.*

Thankfully, Julia had come to the rescue and found her the job teaching Thomas, which was far more suited to her skills and was what she loved doing. She'd been a second-ary school languages teacher back in Germany, before the Nazis' regulations against Jewish people had stripped her of her job too. Gardening might not be something she was used to, but it had to be better than working as a domestic servant, and if it was for someone Julia considered a good person, then it was worth a try.

'All right, I will try it if your friend is willing, but you must tell her that I do not have any gardening experience. I will need to be shown what to do, but I am a quick learner and will work hard.'

'I'm sure you'll be fine with Thea. I'd go and help her myself if I didn't have other work lined up. I'll be leaving London soon to work in a Quaker evacuation hostel for the elderly.' Julia took a sip of tea. 'So, I'll write to her tonight and we'll see what she says. Let's enjoy our tea and buns and then I'll take you back to my house and get you settled in.'

Anna smiled at her friend. 'Thank you. I really appreciate your help.'

'You know I'm glad to do it. I only wish that it hadn't been necessary for you and so many others to flee your homeland.' Julia picked up her teacup and took a sip. 'It's more important than ever to help each other.' She paused for a moment, before gently asking, 'Have you heard any news from your father?'

Anna shook her head. 'Nothing, not since he was arrested by the Nazis in October. His friend, Uncle Ludo, wrote and told me what had happened. He had to send it through a friend in Holland . . . I have not heard anything since.' Her eyes filled with tears.

Julia reached across and patted her hand. 'Don't give up hope, my dear.'

Anna nodded and did her best to smile. She was becoming quite the expert in hoping these days. For now, it was all she could do. The fate of her father was out of her hands and with those who would wish him harm.

Chapter 2

Norfolk

'Are you excited about tomorrow?' Thea Thornton asked her nephew, Edwin, as they shooed the last of the stragglers into the hen coop. She peeped in at the chickens who'd already taken themselves off to bed and were now sitting happily on their perches, feet tucked away out of sight under fluffed-out feathers. Satisfied that everything was as it should be, she closed the door securely, not wanting to lose any to the local foxes.

'Yes, but nervous as well,' Edwin admitted. 'I've been waiting to get started and now it's almost here it feels ...' he shrugged.

'You're moving to a new place and doing something you've never done before, so it's only natural to feel like that.' Thea linked her arm through his as they left the orchard to head back to Rookery House. 'I felt the same when I left to drive ambulances in France. It was a big step, but I never regretted it.'

She was very proud of Edwin – he'd stuck to his principles when he'd registered as a conscientious objector last autumn, in spite of what it had cost him personally. He'd since been thrown out of his home by his father, Victor, and had lost his job as well, since Victor was also his boss. She'd gladly given him a job and a home, and it had been a joy to work alongside him for the past few months. She was really going to miss him when he left tomorrow to start training for the Friends Ambulance Unit.

'You will keep an eye on Ma for me, won't you?' Edwin's breath plumed in the cold air as the temperature dropped along with the sun.

Thea nodded. 'I always do, don't worry.' Keeping an eye on her sister, Prue, was one of the reasons why she'd moved back to Great Plumstead last year, as well as to buy Rookery House, the home of her dreams, which she'd wanted to live in since she was a small girl.

Hopefully, Prue would be waiting for them in the house, along with their other sister, Lizzie, and the rest of the family, for Edwin's surprise leaving party. They couldn't let him go without some sort of celebration to send him on his way.

'I'm going to miss this place.' Edwin looked around at the garden. 'I've really enjoyed working here and being outside in the fresh air instead of stuck in Father's shop. Now I'm going to miss the start of the growing season and the cow arriving next month.'

'You've been a big help; I'd never have got this much

work done on my own.' Thea glanced at the large, freshly dug vegetable beds which Edwin had prepared for the coming year and were now ready for planting. 'You'll get to meet our cow when you come home again, and I'll tell you all about her and how everything's going in my letters.'

Thea was looking forward to expanding what they produced here with the arrival of a house cow next month, which her brother, Reuben, had arranged. It meant that they would be self-sufficient in milk, butter and cheese. It was a pity Edwin wouldn't be here to see her arrive; he'd worked hard on preparing the byre for her.

'Will you be able to manage all this on your own?'

'Of course, and I can get more help if I need it,' Thea reassured him. 'Marianne and Hettie said they'll pitch in too. You've already done the hardest work doing the digging. We'll get to sow the seeds and see them grow.'

Secretly, Thea *was* concerned with how she would manage her new enterprise without Edwin's assistance, but she wasn't going to admit that to him. It didn't help that she'd recently joined the Women's Voluntary Service and was doing regular shifts in one of their mobile canteens. She enjoyed it very much and wanted to do more for the war effort, but it did take her away from the work that needed doing in the garden.

Marianne and Hettie had offered to help her, but realistically what they'd be able to manage was limited. Marianne had a young baby, Emily, to look after as well as doing her dressmaking work – she'd been evacuated from London last September as an expectant mother and billeted with Thea. Hettie – who'd come to live with Thea after she'd retired from her job as cook at Great Plumstead Hall, having been a close friend of Thea's mother, and in turn with Thea as she grew up – was busy in the house, and at sixty years old, was less energetic than twenty-year-old Edwin. She'd see how they got on, but would be getting extra help if necessary.

When they reached the house, they went through the door leading into the scullery and took off their outside boots. Thea made sure to spend more time than usual washing and drying her hands, so that Edwin would be the first to go through the connecting door into the kitchen. He did so, to be greeted by a burst of cheering and clapping that signalled the start of his leaving party.

Following behind him, Thea smiled at the sight of Edwin being tightly hugged by her sister, Lizzie, who'd arrived here from Norwich, and his own sister, sixteen-year-old Alice. Thea's brother Reuben's dog, Bess, danced around them, nudging at Edwin's leg, eager to be included.

The kitchen looked warm and inviting, with the soft glow of the oil lamps and the decorations that had been put up by Hettie and Marianne this afternoon. Bunting made from string and triangles of newspaper hung around the kitchen walls, and a feast of Hettie's delicious cooking was spread out across the table for them all to enjoy. Edwin's final night here at Rookery House was going to be filled with fun, laughter and good company, spent with all those who were important to him – with the exception of his father, Victor, who Edwin had had nothing to do with since he'd thrown him out, and his elder brother, Jack, who was away serving with the British Expeditionary Force somewhere in France.

Sitting around the large kitchen table a little while later, everybody full of good food, Thea held up her glass of blackberry wine to propose a toast. 'We wish you every success in your new role. To Edwin and all the people that he helps.'

'To Edwin!' everyone chorused, raising their glasses in the air, then sipping at the wine, which was best drunk with caution as it packed a powerful punch.

Edwin smiled, his face glowing with happiness. 'Thank you. I'm going to miss you all very much, but I'm excited about finally being able to start my training and do my bit, my way.'

'Hear, hear!' Hettie cheered, her cheeks rosy, her blue eyes bright behind her round glasses, no doubt the effects of her potent homemade wine combined with the emotion of the occasion. 'Make sure you write to us often and let us know how you're getting on.'

'I promise.' Edwin put his arm around Hettie's shoulders as she was sitting next to him. 'As often as I can.'

They were all going to miss him, Thea thought. She glanced across at her sister Prue. Edwin's mother was smiling at her son, but Thea could tell that she was wishing he wasn't leaving. No doubt she'd be worrying about him and, knowing Prue, would channel that into working hard to help others, keeping herself so busy that it distracted her from fretting about her children.

At the far end of the table, Reuben looked thoughtful, perhaps remembering the night before he'd gone off to join the army during the Great War. He and Edwin were close, even more so since the young man had come to live

13

here. Reuben lived in the garden right by the orchard, in an old railway carriage that he'd converted into a home, and the two of them would often spend evenings chatting over a game of draughts. When Reuben had gone off to war no one had imagined that the next generation of young men would be having to do the same thing again just over twenty years later. At least in Edwin's case he wouldn't be fighting on the front line, but going to work for the FAU wasn't an easy option. He'd be faced with sights that no one would ever want to see, and might well be sent into fighting zones to rescue injured soldiers. He really was as brave as any soldier. Going against the flow to stand up for his beliefs as a conscientious objector hadn't been easy, and the path he was choosing to take wouldn't shield him from the horrors of war. Everyone sitting around the table was immensely proud of Edwin and wished him nothing but happiness and a safe return, but Thea knew all too well there were no guarantees in wartime.

Chapter 3

Going to the station to wave people off was becoming a bit of a habit, Prue thought, as she waited with Edwin for his train. It was always a bittersweet time, eking out every moment she could with her sons, dreading having to say goodbye and watch them be carried away, not knowing when she'd see them again or even ... *No!* She reined her thoughts firmly in; she wouldn't even give that any consideration.

'Here it comes.' Edwin pointed to the puffs of smoke visible in the distance, as the train headed for Great Plumstead station. He turned to face Prue and smiled at her. 'This is it then, Ma.' He paused, biting his bottom lip. 'I know I'm doing the right thing and I can't wait to get started ... but the hardest thing is having to leave you and everyone else to go and do it.'

Prue reached out and took hold of his hand. 'We'll be fine. Don't worry about us, just concentrate on looking after yourself and keeping safe.' She was immensely proud of her son for wanting to help others. 'Write and let us know how you're getting on, and if you need anything I can send it on to you – even money. I know you won't be paid more than pocket money.'

'Thank you, but I won't need much. I'll get my bed and board, and what more will I need? I can borrow books from libraries and won't need to buy much more than stamps to send letters.'

'I know, but if you do just ask.' Prue glanced at the train as it slid into the station and came to a halt with a rush of steam along the platform.

Edwin threw his arms around her and squeezed her tightly. 'I'll miss you.'

'And I will miss you.' Prue closed her eyes, imprinting the feel of her son in her arms.

He picked up his suitcase and kissed her cheek before climbing into a nearby compartment, slamming the door behind him and leaning out of the window.

Prue forced herself to smile, clasping her hands tightly together in front of her, determined to send him off with a happy face rather than the tears that were threatening to fall. 'Have a good journey and remember what I said . . . if you need *anything*.'

Edwin smiled back. 'I will.'

The guard blew his whistle and Prue reached out her hand to his, grabbing his fingers as the train started to move, walking along with it a few yards until they were forced to break their hold as the train picked up speed. Edwin kept looking back at her, waving out of the open window, and she waved back, watching until the train rounded the bend and disappeared.

Prue sighed heavily. It never got any easier seeing them off.

She pulled out her handkerchief and wiped away the escaped tears, proud of herself for not letting Edwin see them. Then she turned and headed towards the exit. There, to her surprise, her sister Thea stood watching, dressed in her green WVS uniform.

Why was she here? Was there a problem? Prue hurried over to her.

'Thea, what are you doing here? I thought you were going out with the mobile canteen this morning.'

'And so I am, but there's a problem. Pat, my usual partner, is ill and can't do it today, so I wondered if you'd be able to lend a hand. It's only for a few hours, going around to some of the isolated troops. It's fun.' Thea smiled encouragingly. 'You might feel like a change today.'

Prue considered it for a moment. It would be good to do something completely different today; all she had planned was catching up on the housework. She'd thought it might be best to be alone with her thoughts and feelings, but perhaps getting out and about with Thea would be a good idea. Only there was a problem. 'But I'm not a member of the WVS, am I?'

Thea gave a shrug of her shoulders. 'No, but this is a bit of an emergency and you'd be stepping in to help. I don't think any of those in charge would mind, just this once, and you'd be doing the WVS a favour. If I have to go on my own, it's going to be a struggle to get everyone served; the troops depend on us getting out to them to bring them drinks and food, and I don't want to let them down.'

'All right then, I'll do it!'

'Excellent!' Thea put her arm around Prue's shoulders and marched her out through the station ticket office to where she'd left the mobile canteen parked.

This might be fun, Prue thought, as she climbed into the cab of the canteen, which had been converted from a delivery van. It could be just what she needed today to take her mind off things.

'Where are we heading to?' she asked as Thea started the engine.

'A searchlight detachment first, and then on to several isolated troop stations. We have a set route we do on a Monday.'

Thea pulled away smoothly to the entrance of the station yard, from where she proceeded to head out of the village. 'We serve them food and drink, as well as selling them things they find hard to get where they're stationed. We're a bit of a mobile shop as well as a canteen.'

'What else do you sell?' Prue asked.

'Things like stationery, matches, soap, stamps, candles, pencils, tea, even razor blades, as well as chocolate, cigarettes, biscuits and fruit.'

Prue nodded. 'It's quite a service you provide.'

'It helps make the troops' lives a bit easier.'

'Are you happy driving such a big vehicle?' Prue felt much higher above the road than in her little car, and the canteen was wider and clearly a very different beast to drive.

Thea glanced at her and smiled. 'Absolutely. Remember,

I drove ambulances in France. At least the roads here are smooth and not pitted with huge holes like we had there. I enjoy driving the canteen around.'

Arriving at the searchlight detachment a short while later, Prue could instantly see why the crew would appreciate a visit from the WVS canteen: they were set up in a field with no facilities of their own.

'Right, time to get the tea on and some soup as well. It will probably be a good idea to have some for sale too – it's cold today.' Thea steered the canteen in through the gateway and brought it to a halt, waving out of the window to the crew who looked delighted to see them.

Prue was impressed with the layout inside the canteen. Its design had been well thought out with cupboards fitted along each side, their tops forming a surface to work on, and large urns for boiling water and a small oven for heating up food. All available storage space was used; items of crockery were stored in slide-out drawers to keep them safe while on the move, each cup placed within its own separate little compartment so that they didn't bump against each other. One side of the canteen could open to form a serving hatch.

'What do you think?' Thea asked, passing Prue a green apron with the initials WVS embroidered in red on the chest pocket.

'It's very nice, so well organised.'

Thea laughed as she tied the strings of her own apron around her waist. 'I thought you'd like it. Everything in here must serve a purpose. Right, I'll get the water boiling for the tea, coffee and soup, if you can start setting out cups – and there are some meat pies that need to go in the oven.'

Prue did as she was asked and, fifteen minutes later, when they were ready to start serving and open the hatch, they found a queue of customers already waiting.

'Morning, ladies,' the soldier at the head of the queue said, beaming at them. 'Have you got any of those meat pies and some soup today?'

'We certainly do.' Thea took a mug and poured out a serving of tomato soup from the urn, then reached for one of the warm meat pies that had come out of the oven. 'There you are.'

Prue smiled down at the next soldier in the queue. 'What can I get for you today?'

It was a busy twenty minutes serving the searchlight crew, who clearly enjoyed the meal they provided and also stocked up on some of the goods they sold. Quickly washing up the used mugs after they'd finished, they dried them and stored them safely away ready to move on to the next stop.

'What do you think then?' Thea asked when they were back in the cab and on their way. 'Did you enjoy it?'

Prue smiled at her sister. 'I did, very much. You feel like you're making a difference to them, helping them. It can't be easy stuck out in the middle of the countryside with no proper canteen facilities of their own and miles from the nearest shop.'

'Exactly. You could always come and help again, you know.'

'But I'm not a member of the WVS,' Prue said.

Thea slowed down as they came to a junction. 'You *could* be though. There's plenty of other work that the WVS do, it's not just running mobile canteens, though you already do a lot with the WI.'

'I could always do more. I'll think about it.' *The WVS do have a rather nice uniform as well*, Prue thought, glancing at Thea's double-breasted overcoat made from grey-green tweed. Combined with the green felt hat with its red band around it, the ensemble was rather smart. It spoke volumes about the wearer – someone who was there to help as part of the war effort. Perhaps it was time for her to take on another role, too.

Chapter 4

It was almost dark by the time Thea set off to walk to Rookery House from the village station. She and Prue had taken the train back there after returning the mobile canteen to its base in Wykeham. She'd offered to drop Prue home first, but her sister had insisted on finishing the job with her and had helped her clean the canteen, leaving it ready for the next day's WVS volunteers to take out.

She suspected that her sister might well join the WVS now, as she'd clearly enjoyed herself and had quizzed her about the other things that the volunteers did as they'd driven along. With Edwin now gone and Prue's daughter, Alice, soon to be leaving school, she probably felt the need to fill her time as much as she could, keeping herself busy to avoid worrying about her absent sons – and to make up for being married to Victor. Thea worried about Prue, who she knew wasn't happy in her marriage, her face taking on a haunted look whenever anything to do with her husband

22

was mentioned. Joining the WVS would help distract her from that unhappiness.

Turning in through the gates of Rookery House, Thea was looking forward to a cup of tea to warm her up. It was cold outside, with a clear sky overhead in which pinpricks of bright stars were beginning to show, and no doubt there'd be a frost later. A mouth-watering smell of herby stew met her as she walked into the warm kitchen, where the heat from the cooking range and the soft glow from the oil lamps made for a pleasant welcome.

'How did you get on?' Hettie asked, reaching for a clean cup from the dresser and pouring her a cup of tea from the brown teapot that was huddled underneath its brightly coloured knitted tea cosy. 'Did Prue go with you?'

Thea took her cup of tea and added some milk, cradling it in her hands, glad of the warmth as it seeped into her cold fingers. 'She did.' She smiled at the older woman. It was Hettie who'd been the one to suggest getting Prue involved in the first place. 'She enjoyed herself, and I have a feeling she'll be joining, too.'

'Knowing Prue, she'll get involved with plenty of their schemes and do an excellent job. Hopefully, it'll keep her busy and stop her worrying about Jack and Edwin so much.' Hettie took the lid off the saucepan of stew, which was simmering on the top of the range, and gently placed some uncooked dumplings on the top. 'Tea won't be long, so can you give Marianne a shout – she went upstairs to change Emily. Oh, before I forget, there's a letter for you on the hall table. It came in the afternoon post.'

Thea took her cup of tea with her, stopping to collect the

letter on her way. She glanced at the writing on the front of the envelope and recognised immediately that it was from her friend Julia in London, who'd lived in the next-door flat to her for many years. They'd become good friends and had kept in touch since Thea had returned to live in Great Plumstead.

Upstairs, she tapped on the door of Marianne's bedroom.

'Come in,' Marianne called.

She went in and saw that the young woman had just finished changing her baby daughter. Emily lay on the bed kicking her legs in her long, white flannel gown and waving her delicate fingers in the air. As her blue eyes settled on Thea she gave her a gummy smile. At eight weeks old she was a delight and growing so fast.

'Hettie's just put the dumplings in to cook, so tea will be ready soon.' She reached out to Emily, who immediately wrapped her fingers tightly around one of Thea's. 'Hello, lovely. You're getting bigger by the day.' Thea smiled at Marianne. 'It's such a joy to watch her grow. I'm so glad you're still living with us.'

Marianne had married her husband Alex just a few weeks ago and could have gone to live elsewhere, but the pair of them had accepted Thea's offer to stay at Rookery House as long as they wanted. With Alex off training to be a pilot he'd been glad that Marianne and Emily could stay in a place where they felt at home, and where he knew they would be looked after.

'We love it here, don't we, Emily? If we can't be with Alex, then there's nowhere else we'd rather be.' Marianne smiled back at Thea as she reached down and picked up

Emily, who shot her hand out and grabbed a fistful of her mother's dark, wavy hair.

'Right, I'd better get changed before we have tea. I'll see you downstairs in a few minutes, then.'

In her bedroom, Thea quickly put on her normal clothes, hanging up her WVS coat and long-sleeved dress, then sat down on the chair at her dressing table and opened the letter from Julia, thinking that she'd have a quick glance through it before going down for tea. She'd expected it to be one of her friend's usual chatty letters, full of news of what she'd been doing and life in London, only this one was different – it had something to ask of her. The request sparked an immediate yes from Thea, but it might not receive the same reaction from Hettie and Marianne. Folding the letter back in its envelope, Thea put it in her pocket and went downstairs, knowing that it was only right that, since they lived here too, their opinions be taken into consideration before she made a final decision.

Thea waited until they'd finished eating, the plates cleaned of stew, dumplings, mashed potato and carrots, before she spoke about what Julia had asked of her.

'My friend Julia in London has written to me to ask if I could give a job and a home to a young woman called Anna, who could replace Edwin in the garden. Only I need to ask what you think, as it's not quite straightforward.'

'What do you mean?' Hettie asked, her blue eyes concerned behind her round glasses.

'The young woman is German. She's—'

'*German!*' Hettie pulled a face. 'What's she doing here then?'

'She's a Jewish refugee. She had to flee her home because of the way Nazis are treating Jewish people, even if they are fellow Germans. I know what I would like to do, but if I say yes, it will *only* be if you're both happy with her coming to live here as well.'

Marianne frowned. 'What must it be like to have to flee your home and leave everything you know to go to a strange country? I'm happy for her to come here, Thea. You gave me a home when I needed one, and now she needs one too. She's not the enemy, Hitler is.'

Thea nodded and smiled at her. 'Thank you. What about you, Hettie?'

'Well of course she must come!' Hettie said firmly. 'There's no question about it. I know there'll be some in this village who'll think she shouldn't be here, but we'll deal with them when the time comes.' Hettie puffed herself up in her chair like an indignant hen. 'Remember the fuss some of them made about having expectant mothers from London. Goodness knows what they'll think about having a German woman come and live in the village.'

'Then we'll just have to educate them, won't we?' Thea said. 'I'll write back to Julia tonight and tell her that Anna Weissenborn is most welcome here at Rookery House.'

Chapter 5

Anna stood waiting by the carriage door as the train slowed and came to a halt alongside the platform of Great Plumstead station. The guard had informed her that her stop was coming up next, so she'd been watching eagerly out of the window, searching the countryside for the first glimpse of the place that would become her new home. Now she'd arrived, it felt like a swarm of moths were doing circuits around the inside of her stomach. She was about to start again, for the third time since she'd come to England, and it didn't get any easier.

She took a steadying breath, opened the carriage door and stepped down onto the platform, looking around for Thea, who was supposed to meet her.

'Anna?' A cheerful-looking woman, with dark brown curly hair cut into a short jaw-length bob, a red and white polka-dot scarf tied around it, the bow on top of her head, came striding over to her.

She nodded. 'Are you Thea?'

'Yes, I am.' Thea held out her hand to her, smiling warmly. 'Welcome to Great Plumstead. I'm so glad you're coming to stay with us, and I hope you'll be very happy here.'

'Thank you. I am pleased to be here.' Anna shook her hand, instantly liking the older woman who exuded an air of warmth and friendliness.

'Let me help you with your suitcases.' Thea held out her hand to take one. 'I brought my bicycle to help carry them back to Rookery House,' she explained as they walked out through the booking hall into the station yard.

With one suitcase strapped onto the carrier on the back of the bicycle and the other balanced on top of the wicker basket and handlebars at the front, they set off walking side by side, Thea pushing the bicycle rather than riding it.

'This is the main street with all the shops,' Thea said as they passed by them. 'We'll need to register your ration book in the grocer's and butcher's, though we're lucky here in the countryside that rationing hasn't hit us as hard as people in towns, as we can supplement our rations with what we grow and forage. Turning over the gardens of Rookery House to grow more fruit and veg is helping that, and hopefully it will provide an income as well.'

'Julia told me that your nephew used to help you in the garden,' Anna said.

Thea glanced at her and nodded. 'That's right, he did a lot of the hard work over the winter, preparing new beds for planting. But he's gone to join the Friends Ambulance Unit now, so I needed someone else to help – you.'

'Even though I do not know anything about gardening! But I promise I will do my best to learn, I am a quick learner and listen to what I am told.'

Thea stopped and turned to face Anna. 'Please don't worry about not having done any gardening before. I'm learning as well and anything I don't know I ask my brother, Reuben. He keeps an eye on what I'm doing, and so far we've managed very well, which I'm sure we'll continue to do with your help.' She smiled warmly at her. 'It's a lovely job to do. I enjoy being outside, seeing the changes as things start to grow, and I hope you'll enjoy it too, although it will be a big change from what you've done so far. Everyone is looking forward to meeting you.'

'Julia told me that you live with others at Rookery House,' Anna said as they set off again.

'Yes, the house is far too big for just me, and it's nice to share it. There's Hettie, who's the retired cook from Great Plumstead Hall. I've known her all my life so she's as good as family to me – she loves to cook and of course is excellent at what she does. And there's Marianne and her baby, Emily. She's been living with us since last September after she was evacuated out here from London. Her husband's in the Royal Air Force training to be a pilot. They all live in the house with me,' Thea explained as they took a turning that led out of the village.

'Then there's my older brother, Reuben, who has his own home by the orchard, which is made from an old railway carriage. I offered him a room in the house too, but he wanted his own place and peace and quiet, and he's still close by. His wife died a couple of years ago, and with him being nearby I can keep an eye on him, although he's very independent and would hate to think I'm doing that.' She laughed. 'I daresay he's looking out for me as much as I am for him. He works on the Hall's estate so he isn't around during the daytime. I'll introduce you to him tonight. Do you have any brothers and sisters?'

Anna shook her head. 'No, it was just me, Mama and Papa, but Mama died five years ago.'

'I'm sorry to hear that. Is your father in England, too?'

'No. I am not sure where he is. The Nazis arrested him in October, a friend of his wrote and told me . . . '

Thea halted and reached out to Anna, putting her hand on her arm. 'I'm sorry, that must be so hard.'

'Yes.' Anna looked down at the ground for a few moments before glancing up and meeting Thea's bright blue eyes. 'I did not want to leave him behind to come to England, but he insisted I should get out while I had the chance, he was frightened that things would only get worse and worse for people like us. He said he would follow on . . . he tried to get out before war was declared . . . but he did not make it . . . I have not heard anything from him since he was taken.' She swallowed hard. 'I just hope he will be released and that we will be together again sometime.'

'I'm sure that knowing you're safe here in England is of great comfort to him,' Thea said gently. 'I hope that it's only a matter of time before you can be together again, and all this madness will be over.'

Anna nodded and did her best to smile. 'Until then I have learned that we just have to hope and carry on.'

Thea returned her smile. 'Yes, you're right. Please do ask me if there's anything I can do to help you, all right?'

'I will, thank you.'

'Good. Come on.' Thea set off again, pushing her bicycle. 'Hettie will be wondering where we've got to – she's baked a cake to celebrate your arrival.'

Anna liked the look of Rookery House the moment she set eyes on it. It was a little way out of the village, surrounded by fields, with a stand of tall elm trees just down the road, which Thea told her were home to rooks' nests which gave the house its name. It was built of red brick, with two bay windows sticking out either side of the front door in the middle downstairs and three windows above it on the floor above.

'We usually go in around the back,' Thea explained as she wheeled her bicycle in through the gates and headed round towards the rear of the house.

'We're home!' Thea called, opening the back door and standing aside to usher Anna inside.

Stepping into the kitchen, Anna was immediately struck by how warm and cosy the room was – and the sight of the small, plump woman with curly grey hair and bright blue eyes that twinkled behind round glasses, hurrying towards her with a warm smile on her face, made her feel very welcome.

'Hello, I'm Hettie.' The older woman held out her hand to Anna. 'Welcome to Rookery House.'

Anna shook her hand. 'Thank you, it is very nice to meet you and to be here.'

'I'll put the kettle on to boil and we'll have a cup of tea and a slice of cake.' Hettie went over to the black range that was sunk into the chimney breast at one end of the kitchen.

'Where's Marianne?' Thea asked, putting down Anna's suitcases.

'She's just taken Emily upstairs to put her down for a nap, she won't be long,' Hettie said.

'I'll give you a quick tour of the house and take you up to your bedroom,' Thea told her. 'Then we can sit down and have our tea and cake.'

'Thank you.' Anna liked what she'd seen so far of Rookery House and she was particularly looking forward to seeing her room, the place that would be her own space to rest and sleep in. It would be especially welcome tonight, for the journey from London and the inevitable anxiety over coming to a new place and meeting new people had tired her out.

'So, this is the kitchen.' Thea smiled. 'We spend most of our time in here as it's the warmest room.'

Anna looked around, liking what she saw. There was a large scrubbed wooden table in the middle of the room, standing on the floor of red quarry tiles. A deep stone sink with a hand pump was by the window that looked out over the back garden. Pretty yellow curtains with blue flowers framed it. Two dressers lined the walls, holding blue and white patterned cups and plates, which looked fresh and cheerful.

'The pantry's in here,' Thea said, opening the door at one end of the kitchen.

Anna looked inside and saw that it was a good size, its shelves lined with food, such as pickles, jam and honey.

'It's this way to the scullery and bathroom,' Thea said, leading her across the kitchen to another doorway, which led into a single-storey wing. 'We do the laundry in here.' Thea indicated the copper for heating water and a sink. There was also a mangle for squeezing the water out of washed clothes. 'We often come in and out of the garden through this way too.' She nodded to the outside door. 'Keeps muddy boots and wet coats out of the kitchen.' She walked across to the far side of the room and opened another door, stepping aside so Anna could go in. 'This is our little bit of luxury. I had it put in after I moved here last summer, otherwise we'd have been having to bathe in a tin bath in front of the range in the kitchen. And the indoor lavatory saves us having to traipse to the outside one on a cold winter's night!'

'It looks very nice.' Anna had grown up in an apartment in Berlin that had a bathroom, but she knew that not everyone was so lucky.

'I must warn you that we don't have electricity here. Some houses have it in the village, but it hadn't yet reached us out here before war was declared, and it's hardly a priority now, so we won't be getting it any time soon.' Thea gave a shrug. 'So, it's oil lamps and candles once it gets dark. I rather like it though, it's cosy. Right, I'll show you your bedroom next.'

Passing through the cosy kitchen again, Thea led Anna into a bright hallway where the afternoon light streamed in through the stained glass of the front door, splashing the black and white tiled floor with colour.

'Oh, and that's the sitting room,' Thea pointed to the

33

nearest door leading off the hall, 'and the dining room is down there.' She indicated a door on the opposite side of the hall beyond the staircase at the front of the house. 'Though we don't use it very often as it's much cosier and easier to eat in the kitchen, and Marianne often uses the table for her dressmaking commissions. She's a talented dressmaker and designer and is in demand making clothes for people in the village,' Thea explained, leading the way up the stairs, which were painted white and had a dark-red carpet runner secured with brass stair rods running down the centre.

'That's my room,' Thea pointed to a door at the front of the house, 'and Hettie's opposite. That's Marianne's,' she said, signalling to the door on the right as they walked along the landing, 'and this will be yours.'

She opened the door of a bedroom on the left at the back of the house and stepped aside to let Anna in. 'I hope you'll be comfortable.'

Anna stepped inside and loved what she saw. There was a single iron bedstead with a comfy, plump pillow and a colourful patchwork quilt, with a rag rug on the floor beside it, a chest of drawers and a small bedside table. The room smelt of lavender and beeswax polish.

She turned to Thea and smiled. 'It's lovely, thank you.'

'I'm glad you like it.' Thea walked over to the window and Anna joined her looking out. 'You've got a nice view of the back garden and meadow; we've got a cow coming soon who'll graze in there and produce milk for us.' She pointed in the other direction. 'And if you look that way, you can see the orchard where the chickens and bees are – and

Reuben's home. You'll see he's built a bit on the back of the carriage to extend it, so it's very cosy in there and the perfect size for him.'

Anna stared at the low building. Painted in a bottle-green colour, it still had the look of a railway carriage at the front, but a veranda had been added around the sides facing Rookery House. 'I have never seen a house like that before.'

'There are quite a few homes around here that are made from old railway carriages – easier than building a brick house,' Thea explained. 'You can have a look round later when Reuben comes home.'

'I would like that.'

Arriving here at Rookery House was turning out to be different from what she'd expected in so many ways, but she liked it very much. The people were friendly and the house felt welcoming and homely.

A gentle tapping on the door made them turn around, and a young woman with shoulder-length curly brown hair popped her head in.

'Hello, I heard you come up while I was putting Emily down for a nap.' She came into the room, smiling and holding out her hand to Anna. 'I'm Marianne, it's lovely to have you come and live with us.'

Anna shook her hand. 'Thank you. I am pleased to meet you.'

'Come on, we'd better go down or Hettie will be wondering where we've got to,' Thea said, heading for the door.

Downstairs in the kitchen, Hettie had set out some small plates on the table, and there was a delicious-looking cake ready to be sliced, and a brown earthenware teapot snuggled under its brightly coloured knitted cosy.

'Sit yourself down,' Hettie said, pouring out cups of tea and passing one to Anna. 'Would you like a slice of cake? It's apple and cinnamon, made with apples from our orchard.'

'Yes, please, that would be lovely.' Anna smiled at the older woman.

'I'll show you the orchard later,' Thea said, adding some milk to her tea. 'We had a good crop of apples and plums last autumn, and it's where we keep our flock of hens and my beehives.'

Anna took a bite of her cake, which was delicious. 'This is lovely.'

Hettie smiled. 'I'm glad you like it. Your English is very good. I was worried you might not be able to understand what we say – and I can't speak a word of German!'

'I love speaking English.' Anna smiled at her. 'I was a teacher of languages in Germany: I taught English and French.'

'Did you get a job in a school here?' Marianne asked.

'No, I was not able to, the only way I could come to England was with a domestic permit, so I had to get a job as a domestic worker in a house,' she explained.

'A servant!' Hettie said. 'That's a waste for someone who's a qualified teacher. Not that there's anything wrong with being a servant, I was one all my working life, but if you've got the skills to teach then that's what you should be doing.'

'I only worked as a domestic maid for a while, and then got a job as a governess to a boy called Thomas. His father is going abroad so Thomas had to go to boarding school and I came here.'

'And very welcome, too.' Thea smiled at her. 'I hope you're able to teach again one day, if you'd like to.'

'Thank you. Yes, I hope I can, I love to teach. Until then I am very happy to be here.' Anna took a sip of her tea. 'I must go to a police station to register that I am living here, where is that?'

'Wykeham's the nearest. We're going there tomorrow as it's market day, so if you come with us I can take you there,' Thea said.

'Why on earth have you got to do that?' asked Hettie. 'You're not a criminal.'

'It is fine, all enemy aliens like me have to do this.' Anna shrugged. 'It is so the authorities know where we are living. I am lucky to be here – it is a small thing to do, I do not mind.'

Hettie frowned. 'Well, I don't think it's very nice.'

'It is what I had to agree to at my tribunal because I am a category C enemy alien,' Anna explained. 'It is much worse for people who are category A or B.'

'What happens to them?' Marianne asked.

'Category A are interned straight away because they are a risk to the country. Category B are still free, but have travel restrictions and are not allowed to own a car or a camera, and Category C – like me – are no risk but still have to report to the police when they move to a new place.'

'It could be worse, then.' Hettie smiled at her.

'Yes.' Anna returned the older woman's smile. It could be a lot worse, and it certainly was back in Germany for her father and her Jewish friends, but she didn't want to spoil this welcome tea by talking about that. 'It is a small thing to do,' she repeated.

'We can do that as soon as we get to Wykeham in the morning and then you can have a look around the town,' Thea said. 'It's a busy place on market day with lots to see.'

Chapter 6

Market day in Wykeham was in full swing. Many stalls were set out in the marketplace, which was thronged with shoppers, people from surrounding villages like them as well as the local townspeople. Leaving her shopping until later, Thea headed for the police station with Anna.

'I'll introduce you to one of my sisters when we're done in here,' she said as they approached the police station. 'Prue should be manning the WI stall with Hettie.'

Hettie had come into Wykeham with them and had gone straight to the stall to take her turn selling the baked goods and produce from Great Plumstead's WI members.

'My younger sister, Lizzie, lives in Norwich. You'll get to meet her some other time.'

Thea halted outside the police station and looked at the slight young woman. Anna appeared calm, but Thea supposed that she was used to having to do this, whereas, for Thea, a sense of indignation was welling up inside. Anna should not have to subject herself to this, as if she had done something wrong, as if she were a criminal.

'I'm sorry that you have to do this every time you move somewhere new. Your tribunal decided that you're not a threat to the country, so it seems . . . ' Thea shook her head. 'Unnecessary to then keep track of you like this.'

Anna smiled at her. 'It is fine, Thea. I'm used to it, and I am grateful to be living here in England safe from the Nazis. That is what really matters. Things were much worse for me back home.'

What must it have been like for her? Thea wondered. Now wasn't the time to ask, but perhaps Anna would talk about it when they got to know her a bit better. As it was, the young woman's reaction had put Thea's feelings into perspective: they were lucky here in England not to be subjected to Nazi rule, and she desperately hoped that would never change, although Hitler might have plans for spreading his empire further, since he'd already taken over Poland and Czechoslovakia. Was England on his list of countries to eventually conquer as well? Though if it was, he'd have a challenge on his hands.

'Let's get it over with then.' Thea opened the door and ushered Anna in, following behind her.

Anna liked the busyness of the marketplace, the stalls and their brightly striped awnings making it look very cheerful despite the grey sky overhead. Women were bustling about doing their shopping, their baskets full of items bought from the stalls. Most people seemed in a good mood, often greeting people they knew and stopping to chat.

'All sorted?' Hettie asked when they arrived at the WI stall, which was well stocked with goods from vegetables and eggs to a pyramid display of jars of dark purple jam.

'Yes.' She smiled at the older woman. Anna had taken an instant liking to Hettie yesterday; with her twinkly eyes behind her round glasses, she exuded good cheer and warmth. 'The policeman was very nice.'

Hettie rolled her eyes. 'Bit of a palaver if you ask me, but now it's done you can forget about it I suppose.'

'Anna, this is my sister, Prue, she lives in Great Plumstead too,' Thea said, introducing her to one of the other women behind the stall, who'd just finished serving a customer. 'And Gloria, who was evacuated to the village with Marianne last September,' she continued.

Gloria, who was in the middle of helping a customer, gave her a beaming smile and a friendly wave.

Anna returned her smile and wave, thinking how different Gloria looked to the other women in her bright red dress and matching lipstick, her bottle-blonde hair in a pompadour hairstyle. She was like a bright, glistening jewel.

Prue smiled warmly at her and held out her hand. 'Very nice to meet you.'

'Thank you, it is nice to meet you, too.' She shook Prue's hand. Despite her having ash-blonde hair, which she wore tied back with a clip at the nape of her neck, instead of brown hair like Thea's, there was no doubt that the pair of them were sisters. They shared similar features and their eyes were the same shade of blue.

'You're taking over from my son, working with Thea. He enjoyed it very much and I hope you will too,' Prue said warmly. She was about to say something else but was distracted by a customer wanting to buy some jam. 'Excuse me.' With an apologetic smile she turned away to serve them.

'Do you want to come and help me with the shopping?' Thea asked. 'I need to get some more seeds to sow this week, and Marianne asked me to get some things from the haberdashery.'

Anna nodded. 'Yes, I'd be glad to.' She wanted to embrace this new place she'd come to. It was different from what she'd left behind in Oxfordshire, where she worked with Thomas. She'd spent most of her time there at the house, with the exception of daily walks. Here, she already felt that she was outside and doing more, mixing with others, and she liked it very much.

They were halfway across the market square when a woman dressed in a dog-toothed check jacket and skirt called out to Thea, hurrying over towards them.

'Good morning. I was hoping to see you here today.' Her gaze rested on Anna briefly before she returned her attention to Thea. 'Do you know if Marianne has any time to do an urgent commission, only I've been invited to my nephew's wedding and I would love a new outfit.'

'I'm not sure, Blanche,' Thea said. 'I'll tell her you asked and if she has time she can get in touch.'

'All right, thank you.' She nodded, and looked at Anna, her eyes appraising her. 'And who might you be? I've not met you before.'

'This is Anna, who's come to work for me, taking over from Prue's son.' Thea introduced her. 'Anna, this is Blanche Stimpson. Her husband runs the post office in Great Plumstead.'

'Pleased to meet you.' Blanche held out her hand to Anna.

'And you, too. I am Anna Weissenborn.' Anna reached out to shake Blanche's hand, but the woman had dropped hers, her face draining of colour, becoming pale to match her grey hair.

'Are you a *German*?' Blanche spat out the question.

'Yes, Anna is a refugee from Nazi persecution,' Thea explained.

Blanche took a step backwards, clutching her wicker basket to her chest. 'Are you sure you know what you're doing, Thea? She might *say* she's a refugee, but how do you know for sure? She could be a spy for all you know.'

Anna's joy at being here in this delightful place vanished. It wasn't the first time she'd been accused of being a spy, but she'd hoped things would be different here. However, clearly just being German marked her down as a possible enemy agent. If only this woman knew how far from the truth that was.

'Now look here, Blanche,' Thea said, keeping her voice low but emphasising each word in an angry tone. 'Anna is no spy, she's had to flee her country because of what's happening there. Shame on you for thinking that way.'

'So she says . . . but that might just be a story made up to hide the truth. A spy is hardly going to admit they are one, are they?' Blanche's words dripped scorn. 'You should think more carefully about who you bring to our village, Thea.' She narrowed her eyes. 'I thought you had more sense. And you can forget about that dress.' With a final glance at Anna, making her feel like she was something nasty that Blanche had discovered on the bottom of her shoe, she turned and hurried off.

Thea sighed heavily and turned to Anna. 'I'm so sorry that you had to hear that. I promise you that is not what everyone here is thinking.' She put her hand on Anna's arm. 'Blanche is narrow-minded and suspicious of anyone new, and with things how they are now . . . ' She shrugged. 'It's easy to look for someone to blame and be distrustful of, but she is wrong!'

'It is all right. I have been told it before, Blanche was not the first.' Anna smiled at Thea to reassure her. 'Many German refugees have this happen. I know I am *not* a spy, and that is what matters.'

'And I know you're not, and Hettie, Marianne, Reuben and Prue, for starters.'

Anna nodded. 'That is a good group to start with. Please do not worry, Thea, there are much worse things that can happen . . . they do in Germany . . . so I just . . . ' She shrugged. 'I carry on doing my job and ignore them.'

'You're very noble to do so. I'm not so sure I could stop myself from arguing back.'

'I am an enemy alien in another country, and glad to be here. I will not make a fuss.'

'I understand, but I'm ashamed of how Blanche behaved towards you. She is the exception rather than the rule around here.'

Anna smiled. 'We have some shopping to do for Marianne from the haberdashery, yes?'

'We do.' Thea linked her arm through Anna's. As they

resumed their walk across the market square, Anna caught sight of Blanche talking with another woman at the far side, both of them staring at her with looks of hostility on their faces. She was grateful for Thea's supporting arm and positive words; it was a horrible sensation knowing that some people thought so badly of you just because of where you came from. It was the same in Germany, only not because of her nationality, but her race.

Chapter 7

Prue stared at her reflection in the wardrobe mirror, liking what she saw. Smoothing down the front of the green herringbone weave jacket, with its nipped-in waist, she twirled from one side to the other, her matching skirt moving with her. The dark red blouse that she wore underneath the jacket went very well with the suit, giving a subtle pop of colour. In fact, the whole combination of colours suited her complexion and blonde hair very well.

Picking up the final piece of her new uniform she carefully placed it on her head, tilting the green felt hat this way and that until she found an angle that she was satisfied with. She smiled again at her reflection – she looked like a smart, capable member of the WVS, someone who could be relied upon to do her bit. She might have only just joined, but she was ready and eager to get started, and this afternoon she could do one job on the way to sorting out another.

*

'What's this then?' asked Grace Barker, who ran one of Great Plumstead's grocery shops, as Prue handed her a poster.

'The latest anti-gossip notice,' Prue explained, taking another rolled-up poster out of her basket and unravelling it to give Grace a proper look. It featured a cartoon of two women sitting having a chat, unaware that Hitler and Goering were two rows behind them listening in. The words 'You never know *who's* listening!' had been added to get the message firmly across.

'The WVS are responsible for distributing them. I've already put some up at the station and village hall. Would you be able to put one in your shop window, please?'

'Of course.' Grace looked at the poster. 'There are some people in the village who need to be reminded about the perils of gossiping!' She laughed. 'You know what they're like around here, interested in other people's business and only too happy to give an opinion on it, whether they've been asked to or not. And they love talking about the latest goings-on in the war and what's happening around here with troop movements and such.'

'Thank you,' Prue said. 'We've all got to be careful. None of us know where there might be spies – they're not going to go around looking obvious, are they?'

'Certainly not! I'll put it up straight away.' Grace took a reel of tape out from under the counter and made her way over to the window where, with Prue's help holding the poster in place, she could display it so that passers-by would be able to see it. 'How's that?'

'Perfect, thank you.'

47

'I didn't know you were a member of the WVS.' Grace smoothed down the last strip of tape and stood back. 'I must say you look very smart in your uniform; it suits you.'

'Thank you. I've only just joined, but I wanted to help out with some of the things the WVS are doing for the war effort. I'm planning to get more things set up in the village to help.'

'Well let me know when you do and I'll come along if I can, shop hours permitting of course. I'm tied to this place most of the day, but I can do things in the evening if you're having a knitting or sewing bee for the troops.'

'Don't worry, I will.' She smiled. 'I'll probably be asking you to put up more posters soon enough.'

Grace nodded. 'I'm happy to do that for you.'

At Rookery House, Prue found Thea and Anna working in the greenhouse, the pair of them busy sowing seeds into neatly labelled pots.

'Hello! Hettie told me I'd find you out here.'

Looking up from the bench where she was working, Thea's face broke into a wide smile at the sight of Prue. 'Look at you! Don't you look smart.'

'I went to Norwich and joined at the WVS office there, then I went and bought my uniform straight away.' Prue smiled. 'You know me, I was keen to get started as there's so much to be done. I was talking to one of the organisers at the office about setting up salvage collections in the village and perhaps a second-hand clothing depot. That would be really helpful for our evacuee mothers, what with their babies growing so quickly and needing bigger clothes.'

'My sister likes to keep busy,' Thea said to Anna. 'What about the WI? Are you giving that up?'

'No, of course not! I'm going to do both, I just need to be organised. Working for the WVS as well as the WI means that I can do a wider range of things, it's not a conflict of interest at all, in my opinion. I'll be able to encourage people to contribute to the work of the WVS at the WI meetings, remind them to save stuff for a salvage collection, that sort of thing. Anna, I hope that you'll come along to the WI meeting next week, you'll be very welcome.'

'Thank you,' Anna said. 'What will happen there?'

'It's going to be a first-aid demonstration and practice – a good skill to learn. Whatever we do, it's always a nice meeting and it will be a chance to meet people from the village. Hettie and Marianne always go.'

'Do you go, Thea?' Anna asked.

'I'll be here looking after baby Emily for Marianne,' Thea said. 'You should go along with Hettie and Marianne and try it.'

Anna smiled. 'All right, I will. Thank you, Prue.'

'I look forward to seeing you there.' Prue returned the young woman's smile. 'Thea, I was hoping I could come out in the mobile canteen with you again, if you need help. If your usual partner is ill again you will ask, won't you?'

Thea nodded. 'You'll be first on the list, don't worry. We made a good team the other day.'

Prue smiled. 'We certainly did, and I enjoyed it very much.' She glanced at her watch. 'Right, I'd better get going, I need to finish distributing these anti-gossip posters,' she nodded at the remaining rolled-up posters in her basket, 'before I go home to cook the tea.'

Chapter 8

Thea stirred a spoonful of honey into her porridge, glancing down at the list of jobs which lay on the table beside her. It was gratifying to see that more things were being ticked off each day, now that Anna was working alongside her in the garden. The young woman might not be experienced, but she was eager and quick to learn. Together they had got through a lot of seed sowing, and over the next few days Thea planned on catching up with everything else that needed to be done.

Across the table, Anna was tucking into her own bowl of porridge, and beside her sat Marianne, who had Emily against her shoulder and was gently patting the little girl's back to wind her after her feed.

'More tea?' Hettie said, offering the teapot.

'Please.' Thea held out her cup.

'What's the—' Hettie began, but was silenced by the ringing of the telephone out in the hall.

Who could be ringing at this time? Telephone calls at half past seven in the morning weren't the sort you got for no reason. Was there a problem?

Thea began to get up but was halted by Hettie, who was already on her feet. 'I'll get it.'

Thea glanced at Marianne, whose face had gone pale, no doubt thinking the same thing. With her husband training to be a pilot, Thea knew the young woman worried about him. She strained to hear Hettie's side of the conversation in the hall, but it was brief and gave no clue.

'They want to talk to you, Thea,' Hettie said, hurrying back into the kitchen. 'Wouldn't say what it was about.'

'Who is it?'

'They wouldn't say that either.' Hettie tutted.

Thea hurried through to the hall and picked up the receiver, uncertain about the news that awaited her. 'Hello, Thea Thornton speaking.'

'Good morning! This is Mrs Hewitt from the WVS headquarters in Norwich.' Her voice immediately conjured up a picture of a no-nonsense looking woman in Thea's mind. 'We've been asked to supply mobile canteens for an ARP exercise tomorrow and would like you to man the one stationed at the starting point.' She named the village three miles away from Great Plumstead. 'I know it's very short notice, but I'm sure you and your partner can meet this target. It's important, and one must remember that if the country is invaded we may get very little notice, so we must count this as a good chance to practise. You will of course need to have plenty of supplies on board – those taking part are going to be hungry and thirsty and very much in need of sustenance.'

This was going to be much more than their usual drive around various isolated troop posts, Thea thought. Supplying the men taking part in an exercise was a far bigger job, and the fact that only twenty-four hours' notice had been given was going to make it even more tricky, but as Mrs Hewitt said, if such a thing happened for real they wouldn't get much notice then either. This would be as much a training exercise for the WVS as for the ARP.

'Of course. We'll be there, and we'll make sure we have enough food and drinks for everyone.'

'Excellent. I have every faith in you. Good luck!' She hung up, leaving the buzzing tone in the receiver, which Thea gently replaced as her mind raced ahead with what she'd need to do in preparation for tomorrow.

Her plans for working in the garden had well and truly flown out of the window. She was going to need help with this and there was one person that she could absolutely rely on.

Picking up the receiver, she waited until the operator asked what number she wanted to be connected to. Thea told her Prue's.

Chapter 9

Reaching the end of the row, Anna stood up and bent gently backwards, rubbing her hands against the small of her back to ease the unaccustomed ache brought on by today's job of planting potatoes. Closing her eyes, she raised her face towards the sky, enjoying the warmth of the April afternoon. There was a definite feel of spring in the air, and all around the garden nature was bursting back to life after the cold winter months. She smiled as she listened to the cawing sound coming from the rookery in the tall elms where the rooks were busy at their nests, the sound oddly comforting. She sighed happily.

She'd only been here a few days, but already felt very much at home. Thea, Hettie, Marianne and Reuben had made her so welcome. Even the work she was doing was proving to be much more satisfying than she'd imagined – although it was far more physically tiring than teaching Thomas had been, and her muscles were being challenged in ways they never had been before. She was going to write to Thomas at his school tonight and tell him about what she'd been up to, and a letter to Julia too, to let her know she had settled in well and was enjoying her new gardening job. She was looking forward to sharing it with them.

'How are you getting on?'

Anna opened her eyes and saw Marianne parking Emily's pram nearby.

'Fine, just easing out my back. It is not used to so much bending!'

'I've come to give you a hand now Emily's fast asleep. With Thea having to go off and sort out the provisions for the mobile canteen for tomorrow, it looks like you'll need all the help you can get.' Marianne picked up a trowel and one of the trays of chitted potatoes, with their delicate green shoots that were ready to be planted, and joined Anna at the end of the next row. 'Hopefully, between us, we can get them all planted this afternoon.'

Anna nodded. 'I'm sure we can. Thea was worried about me falling behind without her.'

'She's worked very hard to get it ready and there's still plenty more to do.' Marianne smiled at her. 'I'm glad that you've come to work here, Anna. Having someone else working with her is a big help to Thea. Hettie and I do as much as we can, but we can't be outside in the garden all the time.'

They began to work side by side, each bending down and digging out a hole in one of the pre-marked rows and gently placing a chitted potato in it, then covering it with soil before moving on and repeating the process.

'How are you settling in?' Marianne gently placed another sprouted potato into a hole and started to fill it in. 'I know it's not easy moving to a new place and living with people you've never met before.'

Anna glanced at her. 'Good. It feels like I have been here longer than just a few days.' She smiled. 'I like it here very much – everyone is kind and friendly. It is one of the nicest places I have lived in since I came to England.'

'Yes, we're lucky to be here,' Marianne agreed. 'If I can't live with my husband, then there's nowhere else I'd rather be. Rookery House is my home now, and everyone who lives here has become family to me.'

'Where did you live before?' Anna asked as she dug another hole with a trowel.

'In London, but I come from Kent originally. I only moved to London when I was offered a job as an apprentice dressmaker. I was evacuated here last September when I was expecting Emily.'

'And now you work as a dressmaker here?'

'Yes, but not as much as I did before Emily was born. I have her to look after now, but I'm still doing some as I love it so much. Where was your first job when you came to England?'

Anna picked up her box of potatoes and shifted a little further down the row before answering. 'In Richmond. That was working for the elderly couple. Although the house was nice, they weren't!'

Marianne looked up at her, frowning. 'What happened?'

'They thought they could save money by just having one servant in place of the two they used to have. I had to run the house *and* cook as well – there was too much for me to do.' She shrugged. 'I worked very hard, but it was impossible to manage by myself, and when I asked for help they threatened to send me back to Germany for Hitler to deal with.'

Marianne gasped. 'That's horrible! What did you do?'

'I left and found another job as a governess, which was wonderful.' Anna recalled the joy at moving from such an awful job to one she loved. 'It was a pity it came to an end.'

Marianne, who'd moved herself along the row and was working close by, reached out and touched Anna's arm. 'Well you certainly won't be threatened with being sent back to Hitler here, I can promise you that. Would you like to get another teaching job in the future?'

Anna nodded. 'Yes, but in the meantime I am happy to garden and grow things. I am enjoying it even if it is making my back ache.' She laughed, rubbing her back. 'I am feeling muscles ache that I have never felt before, but being outside in nature is lovely.' She paused, listening to the sound of large bumblebees busy in the daffodils grow- ing nearby. 'I am learning things I never knew before and enjoying it very much.'

Marianne smiled at her, grateful too that she'd been given the chance to come to live and work at Rookery House.

Anna agreed with Marianne – if she couldn't be at home in Germany with her father, then life here at Rookery House really was a good place to be. But she couldn't wait to return home and be with him once again.

Chapter 10

'And he's finally got the hang of envelope corners.'

Thea glanced across at Prue, who was reading snippets from Edwin's latest letter, delivered by the postman just before they had set off to Wykeham in the mobile canteen ready for today's shift.

Now they were on their way to the railway station, which was to be their rendezvous point for the ARP exercise. Her stomach was fluttering with nerves as she worried if they'd be able to cope, so hearing about her nephew's progress at the Friends Ambulance Unit training camp was a good distraction.

'What else has he been doing?' she asked.

'More PT training runs, lectures, bandaging practice.'

'He told me in his last letter that he's been learning to drive as well, so he'll be able to drive ambulances once he's fully trained.'

'Just like you did.'

'Edwin always did like listening to tales of my ambulance driving days during the Great War, it must have rubbed off on him.' Thea smiled at Prue. 'I'm glad he's found his way.'

Prue sighed. 'If only Victor would look at it like that. Whenever I try to talk to him about Edwin, he just walks away. It's like he's wiped him out of his life.'

Victor hadn't seen his son since last autumn when they had bumped into each other in Norwich after coming out of Edwin's conscientious objector hearing. That had been a shock, and not just for her and Edwin, Prue thought, recalling the look of horror on Victor's face when he'd seen them walking along on the other side of the street towards him. It turned out that apparently he'd had to go into the city for an emergency meeting of one of his committees. Prue had asked him how the meeting went later on when he came home, but he'd been very dismissive of it; he hadn't wanted to talk about it at all. Since that unexpected brief meeting he'd made no attempt to see Edwin before he left for his training and didn't want to hear about him from Prue either.

'Well, he's a fool and the one who's losing out!' Thea had no patience with her selfish, opinionated brother-in-law. Victor's reaction to Edwin's registration as a conscientious objector last year had been disgusting. Edwin was a young man of principle and honour, and Victor should've been proud of him for standing up for what he believed in, doing his bit for the war effort in a way that suited his principles. It would be far from an easy ride – she knew that from her own experience.

'I quite agree,' Prue said. 'But let's not waste time talking about Victor. We've got a busy day ahead of us and I'd rather focus on the positives in my life, not the unpleasant bits.'

Thea threw a look at her sister, who was staring resolutely ahead. It was the first time that she'd talked about Victor in such a way; she'd always defended her choice to marry him, downplaying the unhappiness that clearly came with being married to such an unpleasant man. Perhaps the worm was beginning to turn.

'Of course. It's going to be busy, but I hope it will be enjoyable too. We make a good team in here.'

Pulling up in front of the station a short while later, Thea spotted other civil defence volunteers. The exercise had already begun; ARP wardens were directing stretcher bearers carrying casualties into a large tent that had been set up as a makeshift first-aid station.

'Right, we'd better get cracking,' she said, pulling on the handbrake and switching off the engine.

Inside the back of the canteen they got to work. Thea started heating up the urns, one for tea, another for coffee and a third for soup, while Prue busied herself putting pies and sausage rolls in the oven to warm through. Then they set out the split bread rolls that had been filled with a scraping of margarine and fish paste. There were also plenty of buns baked by some of the WVS members from Wykeham, who'd brought them to the canteen this morning before they set off. They had plenty to feed people with, but needed to get everything ready before they could open the hatch and start serving.

After setting out the cups, Thea leaned closer to the urns, willing them to hurry up and come to the boil. She tumbled tomato soup cubes into one and then made tea and coffee in the others.

'Are we nearly ready?' Prue said. 'Only I can hear mutterings out there.' She nodded outside the canteen, where voices could be heard as people were gathering, clearly ready for some refreshment. The sisters had kept the hatch down until they were fully prepared.

Thea gave a final look around to check everything was in place and ready. Once they opened for business it would be non-stop – they needed to work efficiently and have everything to hand.

She nodded. 'Looks like it. This will be different from the runs out to army outposts – no selling stamps or pens here, just food and drink, and plenty of it. Ready then?'

Prue smiled. 'Absolutely!'

Together they opened up the hatch and were met by a cheer from the waiting customers, some of whom were swathed in bandages, acting as casualties for the exercise, and had abandoned their stretchers for something to eat and drink.

'What can I get for you?' Thea asked a man who had a label that read *fractured femur* dangling from his jacket buttonhole.

'Cup of tea and a meat pie, please,' he said. 'Oh, and a bun for afters as well. I missed my breakfast this morning.'

The next few hours passed in a whirl of dishing out drinks and food. Extra water was delivered from the stationmaster's house to boil more urns of tea, coffee and soup. Food supplies dwindled as more customers arrived, some in ambulances, and Thea quickly grew used to the sight of mock casualties coming to their serving hatch. By the time the exercise was drawing to a close, they had sold out of almost all the food they'd brought. Now they had to catch up on the washing up – they'd been so busy it had been impossible to keep up with it and serve at the same time, and it was piled up on the worktops running along each side of the canteen.

'Here, let's have one of these and a cup of tea before we tackle that lot.' Thea held out the plate with the last two buns on. 'We could do with something to keep us going and I reckon we deserve a treat after being rushed off our feet.'

Sitting in the open doorway at the back of the canteen, legs swinging above the ground, they munched the buns and sipped the stewed tea and relaxed for a few minutes.

'We did a good job today,' Thea said. 'It was quite a rush, but with everything organised beforehand I think we managed really well.'

Prue nodded, chewing on a mouthful of bun. 'It makes you think though, we might have to do this for *real* one day. Today was just an exercise . . . just imagine if those casualties were real and there'd been some bombing.' She shivered. 'It's a sobering thought.'

'And precisely why we need to practise on days like this.' Thea took a sip of tea. 'We can't stop what might happen, but we can be prepared to deal with it *if* it does.'

'It's what being a member of the WVS is about – it's not just the nice uniform.' Prue nudged Thea with her elbow. 'I feel like I'm doing something really worthwhile, it gives me something to focus on and keep busy.'

Thea raised her eyebrows. 'As if you weren't busy enough before, what with the WI and the mother's day club and being billeting officer.'

Prue laughed. 'Well you know what they say, if you want something done, ask a busy woman. So come on, drink up. We've got a mountain of washing up to get through before we can go home.'

Chapter 11

Anna hadn't been into the village much since she'd come to live here in Great Plumstead and was both looking forward to and feeling uncertain about tonight's WI meeting in the village hall. After Blanche Stimpson's hostile reaction to her when they'd met on market day, Anna was worried that there might be others who would think the same. Now that they were on their way, the nearer they got the more she wanted to turn around and retreat to Rookery House.

Hettie, who was walking on one side of her, must have sensed her hesitation as she slipped her arm through Anna's.

'Don't worry, you'll be fine,' Hettie reassured her. 'Marianne was nervous her first time, weren't you?'

Marianne, who was on Anna's other side, nodded and linked her other arm so that she was firmly supported between the two women. 'Yes, people will notice you as you're new, but that happens with everybody. Just smile at them.'

It was as Marianne said. Her arrival in the hall was observed by many members, but Anna did as she'd suggested and smiled, Hettie leading her straight to some empty seats in the front row as it was time for the meeting to start. They sat down opposite the table, where she saw Prue was busy organising bits of paper in front of her.

'All right?' Hettie said softly as they settled into their seats and waited for the meeting to begin.

Anna nodded and smiled at the older woman.

'Good evening, everyone.' The very smartly dressed woman sitting next to Prue stood up, her loud voice silencing the seated audience who focused their attention on her. 'Welcome to all members and visitors. To those who don't know me, I am Mrs Baden, the president. Mrs Wilson here is my vice-president.' She nodded at Prue. 'Tonight's first-aid training could be of vital importance, so please be sure to give it your full attention.' She sat down again, her duty done.

Prue stood up and smiled at the women. 'Good evening. Tonight we're delighted to have Nurse Williams with us.' She gestured to a woman in a nurse's uniform, sitting in the front row on the opposite side of the hall from Anna. 'She's here to teach us some basic first aid which will prepare you so, in the event of attack by the enemy or even accidents in the home, you know what to do.'

She handed over to Nurse Williams, who came to stand at the front of the hall as the audience politely clapped.

'Good evening, ladies. You'll be working in pairs tonight, taking it in turns to do basic first aid to treat cuts, bleeding, broken bones and burns. By the end of the session my aim is that you will be able to deal with any of those situations with confidence. If you want to learn more then I will be running further classes here in the village hall for the next four weeks and would be very pleased if you'd sign up to take them. So ...' she looked around expectantly, 'can I have a volunteer?'

Gloria, who Anna had recognised from the WI market stall, put her hand up and was gladly accepted by Nurse Williams.

'That's Gloria,' Marianne said quietly, leaning closer to Anna as they watched the nurse slip off Gloria's high-heeled sandal and start to talk through and demonstrate how to feel for broken bones or sprain, and how to treat them. 'She was evacuated here the same time as me, and so were the other women in the front row. We all like coming to the WI and joining in with its activities in the village.'

By the time the tea break arrived, Anna felt rather like an Egyptian mummy, with her legs and arms having been bandaged by Marianne following instructions from Nurse Williams.

'How does that feel?' Marianne smiled at her.

'Firmly secure.' She laughed. 'I do not think I would be able to run away in these, but if I had a broken bone I would be quite safe until I could get to hospital.'

'That was the aim!' Marianne grinned. 'Right, let's get you out of them and we can have a cup of tea and a biscuit before it's your turn.' Marianne began to unwind the bandages, rolling them up neatly again.

Anna helped as much as she could, pleased to be enjoying herself and looking forward to putting what she'd learned from Nurse Williams into practice after the tea break.

Once Anna was free of bandages, she and Marianne joined the queue for refreshments. While they stood waiting, Anna became aware that she was being watched by a group of women sitting together across the other side of the hall. In the middle of them was Blanche, and they were giving her unfriendly glances and making her feel uncomfortable. She tried her best to ignore them, and once she'd got her cup of tea followed Marianne over to some empty seats and did her best to focus on what she'd learned so far.

She'd almost finished her tea when the general hubbub of the members chatting was broken by a loud, indignant '*No!*' which immediately silenced the women, all of them turning to look where it had come from.

It was Hettie who'd said it. She was standing by Blanche's group with a tray in her hands as she'd been going around collecting used teacups.

'Listen to yourselves, you should be ashamed!' Hettie's voice rang out loud and clear in the silent hall, the small woman seeming to have puffed herself up with indignation. 'You have *no* idea, so don't you *dare* go pointing fingers about things you know nothing about.'

'What on earth is going on?' Prue went hurrying over from where she'd been talking to the WI's president at the front of the hall.

'This lot should be ashamed of themselves for what they're thinking and saying.' Hettie's cheeks were flushed.

'And what exactly have they said?' Prue asked.

'Nothing, let's just forget it,' one of the women said, while most of the group looked embarrassed, but not

Blanche, Anna noticed. She sat with her arms firmly folded across her chest, an obstinate look on her face.

'No, if something like this is left to fester it will only get worse.' Hettie glanced across at Anna. 'I'm sorry to say that these ill-informed women are prejudiced and being narrow-minded through their ignorance, and if they aren't taught the truth they'll just carry on thinking the way they do and spreading wicked lies.'

Anna felt sick. She knew what Hettie was hinting at from the few words she'd heard. The women clearly thought she was here in England to spy for the Nazis.

'Come with me, please.' Prue put her arm through Hettie's and led her over to where the president was sitting. While the three of them spoke together in a huddle, the room erupted into loud chatter as the women discussed what had happened.

Anna felt a hand on her arm. 'Are you all right? This sort of thing doesn't usually happen at WI meetings,' Marianne said.

She nodded. 'I think it is probably best if I go back to Rookery House.' She stood up to leave, but was halted by the arrival of Prue and Hettie.

'Did you understand what that was about?' Prue asked.

Anna nodded. 'I think so. I heard a few words and they were looking at me a lot ... and I met Blanche at the market in Wykeham, she told me what she thought of me then.'

Hettie's face went white. 'You never said. Why didn't you tell me?'

'I did not want to make a fuss. It was not the first time

it has happened to me since I came to England. I wanted to forget about it. I asked Thea not to tell anyone as she was with me.'

'Thea was there!' Hettie frowned. 'What did she say?'

'She was angry with Blanche and told her what she thought.'

'I'm glad to hear it. But it doesn't make it right, even if it's happened before.' Hettie's blue eyes were bright behind her glasses. 'And we don't want talk or thoughts like that here in this village, and definitely not in our WI!'

'It is all right, I will go home. I am not going to cause trouble, do not worry.'

'No, please don't go!' Prue reached out and took hold of Anna's hand. 'I'm so sorry that you've experienced this before, especially since you came to live here – and from our WI members too! But it's only a few women and, if you're willing, I'd like to take this opportunity to educate the ignorant about their foolish beliefs. We can turn this around – use it as a chance to set things right. Only if you feel you can – I understand if you'd rather not. But with your teaching experience I think you could help them understand why you came to England, what life was like for you in Germany and how it was so bad that it made you want to leave. I could ask you questions, and your answers would educate us all far better than any news report or newspaper article ever could.' Prue paused for a moment. 'I am so very sorry that there are people here who automatically think that because you're German you have the same values and beliefs as those we're fighting against.'

Hettie snorted. 'It's *them* who should be sorry.' She

turned and glared at the women, who had been watching what was going on but quickly looked away.

Anna considered this for a minute. It wasn't the first time she'd encountered English people who'd thought that just because she was a German then she was a Nazi, or a spy here to help the enemy. Though she was a fellow country-woman, the Nazis regarded people like her as the enemy just because she was Jewish. Perhaps it was time to start doing something about it, to educate those who were ignorant of what had happened to people like her back home.

'Yes, I'll do it.'

Prue nodded, smiling at her. 'Thank you.'

Standing at the front of the hall a few minutes later, with Prue beside her, Anna glanced at Hettie and Marianne sitting in the front row, both of whom smiled encouragingly at her. Ignoring the thumping of her heart, which seemed to her so loud that the audience must be able to hear it too, she reminded herself that ignorance was part of the reason that people were prejudiced. They didn't know, they didn't understand, and that could happen anywhere, especially in small rural villages like this one. If she changed the blink-ered opinion of only one person here tonight, then it would be worth doing.

Prue clapped her hands and the hall fell silent as more than thirty pairs of eyes looked in their direction.

'Before we carry on with our first-aid practice, we need to remember what it is that we are fighting for; why we are at war with Hitler and his hideous Nazi party. We are very fortunate to have someone here who can tell us from first-hand experience, educate us about what's going on out there, because there are enough problems without adding to them because of prejudice and ignorance.' Prue looked at Anna and smiled. 'Some of you may have already met Anna, who's working for my sister and living at Rookery House. Anna is German and she came to England as a refugee from Nazi oppression because she is Jewish.' She paused, looking around at the women, her gaze settling on the group who Hettie had been so cross with, before turning her attention back to Anna.

'Can you tell us, when did you come to England?'

'In February 1939. I managed to get a domestic permit and found a job as a maid.' Anna's voice came out shakily at first, but she pushed herself on. 'I had to send many letters to employment agencies, newspapers and other people to find that job. It was not easy.'

'Did you work as a maid in Germany?' Prue asked.

Anna shook her head. 'No, I was a teacher. I taught languages – French and English – but the only way to get a job here was to work as a domestic servant.'

There were mutterings from several of the women who looked at her in sympathy.

'So why did you want to leave Germany?'

Anna bit her bottom lip, memories and feelings of those difficult months before she'd left flooding into her mind. She took a steadying breath and began, 'I left because life was getting more and more difficult for Jewish people under the Nazis' rules. After Hitler came to power, our lives started to change bit by bit. We were not allowed to go to parks, restaurants or swimming pools, then we were banned from having bicycles, not permitted to go to the theatre, concerts or exhibitions. I lost my job as a teacher, then on Kristallnacht in November 1938 Jews started being murdered, synagogues were burnt, shop windows broken.' She sighed. 'My father was insistent that I get out ... he tried to leave too but had not found a job by the time the war started. Without a job to come to, he couldn't get a permit to come here. He was arrested by the Nazis in October ... and I do not know where he is now.' Her voice cracked.

Prue took hold of her hand and squeezed it gently. 'Wherever he is I'm sure it will be a comfort to him knowing that you are safe here in England.'

A woman sitting in the second row put up her hand to ask a question. 'What happened if you didn't stick to the rules? It seems ridiculous to ban someone from going to a park or riding a bicycle just because they're Jewish.'

Many women nodded in agreement.

'I know, but Hitler is so against us that he is restricting our lives, and anyone who opposes him or ignores the rules is soon in trouble. The Nazis encouraged people that were once our friends to turn against us. I fear it will only get worse for the Jewish people in Germany and Austria, and anywhere the Nazis are in charge. I hope they never come here.'

'So do we. If they try, we'll put up a fight!' Hettie said. 'Even if I have to fight them with my rolling pin!'

'Hear, hear!' a woman called from the back of the room.

Anna smiled. 'I might be German, but I promise you that I am no spy, no supporter of Hitler and what he is doing. I am his enemy and want him defeated as much as you do, probably more because of what he has done to my family, friends and country. I am grateful to be here and to have found a home and work with Thea, Hettie and Marianne.'

Hettie and Marianne stood up and started clapping and were quickly joined by every other woman in the room, including those that had made comments about Anna earlier. Even Blanche was standing, clapping loudly.

Sudden tears smarted in Anna's eyes and she smiled and nodded back at the women.

'Well done.' Prue put her arm around Anna's shoulders. 'You have educated these women, and that will filter through to their families as well.'

Anna was finishing the bandaging on Marianne's arm a short while later when she became aware of several women standing watching her. She stopped and looked up at them, realising that they were the group who had watched her with hostility during the tea break.

'We owe you an apology,' said Blanche, who was clearly their leader. 'And *especially* me, for what I thought and said to you on market day. It was wrong, and now I've heard what happened to you, I, and we . . . ' she indicated the rest of the group with her hand, 'know better. Thank you for sharing your story. We really had no idea what was going on in Germany in the name of Hitler's ridiculous rules. You are very welcome here.'

'We're very sorry,' the other women chorused.

'Thank you.' Anna smiled at them. 'When people know the truth, they can understand. I am happy to come and live and work here, and appreciate your welcome.'

Chapter 12

'I must say, you dealt with that unpleasant situation very well, Prue,' Mrs Baden said as the last of the members went out of the door, leaving just the committee behind in the village hall to go through a few items that needed to be arranged before their next meeting.

'It was very diplomatic and put those women who were making comments about Anna to shame,' the secretary added. 'It educated all of us, and I don't think there was a woman in this hall who wouldn't be prepared to do her bit if we were invaded, to stop such horrors happening here.'

'Absolutely!' Mrs Baden added. 'Let it not be said that WI meetings in Great Plumstead shy away from educating women in different ways. Although,' she fixed her eyes on Prue, 'I do hope you're not taking on too much with your new role working for the WVS, as well as your role here on the committee. I would hate to lose you, Prue, you're an important member of this institute.'

Prue smiled reassuringly at her – she'd been expecting something like this. 'Not at all. The WI *and* the WVS both do such good work for the war effort and the community. There's so much to be done and by being in both I can do more. I really don't want to have to choose between them.'

Mrs Baden nodded. 'I understand.'

'And I hope you didn't mind me promoting the WVS salvage collection at the end of tonight's meeting?' Prue asked.

She'd slipped in the latest news about the collections she was organising in the village when she'd given out the notices at the end of the meeting, along with the latest information about the seeds available at a special price for the WI members' gardens and the rota for working on the allotments that they'd been given. She didn't feel there should be a border between what the two organisations did, because it was all for the greater good.

'Not at all.' Mrs Baden smiled. 'I'll make sure I have my paper ready for collection when you come around. Right, let's get on with sorting out what needs to be done for next time.'

Chapter 13

Thea shook the straw, scattering it evenly across the floor of the byre that Edwin had finished preparing not long before he'd left for his training. The walls were painted with whitewash and there was a manger fixed to one of them that she'd already filled with hay. Soon this would become the night-time home and milking parlour of Rookery House's newest resident. The thought of the cow's arrival made Thea feel like a child on Christmas morning again, bubbling with excitement and anticipation. Her grandparents had kept a house cow and she'd often helped with it, learning how to milk by hand and make butter and cheese from the cream with her grandmother. She'd wanted to have a cow of her own when she was older, but with her life taking her to London it had been impossible. Now, moving back here to Norfolk, and with Rookery House having enough land to keep a cow, her long-held dream was about to come true, and with rationing in full force it would be a huge help.

With a final look round to check that everything was ready, Thea went out to wait for Reuben. He would be bringing the cow, who she'd decided to name Primrose, home from where he worked on one of the farms on the estate.

Reaching the greenhouse, where Anna was busy sowing another batch of dwarf bean seeds so that they'd have them ready to pick over several months, she popped her head in the doorway.

'Reuben should be here soon with Primrose. Do you want to come and wait for them by the gate with me?'

Anna smiled at her. 'Yes, I would like that. I never thought I would be doing something like this when I came to England.'

Thea laughed. 'Well I suppose it *is* quite unusual, but then I've never been one to do what everybody else does. I like to follow my own path in life and do things I enjoy.'

She thought about how her innate desire to go her own way and not be afraid to do things differently had worked out well for her. She'd decided to go and live in London after the Great War and start her own business: a catering company that had filled the gap she'd spotted when she'd been working in a boring office job. She'd noticed that other workers like her struggled to find somewhere to buy an affordable, decent meal in their dinner hour without having to pay the higher prices of cafes and restaurants, and from that her mobile catering business had been born. It had been a great success, so when she'd been ready to come back to live here and had heard that Rookery House was for sale, selling her business had allowed her to buy her dream home. And it meant that she could fulfil other dreams that she'd had since childhood too.

They'd just reached the gateway and stood peering down the lane in the direction of the farm when Reuben appeared around the corner, Primrose plodding along at his side, his dog Bess on the other.

The cow looked quite content to have left her home, and stopped occasionally to grab a mouthful of grass from one of the verges, which were growing well in April's warmer weather.

'Oh, she's such a pretty cow,' Anna said. 'I've not seen one like her before.'

Thea smiled at her. 'She's a Jersey. The breed originates in the Channel Islands and they give very creamy milk, which is good for making butter and cheese, and they're also very pretty cows.'

Primrose was toffee-coloured, the fur under her neck and down to her belly blending into a cream colour. Her black nose was rimmed with a white muzzle, her big brown eyes fringed with long lashes. Dainty and pretty, she belonged to the movie-star looking breed of cow.

'Here she is.' Reuben smiled broadly as they came to a halt and he stroked Primrose's flank. 'She was quite happy to come with me. You can take over from here.' He held out to Thea the end of the halter he'd been leading Primrose with.

'Thank you.' Thea took hold and, standing by Primrose, gently stroked her soft, velvety ears. She'd already met her when she went to the farm to choose a cow and had been taken by her gentle nature. 'Everything's ready for her, we'll put her in the meadow for the rest of the day so she can graze and then she can come into her byre at milking time.'

'I'll come back then to help you,' Reuben said, as Thea began to lead Primrose in through the gates of Rookery House and round through the back garden towards her meadow.

'I'll open the gate.' Anna hurried on ahead of them.

With Primrose safely in the meadow, already grazing happily on the fresh grass, Thea leaned on the gate watching her, a wide smile on her face. 'She's a real beauty.'

Reuben nodded. 'Feels right to have a cow here on the land, and you've got a good one there.'

'Is she here?' a voice called.

Thea turned around to see Hettie coming towards them with Marianne, who was pushing Emily in the pram.

Thea smiled at her. 'Come and see.'

Hettie looked at Primrose for a few moments and nodded. 'She looks lovely, and you've got her not a moment too soon.' She frowned. 'It's just come on the wireless that Hitler's troops have invaded Denmark and Norway, and if the Danes can't fight them off, there'll be no more Danish butter or bacon to be had for us.'

Thea sighed. This news wasn't altogether unexpected from the way that Hitler was throwing his weight around, taking over other countries as he saw fit. But the obvious question was, where would it all lead? What country was next on his list?

'Perhaps they'll be able to fight them off, maybe we'll send in troops to help.' She looked at her brother, who didn't appear convinced by her words.

'They'll be lucky if they can get rid of them, Hitler's got

a much bigger army than Denmark. Even if we send troops to help, the enemy will have the advantage.' Reuben took off his cap and scratched his head.

Thea didn't want to think about that right now. There was nothing she could do to change what was happening, she only hoped the Danes would be able to fight off the invaders. What she could do was enjoy what they had here at Rookery House, and the arrival of Primrose. Her milk would help to bolster them from the effects of wartime and its rationing.

'Right, I'll be back later to help you with the milking,' Reuben said. He patted her shoulder and left with Bess trotting at his heels as she always did.

'That's it. You've got it!' Reuben said quietly from behind her.

Thea sat close by Primrose's hind quarters while she milked her, the cow contentedly munching on some hay from her manger. It had been a long time since she'd milked a cow, but somewhere in her mind the memory of what to do and how it felt had quickly returned to her. Now she had settled into a steady rhythm, the jets of milk squirting into the metal pail, where a creamy froth floated on top.

'I was worried I'd forgotten how to do it,' Thea said over her shoulder. 'But I haven't. Though my fingers are beginning to ache a bit – they're not used to this motion.'

'Do you want me to take over?' Reuben asked.

'No, I'll be fine, I need to get used to it.' Thea knew her brother would milk the cow much faster as he was used to doing it on the farm where he worked, but she wanted to be independent. Primrose was her responsibility and she needed to get used to that from the start.

When she'd finally finished, after stripping each quarter of the udder out, Thea stood carefully and pulled the pail of milk away from Primrose's hind legs.

'It's beautifully creamy milk. Hettie's looking forward to making butter and cheese with it.'

'It'll be much in demand around here,' Reuben said.

'I hope so, there'll be more than we can use so I'm planning on selling some. Primrose will be earning her keep.' Thea smiled at her brother. 'Come on, let's go and have our first cup of cocoa made with home-grown milk.'

Chapter 14

Anna kicked off her boots in the scullery and stood them tidily to the side, shrugged off her coat and hung it on a hook before giving her hands a thorough wash. She'd been cleaning out Primrose's stall and now it was ready for the afternoon milking. It was a week since the cow had arrived at Rookery House and she'd settled in well; Anna enjoyed helping to look after her and had even started learning to milk her. Her next job was to do some more seed sowing in the greenhouse, but before that she needed both a tea break and a chance to warm up, as there was a cold April wind slicing across the Norfolk countryside today, the sky heavy with grey clouds that threatened rain.

The warmth of the kitchen was most welcome after the cold outside. Anna pushed the full kettle onto the hot plate on top of the range and lingered beside it while she waited for it to come to the boil, holding her hands out to let the heat revive them, her fingers cold despite wearing gloves. A hot cup of tea would help to warm her up from the inside too.

It was just her here this afternoon – Marianne and Hettie were at the day club in the village, and Thea out on the WVS mobile canteen. Anna didn't bother adding fresh tea leaves to the pot – with tea on the ration they tried to eke the leaves out as much as they could. Leaving it to steep, she fetched the jug of milk from the cold slab in the pantry and a clean cup from the dresser, and was about to pour herself some tea when the letterbox rattled in the hall signalling the arrival of the afternoon post.

Anna hurried through in case there was anything for her. She'd written to her friend Julia again last week and had been expecting a reply. There was just one envelope lying on the mat, and when she picked it up and turned it over she gasped.

It was for her. Sent from Holland with its Dutch stamp.

Was it from her father? Whoever it was from had written to her previous address, and it had been redirected here – the neatly typed words crossed out by the tenants who rented Mr Jeffries' house while he was away, and Rookery House's address written on the envelope instead.

With her heart thumping hard, she tore the envelope open and unfolded the single sheet of paper, immediately seeing that it wasn't her father's handwriting, but from his friend, Ludo. It was dated 23 January 1940.

Dearest Anna, she read in German.
    I'm so very sorry to have to tell you that your father died early this morning.

She gasped, putting her hand over her mouth. No! No . . . she didn't want to read on but was compelled to know more.

He was eventually released by the Nazis last week, but was in a very bad way, very thin and clearly unwell. I had him brought back here to stay with me as his apartment had been confiscated and Dr Cohen and I did everything we could for him, but he was too ill to go on.

Anna let out a wail, imagining what her father must have gone through at the hands of the Nazis. He'd been taken in a healthy man and come out broken, battered and dangerously ill. What had they done to him?

Before he died, he was most anxious that I get word to you and tell you that he'd been freed, and that knowing you were safe in England was what had kept him going in captivity – it gave him great comfort. His worst fear was that the Nazis might have hurt you if you'd stayed here in Berlin, so getting you to safety had been his priority.

He spoke of how immensely proud of you he was and how much he loved you – with all his heart. He died very peacefully, I held his hand and promised him that I would tell you and be there to help you in the future if you need me to, God willing.

Your father was buried in the Jewish cemetery, beside your mother, as he wished to be.

I know this news will come as a shock and bring you much pain, and I wish that it had never been necessary to have to break it to you.

I am sending this via my friend in Holland. I suspect it
may take some time to reach you, but it is the only way I
can contact you now.
Look after yourself.
Fondest regards,
Ludo

Anna slumped down onto the cold tiles, elbows on her
bent knees, and howled, her tears dripping down to form
a wet patch on the legs of her dungarees.

Her father was dead. As good as killed by the Nazis. They
might not have given him the final blow, but they had left him
with a body so broken and weakened that it couldn't go on.

Was that why they'd finally released him? To let him die
somewhere else rather than have the bother of burying him?

The thought that her father had died almost three
months ago, and that she'd known nothing about it, hurt
more than she thought was possible.

Shouldn't she have known, have sensed that he was no
longer alive?

A stab of guilt hit her in the heart, left her reeling with
the news, but her head stepped in and reminded her that she
couldn't possibly have known. The fact that she hadn't been
there with him at the end was hard to bear, that she hadn't
been the one holding his hand as he died, but he'd wanted
her to be free, insisted that she come to England, and Ludo's
letter had told her what a comfort that had been to him.

Anna sat up and leaned back against the wall, her breath
coming in gasps. She closed her eyes and forced herself to
slow her breathing down, or else she'd pass out. Her father

would be upset to see her like this. He would acknowledge her pain, but gently remind her that he had wanted her here, to be living a life not limited by the Nazi regime. She must focus on that, live well, live for those who no longer had the chance to.

She pictured his kind face, imagined how he would smile and take hold of her hand and tell her to go on. To remember his love and their life together before she came here, to be brave and strong . . . words he'd said to her just before she'd left Berlin for the last time.

Her bottom lip wobbled again and she breathed out slowly, counting to ten to try to hold back the tears. It was no good sitting here, she thought, she needed to be *doing*.

Anna stood up, putting the letter in her pocket, and hurried through the kitchen to the bathroom and splashed her face with cold water.

Looking up at her reflection in the mirror, her eyes were red and puffy, and they looked different now, sadder.

She quickly turned away, dried her face and went back to the kitchen, pouring herself a cup of tea, adding some milk and drinking it down quickly.

The desire to sit by the range and drink it slowly, as she'd planned to do just a short while ago, had gone. She needed to get back outside and get busy, try to numb her mind from the news for a while.

Thea instinctively knew something was wrong from the moment she saw Anna working in the greenhouse. The young woman's normally upright posture was hunched, as if she were bearing a heavy weight on her shoulders.

Thea opened the door and went in. 'Hello, how are you getting on?'

Anna turned to look at her from the bench at the far end of the greenhouse, where she was sowing seeds. 'Fine, I am just doing some lettuces.'

Thea smiled and went to stand beside her, looking at all the pots of soil with labels sticking out of them on the bench, each with the name of what had been planted in them written in Anna's neat handwriting. 'You've done a lot this afternoon. Why don't you finish now and go and have a bath before tea, ease your muscles a bit?'

'No, I am fine. I have some more peas to do yet.'

'They can wait till tomorrow.' Thea put her hand on Anna's arm. 'Is everything all right?'

Anna bit her lip and her eyes filled with tears. 'My . . . my . . .' She shook her head and started to cry, and rather than trying to say anything else took an envelope out of her pocket and handed it to Thea.

Looking down at the address, Thea saw that it had been sent from Holland. 'Is it from your father?'

Anna shook her head, her eyes swimming with tears. 'My father is dead . . . he died in January.'

Thea threw her arms around her and hugged her tightly, while Anna's slim frame shook with her sobbing. 'I'm so very sorry.'

She held on to her, gently patting her back for some time, letting her cry. 'Is the letter from your father's friend?' she asked as Anna's crying subsided. Thea stood back and held on to the young woman's arms, looking at her.

Anna nodded. 'He said that my father was finally freed

in January, but was so weak and ill that he died a few days after.'

Tears filled Thea's eyes. 'I'm so sorry, Anna. I had hoped you would be reunited again when all this mess is over.'

'So did I, but that will not happen now ... he is gone and my home in Berlin too.'

Anna looked completely lost. The usual spark had gone from her eyes, the news destroying the hope that she'd been clinging to since she'd left Germany a year ago.

'I know it can never make up for losing your father and the home you had with him, but this is your home for as long as you want it to be, Anna. Whatever happens in the future, you are always welcome here.' Thea put her arm around the young woman.

'Thank you.' Anna laid her head on Thea's shoulder for a moment.

'Come on, let's go in.' Thea led her out of the greenhouse towards the house. 'You need a hot drink and perhaps a bath and then a rest.' They were simple measures to help her right now, but it would take a long time for Anna to come to terms with what had happened. Thea would be keeping a close eye on her to help her through this.

Chapter 15

Prue wrote down another item on her shopping list, munching on her toast whilst keeping an eye on the eggs boiling on the cooker for breakfast. It was going to be a busy day and she didn't want to forget anything. She planned to drop her shopping list and ration books in at Barker's Grocers this morning before she went to the village hall to meet the Girl Guides who were helping with today's salvage collection.

'What's happened to my best shirt?' Victor said, coming into the kitchen without so much as a good morning, sitting down at his place at the table and reaching for a piece of toast. 'It's not in my wardrobe where it *should* be.'

Prue glanced at him. 'It must be in the laundry basket then.' She turned her attention back to the eggs, which were almost ready.

'Well, I need it for tomorrow, for my meeting in Norwich.' Victor spoke through a mouthful of toast.

Prue turned off the cooker and carefully spooned the eggs out of the boiling water and into the waiting egg cups. She took them over to the table and put one in front of Victor and the other in her place, and sat down at the table ready to eat. 'I'm not sure that I'll have time to get it ironed today, I've got a lot to do. You've got plenty of other shirts you can wear.'

Victor stared at her for a moment, his cold, ice-blue eyes fixed on her face. 'I *need* it tomorrow, Prudence. Is it too much to ask that I have a shirt ironed ready for going to an important meeting?' Red blotches were blooming on his cheeks, a tell-tale sign that his temper was about to erupt.

Prue sighed. 'Honestly, Victor, no one's going to care about what shirt you wear. If it's such an important meeting, everyone will be focused on the agenda, not who's dressed in what!' She smashed the top of her boiled egg with a spoon, cracking the shell, thinking he really was making a ridiculous fuss. Victor had become such a fusspot over his shirts. He wasn't usually so particular about his clothes, but perhaps it was because it was a meeting in the city and he was mixing with people he wanted to impress. 'If it really is *so* important to you, then you could always iron it yourself.'

The words were out of her mouth before her brain had time to catch up with her tongue, and an immediate feeling of dread filled her stomach. Speaking that way to Victor was akin to jabbing a stick in a wasps' nest.

He slammed down on the table the knife he'd been using to cut the top off his boiled egg and leaned forward, glaring at Prue.

'I'm out working all day, earning the money to pay for all

this.' He threw one hand in the air in a gesture intended to encompass the house and their lifestyle. 'If we were relying on what money *you* bring in then we'd have been living in the workhouse long ago,' he sneered.

'I might not earn any money, but I'm working for the war effort, contributing to the community we live in.' Prue fought to keep her voice calm, not betray the racing of her heart.

'Well charity begins at home, don't forget that. You're spending too much time doing stuff for other people and neglecting your family.'

Family! Prue thought. *He's a fine one to talk about family, the way he's treated Edwin.*

'You've got a daughter and husband to look after, it's your duty to make them your priority, not running a day club for some East End women and their squalling brats, or going around collecting up rubbish like some rag and bone man,' he said, counting each item out on his pudgy fingers. 'Or careering around the county in a canteen with your sister! You spend more time looking after others than you do your family. You need to get your priorities right, Prudence.'

'I *do* look after my family.'

'Then you'd better make sure that shirt is ironed and ready for me by tomorrow morning.' Victor spooned the last mouthful of egg into his mouth and, grabbing a piece of toast, stood up and left the kitchen, slamming the door behind him.

Prue sighed, her shoulders drooping, the weight of Victor's words seeming to press down on them.

Was she doing too much out of the home and neglecting her family?

His words had planted a worrying seed of guilt. After all, she'd just taken on more work by joining the WVS and getting involved with their various campaigns, and that was on top of what she already did for the WI and the mothers' day club. Was she stretching herself too thin?

She jabbed a toast soldier into the runny, golden yolk and popped it into her mouth, chewing slowly. Why *did* she take on these jobs, volunteer to do so much?

The answer was simple: because it filled her time and stopped her thinking too much about the hollowness of her life with Victor. Their marriage was an empty shell; it looked solid enough from the outside but in reality there was nothing there, no substance to it, and certainly no love.

And as for the family, there was only Alice left at home, and she was out most of the time these days, at school or seeing her friends or over at Thea's. Prue always had meals cooked for Alice when she came home, or left something ready for her if she was out. Her clothes were washed, her bed changed, she was far from being neglected.

Victor wanted his own way and was an expert at getting it, knowing exactly how to make her feel guilty because her family was her weak spot. But most of them were gone now and she wasn't needed by her children the way she'd once been. Her husband only wanted her to be a domestic slave and for the appearance of having a wife.

She took a sharp breath, a flame of anger flickering into life and growing stronger at Victor's audacity. If he wanted that shirt so much then he could jolly well do it himself. She had more important things to do today.

Chapter 16

Anna slipped her right knitting needle into the next stitch on her left needle, wound the wool around where they crossed and then carefully lifted the new stitch she'd just created off onto her right needle. Then she started the process all over again. At the rate she was going this scarf would never be ready to send with the rest of the garments to the RAF in three weeks' time.

As if sensing her thoughts, Hettie, who was sitting next to her, her fingers deftly flying over the sock that she was knitting with four double-pointed needles, leaned closer to her and said, 'Keep going, you're doing really well.'

Anna looked up and met Hettie's blue eyes, noticing that the older woman was still knitting without even looking at what she was doing. 'I'll never be able to go as fast as you.'

Hettie laughed. 'I remember thinking the same thing when I first learned to knit. My granny's fingers were a blur over the needles while I was labouring over every single stitch and kept dropping them and making big holes, my knitting getting narrower as I went up ... But I gradually got better – the more I practised, the better I got.' She smiled. 'And so will you. Don't be so hard on yourself. It's only been a few days since I first taught you what to do, and look at you now, knitting a fine scarf that any airman would be proud to wear.'

She reached across and ran her fingers over the three inches of stocking-stitch scarf that Anna had made in grey wool. 'See, look, there are no holes and you haven't lost any stitches or made any where there shouldn't be. Just keep on going and your fingers will start to remember what to do and you'll gradually get quicker.'

'Will I be finished in time?' Anna asked. She wanted to contribute, and for the time and effort that she was putting into her knitting to not be for nothing. Since Prue had put the call out a few days ago for knitted garments for the RAF, the women of the village had stepped up to the challenge, and Anna was enjoying being involved and wanted to finish what she'd started. Today's knitting bee here at the village hall was just part of the three-week drive for knitted garments – there was a lot of work towards it going on in homes around the village as well. The coming together of women this afternoon, with everyone busy and productive, was something that Anna hadn't experienced before, except for her visit to the WI; she loved the happy atmosphere, the industriousness while everyone was enjoying themselves. Being part of it was being part of the community.

'Of course you will. You've got time and if you pick up

your knitting whenever you can, when you're listening to the wireless in the evening or on your tea break, it will all add up, bit by bit,' Hettie reassured her.

Anna nodded. 'Thank you.'

Hettie chuckled. 'It's a pleasure. I'm enjoying teaching you and seeing how you're getting on. I never had a daughter, so it's lovely to be able to teach you ...' She paused, her attention caught by the rattle of cups, where Prue and Thea were carrying trays of tea things into the hall. 'Looks like tea's on its way.'

'Would you like a biscuit?' Blanche asked, offering them the plate of homemade oat and honey biscuits which she was taking around to the knitters, after Prue had brought them both a cup of tea. 'I know you made them, Hettie, so they'll be tasty.'

Anna took one. 'Thank you.'

'Not for me,' Hettie said. 'I had one earlier, had to test them after they were cooked to make sure they were up to standard.' She smiled. 'And they were.' She stood up. 'In fact, why don't you sit down and have one yourself and I'll finish taking them around. You can have my tea as well, I haven't touched it. I'll get another cup in a minute when I've done the rounds.'

'Oh, all right, thank you.' Blanche took the offered cup of tea, and a biscuit from the plate, and sat down in Hettie's vacated place next to Anna.

As Blanche settled herself down, Hettie gave Anna a wink and a smile before moving off to offer around the biscuits – she was deliberately leaving her with the other woman! Anna wasn't sure if this was a good idea or not, but it would be rude to get up and leave herself. Blanche had been polite, quite unlike their first meeting.

'This biscuit is delicious,' Blanche said after taking a bite. 'You're very lucky to be living with Hettie and getting to sample her cooking every day.'

Anna nodded. 'Yes, she is a very good cook. She told me she used to be the cook at Great Plumstead Hall.'

'Yes, she even cooked for the King and Queen when they visited there.' Blanche smiled at her. 'How are you settling in here?'

'Very well. I like it here very much and Thea is good to work for, I'm learning a lot.'

Blanche looked uncomfortable, biting her bottom lip, before turning in her seat so that she faced Anna. 'I am really sorry that I treated you so badly when we first met, Anna.' Blanche's eyes met hers. 'I am ashamed of what I thought and said, and I've been thinking a lot about what you told us at the WI meeting. I'm glad you escaped to England to get away from the Nazis' persecution – understanding what's going on there makes it even more important that we stand up to Hitler and put a stop to what he's doing.'

'Thank you.' Anna smiled at the older woman. 'I do understand how easy it is to believe untrue things when you do not know the whole story. The important thing is to learn and change when you have the knowledge.'

'Yes, and I've been telling people about it, what's going on over there, because we need to know. And by spreading the word, it will help stop more people thinking like I did.' She took a sip of tea. 'So how's your knitting going?'

'Slowly!' Anna held up her scarf so Blanche could see.

'Hettie tells me to keep going and I will get there. At least there are no holes in this one.'

'You're doing well. It took me a long time to get the hang of knitting. I'm left-handed you see, and my mother was right-handed and had an awful job of teaching me to knit. The mess I used to get into and the dropped stitches, my knitting was more hole than wool, but I got there in the end. I'm always knitting now when I get the chance to sit down, so it's lovely to come here and have a reason to sit and knit and chatter. One good thing about this war is it's bringing us women together to do things like this. We did a big blackberry picking and jam making session with the WI last year, it was good fun, I'm hoping we'll do it again. Then there are the evacuee mothers who've come to live in the village, they've joined in everything, too.' Blanche looked over to where some of the mothers were having their tea break, while gently rocking their babies in the prams to send them to sleep.

'There must have been a lot of changes here in the village since the start of the war,' Anna said.

'Yes, there have been. Some of them have been hard with sons going off to join the forces, but it's brought some good ones too, new people coming to live here, and us working together to achieve things. Prue's enlisted me to help with her WI allotment and I'm enjoying that, but I'm not sure if I've developed green fingers yet!'

Anna frowned. 'Green fingers?' She looked down at Blanche's hands, which were perfectly clean.

Blanche, seeing her glance, laughed. 'It's a saying. It means you're good at growing things.'

'Ah, I see. It is an idiom. I know some of them, but there are such a lot in English to learn.' Anna smiled. 'I like that one, very much. Perhaps I will get green fingers working for Thea!'

Chapter 17

Listening to the six o'clock news on the wireless had become a daily necessity for Prue in her attempt to keep up with what was happening on the continent and how it might be affecting her son Jack. His letters were sporadic and told her very little, and she wasn't sure where he was now, not even which country he was in. She knew from not-so-subtle references that he'd made in his first letters that he'd landed in France to begin with, but he'd been moving around and whether he was still on French soil, she had no idea. But having heard tonight's announcement by the newsreader that Holland, Belgium and Luxembourg had been invaded by the Nazis, her mind was in turmoil wondering if Jack was in one of them, facing the onslaught of a tide of Nazi troopers that seemed unstoppable.

On top of that worrying news, it had also been announced that Neville Chamberlain, the Prime Minister, was resigning, and that Winston Churchill would be taking over the leadership of the country.

She realised that she had stopped washing the plate in her hands. Standing with her back to the room at the kitchen sink, she bit her bottom lip to stem the tears that were threatening because she was frightened for her son.

'They won't get much further with our British Expeditionary Force waiting for them.' Victor's voice sounded loud and jarring in the confines of the kitchen. They'd just had their evening meal and he'd remained in here to listen to the news. 'Jack will send any Nazi soldier he meets packing – they'll be turning on their heels and scuttling back to where they came from if they've got any sense.'

Prue closed her eyes and leaned against the sink, biting down on the urge to scream at her husband. How could he talk in such a blasé fashion about their son coming face-to-face with a determined and ruthless enemy that had mercilessly swept aside those who had tried to oppose them in other countries? It wasn't a game out there, and Victor's gung-ho talk about Jack made her feel sick.

She turned around and faced Victor, water dripping from her hands onto the rug on the floor. 'I hope to God that Jack's nowhere near them.'

Victor put down the cup of tea he'd just taken a sip from and frowned at her. 'He'd want to be in the thick of it, it's why he joined up, and if I were a younger man, I'd want to be there too. They need to be stopped or they might come knocking on our door before long. I'd say Hitler's got his eye on our country as well.'

Prue narrowed her eyes. 'You didn't even do any fighting

in the Great War, Victor, remember? You spent it safely behind the counter of the army stores on British soil, you never even went to France. So how can you say you'd be there fighting now if you had the chance? Because you didn't when you were a young man.'

A flush appeared on Victor's cheeks and Prue instantly regretted that last jibe, knowing how her husband's mood was likely to take off like a rocket if something annoyed him. She really didn't feel up to having to deal with him being like that tonight.

But why shouldn't you speak the truth? a voice said in her head. It was all too easy to make ridiculous comments from the safety of your chair, miles away from the advancing enemy. She was more concerned about the safety of her son, and if he had any sense, so should Victor be. But then he'd always been one for show, caring about what people thought more than the reality of what went on behind the scenes in his home.

To her surprise, Victor snorted, shaking his head as he looked at her with amazement on his face. 'At least Jack's out there doing his bit, unlike that lily-livered brother of his.'

'Edwin is doing his bit. You don't have to carry a gun to do your part for the war effort,' Prue said. 'Ambulance crew are needed just as much as soldiers. If Hitler sends his bombers over here, then who's going to be rescuing casualties? It will be ambulance crews, and the injured will be grateful to have them, and that might be you one day, it could be any of us, so don't belittle what Edwin's chosen to do. I'm very proud of him.' Not waiting to see how Victor responded she turned her back on him and resumed washing up, scrubbing the plate far harder than was necessary. She was extremely proud of Edwin, who'd successfully completed his training course and had now been sent to a hospital in the East End of London, where he was working long hours as an orderly on the wards. His letters were full of enthusiasm; he was enjoying what he was doing and learning a lot, while still being of service to the country.

To her surprise, Victor didn't respond. She just heard the scraping of his chair on the tiled kitchen floor and then the opening and shutting of the kitchen door as he headed for his study as he always did, no doubt to go over his precious figures from the day's takings at his agricultural and seed merchant's shop in Wykeham.

She rinsed the clean plate, put it on the drainer and then leaned against the sink, hanging her head and sighing. Sometimes it was very hard not to scream and shout and let her tears of worry and frustration fall; sometimes she wanted to just go up to her bed, crawl under the covers and not come out because of the sense of helplessness which steadily crept up on her. It seemed hard to comprehend what was going on over the other side of the Channel; what terrors the Nazis were inflicting on the countries they invaded, when outside spring was in full swing, trees were coming into leaf and colourful flowers blossoming with the warmer days. Nature was carrying on as normal, beginning her annual bloom, while the man–made war was getting worse and creeping ever closer to home.

Tears seeped out and slid hotly down her cheeks. Prue took some shuddering breaths and stood up straight. This wasn't going to get her anywhere – of course she was worried about Jack and Edwin, about all those she cared for, wherever they were and however they were being affected by this horrible war, but moping and feeling miserable wasn't going to help. She needed to keep focusing her energies on what she *could* do to make a difference, all the while hoping that Jack would be safe and come home in one piece someday.

Chapter 18

Thea stood leaning on the gate that led into the meadow watching Primrose graze, swishing her tail against the flies, in the soft light of the beautiful May evening. The blue sky overhead was clear of clouds, the air still, and a blackbird sang its beautiful fluting song high on a branch in the tall oak tree. She enjoyed this relaxing time when she checked on the gentle cow before turning in each night. With the weather being warmer now, it was fine to return Primrose to the meadow after evening milking so she could continue grazing and settle down to sleep wherever she pleased, often under the spreading boughs of the large oak tree standing in the hedge. It was only a few weeks since Primrose had arrived here at Rookery House, but it seemed like she had been here for ever, her needs fitting seamlessly into the routine with her twice-daily milking, which Thea really enjoyed, a quiet rhythmic task that was always calming.

'Primrose all right?' Reuben's voice made her turn

around and she saw her brother and Bess coming towards her. Bess ran ahead to greet her, the tip of her tail wagging like a white flag, and she leaned against Thea's legs as she patted her head, stroking her silky ears.

'Yes, she's looking well and very contented.' Thea smiled at her brother as he came to lean against the gate beside her. 'She's made a big difference, helping us provide for ourselves, plus selling the milk, butter and cheese for income is a bonus too.'

They fell into silence watching swallows flitting back and forth over the meadow, hawking for insects.

'I'm going to go and make a cup of cocoa and listen to the nine o'clock news,' Reuben announced. 'Do you want to join me? We can listen to what's been going on today.'

Thea nodded. 'Yes, that would be nice, thank you.'

They headed over to Reuben's railway carriage, which stood on the far side of the garden near the orchard, and while her brother busied himself heating up a saucepan of Primrose's milk on the stove, Thea turned on his wireless set to give the valves time to warm up ready for the news. Sitting down in one of the two armchairs, Thea looked around at her brother's little house. It was neat and tidy, with everything well thought out to make the most use of the space. You could still see the outline of the carriage where the two bedrooms were. The kitchen area where she sat had been built on to the back and contained the stove, the sink and a table; with a pantry leading off it, it had everything that anyone would need to live quite happily. It was cosy and she always liked spending time here.

With a mug of cocoa each and Bess lying on the worn

rag rug in front of the stove, they listened to the news. As always these days, it charted the advance of Hitler's troops across the continent and made for worrying listening. It was four days since they'd invaded Holland, Belgium and Luxembourg, and although the British Expeditionary Force was fighting hard, they hadn't managed to push them back – and going by what had happened in the past, Thea couldn't help thinking it was unlikely that they could. Hitler's army was huge and so far had the unstoppable ability to overpower any country they invaded. Who would be the next to fall – France? And then would Hitler turn his greedy eye on Britain? Only he wouldn't find it as easy as he had so far, because they were an island, and invading Britain wouldn't be such a simple matter as rolling across an imaginary borderline.

The news came to an end and it was announced that the War Minister, Anthony Eden, was to make a broadcast. Immediately Thea's heart sank. What was he going to say, what had happened? Was an invasion imminent? Surely they would have said so on the news, wouldn't they?

Thea glanced at her brother who, from the look on his face, was clearly thinking along similar lines.

'*Since the war began,*' Eden's voice came out of the wireless set, '*the government have received countless enquiries from all over the kingdom from men of all ages, who are for one reason or another not at present engaged in military service and who wish to do something for the defence of their country. Well, here is your opportunity. We want large numbers of men in Great Britain, who are British subjects, between the ages of seventeen and sixty-five, to come forward now and offer their services. The name of the new force that is now to be raised will be the Local Defence Volunteers. This name describes its duties in three words. You will not be paid but you will receive a uniform and you will be armed. In order to volunteer, you must give in your name at the local police station; and then, as and when we want you, we will let you know. Here, then, is the opportunity for which so many of you will have been waiting. Your loyal help, added to the arrangements which already exist, will make and keep our country safe.'*

'What do you think of that?' Thea asked as the BBC announcer introduced the next programme.

'It's a good idea and if there is an invasion it could make all the difference.'

Thea nodded. 'Are you going to volunteer?'

'I reckon so.' Reuben smiled. 'Might as well put all that experience I got in France to good use.'

'I'm sure they'll get lots of volunteers, no one wants what's happened to Holland and Belgium to happen to us.' She stood up. 'I'd better get going, I'll see you tomorrow. Thanks for the cocoa.' She squeezed her brother's shoulder as she left, knowing that, although he'd not made a fuss about it, joining something like the Local Defence Volunteers would help him feel he was doing more to help with the war effort.

She was almost back at the house when Bess came charging up to her, her wet nose touching her hand. She turned around to see Reuben following on, pushing his bicycle.

'Where are you off to?'

'To put my name down at the police station in Wykeham. Would you keep Bess with you while I'm gone? I don't want her following me.'

'Of course, but why go now? Why not wait until tomorrow?'

Reuben shrugged and smiled. 'I just want to get my name down quick.'

She laughed, knowing that she'd been right in thinking he'd be eager to do his bit. Her brother might not say much but she knew him well enough, and despite what he'd experienced in the last war, he would do all he could to help defend the country this time around too.

'I'm not sure they're expecting people to sign up tonight, it's after nine o'clock.'

'I'll sleep better if I know my name's on the list. I'll pick Bess up on my way back.'

'All right.' Thea took hold of Bess's collar to stop the dog following him, and watched as Reuben hurried off to sign up, noticing that he had a spring in his step.

Chapter 19

The bell above the door of Barker's jingled as Prue pushed it open and went in. Her arrival was instantly noticed by Rosalind and her friend Sylvia, who were talking to Grace, the shop's owner.

'Good morning, Prue,' Grace said, looking pleased to see her. No doubt she was relieved to have someone else here to dilute the effect of Rosalind and Sylvia's gossiping, which was renowned in the village.

Prue smiled at Grace, going up to the counter where she was cutting a piece of cheese. 'Good morning Rosalind, Sylvia.' She nodded at the two other women who had ceased their gossiping. 'Grace, I was wondering if you'd put up one of my posters advertising the WVS Salvage Week, which starts on Monday? We'll be doing collections around the village. The Girl Guides are going to help, and some of our evacuee mothers with their prams.'

'Of course. I'll make sure it's put in a prominent position

in the window. If you leave it on the counter, I'll see to it as soon as I can.'

'What are you collecting?' Rosalind asked, craning her neck to read the poster as Prue put it down on the counter.

'Waste paper, bones, rags, glass jars and scrap iron,' Prue said. 'Every bit helps. We've run a collection before for waste paper, but this one's much bigger and for more types of salvageable materials. I hope most households will be able to contribute.'

Rosalind nodded. 'We must all do what we can. My husband's going to sign up today for the Local Defence Volunteers, his experience in the Great War will no doubt be of great use. He was a captain, you know – led his men into battle many times. He knows how to fight the enemy.'

'It was quite a surprise hearing the announcement about the Local Defence Volunteers after the news last night,' Grace said, placing the wrapped portion of cheese on the counter and checking the next item on Rosalind's list.

'Victor's going to sign up today as well,' Prue said. 'I don't think they'll be short of volunteers around here.'

'I just hope that the government haven't left it too late,' sniffed Rosalind. 'We could be invaded any day now and be overrun just like Holland and Belgium.'

Prue frowned. 'Well, if they do come, they won't find it as straightforward as they did there. They've got a sea to cross to get to us first.'

'My husband says Hitler will send troops in by parachute first.' Rosalind pinched her mouth into a thin line. 'So what would we do then? Do we stay or do we go? The government haven't bothered to tell us, and I'm certainly not going to sit around and wait for some Nazi paratrooper to come bursting into my house. I've taken my car out of storage and filled it with petrol so it's ready to go if the time comes.'

Prue glanced at Grace; from the look on her face, they were both thinking the same thing. True to form, Rosalind was concerned only for herself. 'I'm not sure if that's a wise thing to do. Your car could be used by an enemy paratrooper to get around.'

Rosalind frowned. 'What else am I supposed to do? I'm not going to wait around like a sitting duck. If the enemy comes, I'm not going to stay put and wait to surrender. No doubt there are spies here already, just waiting for the invasion to begin. They'll be gathering information that will help the invading troops. That young German woman your sister's got living with her could be one for all we know, her story about what happened to her might just be a front to throw us off guard. A spy is hardly going to look like one, are they?'

Prue bunched her fingers into a fist. 'Anna is *not* a spy, I can assure you of that, Rosalind. Didn't you listen to what she told us at the WI meeting? And since then she's heard that her father's died because of the Nazis. She would *never* help them!'

Rosalind shrugged. 'As I said, it could all be just a story and she a good actor.'

'Well it's not a story, it's fact,' Prue snapped. 'And shame on you for still thinking otherwise. Hitler would be delighted the way fear and suspicion is sneaking into our communities, it's playing right into his hands.'

'Well, really!' Red spots had appeared on Rosalind's

111

cheeks. 'I'll come back and collect my shopping in a while.' She directed this last comment to Grace. 'Come on, Sylvia.' And with a final glare at Prue she stalked out of the shop, slamming the door behind her making the bell jangle loudly.

'Oh dear!' Grace raised her eyebrows, a smile playing on her lips. 'I think you've offended Rosalind.'

Prue laughed. 'I think I have, but that woman never fails to astonish me with her bigoted, narrow points of view. If the Germans do come, we know she'll be the first to turn tail and run for it rather than doing something to stop the invaders.'

'Let's hope they get the Local Defence Volunteers up and running soon then. I don't like Rosalind's attitude, but she's right: if they do come, what *should* we do, what's the best thing?'

Prue sighed. 'I'm sure that thinking just of yourself like Rosalind isn't right. If everyone did that it would create chaos and play into the enemy's hands. But *what* the right thing to do is, I don't know, and faced with the situation who knows how any of us would react. Let's hope we never have to find out.'

Chapter 20

Now, with spring in full advance, and with the recent arrival of fine, warmer weather, the evenings had been too nice to spend inside. Tonight Anna was enjoying listening to the Mozart concert on the Home Service while sitting in a deckchair outside in the garden of Rookery House, alongside Hettie, Thea and Marianne. Bess was with them too, lying contentedly with her head on her paws, eyes closed, as Reuben had gone to the first meeting of the LDV in the village. The half-glass double doors of the sitting room had been thrown wide open, and the wireless in there turned up so it could be heard outside, the glorious music spilling out into the garden. When the announcer had introduced the concert, he'd spoken about how Mozart had originally intended the music to be performed in the open air, and so it was all the more fitting that they should be here listening to it in the garden. Its melodies were reminiscent of the German folk songs that she'd grown up with, had sung at school, and it was a sweet reminder of her early life back in her homeland before things had turned sour.

Anna sighed happily, her eyes closed enjoying the soothing music, to which a blackbird on top of the house added its clear fluting notes. This was the perfect end to the day, her body pleasantly tired from a day of physical activity in the garden, and she'd had a lovely letter from Thomas in the afternoon post, full of news about school and how much he was enjoying it. Now, sitting with the pleasure of the company of people who had quickly become good friends, she was full of contentment.

All too soon the concert came to an end, and the beeps of the time signal heralded the nine o'clock news, stirring all of them from their relaxed state.

'I'll just listen to the headlines then go and make us some cocoa,' Hettie said.

As usual, the news was centred around the war. It often wasn't pleasant to listen to, Anna thought, but it was necessary to keep abreast of what was happening. The newsreader spoke of the latest battles fought by the British Expeditionary Force in Belgium and then turned to news on the home front.

'*The Home Office today announced that the Home Secretary has, as a further measure of precaution, directed a temporary internment throughout Great Britain of all male Germans and Austrians over the age of sixteen and under the age of sixty whose present classification as a result of examination by a local tribunal or regional advisory committee is B.*'

Anna sat bolt upright in her deckchair, clasping her hands together tightly. All the mellow, relaxed feeling from listening to the concert had vanished, and Bess, sensing her distress, came to sit beside her, leaning on her legs, while Thea reached across from where she sat and gently touched Anna's arm.

'*The round-up began in London immediately after the Home Secretary's order. The greatest secrecy had been maintained until it was in progress.*'

As the newsreader spoke in his neutral tone about how the police had collected the aliens and taken them to internment camps, describing how many of them were refugees, Anna's imagination pictured how it must have been for the men who were rounded up, memories of hearing how friends of her family had been taken by the Nazis providing fuel. Her fingers sought out Bess's butter-soft ears, stroking them as she imagined how it had been when the Nazis had come for her father, the knock on the door of their Berlin apartment, the harsh way they would have treated him, marching him away like a criminal.

She, and so many of those men that had been rounded up today, had fled to this country to escape such treatment in their homeland, but now it was happening here too. It might not have been the Nazis rounding people up, but once again they were being targeted. Wherever people like her went, it seemed that they could never be allowed to live peaceful lives.

As soon as the newsreader moved on to the next item, Thea leapt up from her deckchair and hurried into the sitting room to turn off the wireless, leaving just the sound of the blackbirds singing out across the garden.

Thea came back and crouched down in front of Anna. 'Are you all right?'

Anna's mouth felt dry and she swallowed before speaking. 'Why did they have to do that? Most of those men will have been refugees from Nazi oppression like me.'

'They said it's as a precaution.' Thea sighed. 'I don't like what they're doing either, but the way things are going the government must think it's necessary, and they're only interning Category B – men they already weren't sure about, and it's temporary.'

'I'll go and make that cocoa, a nice hot cup will make you feel better.' Hettie patted Anna's shoulder as she went past.

'Do you think they'll intern women as well?' Anna asked. The Nazis didn't appear to discriminate as to gender.

Thea's blue eyes met hers. 'I hope not, but if they did it would only be the Category B ones, like with the men. The government knows that women who were given a Category C at their tribunals, like you were, do not support the Nazi regime in any way, and have in fact suffered because of it.'

Anna nodded. She knew what Thea said was true, but she'd lived through the steady, insidious creep of rule changes back in Berlin. First the Jewish population were stopped from doing one thing, which was fine, then something else was brought in and then another. Bit by bit things changed for the worse. She desperately hoped that wasn't going to happen here in Britain. The news had left her feeling helpless, her fate in others' hands, and it had deeply unsettled her just when she felt she'd finally found a proper home here at Rookery House.

Chapter 21

The village hall in Great Plumstead was, this Saturday morning, acting as the headquarters for Prue's salvage week collection. Today was going to be the culmination of her efforts as part of the WVS to raise awareness among the village's housewives, teaching them not to throw out items that had become valuable to the country's war effort. They needed to think of it as salvage, which could be recycled and put to good use making new things instead of being thrown away as rubbish.

Dressed in her green WVS uniform, she smiled at the Girl Guides and three evacuee mothers who'd gathered outside, ready with an assortment of handcarts, wheelbarrows and empty prams that they'd brought along to help the collection. The mothers had left their babies inside the hall where they were being looked after by other evacuee mothers. Prue was delighted that they had volunteered to help, working together as a team to make sure their children were cared for while they did their bit; she had even persuaded Alice to come along and help too.

'Thank you all for coming this morning.' Prue smiled at the eager-looking girls, smartly dressed in their Guiding uniform, and the mothers who had become part of the community since they'd arrived here last autumn. 'I've divided you up into groups to collect from houses in different areas of the village, that way you'll be more efficient and can cover more ground.' She held up a map of Great Plumstead that she'd drawn and, consulting her list, began to explain who would be going where. 'When you've finished your area, or when your handcart or pram is full, bring your salvage back here and sort it into these boxes.' She indicated the row of boxes standing by the wall, which she'd labelled for each of the types of salvage they'd be collecting. 'Rags can go in the sacks and bones in the metal dustbin at the end.' She'd persuaded Victor to donate a dustbin from his hardware shop, arguing that since she'd have to take them to the nearest depot in her car, it would be a good idea to put any bones in a solid container with a lid, otherwise the inside of her car might never smell of anything else again. Her husband, no doubt thinking of the car's resale value in the future, wouldn't want to put its condition in jeopardy.

'The bones for our group are going in 'ere,' one of the evacuee mothers said, pointing at the metal pail tied to the handle of her pram with string. Prue had put them all in one group to work together. 'Don't want smelly old bones in my pram!'

'Good idea.' Prue smiled at her. 'Right, is everybody clear where they need to go?'

They all nodded. 'Right, good luck everybody and let's hope the villagers of Great Plumstead will have done themselves proud.'

The guides and mothers quickly dispersed in different directions, in groups of three or four with their carts, barrows or prams, leaving Alice and Prue with their handcart.

'Do you want to push or should I?' Prue asked.

'I'll push for now, but we might have to take turns if it gets too heavy with salvage.' Alice smiled at her.

Prue laughed. 'I do hope so.'

They headed off in the direction of Rosalind's grand house – The Grange – which stood on the outskirts of the village, Prue having been very careful in deciding which groups should collect from which areas. If there was one person in the village who was likely to be difficult it was Rosalind, and it was better that Prue herself deal with her rather than some young Guide who might be upset by the woman's brusque manner. In fact, she wasn't sure how seriously Rosalind would take salvage week. The last time she'd spoken to Rosalind she was very much in favour of looking after herself, so saving scraps of waste paper and glass jars would probably come very low down on her list of priorities right now.

Knocking on the front door of Rosalind's house a short while later, Prue stepped back and waited, noting that Rosalind hadn't bothered to follow the clear instructions on the posters, requesting householders to leave the salvage outside their homes so that it could be collected without having to disturb them.

Either Rosalind had no salvage to collect or she expected

them to knock on her door. Regardless, Prue was doing her best not to get annoyed. Someone with Rosalind's standing in the community – and her habit of voicing her opinions – should be setting a good example, encouraging others by what she was doing.

The door opened and Rosalind's housekeeper, Joan, who was a staunch member of the WI, smiled at her. 'Good morning, Prue. Have you come to collect the salvage?'

'Yes. I'm sorry to have to disturb you, only it's not been left out.'

Joan stepped forward, nodding her head back into the house and whispering. 'She wouldn't let me leave it outside, said it would look common.' She raised her eyebrows. 'So I've put it by the back door, if you want to bring your cart around.'

Prue nodded. 'Of course.'

Alice pushed the handcart around the side of the house to where Joan was waiting for them.

'I've had a good sort out this weekend and found quite a bit.' Joan helped Prue and Alice load the salvage into the cart. She had neatly separated it, tying the bundles of waste paper with string and putting the glass into an old cardboard box. 'Where do you want these?' She held up a bowl with some bones in.

Prue took the lid off the metal pail that she'd brought along, not wanting the bones to contaminate the rest of the salvage or attract flies. 'In here, please.'

Joan tipped them into the pail, the hard bones clanging as they hit the bottom. 'What will they use them for?'

'To make glue, explosives, soap, fertiliser or animal feed,

so I've been told,' Prue explained. 'Plenty of uses for something we'd normally throw out. Thank you for collecting all this.'

'I'm glad to help, I did it of my own accord. I did ask the boss, but she wasn't interested so I just got on with it. If we all do a bit, together it makes a lot.'

'Exactly.' Prue smiled at her, thinking she must have the patience of a saint to work for Rosalind. If it were her, she wouldn't last five minutes in that house. 'Thank you very much, and though this week's salvage week is to raise awareness, it's not a one-off. We'll still be doing regular collections, so please don't throw out any bits that can be recycled.'

'Don't worry, I won't.'

After Rosalind's house, they called at the others on the road as they headed back to the village hall. Prue was pleased to find that every house had some salvage waiting outside for them. The cart had grown heavier with each stop, and she and Alice had to push it together.

Back at the hall, a substantial amount of salvage had been collected and sorted into different categories. Prue had hoped that the housewives in the village would take notice of her posters and find materials in their homes that could be recycled, but she hadn't expected that there would be quite so much. It was heartening to see, and her little car would be packed full when she took the salvage to the depot this afternoon.

Chapter 22

Walking into the police station in Wykeham at ten minutes to midnight wasn't what Thea had expected to be doing tonight. Normally, she'd be tucked up in bed by now, but the request for help had come and she'd responded, although what it was for she didn't yet know. The WVS organiser in Norwich, who'd telephoned Rookery House while they'd been listening to the evening news on the wireless, had been sworn to secrecy. All she could tell Thea was that it was an important job that WVS members had been specifically asked to assist the police with, knowing that they could be relied on to do excellent work. Any more than that she wouldn't say.

The policeman on the front desk looked up from the newspaper he was reading and smiled at her as he took in her green WVS uniform.

'Miss Thornton?' he asked.

She smiled at him. 'Yes, that's me, reporting for duty for

whatever it is . . . .' She raised her eyebrows, hoping he might give some sort of hint, but instead he beckoned her to come through the door that led into the back of the police station.

'If you go and wait in the staff room on the right.'

'How long for?'

He gave a shrug. 'I'll bring you a cuppa to have in the meantime.'

Thea did as she was told, and was reading the posters on the wall when he returned a few minutes later with a steaming mug of tea and a couple of biscuits on a saucer.

'Thank you.' Thea took the tea and biscuits from him. 'Can you tell me what I'm going to be doing?'

He shook his head. 'I'm afraid not. You'll be told when it's time, so I'd make yourself comfortable if I were you, get a bit of kip while you can. I'll see to it that you won't be disturbed in here.'

Left on her own, nibbling on a biscuit, Thea's mind was racing with ideas about what could be going on here. What was she needed for? And why the secrecy?

The clock on the wall slowly ticked around and one o'clock came and went. She made herself as comfortable as possible in one of the armchairs and must have dropped off, the day's hard work in the garden catching up with her.

A loud cough woke her up with a start and she saw a different policeman standing in the doorway with another mug of tea in his hand.

'Miss Thornton.' He smiled at her, coming into the room. 'I'm Sergeant Grayson, you'll be working with me this morning. We need to be going shortly. I've brought you a drink and if you'd like to use the facilities and freshen up before we leave, I'll meet you at the front of the station in a quarter of an hour.'

She glanced at the clock and saw it was now a quarter past five. She heaved herself out of the chair, her limbs feeling stiff from sleeping in an awkward position.

'Yes, of course. Where are we going?'

'I'll explain on the way.' He handed her the mug of tea. 'I'll see you in front of the station then,' he said briskly, and left before she could quiz him further.

When they drove away from the police station a short while later, the sun had risen and the blue sky overhead promised a fine day. As they passed through the silent streets of the market town, heading south, Thea asked again, 'Can you tell me now what you need me to do?'

'It's a job of national importance, apparently. Orders coming from the top.' Sergeant Grayson cleared his throat. 'We've been ordered to detain a woman enemy alien who's living in the district.' Thea's stomach plummeted down into her sturdy lace-up brown shoes, her thoughts immediately going to Anna. 'You and I are going to collect a young woman living in Great Plumstead.'

'Anna Weissenborn?' Thea's voice came out in a squeak.

He glanced at her. 'You know her?'

'Yes, she lives in my house and works for me.'

Sergeant Grayson brought the police car to a halt and drummed his fingers on the steering wheel, frowning. 'This is a fine turn-up for the books . . . you shouldn't have been asked to do this, I'll take you back to the station and go and get her with a constable.'

'No! If you're going to take Anna, then I'm coming with

124

you. At least if I'm there it will be easier for her; I'm a familiar face and I can look out for her,' she said firmly. 'But I don't understand why you're detaining her, she's a category C and not considered a threat. She's a teacher, for goodness' sake, who had to flee from Germany because she's Jewish. The Nazis caused the death of her father. She's as much an enemy of Hitler as you or me, *more* so in some ways.'

Sergeant Grayson sighed. 'It's not my decision, but we're near enough to the coast where they've been evacuating people from because of the threat of invasion, so I suppose those that make the orders consider *any* enemy alien within the vicinity might potentially be on the enemy's side. With any luck, she won't be held for long and she'll be returned home to you in a day or two.' He put the car into gear. 'Well, if you're sure you want to come with me, we'd better get going.'

'I'm sure, although I don't agree with it at all ... but I'm not sending Anna off on her own, not when I can be with her. Can I please tell her what's going on? If you go barging into her room to wake her up it will frighten her and make matters so much more difficult.'

Sergeant Grayson nodded. 'That's a good idea. We don't want to make this any harder than it already is.'

Arriving at Rookery House, Thea led Sergeant Grayson in through the back door and into the kitchen. She was grateful that the house was quiet, everybody seemingly still sleeping.

'This way.' She headed into the hall and up the stairs, aware that the policeman was following her, the heavy

125

clump of his boots on the stairs seeming even louder in the quiet. Stopping outside Anna's bedroom door she looked at him, and he returned her gaze with a nod of his head.

'I'll wait here.' He kept his voice low. 'You need to tell her to pack a suitcase of clothes and anything she might need.'

Thea was about to tap gently on Anna's door when Hettie's bedroom door burst open and her friend came bustling out, tying the cord of her dressing gown around her, her eyes going from Thea to Sergeant Grayson and back again, a look of horror passing over her face.

'What on earth's going on? What's a policeman doing here at this time of the day?' She frowned. 'I thought you were going out on WVS business?'

'I won't be a minute,' Thea said to Sergeant Grayson before putting her arm around Hettie and steering the older woman back into her bedroom. 'You're not going to like this any more than I do, but orders have been given to detain female enemy aliens, and that includes Anna.' Hettie gasped; her blue eyes widened with horror. 'The WVS have been asked to accompany them to wherever they're being taken to make sure that they're looked after and well treated.' She sighed. 'I don't agree with what's going on, but at least I can be with her and make sure she's all right – better that it's me with her than some stranger.'

'But she's *not* a danger or a spy!' Hettie was puffing up like an indignant hen, a blotch of red appearing on each cheek. 'Whose bright idea is this?'

Thea shrugged. 'I know that, and you know that, but this order has come from on high. With any luck they'll see sense and she'll be back here very soon. And in the meantime, I'll do what I can to make this as easy for her as possible.'

'I'll go and get some food ready for you to take, make some sandwiches so at least you have something to eat. Do you know where they're taking her?'

'No. I didn't know anything about this until a short while ago, it was kept a secret with only those who needed to know being told. I'll find out where we're going when we get there, I suppose. The main thing is to be with Anna, keep her calm and find out as much as I can so I can help her.'

Leaving Hettie to go down to the kitchen, Thea tapped gently on Anna's bedroom door and went in, while Sergeant Grayson maintained his watch on the landing. It was dim inside her room, as the sunlight from outside was blocked by the blackout curtains, but Thea could see and hear from her slow, steady breathing that Anna was still asleep. Rather than waking her by shaking her shoulder or calling out to her, Thea went over to the window and opened the curtains, allowing the morning sunlight to stream into the room, and that, combined with the sound of her moving about, made Anna stir. She opened her eyes and at the sight of Thea she sat up, looking puzzled.

'Thea, is everything all right? Did I oversleep?' She glanced at the clock on the chest of drawers beside her bed and seeing that it was only six o'clock, frowned.

'No.' Thea sat down on the side of Anna's bed and took hold of one of the young woman's hands, looking her straight in her brown eyes. 'I'm afraid that orders have been

given for women to be detained, like the men were, and ...'
She paused for a moment to steady her voice, trying to keep
calm. 'A policeman is here to escort you, but I'll be going
with you.' She smiled, trying desperately to look positive.
'This is what the secret WVS job was about. I only found
out on the way here and I wish so much that this wasn't
necessary, but at least I'll be with you, you won't be alone.'

Anna stared at her for a few moments, clearly in shock
at the news, then her eyes filled with tears as she shook her
head. 'No, no, that cannot be right. I am a category C.' Her
tears spilled over and ran unchecked down her pale cheeks.
'I thought ... I thought I was safe here in England.'

Thea squeezed her free hand into a fist as she fought back
her own tears. She couldn't cry, she *mustn't* cry. She had to
stay strong for Anna's sake.

'No one's going to hurt you.' She handed Anna a clean
handkerchief. 'The police are just acting on an order from
higher up. I'm sure once they realise that you're not a threat
you'll be back here.'

'I am not a spy!' Anna wiped her eyes.

'I know that, and they soon will as well. I think those in
charge are just panicking because of the threat of invasion,
and they're overreacting by sweeping up anyone who isn't
from here, men or women.'

'Where are they taking me?'

'I don't know, but wherever it is I'm going with you
to make sure that you're looked after. I'll be with you, I
promise. Now you need to get up and pack any clothes you
want to take and anything that might be useful, like some
books or pens and paper, that sort of thing.'

Anna nodded. 'How long will I be gone?'

'I don't know, so take a mixture of clothes and something to do to occupy yourself.' She stood up. 'Hettie's making us some food to take with us.'

Downstairs in the kitchen a short while later, Hettie handed over the basket of food and drink to Thea and flung her arms around a subdued and tearful Anna.

'You'll soon be back here again, don't you worry. Once they realise that this is all a dreadful mistake,' Hettie said, finally releasing her.

Marianne, who'd been woken up by the goings-on and had come downstairs, hugged Anna tightly too, saying, 'Thea will look after you.'

Sergeant Grayson, who was carrying Anna's suitcase, cleared his throat. 'We need to get off.'

Thea nodded at him, grateful that he'd shown some compassion and had allowed Thea to shield Anna from as much distress as possible. He was clearly uncomfortable with what he was having to do, and while Anna had got up, washed, dressed and swiftly packed a suitcase, he'd maintained a discreet distance. He had even allowed her to have a quick breakfast, although the poor girl had been unable to swallow more than a few mouthfuls of bread, butter and honey that Hettie had given her. Now it was time to go, and Anna was clearly fighting to maintain her composure as Marianne and Hettie hugged her tightly.

'Don't you worry, you'll soon be back with us,' Hettie croaked, her eyes filling with tears as she grasped Anna's hand.

Anna nodded at them, unable to speak, her eyes bright with tears.

'Let us know what's happening.' Hettie put a hand on Thea's arm.

'Of course I will.' She had no idea where they were going, or how long she'd be away for, so she'd put some bare essentials for an overnight stay in her bag just in case she couldn't get back for a day or so. However this was going to play out, she was determined to do whatever she could to help Anna and bring her home after this whole sorry mess was sorted.

'Ladies, we need to get going,' Sergeant Grayson said from the back door.

Thea took hold of Anna's hand and together they left Rookery House's homely kitchen and followed the policeman out to his car, which was waiting on the drive in front of the house.

Sitting beside her on the back seat as they drove off, Thea kept hold of the young woman's hand, hoping that her touch was some reassurance. Anna was very quiet and subdued and, Thea suspected, in shock. Thea knew that if the situation were reversed she'd be kicking up a fuss and not going quietly, but then if she were regarded as an enemy alien in a country that had given her refuge, perhaps she'd do as she was told for fear of making it so much worse for herself. As awful as the situation was, she was grateful that she was here with Anna and hopefully would have the chance to do something about it quickly and bring her home again.

'Can you tell us where you're taking us now?' Thea

asked, leaning forward towards Sergeant Grayson in the driver's seat. They'd driven back through Great Plumstead and were heading out into the open countryside on the far side of the village.

'To Norwich.' That wasn't so bad, Thea thought. It wasn't far away and being on home ground would make it easier to get this sorted out. 'To Thorpe station,' he added.

The reassurance she'd felt only seconds before instantly evaporated. If they were going to that station it meant that they must be taking a train out of the county.

'And we're getting a train to where?' she asked.

'That I can't tell you. You'll see when we get there.' Sergeant Grayson glanced round briefly and shrugged. 'I'm sorry, but orders are orders. I'll be going with you though, don't worry.'

Thea slumped back in her seat and looked at Anna, who was staring out of the window at the passing countryside, which in its colours of fresh spring green looked so beautiful in the sunshine and contrasted starkly with the heavy grey feeling that had settled in Thea's heart.

Arriving at Norwich's Thorpe station, Sergeant Grayson parked the police car and shepherded them through the grand Victorian entranceway. After buying a newspaper from a vendor, he took them to the ladies' facilities and waited outside, before leading them onto the long train waiting by platform one which was London bound, and into a compartment that had been reserved for them.

'It will only be us in here,' he said, sitting down just inside the sliding door as if to keep guard. 'Orders again that we should travel in a sealed compartment with no other passengers. This will help pass the time.' He handed the newspaper to Thea.

She took the paper, knowing that he must feel awkward about doing this. At least he hadn't been unkind, but had shown patience and consideration. 'Thank you, we can do the crossword between us.'

He nodded. 'You know where you're heading?'

'London, but it's a big place . . . ' She raised her eyebrows. 'I don't suppose you can tell us where exactly?'

He shook his head and, leaning back against the seat, crossed his arms and closed his eyes.

Thea looked at Anna, who sat opposite her next to the window and was watching the comings and goings out on the platform. What must she be feeling right now?

Thea leaned forward and touched the young woman's hand. 'Are you all right?'

Anna nodded. She seemed calmer now than she had been when they'd left Rookery House, accepting almost, but then what choice did she have? Resisting government orders could make matters far worse for her.

As the train pulled into Liverpool Street station several hours later, Thea's mind was racing with the possibilities of what would happen next. She'd done her best to keep calm on the journey here, glad of the food and drink that Hettie had packed for them. Serving that out to Anna and Sergeant Grayson had given her something to do as well as reading the newspaper, but the journey now being over, and arriving in a city so far from Rookery House, made her feel as if the situation were fast slipping out of her hands.

Wherever Anna was destined to be taken here in London, it was going to be harder to deal with than if she'd been detained in Norwich.

'I'll be escorting you to a police car and it will take you on to your final destination,' Sergeant Grayson explained as he stood up. 'I'll be returning home on the next train to Norwich.'

'Can you at least tell us where Anna's being taken?' Thea asked.

'I'm not sure. My instructions were to escort her here to Liverpool Street and then hand her over to the London police, beyond that I don't know. Honestly I don't.' He looked at Anna. 'I'm sorry to have had to bring you here, Miss, really I am. I hope that it gets sorted out quickly so you can come home again.'

Anna nodded. 'Thank you.'

'Well, I'm not going back. I'm staying with you until you come back with me or I'm forced to leave.' Thea took hold of Anna's hand as they followed Sergeant Grayson out of the compartment and along the corridor. They finally stepped out of the carriage onto the crowded platform, where the noise and busyness of London felt overwhelming after their quiet village life.

A London police car was waiting to meet them near the taxi rank and Thea and Anna were soon being driven through the busy streets. Thea noticed the changes that had taken place since she'd left London almost a year ago, just a few months before war had been declared. Now evidence that the country was at war was all around, with sand-bagged buildings, windows criss-crossed with anti-blast tape and so many people dressed in service uniform of one sort or another.

'Can you tell us where we're going?' Thea asked the young police constable driver while they were stopped at a traffic light.

He turned around and looked at them. 'Holloway Prison.'

Thea felt Anna tense beside her and glanced at the young woman, whose face had drained of colour. She squeezed her hand reassuringly.

'But why? She's not a criminal.'

The policeman shrugged. 'Those are my orders.' Thea clenched her free hand tightly, the nails digging into her palm. Damn the stupid orders, she wanted to shout at the policeman, but knew if she did that she was likely to be deposited on the pavement and Anna taken to Holloway on her own. 'It's where all the female enemy aliens are being taken,' he added.

'Then I'm going in too,' Thea said.

The policeman shrugged and returned his attention to the road. The traffic lights had changed and they moved off again.

'I'm not going to leave you,' she whispered to Anna.

The young woman nodded, and when her brown eyes met Thea's she could see that Anna was frightened, understandably so. It was bad enough that she'd had to leave her family and country and flee to England, but now to be treated like this . . . Thea was utterly ashamed and horrified at her own country's government.

Arriving outside the imposing façade of Holloway Prison, Thea felt sick at the thought of what lay beyond the doors. Would Anna be admitted like a criminal when she'd done nothing wrong?

They got out of the police car and, hand-in-hand, were ushered towards the door by the policeman, who carried Anna's suitcase for her. But when the door was opened to admit them, the woman prison warder standing in the entrance didn't look very friendly.

'Another enemy alien for you,' the policeman said. 'Anna Weissenborn.'

The prison warder's eyes fell on Anna, and Thea could feel her hesitation through her hand. 'We'll take her from here.' She directed this at Thea, who in her green WVS uniform appeared only to be there in an official accompanying role. She had no idea that, in this case, it was far more personal.

'It's all right, I can come in and help because we need to get this sorted out,' Thea said. 'This is a terrible mistake. Anna shouldn't be here, she was given a category C at her tribunal, she's no threat to national security.'

The prison warder folded her arms and sighed. 'If the order came through for her to be detained, then that's what's going to happen until we are told otherwise. Now take your suitcase and come inside, we're busy enough today without having to argue over whether or not you should be here.'

The policeman went to hand Anna her suitcase, but Thea snatched it from him. 'I can at least come in and help settle her in.'

The police constable put out his hand to bar her way. 'Your job is done, go home and get on with whatever else you have to do. She's Holloway's responsibility from here on.' He grabbed the suitcase back from Thea.

Thea glanced at the policeman and he gave a small shake of his head to tell her that there was nothing she could do about it now, his eyes boring into hers. Reluctantly she knew this battle was one she couldn't win. 'Can I come back in the morning, then?'

'You can, but I doubt it will make much difference.' The prison officer shrugged. 'Come on.' She held out her hand to guide Anna in.

A wave of panic washed over Thea. She wanted to stop this, to grab Anna and run away with her as fast as they could, but that would only make things worse and she could be arrested herself.

No, she had to deal with this carefully and for the moment cooperate. She turned to Anna. 'I promise I'll be back tomorrow to try to get this mess sorted out so you can come home.'

Anna nodded, her eyes bright with tears.

Thea threw her arms around her and hugged her tightly. 'Keep strong,' she whispered in her ear. 'I promise I'll get you released; I won't give up until you are.'

Thea's throat was aching with a mixture of fury and tears as she watched Anna carrying her suitcase in through the heavy wooden door. The solid clunk it gave as it closed behind her seemed to echo through Thea's body.

'Would you like a ride back to Liverpool Street station?' the policeman asked kindly.

She looked at him and shook her head. 'Thank you, but I'm not going home tonight, I'm going to stay in London so I can come back tomorrow and sort this out.'

'Can I give you a lift somewhere else then?'

'All right, thank you. I'm going to my friend's in Holborn, so if you drop me near there it would be very helpful. It's been a difficult day and I appreciate your help.'

The policeman nodded, shifting from foot to foot. 'You know I don't like having to bring in people like Anna. I hope you can get her out soon.'

Thea smiled at him. 'Thank you.'

Chapter 23

'Wait in here and they'll sort you out,' the prison warder said, opening the door to a room and gesturing for Anna to go inside. Other women, who'd clearly been brought in today, were already waiting. There must have been at least thirty of them, and there was a low hum of conversation as they spoke to each other in pairs or small groups. From the expression on their faces they were clearly as unhappy about being here as she was.

She stepped inside, doing her best to suppress the rising panic that was welling up inside her; it had been growing since they'd arrived outside the prison, and since Thea had been forced to stay outside it was getting worse, making her shaky and nauseous. She never thought she'd end up in a prison when she came to England. Coming to this country had been about escaping being persecuted because of her religion but now it appeared that her nationality was against her too.

Looking around, she spotted an empty seat beside an older woman who was sitting reading, apparently oblivious to the chatter going on around her. Anna made her way over to her.

'Do you mind if I sit here?' she asked, her voice sounding wobbly.

The woman looked up at her and smiled, her face immediately becoming softer and more friendly than her severe, short, grey-streaked bob suggested. 'Please do.'

Anna sat down, glad to be off her legs which were threatening to give way as her anxiety worsened.

'Eva Groszmann.' The woman held out her hand.

Anna shook it. 'I am Anna Weissenborn.'

'Good to meet you ... though ...' Eva cast her eyes around the room before returning them to Anna's face, 'perhaps not in such pleasant circumstances.' Her English was good but had a strong trace of a German accent.

'I should not be here, I was given a category C at my tribunal, I am not a danger ... I am not a criminal ...' Anna's voice cracked, and she clasped her hands tightly in her lap. 'I shouldn't be put in prison.'

Eva's calm grey eyes held hers. 'I am the same, a category C ... I had plans to do much more important and interesting things today in my laboratory.' She shrugged. 'It is what it is, and we have to go with it for the time being.' She laid a thin hand on Anna's arm. 'Nothing lasts for ever ... you will not be here for the rest of your life, things will get sorted out, we just have to be patient. Till then we should make it as pleasant as possible for ourselves, keep ourselves occupied and busy. Try not to worry.'

'What will they do with us here?' Anna asked, focusing her attention on Eva as a distraction from the loud thudding of her heart inside her.

'We have to wait until our name is called and then we are taken and given a room. We just have to be patient.'

Anna nodded and racked her brains for something to ask, to divert her thoughts from the situation she was in. 'Where do you live?'

'Here in London, not far from the university where I work. They came banging on my door at six o'clock this morning, saying I must pack a suitcase and get ready to leave.' Eva shook her head and pulled a face. 'If I had known they were coming I would have risen early and gone out before they arrived.'

'The same happened to me. My friend, Thea, who is also my boss and whose house I live in, was accompanying the police – she is in the WVS and was asked to help, but did not know what it was about until just before they came to get me.' She recalled her surprise at waking up and seeing Thea in her room, dressed in her uniform; it had been hard to comprehend what was happening at first. 'She tried to come in here with me, but they would not let her, so she has promised to come back tomorrow to get me out.'

'She sounds a fine sort of friend to have, but ... ' Eva's gaze met hers, 'do not rely on your friend being able to get you out. It won't be because she does not try but I think it will take some time. We will not be here for ever, but you need to prepare yourself for a wait and not worry too much about it. Make it as pleasant for yourself as you can. I ... ' She paused as a prison warder appeared in another doorway, looking around the room at the women, who'd fallen silent at her arrival and were staring back at her.

'Dr Eva Groszmann.'

'That is me!' Eva put her hand up to acknowledge the guard and handed Anna the book she'd been reading. 'Here, read this until it is your turn – you can give it back to me later. Don't sit here brooding.' She stood up and smiled at her. 'I will see you soon.'

Anna watched her follow the warder out of the room and instantly felt the icy fingers of panic starting to creep into her chest again, but she ignored it and looked down properly at the book that Eva had given her. She couldn't help smiling when she saw what it was – an English copy of Grimms' fairy tales. A surprising read for such an obviously clever woman, but then perhaps not, because in times of trouble what better to read than stories that you've heard as a child, in a world of comfort and security at home? Like her, Eva must have been read these stories when she was young and had brought them with her here today. Opening the book, Anna ran her finger down the contents and chose a story that she'd loved, remembering snuggling up on her mother's lap as she'd read it to her. Beginning to read, she felt herself transported back to that time and away from the prison, and her body began to relax.

'Miss Anna Weissenborn.'

Anna was pulled out of the story she was reading at the sound of her name, her heart thumping hard again as she gathered her things together and followed the prison warder who'd called her, wondering what was about to happen.

'Take a seat,' the prison warder said, sitting down on the

other side of the desk after she'd led her into a small room. 'Right, let's start with your full name, then your date and place of birth.'

Anna provided her with the details she needed and watched as the woman wrote them down on the form. 'Before we can admit you onto the wing, you'll need to have a medical check and a bath.'

'Do you know why I have been brought here?' Anna asked. 'I was given a category C at my tribunal. I should not be here.'

The prison warder shrugged. 'All we've been told is to admit the women brought here and put them all together on C Wing. I don't know anything about who should be here and who shouldn't.' She smiled sympathetically. 'Hopefully you'll soon be out. But in the meantime, we need to get you properly admitted, so come on, I'll take you to get your medical check and then you can have your bath.'

A short while later, having been given a clean bill of health after a basic medical check by a bored-looking doctor, followed by a comb through of her hair to check for lice, of which of course there were none, Anna was led to the bathroom and instructed to have a quick bath. This was the last step before being taken up to the wing where the women who'd already been admitted had gone. Looking at the dirty state of the bathtub in the chilly tiled bathroom, Anna couldn't bring herself to sit down in it; she was likely to come out dirtier than she'd gone in, at the very least, or more likely catch something. Instead she washed herself using running water so that she was at least clean, because she had no idea when she might have the chance to wash properly again. Did they allow people to keep themselves clean in prison? She'd soon find out.

'Here are your sheets.' The prison warder who'd been waiting outside the bathroom for her handed her two threadbare, greyish sheets. 'If you want them washed, it's up to you to do them. Follow me.'

A sense of gloom and despondency settled over Anna as she was led into C Wing. The tall echoing building was arranged in layers, with a central open area. Metal staircases went from floor to floor and around the perimeter of each floor, where doors led off into cells.

'You can choose your own cell,' the prison warder said, turning on her heel and leaving Anna standing there.

Looking around, Anna could see that most of the cells on the ground floor were already occupied, but before she started her search for a free one she heard her name called from above. She looked up to see Eva peering over the railings at her from the next floor up.

'I saved you the cell next to mine, if you would like it,' Eva called down to her.

Anna smiled at her, and for the first time since she'd arrived here on C Wing she felt a spark of hope ignite inside her. 'Thank you.' She made her way up the metal staircase, her shoes clanging loudly on it with a sound that echoed around the wing.

'It is not the Ritz.' Eva stood beside Anna as she looked inside what was to be her own cell. 'But at least you do not have to share it with anybody.'

That was a definite positive, Anna thought as she took in the iron-framed single bed covered with a thin mattress, the small wooden table and chair, and the bucket toilet in the far corner. There were no curtains at the small, high, barred window.

'You know what I said about keeping busy?' Eva said. 'Well, the prison warder who brought me in told me they will be asking for volunteers once everybody's been admitted. They want people to sweep floors, fetch food from the kitchen, and those who do it will not spend so much time in their cells. I am going to volunteer and you should too if you want to make this as easy for yourself as you can. Keeping busy will help the time pass.'

'I will volunteer as well,' Anna said. 'Thank you for telling me.'

Eva nodded at her and smiled. 'I will leave you to settle in then and make up your bed. I hope your mattress is not as lumpy as mine!'

Left alone, Anna sat on her bed, the wire frame creaking as she did so, and looked around at the small cell. Yesterday she'd been out working in Rookery House's garden in the May sunshine, and now she was in a prison cell. It was hard to believe how drastically her life had been altered in just a few hours.

Chapter 24

Thea pressed the doorbell not knowing if her friend Violet would be at home or not, but she'd instinctively come here after being forced to leave Anna in Holloway. She couldn't abandon her and go home to Norfolk, she needed to be back at the prison the following morning to try to get Anna released. But meanwhile, time spent with her good friend would help.

Violet had asked her to visit when she was in London, only she hadn't expected to be coming here under these circumstances and now it looked like she was out of luck – Violet was most likely at work. Thea knew that she worked shifts that altered every few weeks, and it was probably her turn to be on duty now. She turned away and started back down the steps to the pavement when the front door opened.

'Thea!' Violet stood in the doorway, a wide smile on her face. 'What a wonderful surprise.' She threw her arms out wide and welcomed Thea in a tight hug before stepping back, her hands resting on her friend's upper arms as she looked at her through owlish, horn-rimmed glasses, her brown eyes shrewd as she instantly picked up that something was amiss. 'What's wrong? And why the WVS uniform?'

Thea's eyes brimmed with sudden tears and she shook her head. 'It's a long story.'

'Well, I've got plenty of time to listen, I'm not long back from today's shift. Come on in, I'll put the kettle on and you can tell me all about it.'

Upstairs in Violet's flat – which was actually her brother's, but into which she'd moved now she was working in London and he'd been posted away to serve in Scotland – they settled down into two comfy armchairs in the sitting room with a hot cup of tea spiced with a small slug of whisky each, her friend insisting that they could probably both do with it.

'So, tell me what's brought you to London. I take it from the uniform you're here on official business?' Violet asked.

'Remember I told you in one of my letters about Anna, who came to work for me and lives with us at Rookery House?'

Violet nodded. 'She's a German refugee?'

'Yes. Well, she's just been detained as an enemy alien, even though she was classed as a category C and isn't a threat to the nation. But clearly that didn't matter because for some reason it was decided that she had to be brought in ... and now she's in Holloway Prison.'

146

'*What!*' Violet leaned forward in her chair. 'But that's ridiculous. So you've come down hoping to use your role in the WVS to help get her released?'

Thea sighed. 'Not exactly. I accompanied the policeman to detain her and travelled with her to the prison.' She explained what had happened leading up to her arrival at Rookery House early this morning with Sergeant Grayson.

'It was an awful thing to be involved with, but it was better for Anna to be with somebody she knew rather than a stranger, and I hoped that I'd be able to stop it somehow, make them see sense and release her . . . They sent me away from Holloway, but I'm going back tomorrow morning.' She took a sip of tea, her throat warming with the taste of the whisky.

'Sounds like you were between a rock and a hard place, and if it's any help I think you did the right thing,' Violet said sympathetically. 'I understand the need to detain people who are Nazi sympathisers, but to do it to someone like Anna is extreme. Hopefully they'll see sense by the morning and let her go. If you like, I'll come with you to Holloway. My shift pattern changes tomorrow so I'll be on the later shift.'

'Thank you, I'd appreciate that.' Thea smiled at her friend.

'Try not to worry, though I know that's easier said than done.' Violet took a sip of her tea. 'We should make the most of seeing each other, catch up properly while you're here. It's ironic that after me visiting you in London for years, soon after you left I arrived to live here.'

'That's the war for you, it's brought so many changes to people's lives.' After serving together as ambulance drivers in the Great War, their friendship had carried on over the years, sustained by frequent letters and visits. Violet would come to stay with her brother here in the flat in London and see Thea, while Thea would visit Violet down in Devon too.

'I never thought I'd end up living here, but the chance to work for the ambulance service was too good to miss.'

'Do you miss teaching?'

'Yes, but it's good to be doing something different. I feel like I'm doing my bit, but I'm still in touch with some of my old colleagues. One of them, Louisa, who's now a headmistress, has just moved with her school to Longleat House for the duration. She's getting used to living in grand surroundings, but I much prefer the job I'm doing. It's something directly for the war effort and I enjoy it. You know there'd be a job for you if you wanted it, the ambulance service would be delighted to have someone with your experience working for them, I'm sure – if you ever felt like coming back here again . . . ' Violet raised her eyebrows questioningly.

Thea shook her head. 'My days of living in London are over. I'm enjoying the country life again and I'm doing my bit with the WVS mobile canteen and getting Rookery House's gardens into full production, and who knows what else I'll get involved with. Are you enjoying being a station officer, being the one in charge? I seem to recall you weren't one for sticking to the rules when we were humble ambulance drivers.' She grinned, remembering how Violet had liked nothing better than shirking the rules.

Violet laughed. 'I must admit there's nothing like seeing it from the other point of view.'

'What are the crews like?'

'A real mixture. They come from all walks of life – with more joining all the time.' Violet took another sip of tea. 'There's one young woman who reminds me very much of myself when we were in France in the way she likes to bend the rules, but she's a fine ambulance driver.' She smiled. 'You should come to the station and have a look round, meet the crews.'

'I'd like that, but I'm not sure if I'll have a chance while I'm here. My priority has got to be getting Anna out.'

'And if you can't get her out?' Violet's shrewd brown eyes held hers. 'What will you do then?'

'I don't know.' Thea swirled the last of the tea around in her cup. 'I can't stay in London for long because I've got work to do and WVS commitments back at home. It's a busy time in the garden, and with Anna gone, I'll have even more work to do.' She sighed. 'I don't want to go back without her though.'

'I'll help you all I can. If you can't get her released tomorrow, I'll be able to go and see her, keep an eye on her for you if you like.'

Thea smiled at her friend. 'Thank you. I've only known Anna a short while but she's become important to me and all of us at Rookery House. To have her detained is ... *awful*. She left Germany to get away from that sort of treatment and look what's happened to her now!'

Violet reached across and touched Thea's arm. 'She's lucky to have you fighting her corner. I know you won't settle until she's free again.'

'Absolutely! One way or another I'll help her come home to Rookery House, even if it takes a while. I won't give up trying until she's free.'

Chapter 25

Anna woke with a start, the loud clanging of a bell echoing around the building. She'd only managed to get to sleep a short while ago, unable to drift off any earlier despite feeling exhausted and wrung out by the previous day's events; her mind had refused to rest, going over and over different scenarios of what might happen to her. And now she felt awful, tired and crotchety. She wanted to bury herself under the grey sheets and scratchy blanket and block out this alien world that she'd been forced into, but clearly from the sounds echoing around outside her cell door there'd be no chance of that: a new day was beginning in Holloway Prison.

She glanced at her watch. It was six in the morning, and the warders were making their rounds, their heavy shoes thudding on the metal balcony. It would be a relief to have her cell door unlocked and open again. The sound of it clunking shut last night before it was locked had made such a horrible, heavy feeling settle in her stomach, and knowing that she was locked in and couldn't get out was stifling. She'd never had that sense before and didn't like it, but there was nothing that she could have done about it, though part of her had wanted to kick and scream, bang her fists against the door for them to open it. Anna knew that behaving like that would get her nowhere and would probably only make things worse for her.

She had her jobs to be getting on with today, as she'd volunteered along with Eva, and that was what she must focus on for now.

'Wakey, wakey, rise and shine!' called the warder who'd just unlocked the door as she pushed it open. 'Take your jug to the fountain to get yourself some hot water for a wash,' she added quickly before moving on to open Eva's cell next door.

Anna forced herself to get up, wincing as her bare feet landed on the cold floor, but at least it was a jolt to her senses and acted to make her feel more awake.

'Good morning, Anna.' Eva appeared in the doorway in her long nightgown, her water jug in her hand. 'There is already a queue for water and if you want a chance of it still being hot, you must hurry.'

'Good morning.' Anna slipped on her shoes, grabbed her water jug and hurried out of her cell, following Eva down to join the queue of women waiting their turn at the water fountain.

'How did you sleep?' Eva asked.

'Not very well. I think I only got a couple of hours at the very most.'

Eva nodded sympathetically. 'Same with me, but tonight will be better. We will be so tired that we'll be able to sleep on a knife edge.'

By the time the queue had shuffled forwards and it was their turn to fill up their water jugs, the hot had run to cold.

'That's the first lesson in here. If you want hot water to wash in,' Eva said, dipping her finger into her jug of water, 'then you need to be nearer the front of the queue in the morning.' She shrugged. 'By the time we get out of here, we'll have worked out the best ways to get by in this prison.'

Anna sincerely hoped that she wasn't going to be in here long enough to do that, although she was grateful to have palled up with Eva. She seemed savvy and calm, her temperament, good education and life experiences no doubt helping her deal with difficult situations like this far better than some of the other women. Several were crying, looking bewildered and bedraggled as they waited in the water queue, and everyone looked tired, no doubt having lain awake most of the night like she had. If this was the effect that less than twenty-four hours of prison had on people, then it was important to keep yourself going, keep busy and occupied as Eva had said. She was lucky to have been given jobs to do.

'Do you know when we go to the kitchen to get the food?' Anna asked as they headed back towards their cells with their jugs of water to get washed and dressed.

'It must be soon, so it is ready for the breakfast. We must get ourselves ready quickly, otherwise they might give the job to somebody else.'

Anna wasn't sure what she'd been expecting, but it hadn't been this, she thought as she was handed a pail of porridge and another of tea in the kitchen a short while later. Eva's eyes met hers, obviously thinking the same thing. Clearly, catering for the number of detainees needed large amounts and pails were the obvious way to transport them onto the wing, but it rather reminded Anna of feeding the animals back at Rookery House.

'Mind how you go with them,' said the warder who'd accompanied them down to the kitchen as they set off back to their wing, holding the door open for them to pass through.

'If I drop these, they will probably land marge-side down.' Eva was carefully holding onto the tray she'd been given, which was piled high with slices of bread and margarine – enough for three per person, which they'd been instructed to tell the other inmates had to last them all day until their evening meal tonight.

'Then they'd just have to be picked up and dusted off. There won't be any more what with the rationing,' the warder warned her.

Back in C Wing, they began the job of doling out the breakfast to the internees. Eva ladled the porridge into the bowls and Anna served the tea in cups which had *HMP* stamped on them.

'Take three slices of bread and marge,' Eva instructed each person. 'And do not eat it all at once, you will have nothing else till tonight so ration it out.'

'Is that all?' one woman asked. 'No more food in the day?'

The warder who'd been overseeing what they were

doing stepped forward. 'There is one other choice . . . ' The woman looked at her expectantly. 'You can have nothing. It's bread and marge or go without, your choice.'

The woman clearly wanted to say something but had the sense not to. She took her three slices and sat down at one of the tables to eat.

No one else questioned what they were given or complained, although the breakfast looked neither appetising nor tasty.

'Have your own breakfast and then collect up everyone's bowls and spoons and take everything back to the kitchen,' the warder instructed after they'd served the last inmate. 'You'll need to do the same routine again for tonight's meal.'

'Of course,' Eva said.

With their own portions of breakfast, they headed to a space at one of the tables and sat down next to each other.

'Well, this is not a grand Ritz hotel breakfast, but it is food,' Eva whispered, tucking into her porridge.

'We know what the other option is . . . ' Anna said quietly. 'Go without!'

Eva nodded. 'I can see you are a quick learner. There are rules in this place, and we need to work with them to survive well.'

Anna scooped up a spoonful of porridge. The taste of it wasn't what she was used to. Porridge at Rookery House was made with Primrose's creamy milk and topped with honey from Thea's bees, whereas this prison version was lumpy and bland with the texture of glue. And it was now barely lukewarm, which did nothing to enhance its flavour.

If she were not so hungry she'd leave it, but she ploughed through, doing her best to imagine it was Rookery House porridge. If she tried hard enough her mind might be able to convince her taste buds it was.

Chapter 26

Prue hurried along the street, thinking through all the things she needed to get done today as she made her way to the village hall to set up ready for the mothers' day club, which would start at ten o'clock. The sight of the postman delivering to houses on the other side of the road halted her, her mind immediately switching tack, and she couldn't help the bloom of hope swelling up that today might be the day that he had a letter from Jack for her. It was several weeks since she'd last heard from him; the few scribbled lines hadn't told her much, but at least had reassured her that he was still alive. She tried not to get her hopes up every time a delivery of post came, but her desperation to hear from her son, to know that he was alive and safe — or at least had been when he'd written to her — always won through.

She quickly crossed over and waited for the postman. As soon as he spotted her, she could tell from the look on his face that there was nothing again. Prue didn't even have to ask him, he knew how desperate she was to hear from Jack. Having a son of his own in the forces, he was sympathetic to her worries.

'I'm sorry there's nothing for you today. They're all for Victor.' He rifled through the letters in his leather bag, pulling out several which he handed to her. 'You might as well take these now.'

'Thank you.' She glanced through the envelopes and saw that they were all as he'd said, addressed to Victor.

'Perhaps there'll be one in the afternoon post,' the post-man said kindly. 'Or tomorrow.'

She nodded at him. 'Yes, I hope so.'

Leaving him to carry on with his round, she headed off towards the village hall, thinking that she did rather a lot of hoping these days.

Approaching the hall, Prue saw that Hettie and Marianne, with baby Emily in the pram, were standing outside in the late May sunshine waiting for her.

'I'm sorry you had to wait, only I saw the postman and ... ' She rummaged in her handbag for the key to the hall. 'Still nothing from Jack.'

'He'll write when he can.' Hettie reached out and touched her arm sympathetically.

Prue looked at her, doing her best to smile, and noticed the dark shadows under Hettie's eyes, the drawn look which was so different from her usual cheerful expression. 'Are you all right? Only you look rather tired and not yourself, if you don't mind me saying so. If you don't feel up to helping out this morning, then it's fine to go home again.'

'No, I'd rather be here. We both would, wouldn't we?' She looked at Marianne, who nodded.

'Best to keep busy,' Marianne added.

Something was wrong. 'What's happened?'

Hettie's blue eyes filled with tears behind her round glasses. 'Anna's been interned. She's in prison.'

Prue stared at the older woman for a moment, not quite believing what she'd just heard, but knowing from the look on Hettie's face that it was true. 'When? Why?'

Hettie sighed. 'I'll tell you as we set up, it helps if I keep my hands busy ...' Her voice cracked and Prue slipped her arm through Hettie's and led her into the hall, with Marianne following behind pushing the pram.

Prue listened in astonishment as Hettie told her how Thea had been sent on a mystery WVS mission and had ended up accompanying a policeman to detain Anna from her own home. She stopped unpacking the books and magazines that they were laying out on a table for the evacuee mothers, listening intently to what Hettie was saying.

'Thea telephoned last night to say that Anna had been taken to London and is now in Holloway Prison.'

'Holloway Prison!' Prue gasped. 'But Anna hasn't done anything wrong.'

Hettie sighed heavily. 'You know that, and I know that, and she was given a category C at her tribunal so she's no threat ... she's no spy ...' Her eyes were brimming with tears. 'But some fool in charge decided that she should be one of the women rounded up.' She pulled a handkerchief out of her pocket and dabbed at her eyes.

'What's going to happen to her?' Prue asked.

'Thea's going back to the prison today to try and get her released,' Marianne explained, having just finished putting toys out in the corner for the children. 'She stayed over last night at her friend Violet's.'

'Thea's very upset about it, she won't rest until Anna's free again,' Hettie added.

Prue bit her bottom lip, imagining how her elder sister must be feeling, but if there was anyone that could get this mess sorted out it was Thea.

'Awful as it was for her, I'm just glad that it was Thea who was sent to accompany Anna.' Hettie took the last of the magazines out of the box and arranged them on the table. 'At least Anna had someone she knew with her.'

'She shouldn't have been taken in the first place though,' Marianne said, carrying a box of wool, knitting needles and patterns over from the stock cupboard. 'She's a refugee, not a Nazi-supporting spy! She came here to get away from all that and look what's happened to her.' She put the box down on the table with more force than was necessary, her eyes bright with tears. 'She doesn't deserve to be put in prison, it's not fair!'

Prue went over and put her arm around the young woman. 'It shouldn't have happened, there's more than enough unpleasantness going on with this war without doing unnecessary things like that. Thea will sort it out and make them see that there's been a mistake, you'll see. She'll bring Anna home again.'

Marianne sniffed, nodding. 'I hope so.'

Prue glanced up at the clock on the wall. Only ten minutes left before the mothers would begin arriving for the day club and there was still a lot to be done. Hearing news like this always made her feel angry and frustrated at the unfairness of it; it seemed that with every passing day such events were becoming more and more frequent. But they had to carry on. It didn't mean that they didn't care, or that it didn't matter, but Prue had learned that there were times when you just had to do your best, do what was necessary. There'd be time to dwell on what had happened later, often in the quiet hours in the middle of the night.

'We need to get a move on or the mothers will be knocking on the door and we won't be ready,' Prue said. 'There's nothing we can do to help Anna from here, so let's keep busy and do what we can for the mothers in the meantime and hope that Anna and Thea are home soon.'

Hettie nodded at her and squared her shoulders. 'Best foot forward then. I've promised to demonstrate how to turn the heel of a sock again, the last attempts some of the mothers made were more hole than heel.'

Prue put her arm around Hettie's shoulder and squeezed her. 'It *will* be all right. Thea will sort it out, you'll see.'

Chapter 27

Thea looked up at the two griffin statues topping the columns either side of Holloway Prison's entrance and shivered. Waiting outside the imposing gateway, surrounded by the high walls – which if you didn't know what lay within would have looked like some castle with its small windows, crenellated battlements and tall towers – made her insides feel like they were quivering in fright. How much worse must it be to be incarcerated in here like Anna, and for doing nothing wrong? She squeezed her hands into tight fists and focused on breathing in and out steadily.

'Are you all right?' Violet touched her friend's arm.

Thea licked her dry lips and nodded. 'I'm trying to be.'

Violet glanced up at the solid wooden door that they'd knocked on a few moments earlier. 'It's not the sort of place anyone would ever want to come to unless they had to, is it? Just standing out here gives me the . . . ' She threw her hands in the air and pulled a face.

'Thanks for coming with me, I ...' Thea fell silent as the door opened and a prison warder peered out at them.

'Yes, what can I do for you?' the warder asked.

Thea stepped forward, glad that she was wearing her WVS uniform. It made her look more official than if she'd just been wearing her ordinary clothes. 'I've come to see someone about the young woman I accompanied here yesterday from Norfolk. She's a category C enemy alien and shouldn't have been interned.'

The warder raised her eyebrows. 'You'd better come in then.' She stepped to the side and waited for them to pass through the heavy doors before shutting them with a loud clunk, turning a key to lock them and sliding some bolts into place.

The sound of those doors shutting and being locked behind them made Thea suddenly want to run, to hammer on the doors to be let out, to be free.

'Follow me,' the warder said, leading them through more sets of doors that were unlocked, opened and locked again behind them. The further into the prison they went, the stronger the feeling of being trapped grew inside her. Thea had to give herself a mental talking to; she was here to get Anna out. It would only be for a short while and then she'd be free again.

They were finally led into a corridor and told to sit on some chairs outside a room. The warder knocked on the door, marked 'Governor', and went in.

Thea glanced at Violet, who looked as uncomfortable as Thea felt. 'What must it be like to be locked in here all the time? And this is just the offices, not even the cells.'

Violet crossed her arms across her body. 'Just coming in this far is enough to keep me on the straight and narrow, not that I ever thought of a life of crime!'

The door of the office opened, and the warder stepped out. 'Mr Davies will see you now.' She ushered them in and closed the door behind them.

Mr Davies stood up from behind his desk and held out his hand to each of them. 'Do sit down.' He nodded at the two chairs facing his desk. 'I'm the prison governor, and I understand that you've come about one of our enemy alien internees?'

Thea sat forward in her seat. 'That's right, Anna Weissenborn. I accompanied her here from her home in Norfolk where she works for me; she lives in my house and has done so since March. She's been an excellent employee and has also become a friend, and I have no hesitation in saying that Anna has absolutely no sympathies with the Nazi regime. In fact, it's because of them that her father died and she had to flee her home. She was given a category C at her tribunal and shouldn't have been interned at all.'

Mr Davies nodded. 'I appreciate what you say, but the decision was made to intern her. There must have been a reason.'

'Well, it was wrong!' Thea said. 'Can you free her and let me take her home?'

Mr Davies sat back in his chair, his hands clasped on the desk in front of him. 'I'm very sorry, but in the case of enemy aliens I have no authority to release them. My job is just to detain them and make sure they are cared for whilst they are here. You need to speak to someone who has the power to release your friend. I wish I could help you, but I can't.'

Thea squeezed her hands together hard, fighting back the urge to shout at him in frustration. 'So who *can* help me then?'

'I would suggest you try a government department, the one which arranged for the enemy aliens to be interned in the first place. I wish you luck.' He stood up, signalling that their meeting was at an end.

'Can I at least see Anna?' Thea asked. 'Just for a few minutes to make sure that she's all right?'

Mr Davies shook his head. 'I'm sorry, but that's not possible today, although if she puts you on her list of visitors, you can come and see her on any visiting day.'

'But I live in Norfolk! I can't just come and see her when I want.' She sighed. 'At least tell me how she is,' she said, staying put and ignoring his opening of the office door for them to leave.

'I can assure you that Anna and all our enemy alien internees are perfectly well and will continue to be cared for while they are under my watch. I give you my word on that.' Mr Davies smiled at her. 'Now if you'll excuse me, I really do have a lot of work to be getting on with . . . ' Thea stood up. 'You can write to your friend here as often as you wish. I'm sure she'd appreciate your letters.'

'If you won't let me see her today, can I at least leave her a letter, tell her what's happened so she doesn't think I've just abandoned her here?'

'Yes, of course, I'll see that she gets it,' Mr Davies said, picking up his pen ready to get on with his work.

Thea bit her bottom lip. 'Could I possibly have a piece of paper and pen, please, to write to her? Only I don't have any with me.' She smiled at him.

'Here, take these.' He opened a desk drawer and took out a sheet of paper and a pen and handed them to her. 'Leave the letter with my secretary and I'll personally make sure that Anna gets it. Now I *really* do have to get on.'

'Yes of course. Thank you very much, I appreciate your help.' Taking the paper and pen, and throwing him a grateful smile, Thea followed Violet out of his office and sat down on one of the chairs outside, beginning to quickly write a letter to Anna while the warder stood waiting for them, tapping her foot.

'If you ask Anna to put my name on her visitors' list, then I can come and see her and tell you how she's getting on,' Violet said. 'Give her my address.'

Thea looked up at her friend and smiled. 'Thank you, I will.'

In the letter, Thea explained briefly that she'd been here to the prison this morning and had been unable to either have her freed or be allowed to see her, but that she would not give up trying to get her released. Then, after she'd handed it in to the governor's secretary, they were led out of the prison.

Outside again, after the heavy doors had shut with a clunk behind them, Thea closed her eyes and breathed in deeply. The sense of being out in the free world was almost overwhelming and made it harder to cope with the knowledge that Anna was still inside, locked up behind thick doors, walls and bars.

'I've failed her,' she said, turning to look at Violet.

'No, you haven't.' Violet put her arm around Thea's shoulders. 'You did all you could and were met with a solid wall of rules and regulations. The only way forward is to go to those who are responsible for Anna being in there.' She sighed. 'It's not right what's happened, but there's a lot going on like that now with this war.'

Thea nodded. 'You're right, but I really don't want to leave her here, I want to take her home again with me.'

'That's not going to happen yet.' Violet's voice was gentle. 'You've done all you can here, and you need to go home and get on with your work and write to the government department that's in charge.'

Thea nodded. 'I hate leaving her here, but you're right, if there's really nothing I can do to convince the prison governor to let her go, then I must go home and start writing letters to get her freed.'

Violet smiled at her. 'I know you won't give up till she is.'

Chapter 28

Thea halted in the gateway of Rookery House, remembering how she'd left just yesterday morning, sitting in the back of the police car beside Anna. She hadn't known then where they were heading, assuming it would be Norwich at the furthest, but sadly she'd been very much mistaken. Now Anna was in London, locked up behind bars in Holloway Prison, leaving Thea no choice but to return home alone.

Her failure to get Anna released this morning had hit her hard; she'd felt so frustrated and useless, unable to persuade the officers of their error.

Heading round to the back door, she let herself into the kitchen. She found Hettie standing by the table, using wooden pats to knock a lump of freshly churned butter into shape.

The older woman looked up at her in surprise, dropping the pats onto the board and hurrying towards her. 'You're back!' She looked towards the door. 'Is Anna with you?'

Thea shook her head, pulled out a chair and slumped down on it. 'No, I couldn't get her out! I tried my hardest to persuade the prison governor, to make him see sense, but he wouldn't budge, said it wasn't his decision.' Her voice cracked and she wiped away tears with the back of her hand. 'I had to leave her there and come back. I couldn't stay any longer because there's so much to be done here.'

Hettie put her arm around Thea's shoulders. 'I'm sure you did your best for her.'

Thea nodded. 'I'm not giving up, I'll keep on trying from here. The prison governor told me to write to the government, to someone who has the power to have her freed. That's exactly what I'm going to do.'

'Hopefully they'll soon listen and believe that Anna's not a threat to this country.' Hettie squeezed her shoulder. 'How is she?'

'I don't know, they wouldn't let me see her this morning. The governor said she was fine and would be well cared for. Yesterday she was quiet and upset, and scared when we got to Holloway.'

'I'm not surprised. Poor girl! It's not right what's happened.' Hettie fell silent for a moment and dabbed at her eyes with her handkerchief. 'Do you want something to eat?'

Thea shook her head. 'No, thank you, I need to go and get changed back into my normal clothes.' She was still wearing her WVS uniform, which she'd put on the day before, never imagining where that day would take her. 'Then I need to go and get on with some work.' She stood up. 'Who's been milking Primrose?'

'Reuben.' Hettie returned to her task, picking up the pats

again and smacking them against the bright yellow butter with more force than she usually did.

'I feel awful coming home and leaving Anna in London, but I couldn't stay any longer and burden others with my jobs. Reuben's got his own work to do and on top of that his duties for the LDV.'

'Anna will understand that,' Hettie reassured her. 'Don't be hard on yourself, Thea. What's happening to her isn't of your making. You going with her like you did would have helped her, it would have been far worse if she'd been taken away by strangers.'

Thea nodded. 'I'm sad that someone who's been through so much already in her young life, who had to flee her country, is now behind bars like some criminal when she's done absolutely nothing wrong.'

'I know, but she won't be there for ever, keep that in mind,' Hettie urged her. 'Get changed and get out in the garden for a bit, it will help you feel better. And it will soon be time for milking.'

Hettie was right, Thea thought, as she led Primrose in on the halter to be milked later. Being outside in the garden, doing some weeding, had helped her to calm down, to accept that coming back here wasn't a betrayal of Anna. She'd done what she could and would continue to fight for the young woman's release, targeting those who were in charge by letter rather than banging on the door of Holloway Prison.

Keeping Rookery House's garden going without Anna's help meant she would need to put in a lot more hours as well. She knew that Hettie and Marianne would help where they could, but they already had plenty to do in the house and with looking after a young baby. It was up to her to shoulder the responsibility; she'd just have to work harder and longer.

With Primrose safely installed in her byre and happily munching on some hay, Thea quickly cleaned her teats and sat down beside her on the milking stool, placing the clean metal pail underneath the cow's udder and starting to milk. As the stream of milk plinked onto the bottom of the pail, she settled into a steady rhythm. The jets of milk soon covered the bottom of the pail and the level began to creep up the sides, bubbles forming on the top of the creamy liquid. Leaning her head gently against Primrose's flank, she breathed in the soothing sweet smell of cow, a scent that came from chewed-up grass and plants.

The way to get through what was happening was to take it one day at a time. Worrying wasn't going to get her anywhere. It would only drain her energy, and she was going to need all of that to get through the work and keep fighting to get Anna free.

Chapter 29

Anna was sweeping the floor of a corridor inside C Wing, glad to be out of her cell doing something to occupy her time – and her mind. The internees who didn't have jobs to do like her and Eva had to spend most of their time in their cells. They were only allowed out for meals or to collect water for washing, and they were only permitted one hour outside in the small exercise yard.

Being restricted to her cell for most of the day and night would have been hard to bear now she was used to being outside in the garden at Rookery House. She'd quickly grown to love working outdoors, enjoying the feel of the wind or sun on her face, hearing the song of birds, the buzz of insects, being aware of the world going on around you. In here, she felt so cut off from the life that continued outside the solid walls.

It was astonishing, she thought as she worked her way along, how even the simple act of sweeping the floor had become such an important part of her life. She'd be forever grateful that Eva, who was working her way towards her, sweeping from the far end of the corridor, had suggested that she volunteer for the job. And after seeing that they were both competent and could be trusted to get on with what they were doing, the warders now left them to their own devices.

It was only two days since she'd been brought to Holloway, but it felt like far longer; the days and nights seemed to stretch on in a way they never had before. Her hopes of a quick release had soon been dashed, but it wasn't through lack of trying. Thea had kept her word and visited the prison governor the morning after she'd been brought in, but had been unable to get her freed. She'd learned all this from the letter she'd had from Thea this morning, telling her that she'd had no choice but to return home, but would be continuing her campaign from afar writing letters to whoever might help. She would not be giving up until Anna was free.

'What is wrong?' Eva's voice interrupted her thoughts.

Anna stopped sweeping and looked at the older woman who stood watching her, leaning on her broom.

'You look worried.'

Anna shrugged. 'Just thinking about Thea's letter, that is all.' She'd shown it to Eva, who'd read it through carefully.

'You must be patient, Anna. I know this is hard and life in here is not what we would choose, but it is what it is for the moment. It will not *always* be this way, and if your friend is doing what she can to get you out, then eventually you will be free again. I hope we all will be when those in charge realise that we are not going to do anything to help the enemy . . . ' She pulled a face. 'Far from it.'

'I know.' Anna managed a smile. 'I am going to apply for a visitor's permit so Thea's friend Violet can come and visit me.' Thea had explained that this was possible in her letter and had given her Violet's address so that the prison could send her the permit. 'It's too far for Thea to come and see me often, so it's kind of her friend to offer.'

'Yes, it will be good to see a new face and get news from outside. I'm going to do the same for some friends of mine. We need to keep positive, remember that.' She smiled. 'Come on, we've work to do – these floors will not sweep themselves.'

Chapter 30

Prue stared across her kitchen at the Bush wireless set, her eyes boring into it as if by some miracle it would allow her to see for herself the events being described by the reporter, Bernard Stubbs, who had witnessed the return of soldiers plucked off the beaches of Dunkirk. He talked about the different sorts of ships going back and forth, day and night, across the Channel, in a desperate attempt to rescue the trapped soldiers of the British Expeditionary Force, and how the ships, like the men waiting on Dunkirk's beach, were being targeted by enemy planes, machine-gunned and bombed, as they went to the rescue or waited to be rescued.

Clasping her hands tightly together on her lap, her knuckles standing out white, Prue listened as he described watching the rescue ships dock on the south coast, coming in packed with as many soldiers as they could take; how the soldiers who disembarked were exhausted, bloodstained and bandaged, their uniforms in tatters, but each one relieved to be off that beach and home again.

Many of them had waited three days to be rescued. Out on a beach exposed to the guns and bombs of the enemy, they'd been sitting ducks. Even hospital ships had been hit, their Red Cross symbols giving them no protection from the ruthless attack.

Was Jack among them? Had he been brought back to Britain, plucked from the French beach? Had he even made it as far as Dunkirk?

Prue closed her eyes against stinging tears. She had absolutely *no* idea where he was, or even if he was still alive, and there was nothing she could do to change that or to help him. That feeling of helplessness over the wellbeing of her own son was hard to bear.

She'd have moved heaven and earth to help him if he was hurt or in trouble when he was younger, but like so many mothers there was nothing she could do to help him from here, only wait and hope.

Chapter 31

Thea handed the soldier his paper packet of ham sandwiches and cake ready for his journey to wherever the war was taking him next. 'Hope you enjoy them.' She smiled warmly at him. 'Safe travels.'

The young man nodded and returned her smile. 'Thank you.' He heaved his kitbag up onto a shoulder and marched off to join the rest of his unit, waiting on the station platform for the train to come in.

'Good job he was the last one,' Prue said. 'We've only got two more portions of food left.'

As well as doing their usual mobile canteen run to various isolated military outposts, they'd been asked to provide refreshments at a village station today, where troops were leaving from the local army camp and heading off to a new posting, needing food for the journey as well as hot drinks while they waited.

'We've done really well today, it's better to nearly sell out than have a lot left over.' Thea glanced at her watch; it was just gone three o'clock. 'We might get a few more customers yet for cups of tea, so why don't we have a break ourselves and sit down before we start clearing up. It feels like we've been on the go all day and I could do with a rest before we tackle that lot.' She nodded towards the pile of used mugs.

'Good idea,' Prue agreed.

Sitting in the open back door of the canteen a few minutes later with mugs of tea, enjoying the warmth of the June sunshine, Thea read the headlines in today's copy of the *Daily Mirror*, which one of the soldiers had left behind on the counter. 'We Never Surrender' was printed in large black letters, and underneath it was a report about the rousing speech that the Prime Minister had given in Parliament yesterday.

'I hope Churchill's right about not surrendering, and that we'll never be forced into making that choice,' Prue said, nursing her cup of tea.

'Well, it's what he believes. It was stirring stuff, they've quoted it here, look.'

Prue glanced at where Thea was pointing. 'Read it out, will you? I heard the newscaster reading it last night, but I'd like to hear it again.'

'All right.' Thea took a sip of tea and began to read. '*Even if large tracts of Europe fall into the grip of the Gestapo and all the odious apparatus of Nazi rule, we shall not flag or fail. We shall go on to the end, and shall fight in France, on the oceans and in the air. We shall defend our island, whatever the cost, and shall fight on the beaches and landing grounds, in the fields and streets; we shall never surrender.*'

'It sends shivers up your spine, that bit about fighting on the beaches and in the fields and the streets.' Prue tucked her arm through Thea's. 'Do you think Churchill's preparing for us to be invaded, just like Holland, Belgium and France? That he wants us to fight in our homes if necessary?'

Thea nodded. 'Yes, and that we'll do everything we can, we won't give up. The message is as much for Hitler as it is us. He's telling him that if he does invade then it won't be an easy fight.'

While they sat in silence for a moment, sipping their tea, Thea considered what the future might hold. The threat of invasion was very much on people's minds these days, and with troops having so recently been snatched away from the jaws of the enemy by the brave actions of so many sailors, it seemed very much like they needed to consider *when* it would happen and not *if*.

Her eyes drifted down the article, reading more about what Churchill had said to the House of Commons. The number of soldiers reported to have been evacuated from France was some three hundred and thirty-five thousand, with thirty thousand dead, injured or missing. It made a heavy weight settle in her stomach – there was still no word from Jack or any communication that he'd been wounded, or worse. Which category would he fall into: rescued, dead, injured or missing?

She quickly turned the pages over, not wanting Prue to read those stark figures for herself, because she knew how worried her sister was about Jack. Despite Prue being busy as usual, carrying on with her various commitments, the strain and worry was clearly taking a toll on her – she looked drawn and thinner than she used to.

Prue drained the last of her tea and stood up, having taken barely five minutes' break. 'I'll go and get started with the washing up. You finish your tea and then you can come and dry.'

'I won't be long. Why don't you wait a little longer? We've had a busy day.'

Prue gave a shrug. 'It's all right, I like to keep busy, you know me.' And before Thea could argue, her sister had climbed into the canteen to get back to work.

Thea was in no rush and carried on reading the article, sipping her tea. She had almost finished it when some words quoted from Churchill struck a chord with her.

'*We have found it necessary to take measures of increasing stringency not only against enemy aliens ... I know there are a great many people affected by the order we have made who are passionate enemies of Nazi Germany.*'

Yes, people like Anna, she thought.

'*I am sorry for them, but we cannot draw all the distinctions we should like to do. If parachute landings were attempted and fighting followed, these unfortunate people would be far better both for their own sake and ours in a place of safety ...*'

Thea dropped the newspaper onto her lap and leaned forward, her elbows on her knees, her hands cradling the still-warm mug. Despite the sunny June day she was grateful for the gentle heat that it gave to her hands, because those words chilled her. She was glad that Churchill acknowledged there were those like Anna who'd been swept up in the internment of enemy aliens; innocent people who were as much enemies of the Nazis as any British person, but had been lumped together as possible threats to the country because of their place of birth.

His point about Anna and others like her being in danger from invading troops was a sobering one. She knew that Anna had feared the country being invaded and falling to Hitler just as Holland and Belgium had, and now that France was fighting for its survival too it could happen here. If the invasion came, refugees like her who'd fled because they were Jewish would be just as much under threat as they had been in their homeland.

Was Anna really safer in Holloway than she would be here, though? At least if she was home at Rookery House Thea could do her best to protect her, could even go so far as to hide her away so that the enemy never found her.

But that was all just idle speculation. Right now Anna was still stuck in prison, and despite writing to the government to get her released, Thea had as yet had no luck.

She'd keep on writing letters until they got so fed up with her that they'd let Anna go just to shut her up. In the meantime, she had mugs to dry and a canteen to pack up ready to head back home.

After dropping off the canteen in Wykeham and returning to Rookery House, Thea changed out of her WVS uniform. She was in the middle of the evening milking when she became aware of someone standing in the doorway of the byre and turned her head to see who it was.

'I didn't want to startle you. Or Primrose, in case she kicked the pail over, but ... ' Prue spoke quietly and advanced into the byre a few feet. 'But I had to come and tell you …' Her voice cracked and Thea grabbed the pail and stood up, her heart pounding in her chest, fearing the worst.

'Jack?' Thea asked, moving towards her sister.

Prue nodded and held out a postcard to her, smiling through tear-filled eyes. 'He's alive. Picked up off Dunkirk beach.'

'Oh, thank God!' Thea quickly scanned the brief message on the postcard. In true Jack style, it only said what was necessary to convey his message. But in this case it was a message of huge importance: he'd survived and was back on British soil again.

'That's wonderful news!' Thea threw her arms around her sister and hugged her tightly.

Chapter 32

'You've got a visitor.'

Anna looked up from where she lay on her bed reading, after she and Eva had finished their daily sweep of the floors in their wing, to see one of the warders looking in at her.

'Who is it?' she said.

The warder shrugged. 'They didn't say. I was just told to bring you down to the interview rooms where you can see her.'

Hopefully it would be Violet, Thea's friend, who might have news for her. She quickly stood up and followed the warder out of the wing and to a section of the prison she hadn't been to before.

'There'll be an interpreter in there with you as well.' The warder stopped outside a door.

Anna frowned. 'Why?'

'They're the rules. In case anyone tries to give away information that may be of national importance and affect the war. If you refuse to agree to them being there, then I'll have to take you straight back to the wing.'

'No, it's fine, but there will be nothing to interpret and I have no information to give away, even if I wanted to.'

The warder shrugged and opened the door for her to go in. 'I'll be back to get you in half an hour.'

Stepping inside, Anna saw there were two women in the room, one sitting on one side of the small table, and the other on a chair by the far wall.

'Hello, I'm Violet Steele.' The woman at the table stood up and came to meet her, holding out her hand. 'I'm delighted to meet you, Anna. I've heard a lot about you from Thea.'

Anna shook her hand. 'Hello, thank you for coming.'

'Have you been told about having an interpreter present?' Violet asked, indicating the woman sitting by the wall with a notebook and pencil on her lap, and who now smiled at them. 'Miss Blake will be here to monitor our conversation in case you speak to me in German ... though I should warn you that if you do I won't understand it, so English is best.' She arched her eyebrows behind her round horn-rimmed glasses, her brown eyes twinkling.

Anna nodded, doing her best not to laugh at the ridiculousness of the situation. But as she'd learned in this place, rules were rules, and if it were necessary for an interpreter to waste her time listening to them talk in English, then that's what had to happen.

'Shall we sit down?' Violet settled herself at the table and lifted something wrapped in brown paper out of the basket by her chair. She placed it on the table in front of

Anna. 'I brought you a cake. I thought you might enjoy it, a nice treat.'

Anna's eyes filled with tears. 'Thank you, that is very kind of you, and if you do not mind, I will share it with some of the other women. Since we have been allowed to have visitors, we share out any food gifts we get between us.'

'Not at all, and there are these too.' She took some books out of her basket and passed them to Anna. 'Share them around as well.'

Anna smiled at her. 'I will, thank you. We swap books between us, there is a lot of reading going on as there's not much else to do.'

'I'll bring you some more next time – if you'd like me to come again?'

'Yes, please, it is so lovely to have a visitor. Though I should warn you, they told us yesterday we are going to be moved somewhere new, but they did not tell us when or where to.'

'Don't worry about that, I'll keep coming to see you while you're here. So, how are you?' Violet's eyes searched Anna's face. 'I promised Thea that I'd find out and have a good look at you to see that you're well. She's worried as she hasn't heard from you yet.'

'Oh, but I have written several letters to her.' Anna sighed. 'They are all censored by the governor, so it takes time for them to be sent out from the prison. Will you please tell her that I have written to her and that they are delayed?'

'Of course. Are they treating you well?' Violet's shrewd brown eyes met hers and Anna was aware that the older woman was watching her very carefully for any sign that something was wrong, or that she might be hiding something.

'I am fine, honestly. We are looked after and treated fairly with no cruelty, and apart from being locked up in a prison and not being able to go outside very much – or leave – I am managing. The warders are good, they now let us lock our own doors at night . . . ' She frowned. 'I know that sounds like a strange thing to be happy about, but after the first few nights of being locked in – it is such a horrible feeling, the sound of the door shutting on you – they decided that because we are behaving well and have not actually broken the law, when it is time to shut the doors just before lights out at nine o'clock, we're allowed to lock them ourselves.' She shrugged. 'It makes us feel a little better.'

'I'm sure it does. When your freedom is suddenly taken away, small things can make a big difference.' Violet smiled sympathetically. 'Do you know what's going on with life outside? Do you have newspapers?'

Anna shook her head. 'No, but we do listen to the news on the wireless every night after tea, just like I did at Rookery House. I miss being there.'

'I'm sure you do, and I know they all miss you too. Thea hasn't had any response yet from the government to her letters about you being in here. She's carrying on writing them until you're freed.'

'I really appreciate what she is doing. Not everyone in here has someone on the outside trying to get them out.'

'I know how persistent Thea can be if she puts her mind to something. It's worked well for her in her life so far. It helped her get through some sticky situations when we were working together in France during the Great War.'

'She told me she was an ambulance driver then.'

Violet nodded. 'We both were, that's how we met and became friends. And we've remained so ever since. I'm running an ambulance station this time around.'

Violet was interesting to talk to and the half hour flew by. It seemed as if only five minutes had passed when the warder came in and told them that their time was up.

Violet stood and took both of Anna's hands in hers. 'I'll write to Thea as soon as I get home and tell her about my visit, how you are and that your letters are being delayed.'

'Thank you. And thank you for the cake and books, they mean a lot to me and the other women.' She picked up the gifts and with a final smile at Violet followed the warder out. As she headed back to the wing she felt a lightness that she hadn't experienced since she'd come in here.

Chapter 33

Thea skimmed a spoon across the top of a large bowl of milk, scooping up thick cream from the layer that had risen to the surface, then added it to the sterilised churn ready to be turned into butter. She loved doing this, enjoying how they could transform Primrose's milk into other things to eat, as well as having the milk to drink.

A plinking sound made her glance at the muslin bag hanging from a hook in the ceiling of the cool pantry, which was full of curdled milk, the drips of whey falling out into the pan below it. When the soft cheese was ready, Hettie would add some salt and herbs from the garden and it would be delicious spread on bread.

They weren't the only ones enjoying what Primrose provided. Prue and several other people in the village now bought milk, butter and soft cheese from them and when Hettie's hard cheese was ready, no doubt they'd buy some of that too. Grace Barker had also said that she'd like some to sell in her grocery shop. They were all very proud of the income Rookery House's land was bringing in.

The pantry door suddenly burst open and Hettie hurried in, her cheeks flushed and her blue eyes anxious behind her round glasses. 'Look what's just been delivered!' She thrust the sheet of paper at Thea. 'It's put the wind up me!'

She took the piece of paper in her free hand and read the large printed words across the top: *If the invader comes — what to do and how to do it.*

'It must mean the government think it's really going to happen.' Hettie waved the other envelopes that she was holding in her hand in the air.

'Well, it's a possibility. There's no point kidding ourselves, is there? The Nazis have invaded so many other countries, why should they stop at us? Why don't you finish skimming off the cream while I read it properly?' She offered Hettie her spoon.

'All right, or we'll be late getting the butter made. I've promised Prue there'd be some ready for her this afternoon.'

With Hettie now occupied, Thea read through the leaflet carefully, thinking how, at first glance, it wasn't surprising that its message inspired a sense of panic and fear. But in fact, the content was sensible, and it was far better to be prepared for what might happen than merely hope it wouldn't.

'Well, what do you think?' Hettie added the last spoonful into the churn, screwed on the lid from which small paddles hung down and then began to turn the handle, which cranked the mechanism inside and twirled the paddles round and round through the thick cream.

'It's a scary thought that the Nazis might invade, but this leaflet is to try to stop what happened to Poland, Holland and Belgium from happening to us. Because as it says here,' Thea pointed to the words, 'they were taken by surprise, and because the people didn't know what to do, they fled their homes and blocked the roads, making it hard for their armies to defend the country because they couldn't get around easily.'

Hettie frowned. 'Well, it's only natural to want to run away if the enemy's bearing down on you and you're just an ordinary person, not in the forces with training and guns to defend yourself.'

'Exactly, it's instinct to do just that,' Thea agreed. 'But it gives the invading enemy an advantage, and that's what this is trying to prevent happening here. If they do invade, at least people know from reading this that they need to stay put and do everything they can not to help the enemy. We need to make it as hard as possible for them to find their way around. That's why they've taken down all the signposts – if the enemy doesn't know which road leads where, which railway station is which, what a street or village is called, it could buy precious time for our troops.'

'Well, if a Nazi paratrooper comes knocking on our door, he won't get any help from me. I'll be after him with my rolling pin.' Hettie's usually friendly face looked fierce. 'It would make a good weapon, it's solid.'

'I doubt they'd knock first, but if any did come to Rookery House, we'd put up a fight. Try not to worry too much about this.' Thea waved the leaflet. 'What else did the postman bring? Is there anything for me?'

Hettie delved into the pocket of her apron where she'd tucked away the envelopes. 'There's one for you and one for Marianne, from Alex by the look of it.' She handed them to Thea then carried on churning the cream again.

Thea looked down at the envelope addressed to her and recognised the handwriting.

'It's from Violet,' she said, tearing the envelope open and reading the letter quickly, absorbing what her friend had written.

'What does she say? Did she go to see Anna?' Hettie asked.

Thea nodded. 'She took her a cake. Anna was really pleased with it and said she was going to share it with the other women. She says,' Thea read aloud from the letter, *'Anna seemed in good spirits and has been told that they're going to be moved somewhere else, but she didn't know where or when.'*

'What?' Hettie looked worried. 'That could be any-where. Perhaps we can get her out before that happens.'

'I'm trying!' Thea sighed. 'But so far my letters have had no effect. I'll write again tonight – perhaps they'll get so fed up with me bombarding them that they'll release Anna just to shut me up!'

It was frustrating that her appeals had gone unanswered. Thea hated the thought of Anna being in prison, or wher-ever she was going to be sent next, until somebody saw sense and released her.

'Go and put the kettle on, we could do with a cup of tea,' Hettie suggested. She stopped churning and checked her progress, and Thea could see that small golden granules of

191

butter had formed, which would gradually clump together and separate from the thinner buttermilk. 'This won't take much longer and then I can make it into pats. Invasion or not, we've still got work to do!'

Chapter 34

Reaching the end of the row, Prue leaned on her hoe and looked back at the upright beetroot plants with their pleasing green leaves and purple stems. She was delighted with how her garden was growing; she'd never grown so many vegetables before, having always preferred flowers. The garden was nowhere near as big as Thea's at Rookery House, but it was making an important contribution to her family's fresh food supplies.

As part of the Dig for Victory campaign, Prue had turned most of her garden over to vegetable production, and had dug up the flower beds and the lawn into plots for growing food. She'd taken advantage of the Sutton's vegetable seed collections that were available for WI members and had planted peas, broad beans, beetroot, Brussels sprouts, broccoli, cabbage, leeks, lettuce, parsnips, onions and turnips, to provide food not only for her family, but also to sell on the WI market stall in Wykeham.

Every spare moment Prue had, she was out tending the garden, and she'd even persuaded Alice to lend a hand when she wasn't at school. Prue enjoyed the time she spent out here. It was calming and relaxing and gave her a much-needed break from her busy life – not that she would ever admit that.

'Hello, Prue!' a voice called, making her turn around. Marianne appeared around the side of the house pushing Emily's pram. 'You look content.'

Prue laughed and went to meet the young woman, whom she'd invited round to talk through a new venture she had planned, one that would benefit from Marianne's expertise.

'I enjoy tending my garden, it's rewarding to see how it grows and changes every day.' She looked in the pram at Emily who was fast asleep, her dark lashes resting on her cheeks. She was a beautiful baby. 'She's grown every time I see her.'

'She has a very healthy appetite.' Marianne smiled.

'I thought it might be nice to sit out here and talk, as it's such a nice day. Would you like a cup of tea, or some cordial perhaps? I've got a bottle of Hettie's elderflower, which is lovely and refreshing on a summer's day.'

'Yes, some cordial would be lovely, thank you.'

Prue leaned her hoe against a wall near the back door. 'You sit down.' She nodded to the bench which stood beside her one remaining rose bed. 'I won't be long.'

Returning outside a few minutes later, carrying a tray with glasses and a jug of elderflower cordial, Prue saw that Marianne had parked the pram so it was out of the direct glare of the sun, and she was smelling a pink rose.

'Isn't it the most beautiful scent?' Prue put the tray down

in the middle of the bench and sat down at one end while Marianne sat at the other. 'I couldn't bear to dig it up to plant vegetables there, it doesn't take up much room – it's my one indulgence and it brings me a great deal of pleasure. We need that in wartime, don't we?'

'It's the most fragrant rose I've ever smelt.' Marianne took the glass of cordial that Prue had just poured her. 'Thank you.'

Prue took a sip of her drink and leaned back against the bench. 'How's Alex getting on?'

'Very well, he's enjoying it immensely, so he says. I had a letter from him yesterday ...' Marianne put a hand to her head. 'I forgot.'

She sprang up, went over to Emily's pram and took out some envelopes. Returning, she held them out to Prue. 'I met the postman by your gate, and he gave me these to give to you. I'm sorry, I clean forgot.' She shook her head. 'My memory's all over the place sometimes. I think broken nights waking up to feed Emily play havoc with it – I never used to be like this before I had her.' She smiled. 'Some of the other mothers at the day club say they're just the same, but the ones who have older children told me that it will get better again. I do hope so!'

Prue patted her arm. 'Of course it will. Your body's still recovering from having a baby, and if you're not getting a good night's rest it's bound to take its toll.' She glanced through the envelopes and saw that there was a letter from Edwin; she'd look forward to reading that later. She put them in her apron pocket and turned to Marianne. 'You must have been wondering why I asked you here.'

Marianne was taking a sip of cordial and nodded.

'Well, I'm hoping that you'll be able to help me. I want to set up a clothing depot as part of the day club, to help the mothers clothe their babies and young children. They grow so quickly that the clothes aren't worn out, they just grow out of them, and it's difficult – not to mention expensive – to keep up with what the children need. I thought we could have somewhere mothers could get clothes for their children, which might not be new but that wouldn't matter, and they could return them once their children have grown out of them and swap them for something bigger.'

'It sounds like an excellent idea,' Marianne agreed. 'I can make Emily anything she needs, but not all mothers are able to.'

Prue nodded. 'Through the WVS I've been given some parcels of children's clothes and material that were sent as a gift from the Imperial Order of Daughters of Empire in Canada. I've got them in the house and I need to sort through what they've sent. The material could be used to make more children's clothes, perhaps garments that there aren't any of in the parcels, so that we'd have a good range.' Prue took a sip of cordial. 'I was wondering if you'd be willing to help? I'd help of course, and perhaps some of the other mothers at the day club would be prepared to work on them too. What do you think?'

Marianne smiled at her. 'Of course, I'll be happy to help.'

Prue beamed at her. 'Thank you. You're by far the most skilled dressmaker we have in Great Plumstead, and with you helping we can make the most of the material we have. We could go and have a look at the clothes parcels and material now if you have time – it will give us an idea of what we've got already and what we need to make.'

Marianne glanced over at her daughter, who was sleeping peacefully. 'All right, let's have a look now while Emily's still asleep. She'll be wanting a feed when she wakes up.'

Leaving Emily outside in the pram, parked by the open glass doors that led into Prue's sitting room, they went inside to look through the parcels.

'We're lucky to have been sent them. It's heart-warming to think that women in Canada are thinking about us over here.' Prue knelt on the sitting-room floor and opened one of the parcels to reveal a neatly folded pile of small garments. She picked up a pretty blue and white gingham dress with smocked detail on the bodice and held it up. 'This looks about the size for a one-year-old, do you think?'

Marianne nodded. 'If we put similar sized garments together then we can see what we've got for each age group.' She took a pair of boy's shorts from the pile and shook them out. 'These have been worn, but there's still plenty of wear left in them.' Glancing at the pile of parcels still yet to undo, Marianne said, 'I think the day club clothing depot is going to get off to an excellent start, the mothers will really appreciate it. You've been very good to us ever since we arrived here.'

Prue smiled at her. 'I'm pleased to be able to help you all. I enjoy having you here in the village, you've certainly livened things up.'

'Do you remember when we first arrived? How shocked some of the residents were by what us East End mothers looked like, and how some of us behaved, wanting to go off to the pub?' Marianne laughed.

Prue joined in her laughter. 'I think there's been a lot of mellowing and broadening of minds on both sides since then. It's been good for the village to have evacuee mothers arrive, though it was quite a shock at first as we'd all been expecting children.' Prue recalled the moment last September when she realised that they'd been sent the wrong evacuees on the day that war had been declared. She'd been horrified to find that all her carefully laid plans to welcome evacuee children had been thwarted, but it had all worked out for the best and she'd worked hard to make the mothers welcome.

A sudden loud wail came from the garden through the open doors.

'She's awake!' Marianne got up. 'Do you mind if I bring her in here to nurse her? Perhaps we could talk about what sort of clothes we need to make while she feeds.'

'Please do.'

While Marianne went out to fetch her daughter, Prue gathered some cushions and arranged them in an arm-chair so that the young mother could feed her daughter comfortably.

'She's definitely hungry!' Marianne said, carrying a fret-ful Emily, who was butting her head against her mother's shoulder, eager for a feed.

'Sit yourself down, and use a cushion to lay Emily on, if you like,' Prue said. 'Would you like more cordial, or perhaps a cup of tea? I could bring the teapot in here so you could have as much as you like. I remember how thirsty I used to get when I was nursing Alice.'

'Tea would be lovely, thank you.'

While she was waiting for the kettle to boil in the kitchen, Prue remembered the letters that Marianne had given her and fished them out of her apron pocket. Leaving the ones addressed to Victor on the kitchen table, she opened the letter from Edwin, which he always addressed just to her. Reading through his words, it was as if she could hear his voice speaking to her.

Dear Ma,

I hope this letter finds you and Alice well. I went to see Jack on my day off, he wrote and told me he's at a camp in Kent at the moment so it was easy enough for me to get there and I wanted to see for myself how he was. I'm pleased to be able to tell you that he's fine. He had a scary time of it but has come out of the other side and he thinks he'll be posted somewhere else in the country to do more training, so you don't have to worry about him being sent off abroad again for a while. He said he'll write and tell you as soon as he's at his new place. You know what Jack's like with writing letters, so I thought I'd write and let you know what's going on first so you don't worry.

I'm still enjoying my work at the hospital, we're busy but I'm learning a lot.

I must sign off now if I want to catch the post.

Your loving son,

Edwin

Prue felt her shoulders relax. They'd unconsciously tensed up with worry when she'd opened Edwin's letter, but the news about Jack was a relief. If he was going to be posted somewhere in the country for more training that was good news indeed. With his life now at the command of the army, she'd been worried that he might be shipped off to North Africa – he had to go where they told him to.

The kettle began to boil, and she quickly made the tea and carried it in on a tray to the sitting room, where all was now quiet. Emily was contentedly feeding, and the sight of Marianne and her small baby brought tears to Prue's eyes. Being a mother took you from times like this, knowing exactly where your child was, being able to care for them, keep them safe, to having them grown up and gone and at the whims of the world. Having them grown didn't stop a mother worrying though, that didn't change with the years.

Chapter 35

Thea woke with a start. Bess was barking loudly down in the kitchen. Reuben was out on patrol with the Local Defence Volunteers tonight, and as he always did when he was on duty, he'd left Bess with her at Rookery House. Usually the dog was happy to settle down to sleep on the rag rug in front of the range and they wouldn't hear a peep out of her until the morning, but something was amiss with her tonight.

Thea got out of bed, pushed her feet into her slippers, grabbed her dressing gown off the back of the bedroom door and quickly put it on, tying the cord around her as she made her way out onto the landing and down the stairs, using the small torch that she kept in the pocket of her dressing gown to light her way.

Bess stopped barking as soon as she entered the kitchen, rushing over to meet her, whimpering and nudging at her with her nose.

'What's the matter?' Thea bent down and stroked the dog's head, checking her over to see if she looked unwell, but she seemed in perfect health.

Bess started to whine again and dashed over to the back door, scratching at it with her paw as if to say she wanted to go out. Perhaps there was something in the garden.

Thea went over to the door and grabbed hold of Bess's collar, before opening it and looking out into the moonlit garden. She couldn't see anything but heard the faint rise and fall of the air-raid siren coming from Wykeham, four miles away. Instantly her heart started to race – that's what Bess had heard!

Enemy bombers could be heading this way, they must get to the Anderson shelter. Thea had to quickly wake the others. There'd been a few sporadic air raids in the past few weeks with bombs falling in rural areas throughout Norfolk, so if the siren was going here, it was time to take cover just in case . . .

She hurried through to the hall and met Hettie coming down the stairs, a candle lighting her way.

'The air-raid siren's going off in Wykeham, Bess heard it. We need to get to the shelter. I'll go up and get Marianne and Emily.'

Hettie nodded, her face grim. 'I'll get the shelter supplies and meet you in the kitchen.'

'I won't be long.' Thea touched Hettie's arm as she passed her. She ran up the stairs and knocked loudly on Marianne's door before going in.

The room was in darkness, the blackout curtain blocking out the moonlight. Shining her torch around, she saw that Marianne was fast asleep, as was baby Emily in her cot. Bess's loud barks had clearly not woken the pair of them.

'Marianne!' She shook the young woman's shoulder, jolting her awake. 'We need to go to the shelter, the air-raid siren's going.'

Marianne sat up, blinking in the light from Thea's torch. 'What?'

'There's an air raid, we need to get to the shelter. Now. I'll get Emily.' Thea left Marianne to rouse herself and went over to Emily's cot, where thankfully the little girl was still fast asleep. Grabbing a blanket from the nearby chair where Marianne sat while she was nursing her daughter, Thea gently picked up the sleeping baby and swaddled her in the blanket to keep her warm. It might be late June, but it would still be chillier outside than in the house.

'Ready?' She looked at Marianne, who was putting on her dressing gown.

The young woman nodded and held out her hands to take the baby. 'Do you think they'll bomb Great Plumstead?'

Thea shrugged. 'I hope not, but if the siren's going off, we need to get to the shelter, no point in taking chances.'

Down in the kitchen, Hettie was waiting with a wicker laundry basket filled with blankets, pillows, candles and matches, and other items that were useful to have in the shelter.

'You lead the way, Hettie, and I'll bring this.' Thea picked up the basket and followed the others, with Bess at her heels. Outside, the waning three-quarter moon bathed the back garden in a cold light, turning the world into monochrome grey instead of the vibrant assortment of summer greens that filled the garden during the daytime.

The Anderson shelter was half-buried in the ground, its curved top covered with soil like some giant mole, with shoots coming out of it where Thea had planted seeds on it. She remembered the day that Reuben, Jack and Edwin had installed it, first digging a huge hole and then bolting the curved pieces of metal together. They'd worked hard to make it as comfortable as possible, putting in steps to make it easier for them all to get in and out, and adding benches along the sides for them to sit or lie on. That had been at the start of the war back in September last year, and since then they hadn't had to use it. But things had moved on; the phoney war was over and with the siren going off in Wykeham they might be under attack.

Inside the shelter, Hettie lit the oil lamp and hung it from the hook in the roof which Reuben had put in especially for that purpose, painting them all in a soft glow of light and throwing their shadows in distorted arcs onto the curved walls. Hettie checked that the blackout curtain hung across the door was firmly in place to stop light spilling out; meanwhile Thea emptied out the basket, except for one pillow to act as a mattress and a blanket, and stood it on the bench that ran along the back wall, in which Marianne laid her still-sleeping daughter.

'I'm glad she hasn't woken up,' Marianne said, tucking the blanket around her so that she'd be warm and cosy.

'Hopefully she'll stay that way until she's ready for her next feed,' Thea said, handing a blanket each to Hettie and Marianne.

'How long do you think we'll be in here for?' Hettie wrapped herself up and sat down on a bench.

'I have no idea.' Draping a blanket over her shoulders, Thea sat down next to Marianne, who was also similarly wrapped up. 'We'll just have to stay here until the all-clear goes as usual.'

'What if we don't hear it?' Hettie looked anxious. 'We didn't hear the warning siren. If it hadn't been for Bess, we'd still be fast asleep in our beds.'

'Bess will hear it, she'll let us know like she did earlier. Her hearing's much better than ours.' Thea looked at the dog, who was lying across the width of the shelter by the blackout curtain, her head on her paws. Her eyes were closed, but from the way her ears were twitching she was still listening to what was going on.

'We ought to have a siren here in Great Plumstead,' Hettie said. 'It's too far away in Wykeham, and if the wind happened to blow in the wrong direction we definitely wouldn't be able to hear it. We could be bombed in our beds!'

'I doubt very much they'll ever put one here, they can't have them in every village. I don't think we're a target, it's not like there are important factories building aircraft or government buildings around here, is it?'

They fell into silence for a few minutes and Thea found herself straining to catch any noise of approaching planes. But there was nothing, just the usual night-time sounds of the tawny owls calling to each other.

'I forgot to bring my knitting,' Hettie said. 'It would help pass the time. I'll nip back and get it; I won't be long.'

'*No!*' Thea and Marianne chorused.

'It's not worth the risk,' Thea said.

'Why don't you try and get some sleep?' Marianne suggested. 'We could be here for some time, and you'll lose out on your rest and be tired tomorrow.'

Thea glanced at her watch. 'It's almost midnight, so why not at least lie down.' She passed a pillow over to Hettie. 'Even if you don't sleep, you'll be resting.'

'All right.' Hettie took the pillow and arranged it on one end of the bench she was sitting on, and then lowered herself down onto it.

'Perhaps if I dim the lamp a bit it will help us drift off. We should get what rest we can.' Thea reached up and turned the lamp down so that it gave out just enough light for them to see by.

Leaning back against the walls of the shelter, even with a pillow between her and the metal surface, wasn't the most comfortable way to spend the night, but even so after a day's hard work in the garden, Thea felt herself beginning to drift off, her eyes growing heavy and her head nodding downwards. A dream was just beginning to take hold of her when Bess began to growl, snapping her instantly awake along with Marianne and Hettie.

'What's the matter with her?' Hettie said.

'Shhhh! . . . Listen!' Thea got up and went over to calm Bess, stroking her silky ears and listening hard. And then she heard it – the sound of a plane's engine. They'd heard enough of them over the past few months, what with the RAF flying from the nearby aerodromes every day, and one of them had even crash-landed in the field opposite Rookery House last autumn.

'A plane!' Hettie's voice came out in a squeak as she struggled into an upright position again. 'Do you think it's a bomber?'

Marianne reached across and took hold of Hettie's hand. 'We're safe in here, it's probably just flying over on its way home.'

The sound of the plane was growing louder and there was no doubt that it was coming in their direction. Thea listened to every thrum of the approaching plane, noticing how it sounded different from the engines of the RAF's planes; this one made a *vroom, vroom* sound which to her ear seem to match the anxious beat of her heart, and felt unsettling and menacing. The atmosphere in the shelter grew tense and Bess leaned heavily against Thea, nudging her wet nose against her hand if she stopped stroking even for a moment. The dog clearly needed comfort as much as the rest of them.

And then the sound began to grow fainter, the plane heading away, perhaps having changed direction, and Thea relaxed. It had passed over. She was about to get up and return to her seat next to Marianne when the crumping, thumping sound of a distant explosion echoed out across the night, sending a trickle of ice down Thea's spine. She'd heard sounds like that before, during the Great War when bombs and shells had been set off.

Hettie let out a yelp and covered her mouth with her hand, while Marianne moved to sit next to her, putting her arm around the older woman.

'Was that a bomb?' Marianne asked, looking at Thea.

Thea shrugged. 'Maybe, it sounded like an explosion.'

Nobody spoke, all of them straining to hear, waiting to see if there were any more noises. Thea carried on stroking Bess's ears, glad of something to do with her hands and for the gentle comfort that the dog gave her. The minutes ticked by but there was no sound of the plane returning, and no more sounds of explosions, just the familiar night-time sounds of the countryside once again.

Up on the tower of St Andrew's Church in the middle of Great Plumstead, Reuben and his fellow local defence volunteer, Fred Parker, were at their observation post on lookout duty watching out for enemy activity. Sitting on the deckchairs that they'd hauled up the twisting tower steps, high above the graveyard, with the village spread out beneath them and the air-raid siren having just gone off, they felt rather exposed and vulnerable.

'Do you reckon we're in for some bombing here tonight then?' Fred asked, his face ghostly pale in the moonlight, his eyes scanning the sky. 'Perhaps we should go down and shelter in the crypt.'

Reuben glanced at him, holding back a smile. Fred was usually full of gung-ho talk, boasting about what he'd do if the enemy landed, but now he sounded exactly the opposite.

'I've no idea. If the siren's gone off then presumably enemy aircraft have been spotted, but whether they've come to bomb us . . . ' He shrugged. For the past month there had been sporadic air raids, with high explosive bombs dropped around the county, sometimes one or two, other times far more. There was no way of knowing when or where the next bombs would fall, there was no pattern. It seemed entirely up to where the pilots decided to jettison their bombs as they flew over the county, so any air-raid warning had to be taken seriously. If you didn't you might live to regret it. Or perhaps not, if you were unlucky.

'Whatever happens, it's our duty to stay up here and keep a look out, that's the order. If the planes have come to drop paratroopers then we need to be here to see them. If we're hiding down in the crypt we won't.'

'I see what you mean.' Fred put a Woodbine in his mouth and quickly lit it, shielding the match flame which flared briefly before he shook it out, and then sucked in a deep lungful of smoke, taking care to shield the red glowing tip with his hand.

'Good job the ARP warden can't see that up here, or our captain. You could be giving our position away to the enemy.'

Fred blew out a long stream of smoke. 'I need it to steady my nerves. We're like sitting ducks up here.'

'Well, we're in a good position to see any bombs falling.' Reuben leaned back in his deckchair, his eyes on the sky and his ears straining for the sound of aircraft engines. He was more concerned that there might be people still in their beds who hadn't heard the air-raid siren. It was a still night and the rise and fall of sound from their nearest siren in Wykeham had been faint, so anyone in a deep sleep was probably blissfully unaware that an air raid could be imminent and hadn't sought shelter.

Bess, he knew, would have heard it. Her hearing was

much sharper than any human's and he was sure that she would have let Thea and the others know. They'd have gone to the Anderson shelter in the garden.

'Listen! Do you hear that?' Fred grabbed Reuben's arm. 'Engines.'

Reuben listened hard. There was no doubt, the sound of a plane's engines thrumming in the sky was growing louder by the second.

'It doesn't sound like one of ours,' Reuben replied. The RAF's engines were smooth, the engines synchronised to give a steady beat, whereas these made an unsettling *vroom, vroom* noise which he knew was typical of the enemy's planes.

'What do we do?' Fred's voice had a rising note of panic.

'We watch and wait.' *And hope*, Reuben added silently as he scanned the sky looking for the first sight of the plane. It was difficult to spot against the inky black sky, which was peppered with only the brightest stars as the moon reflected its ghostly light. But then he saw it as it passed across the moon, a single dark shape silhouetted against the silvery face. The hairs on the back of his neck stood up and time seemed to stand still as he waited for what was to come.

'Bloody hell,' Fred said as the plane disappeared against the darkness of the sky once more. They had to rely on their hearing again to tell where it was, and with the engines growing ever louder, it was heading their way.

'Just keep on going past, you bastard,' Fred muttered before taking another deep drag on his cigarette.

With his heart banging loud in his chest, the beat seeming to mirror that of the plane's engines, Reuben found himself willing it to go quicker, to pass over them and be gone before it could drop any bombs.

What was there in Great Plumstead to merit being blown up? There were no ports or factories building tanks, no airfields full of fighter planes. The village might be in darkness from the blackout, but with the moonlight shining down there was no doubt that the huddle of dark buildings with their unnatural square and rectangular forms would be visible from up above.

Then the engines' tone changed and their drone began to grow fainter. The plane must have changed course and was now heading away from them. Reuben let out a breath that he didn't realise he'd been holding.

'They're going!' Fred leapt to his feet. 'Bugger off back to where you came from.' He shook his fist in the air.

Reuben laughed.

'I don't think they can hear you, Fred.'

'I don't care, it makes me feel better. They scared the living daylights out of me.' He sat back down in the deckchair and sighed deeply. 'I ought to be getting used to the idea of planes coming over here and dropping a bomb or two, but I'm not. It's not right, it's bringing war to innocent people, not soldiers on a battlefield like when we were in the last lot.'

'Things could and probably will get a lot worse. I expect Hitler's got plans to send a lot more planes to bomb us where it will hurt the country most. It'll be the cities that will get hit hard. London's got to be a prime target, why else would they have evacuated children and expectant mothers from there? I—' Reuben halted as a sudden flash of light, closely followed by an explosion from several miles the other side of Wykeham, shattered the peace of the summer night. A sense of dread settled heavily in his stomach.

The plane must have dropped a bomb.

They both got to their feet and stood staring out towards where they'd seen the flare of bright, white light.

'Where'd it hit?' Fred asked.

'Difficult to say. It looked like it was the other side of Wykeham, but it's hard to judge at night and there's nothing to see now.' At least there was no orange tint to the sky to suggest that something was on fire after being bombed. 'Let's hope it fell in a field, well away from the houses. We'll find out soon enough.' Reuben sat down again and reached for the flask of hot tea that he'd brought out with him. He could do with something warm and comforting right now. They still had several long hours up here before their duty was done, and he hoped that there'd be no more planes and that the all-clear would soon ring out.

'Tea?' He offered Fred his spare cup.

'Thanks.' Fred took it and rummaged in his overalls pocket, pulling out a hip flask. 'We'll have a drop of this in it. Purely medicinal of course, for the shock!'

Chapter 36

With five minutes left to go before seven o'clock, Prue reached over and pressed down the button on the alarm clock on her bedside cabinet, to stop it from going off. The way her head was throbbing she didn't want the loud noise to add to her pain, knowing it would feel like a drill hammering into her skull. The sound was annoying on the best of days, on mornings when she woke refreshed and ready to go – but this morning was most definitely not one of those.

She rolled onto her back and stared up at the ceiling, blinking her eyes to try to ease the gritty feeling in them. After the all-clear had sounded and she and Alice had climbed out of the cellar which acted as their shelter, she'd hoped to be able to get some much-needed sleep. But it had evaded her, her mind refusing to rest as it went over the worries and concerns which always seemed to be present these days, lurking in the back of her mind waiting to pounce on her thoughts and taunt her if given a chance.

Her main worries were about Jack and Edwin, of course, but then there was the work she did for the WVS. She enjoyed it very much, but she always had the nagging feeling that there was so much more to do. Then there was the WI; if only by some miracle there were more hours in the day. The state of her marriage had also elbowed its way into her thoughts, and with it her lack of happiness, but that came very low down on the list. She'd rather not think about that too much – far better to worry over other things.

The one person she didn't worry about during those long waking hours was Victor, who'd been out on patrol with the Local Defence Volunteers last night, probably right in the middle of the air raid. Most wives would have been concerned about their husbands doing that – and she would have been once. But years of living with him, with his dominant behaviour and his awful, dismissive attitude to her, had eroded that. She wouldn't wish him to come to harm, but she wasn't going to waste precious mental energy worrying over him.

Prue sighed. Victor would be home soon and wanting his breakfast before heading off to work. Bracing herself, she took a deep breath, rolled over onto her side, swung her legs out of bed and stood up. Tired or not, she had work to do.

Downstairs in the kitchen, she started cracking eggs from Thea's hens into a bowl, marvelling at the rich orange yolks, when she heard the front door open. Victor was home. She found herself tensing, wondering what sort of mood he'd be in. Sometimes he came in from a night's LDV duty in a good mood; other times he'd be ratty from tiredness and complaining about the incompetence of their captain – he was still smarting that *he* hadn't been put in charge of their village platoon. It wasn't surprising of course; the captain had experience of leading men in the trenches of the Great War, whereas Victor's war experience had been handing out uniforms and equipment to new recruits. That hadn't stopped her husband wanting to be in charge. His business, council and various committee roles had given him a rather inflated opinion of his authority and experience, she thought, although she knew better than to tell him as much.

She focused her energy on whisking the eggs, breaking up the golden orbs with a fork, and braced herself.

The kitchen door opened and Victor looked in. 'I'll go and get changed ready for work first,' he said before disappearing again, and she could hear his heavy tread going up the stairs. Prue sighed with relief. She'd learned to read him like a book over the years and he seemed in a reasonable mood. All she had to do was provide him with breakfast and then he'd go off to work and she'd be free of him again until this evening.

She'd made scrambled eggs and was keeping them warm alongside some buttered toast in the top of the oven when Victor returned, his face freshly shaved and his dark hair slicked back with brilliantine so that it glistened like some oily hat.

'Did you make sure Alice sheltered in the cellar last night?' Victor asked, sitting down at the table.

Prue put the plateful of eggs and toast down in front of him. 'Of course.' Victor had deemed the cellar perfect for an air-raid shelter, though she wondered how it would be for them if the house took a direct hit and collapsed on top of them. She'd have preferred an Anderson shelter in the garden like Thea had. At least it would be some distance away if the house were to be bombed, and they'd stand a chance. But shelters cost money and Victor, being Victor, would rather not spend a single penny unless he had to. He'd declared the cellar good enough and that was that.

'It was lucky I was up getting a drink or I doubt I'd have even heard the siren, it was so faint last night.' She poured them both a cup of tea and passed Victor's over to him. 'I heard the plane's engines though; it went over, and no harm done this time.'

Victor was about to take a mouthful of the scrambled egg speared on his fork, but he paused it mid-air. 'A high explosive bomb was dropped the other side of Wykeham.'

Prue's hands gripped the arms of her chair, a heavy lump of dread weighing down her chest. 'Was anyone hurt?' Visions of it landing on a house flashed through her mind.

Victor chewed slowly on his mouthful, swallowed and then took a drink of tea before answering. 'No, it fell in open countryside, just made a crater in a field.'

'Thank goodness for that.' Prue picked up her cup of tea and leaned back in her chair, nestling the cup in her hands and enjoying the heat from it warming her up. The raiders that had come over during the past month, loosing their bombs willy-nilly over the countryside, were unsettling. It felt like war was clawing its way into their land and that nowhere was safe now.

'I'll be late home tonight, I've got the first invasion committee meeting. I don't know what time it will end, there's a lot to talk about.' Victor took a bite of his toast and chewed methodically.

An invasion committee. It wasn't the first time Prue had heard about it, but the very thought of a small market town in rural Norfolk needing to set up a committee to figure out a plan for when they were invaded – *if* they were invaded, she corrected her thoughts – sent chills through her bones. Though clearly from the fact that it was going ahead in Wykeham and in many other places, invasion by German forces under Hitler's orders was a very real possibility and the country was doing its best to prepare for it. Lessons had been learned after what had happened to Belgium and Holland; but now that France had surrendered just three days ago, becoming the latest country added to Hitler's collection, no doubt his eyes would be turning to Britain. With a mere twenty-odd miles of sea separating the south coast from France it was easily achievable if things went badly for the country.

However, they wouldn't go down without one heck of a fight, and not just from the armed forces. Many of the women she knew would fight, perhaps not with guns, but with whatever they had to hand: broomsticks, rolling pins, even frying pans. She smiled at the thought of an army of women from Great Plumstead defending their village from enemy troops with a variety of makeshift household weapons.

'Do you want me to keep you some tea?' Prue asked, returning her thoughts to the present.

'No, we might well have something to eat at the pub afterwards.' Victor drained his cup and stood up. 'I'd better get to work.' He turned and left, without giving her a peck on the cheek as many husbands would do. He had done so each morning once upon a time, but those days were long gone.

Prue took a sip of her tea. If she didn't have to cook Victor his evening meal then she could fit in some extra work for the WI; she and Alice could manage with a sandwich for their tea. She'd make a start on the WI paperwork when she got back later this afternoon, as she was doing a shift with Thea in the WVS canteen this morning. But first she glanced at the clock. She'd better give Alice a shout or she'd miss the bus and be late for school.

Chapter 37

It was just over a month since Anna had been brought to Holloway Prison and rumours were going around C Wing that transport was finally being arranged to move them. Several women had already disappeared, their names being called out before they were taken off somewhere and not brought back. As much as she wanted to get out of here, Anna was worried about where they might be going, and it was now keeping her awake as her mind came up with different scenarios of what might happen to them.

A gentle knock on her cell door made her start. She sat up as the door opened and a warder entered, lighting up her cell with the dim light from her torch.

'You need to pack your things and get ready to leave here in half an hour,' the warder said quietly. 'I'll be back to fetch you then. And keep the noise down – don't go talking to any other inmates, all right?'

Anna sat up. 'Where am I going?'

'You'll see. I'll be back in half an hour, so be ready.' The warder slipped away as quietly as she'd come.

Anna looked around her cell, which was dimly lit by the moonlight coming in through the high window, giving her just enough light to see by but painting everything in monochrome shades. This small room had become something of a sanctuary, a place of her own where she could read, whisk herself away in stories and allow herself to forget where she was for a little while. Now the time had come for her to leave. But not knowing where she'd be going gave her a surprising jolt of uncertainty because this place was now so familiar.

She hoped she was going somewhere much better, although it might be worse. Wherever it was, one thing would remain the same – she would have no control over it. That decision belonged to others; she could only hope that it would be to her advantage.

Throwing back the covers she quickly dressed and packed her suitcase, making sure that she left nothing behind. Once that was done, she sat down on the bed to wait, wondering if the warder would let her see Eva and say goodbye. They'd become good friends and she had helped Anna cope with being imprisoned. The minutes seemed to tick slowly by, as time always did in here compared within the outside world.

When the warder finally returned, Anna stood and picked up her suitcase. 'Could I speak to Eva in the next cell, please? Just to tell her I am going.'

'That's not possible, I'm afraid. This needs to be done quietly. If you don't want to go you can stay here and I'll ask someone else.'

'No,' Anna sighed. 'Would you tell her I said goodbye, at least? In the morning?'

The warder nodded. 'Come on, follow me and try not to make any noise.'

She led Anna through the prison to an empty wing, which was similar to C Wing only very quiet, no sounds of night-time snuffles and snoring coming from cells. It was eerily silent, and not what she'd been expecting.

The warder stopped outside a cell and opened the door. 'You're in here.'

Anna frowned; she hadn't expected to be swapping one cell for another. 'I thought I was leaving.'

'You will be, but not quite yet. In you go, and I'm afraid you'll have to stay in there for a few days until everything's ready. Your food will be brought to you, but there'll be no chance to go out into the exercise yard, understand?'

Anna nodded, because there was no choice if she wanted to get out of here. 'Can you tell me where I will be taken?'

'No.' The warder folded her arms and nodded her head for Anna to go inside. Knowing that she wasn't going to get any more information, she did as she was told and the door was closed behind her with a clunk.

She looked around the cell and saw that it was very similar to the one she'd just left behind. Her prison life wasn't over yet, in fact it had just got that bit harder now she was shut away from her friend and her routine. A surge of disappointment welled up in her and she had to bite her bottom lip to stop herself from crying. She must keep strong, spend her time reading and exercising as much as she could within the confines of her cell. Anything to keep herself occupied and pass the time, because at least this was one step closer to getting out.

On Anna's second night in the isolated cell, she was woken up by someone roughly shaking her shoulder and shining a torch in her face. It sent her heart racing as a surge of adrenaline rushed around her body.

'What's your name?' a woman's voice asked.

Blinking in the sudden light, she shielded her eyes. 'Anna Weissenborn.'

The torch's beam was removed from her face and directed down onto the floor. It lit up her cell enough for her to see a warder that she hadn't met before. 'Just needed to check.'

Anna sat up. 'Why?'

'In case you were impersonating someone else. It's a security check of sorts.' The warder shrugged and smiled. 'Don't worry, you passed the test. Go back to sleep.' She slipped out of the cell, closing the door quietly behind her.

Anna lay back down, her sleepiness gone after the shock of being woken up like that. Did they really think she could be an imposter? She supposed that waking somebody from sleep suddenly was one way to check, but it hadn't been a pleasant experience.

A cry of alarm came from the next-door cell where she supposed the warder was doing the exact same thing to someone else. Since Anna had been brought in here in the middle of the night, she'd heard other women arrive and be placed in cells, but she had no idea who they were. It was a very odd experience knowing that others were just the other side of the brick walls, yet she couldn't have any contact with them. How much longer it would go on for, she didn't know. She had asked and kept asking, but the warders would never give her a definite answer.

Sighing, she turned on to her side and pulled the covers up, willing sleep to come again.

The ringing of the six o'clock bell that echoed around the wings of Holloway woke Anna with a start. She yawned and stretched, her eyes feeling gritty from lack of sleep; it had taken her some time to drift off again after being woken in such a frightening manner. She was still in bed when her cell door was opened. A different warder came in with a bowl of porridge and a cup of tea, placing them down on the small table by the wall.

'Wakey, wakey. Today's the day you've all been waiting for, so get your breakfast down you, then get dressed, packed and ready to leave. The bus is going at nine o'clock sharp and if you're not ready you'll be left behind.' She smiled at Anna. 'And before you ask, I can't tell you where you're going, you'll find out later.'

The news took a few moments to sink in: she was leaving today!

Anna threw back the covers, quickly washed from the jug of cold water they were given each day, and then dressed. Tucking into her porridge, which she'd grown used to in the weeks that she'd been here, she could hear the murmur of activity coming from the other cells in the wing, where no doubt the other women had been instructed to prepare themselves to leave as well. Although she couldn't see anyone, there was a definite sense of excitement in the air and she hoped that wherever they were being taken it would be somewhere better than a prison. She dreamed of being able to see the sky again and be outdoors as much as possible. That had been the hardest thing to deal with in here – not being able to go outside when she wanted to.

After she'd finished her breakfast, she packed her suitcase, checking carefully to make sure that she hadn't left anything behind – particularly any of her books, which had become even more precious to her since she'd been here. Then she sat on her bed to wait. A little after half past eight, her cell door was opened and the warder beckoned for her to come out. Stepping outside for the first time in three days, her suitcase in her hand, she smiled happily at the sight of familiar faces doing the same thing. To her delight Eva was there, standing in the doorway of a cell three down from hers.

The older woman looked as pleased to see her as Anna was, and mouthed, 'Are you all right?'

Anna nodded and did the same to her. Eva smiled broadly back, seeming none the worse for her isolation.

'Right, listen up everybody. You need to collect a packet of sandwiches each from the tray on your way out,' one of the warders explained, pointing to her colleague who stood by the door with a tray piled high with paper packets. 'Then you'll be taken out to a bus which will take you on to the station. I wish you all the best. If you'd like to follow me.'

The women filed out after her, each taking a packet of sandwiches as instructed. Eva managed to move herself down the line so that she was beside Anna. 'I am so glad you're here, I was worried about you. They took me in the middle of the night so I had no chance to tell you.'

'They did the same with me, three nights ago. I wanted to let you know but they would not let me.'

'Perhaps I had already been brought down here, it looks like they took us both on the same night.' Eva picked up her packet of sandwiches. 'It does not matter now, as long as we are both going together.'

Anna nodded, grateful that wherever they were heading, Eva would be with her. She'd made being interned so much easier to bear.

Sitting on the bus beside Eva a short while later, Anna stared silently out of the window as they drove through the London streets. Her eyes darted this way and that as she drank in the outside world again, and the lack of chatter from the other women suggested they were doing the same. It felt overwhelming to be able to see so much, to see more than a pocket handkerchief patch of sky; looking up to see it sweeping over London, the blue scattered with a few white clouds, made her feel very small. And there were so many people rushing around, walking this way and that along the pavements, queuing outside shops, full buses passing them in the opposite direction on the other side of the road. All this life had been going on while they'd been locked away inside Holloway.

Anna felt a hand on her arm and turned to look at Eva.

'It is quite a shock to see this again.'

She nodded. 'I feel like I've been away in another world and I'm seeing this for the first time. It's so busy, so many people.'

'It is real life. A month ago, before we were interned, we would not have thought twice about it.' Eva smiled. 'But it is so good to be out of that prison. Look at that sky, how big it is, so much bigger than the little square we could see from the exercise yard. What a glorious sight.'

Anna looked up, glad to be free of the confining walls of Holloway. It had been an awful experience, but it had taught her to appreciate space, the sky and freedom. Two of which she now had, the other she hoped would return to her — eventually. Thea would be glad to know that she was now at least out of Holloway Prison; she'd write and tell her as soon as they arrived wherever they were going next.

The bus took them to Euston station, where they were herded onto a platform and boarded a train; certain carriages had been specially reserved for them.

'Can you tell us where we are going?' Eva asked one of the policemen accompanying them, as he sat down in the last empty seat in their compartment just as the guard blew his whistle out on the platform ready for the off.

'Liverpool. So you might as well make yourself comfortable, it's a long journey.' He took off his helmet and rested it on his lap.

'Liverpool?' one of the other women asked as the train started to move. 'Why there? Is that where we're staying?'

'You will be, for one night. And then you'll be boarding a ship which will take you on to your destination,' he said.

'And where is that?' Eva asked.

'I can't tell you that.' The policeman smiled. 'Sorry, you'll find out soon enough.' He leaned back in his seat and closed his eyes, clearly not willing to say any more.

Anna looked at Eva, who shrugged.

'Do you think they are sending us abroad – they must be if we are going by ship?' Anna said quietly. She hadn't expected that, and the thought of having to move to another country again filled her with horror. She'd done it once before coming here from Germany, and that had been hard enough when she'd been free. This time she'd be going as an internee, someone whose life was in other people's hands.

Eva frowned. 'I do not know. Try not to worry about it, just look out of the window and enjoy our train ride.' She turned to stare out of the window as if she was enjoying the view, but her hands were clasped tightly together, her knuckles standing out white.

Eva's words might have been reassuring, but clearly the older woman was worried. Anna leaned back into her seat and closed her eyes, desperately hoping that they hadn't swapped the confines of Holloway for something much worse.

Chapter 38

July had arrived with a glorious blue sky, dappled with fluffy, white clouds that floated over Norfolk on a gentle breeze. The perfect conditions for weeds to grow, Thea thought in the greenhouse, as she tied the stem of another tomato plant to the stick thrust into its pot for support. Much as she welcomed this good growing weather, keeping on top of everything was getting harder. The garden was doing well, but she was having to put in longer hours to get everything done. She desperately missed having Anna to help her.

Moving on to the next tomato plant she nipped out the growing side shoots, tied the stem to another stick, then repeated the process again and again as she worked her way around the greenhouse. After she finished in here, there were the broad beans, dwarf beans and peas to pick. Grace at the village shop had ordered some more lettuces and radishes, and she needed to get those ready to take down this afternoon as well as the beans and peas. And then there were the leek seedlings that were ready to plant out.

None of this was helped by having to go to the shelter again, after the air-raid siren had gone off in Wykeham at half past one this morning. They'd only been in it for an hour, but she hadn't slept while they sat there, and even when the all-clear had sounded and they'd returned to the house, Thea had found it hard to relax. She'd only fallen asleep again an hour before her alarm went off. She was exhausted, but the work still had to be done.

Finishing the last tomato plant, she picked up the tray of leek seedlings which Anna had sown not long after she'd arrived here. Now they looked like round blades of grass and were ready to be planted out. A wave of emotion hit her and she sniffed back sudden tears, thinking how rotten it was that Anna wasn't here to plant them out for herself.

Despite the many letters that Thea had sent, she still hadn't reached someone who would listen to her plea and help with Anna's situation. Now she was being palmed off with useless replies from secretaries who just passed on the problem, leaving Anna in prison. But she wasn't going to give up. She'd write again tonight, and keep on until she finally found someone who'd take notice.

She picked up the wooden dibber, shoved it in her pocket then grabbed a watering can and headed to collect the water she'd need for planting out the leeks.

Out on the prepared soil, Thea quickly found a rhythm, using the dibber to make a hole, then gently placing in a leek seedling before pouring in some water so that the soil

229

settled around its delicate roots, leaving it standing upright and ready to grow bigger. It was a satisfying job, and she'd almost worked her way through the seedlings, and was standing, rubbing her hands on her lower back to ease it after bending forward for so long, when she saw Hettie and Marianne heading towards her, the older woman pushing Emily's pram and Marianne carrying a tray.

'Time for a break!' Hettie announced, manoeuvring the pram so that the baby wasn't lying facing the sun.

'Elderflower cordial or tea?' Marianne asked, holding out the tray. There were mugs of tea on it with a glass of cordial and a plate of freshly baked biscuits, which she could tell were still warm from the mouth-watering smell they were giving off.

'I'll have some cordial first, please.' Thea wiped her hand on the bib of her dungarees before taking the glass from the tray. 'And then some tea, it's thirsty work.' She took a long drink of the cold cordial, which had a slightly acidic kick and was very refreshing.

'I've come to help,' Marianne said. 'Emily has just fed and will be fast asleep for a while.'

'And I brought these out to you. Thought you might want to read them now rather than waiting till you come inside later.' Reaching into the pocket of her crossover blue, paisley print apron, Hettie took out two letters and handed them to Thea. 'Postman brought them just before we came out.'

Thea glanced down at the envelopes and recognised the handwriting on one of them. It was from Violet, and the other looked like it could be from Anna. They'd only had two letters from her so far and each had taken several weeks to reach them. They had clearly been censored, lingering on somebody's desk waiting to be dealt with.

Placing her glass down by her feet, she tore open the envelope and took out the letter. Unfolding it, she saw immediately that it was dated 14 June and had been written a week after her first letter.

'It's from Anna. I'll read it out.'

Thea cleared her throat.

Dear Thea, Hettie & Marianne,

Thank you for your letters, which are very precious to me and make me feel like I have contact with you all at Rookery House. I can imagine you all getting on with things there. The other women and I have settled into a routine and I am grateful that my next-door cell neighbour, Eva, encouraged me to volunteer for jobs as it gives me something to do and helps to pass the time. I have done as you suggested in your letter and applied for your friend Violet to be one of my permitted visitors and look forward to meeting her. Please do not worry that you cannot visit so often because I know how far it is to come and how busy you are with the garden and milking and everything that is to be done at Rookery House. I am safe and well and remind myself that things could be far worse if I were still living back in Germany and had been taken by the Nazis just as my father was.

Thea paused, frowning at the thick black ink strokes that had obliterated the next few lines. She turned the paper over to see if she could work out what had been deemed necessary to delete by whoever had censored Anna's letter, but they had done a thorough job and whatever Anna had written was well and truly unreadable now.

'What's the matter?' Hettie said.

Thea held out the letter for her to see. 'It's been censored. I can't see what Anna said next, but whatever it was they didn't like it. Going by what she said just before it I imagine it was something about what happened to her in Germany.' She shrugged. 'After that she just wishes us all well and signs off.'

'Her letters are taking such a long time to reach us, if she were in trouble we wouldn't know for ages,' Hettie said. 'But at least ours are getting through to her quicker.'

'And they mean a lot to her,' Marianne added. 'We must keep writing to her, telling her about what we're doing, if it helps her. And we know that Violet has been to see her a few times as well.'

Thea nodded, opening Violet's letter to see what her friend had to say about her latest visit to Anna. But quickly scanning down through her friend's neat copperplate handwriting she gasped. 'Anna's gone!'

'Gone!' Hettie frowned. 'What do you mean?'

Thea checked the words once more, but they still said the same thing. 'Violet went to Holloway to see her and was told that Anna was no longer there, she'd been moved. They wouldn't tell her where she'd gone. We did know that was going to happen, but ... ' Thea shook her head.

'We need to find out where she is!' Hettie said. 'Perhaps they brought her back to Norfolk to release her?'

'If that was the case, surely we would have heard something by now. She could have been taken anywhere.' Thea wanted to go down to London and hammer on the door of Holloway until they let her in and told her what had happened, where Anna had been taken, but she couldn't just abandon everything and rush off on what might well prove to be a wild goose chase. If they wouldn't tell Violet where Anna had gone, it was unlikely they'd tell her.

'I'll write to the prison tonight and see if they'll tell me something.'

'Perhaps wherever Anna's gone will get letters out to us quicker than the prison, so we'll find out where she is soon,' suggested Marianne.

Thea sighed, shaking her head. 'I'd go down and find out if I could, but . . .'

'It's all right.' Hettie put her arm around Thea. 'Anna understands how much work there is to do here, you could go all the way down to London for nothing. I know it's hard, but wherever Anna is, she'll be safe, she won't be treated badly, she'll be fed and housed and I hope let go very soon. In the meantime, Marianne and I have had an idea about what we can do here to help with the work. You can't go on working the number of hours that you are.' She paused, her eyes fixed on Thea's face. 'We know there's a lot to do to keep up with everything, but realistically it's more than one person can manage. Remember, that's why you employed Anna in the first place.'

'We're helping as much as we can,' Marianne said. 'But it's not as much as you need, so we came up with the idea of asking the mothers at the day club if any of them would like to come and help – remember how much they enjoyed the blackberry picking last autumn? I know that many of them would be happy to help you, even if they can only do a few hours. Added together it would make a big difference. What do you think?'

Thea nodded. 'I think it's an excellent idea. Thank you.'

'Good.' Hettie squeezed Thea's shoulders. 'I'll ask them this afternoon, and I can deliver the veg down at the shop for you on my way.'

'And I'll get started on picking it,' Marianne said, after draining the last of her tea. 'What was the order for today?'

'Lettuce, radishes, broad beans, dwarf beans and peas,' Thea told her, feeling a great sense of relief that she wouldn't have to shoulder the burden of having to get everything done any more.

Hettie picked up the plate of biscuits and held them out to Thea. 'Here, have a couple of these before you finish off planting out the leeks.' She nodded at the bed where Thea had been working. 'We're not going to go short of them come wintertime.'

Chapter 39

Prue threw her handful of wooden pegs into the bag and pulled the dry sheet off the washing line, deftly folding it up into a neat rectangle, before placing it on top of the pile of dry and folded washing. These warm July days were perfect drying weather and having got up early to get the washing done, she'd pegged it out before going off to her shift at the day club.

Picking up the washing basket, she turned and headed back towards the house, stopping briefly by her vegetable plot, casting her eyes over how things were doing. She'd come out later tonight after tea to do a bit of tending, hoeing or weeding.

'Ma!'

Prue turned to see who'd called her and was stunned at the sight of the figure heading towards her, with his kitbag on his shoulder and a wide smile on his face. 'Jack!' She dropped the basket and ran to meet him.

Jack let his kitbag fall to the ground and scooped her up and twirled her around, laughing. 'The look on your face!' He put her down and, still holding on to her arms, looked at her. 'It's so good to see you, Ma.'

Prue nodded, unable to speak for a few moments as her throat was thick with emotion. She bit her bottom lip as tears filled her eyes and then trickled down her cheeks.

Reaching up she gently cupped Jack's cheek, meeting his eyes, which were bright with a film of tears. 'I can't believe you're here.'

Jack grinned. 'It's not a dream, I really am. I'm home for a week's leave before I have to report to my new posting. A whole week at home.' He closed his eyes and sighed.

'Then where are you going, where are they sending you?' *Not abroad, please not abroad to fight*, Prue hoped. Edwin had told her in a letter that Jack would stay in this country, but the army could so easily have changed its mind.

'I can't tell you. Only that it's up north somewhere, but still in this country.'

The relief she felt was like warm treacle running over her shoulders. 'That's good, and before that I've got you here for a whole week . . . it will give me a chance to feed you up a bit, you've lost weight.' Jack's face had still had the slight roundness of youth when he'd left for France, but now it had lost that boyish look, sharp planes and jutting cheekbones replacing it. He'd gone away a boy and had returned very much a man.

Jack shrugged. 'Mealtimes were a bit hit and miss over there and the rations we carried with us weren't up to much.' He smiled at her. 'I'll enjoy every single one of your meals, Ma. It will be food of the gods.'

Prue laughed, thinking that she'd change her plans for tea and make Jack's favourite instead. 'I'd better get cooking then.'

She went to pick up the dropped washing basket, which thankfully hadn't tipped over, although her carefully folded sheets and pillow cases were no longer in a neat pile. But that didn't matter because Jack was home for a whole week and all was right in her world.

'I'll get that for you.' Jack scooped up the basket. 'Is it all right if I have a bath, please? I was on a train for hours and it will be nice to get out of this uniform.'

'Of course. Take as long as you want.'

While Jack had been having his bath, she'd nipped out to the butcher's and, thankfully, after she'd explained that Jack had come home, he'd produced some mince from the back of the shop and she had enough coupons left to cover it. She'd made a shepherd's pie and another favourite, apple pie, which were now both cooking in the range, filling the kitchen with a delicious smell.

She glanced at the clock and saw it was a little after five. Alice was back from school and had been thrilled to hear that her brother was home. She had rushed upstairs to see him, only to return a few minutes later, changed out of her school uniform, saying that he was fast asleep on top of his bed, clean and dressed in his ordinary clothes after his bath. *I'll have to go and wake him if he doesn't come down soon*, she thought, taking the cooked apple pie out of the oven and placing it on the side to keep warm.

She checked that the table was ready and smiled at the four places, which seemed so much better than the three – or often two – that she was used to laying these days.

Although it should be five places if Edwin were here, she sighed. She lived in the hope that one day he'd be back here, and that all her children could sit down together at the kitchen table once more. It was a problem that she couldn't solve right now, so she should focus on the joy that was having Jack here at home for a while.

Noisy chatter and the sound of footsteps coming down the stairs heralded the arrival of Alice and Jack into the kitchen. The sight of Jack, with his short army hair sticking up from sleep, reminded her of him as a little boy and made her want to fold him in her arms and keep him there safe, protect him just as she'd done then.

'It was the smell of shepherd's pie that woke him!' Alice looked up at her older brother with laughing eyes. 'He might have been off fighting, but nothing's changed regarding Jack and his appetite.'

'Very funny! I've had to make another notch in my belt to keep my trousers up,' Jack said. 'The food in the army's not a patch on Ma's, I'm wasting away.' He patted his stomach and Prue's heart contracted at his thinness. He hadn't been overweight when he'd left to join the army, so it was clear that he hadn't had enough to eat while he'd been in France, though it wasn't surprising with what was going on over there. Serving up hearty meals was hardly a priority when the army were faced with the might of the German forces bearing down on them; the men had to survive on whatever they could get.

'Well, we'll just have to fatten you up a bit while you're here. I—' Prue halted at the sound of the front door opening. Victor was home, and the atmosphere changed. Jack met her eye and an unspoken message passed between them, as everybody tensed waiting to see what mood her husband would be in tonight. But to Prue's astonishment, when Victor came into the kitchen and saw Jack standing there, a look of delight swept over his face.

'Jack!' Victor advanced across the kitchen and held out his hand to shake his son's. 'I didn't know you were coming.'

'I thought I'd surprise you all,' Jack said, returning his handshake. 'I've got a week's leave.'

'Then are you off abroad again?' Victor asked. 'To have another go at the enemy, show them what's what and send them packing?'

Prue nearly dropped the shepherd's pie that she was taking out of the oven, her anger at Victor's words surging through her. The man had a warped sense of the reality of war, not stopping to think that if Jack were sent abroad again he could so easily be killed. But that's what you got from spending the Great War behind the counter of a quartermaster's store safely in England. Ask anyone who had experienced the reality of war for themselves, like her brother, Reuben, and they wouldn't be so gung-ho about sending soldiers back to fight the enemy.

'No, my unit's being posted up north for more training. New engineering designs are coming out and we need to be proficient at setting them up and running them – when men's lives and the outcome of battles rely on us, we can't risk letting them down. So we need to be well practised before we're sent abroad again,' Jack said, deftly dealing with his father.

Putting the shepherd's pie down on the table, Prue pasted a smile on her face, ignoring the urge to say something to Victor about his insensitive comment; she didn't want to spoil Jack's first night home. It probably wouldn't matter if she did say something, because her husband's attitudes were so ingrained it would take a high explosive bomb to get them out of him. Best to just let him stew in his own narrowmindedness and let people who knew him well judge for themselves.

As Jack sat down at the table opposite her, he winked at her, the message coming across loud and clear.

She smiled back at him and dished out a large portion of shepherd's pie and green dwarf beans from the garden and held it out to him. 'Tuck in.'

Chapter 40

It was a little before eight o'clock in the morning of the fourth of July, and Thea was heading into the village on her bicycle, freshly picked vegetables for Barker's grocery shop safely stowed in the basket strapped on the back.

She looked up at the clear blue sky, enjoying the early warmth of what promised to be a gloriously beautiful summer's day, and with a jolt realised that this was the first moment that she'd given pause to admire the world around her. Since she'd been up and out in the garden since six o'clock this morning, milking Primrose and then picking the vegetables for the shop, she'd been fully focused on work.

Hard work was nothing new to Thea, but she usually found time to stand and enjoy the world around her for at least a few moments, and never more so since she'd moved back here and could drink in all the sights and sounds of the countryside.

Lately, with the amount of work there was to do at Rookery House, she'd let that slide, simply needing to get through the ever-growing list of jobs, but she'd be getting help with that workload later this morning as some members of the day club were coming to help out in the garden. She was very much looking forward to it, remembering how much she'd enjoyed the blackberrying with them last autumn.

Many of the women who'd arrived as evacuees had thrown themselves into village life and seemed to enjoy taking part in things that they'd never have done back in London, so when Hettie had asked if any would like to volunteer to help at Rookery House, there'd been a good response. However, nothing would replace Anna, and she remained in Thea's thoughts every day, as did the hope that her letters to various government offices would work by attrition if nothing else.

Although she had hated the thought of Anna being in Holloway, at least Thea had known where she was, but now she had no idea. Like so many people in this country, and many more all over the world who were affected by this rotten war, she had no choice but to carry on, all the while worrying and wondering about those she cared for who were away from home. Sadly, it had become part of normal life.

Reaching the village, Thea waved to several people she recognised who were heading off to work, and on reaching Barker's, she propped her bicycle up against the front and unstrapped the basket from the carrier on its back. Looking through the glass door, where the sign was still turned to closed, she saw that Grace was inside preparing for opening. She tapped gently on it to get her attention.

'Good morning, Thea,' Grace said, opening the door to let her in and closing it behind her. She looked down at the basket of vegetables that Thea held out to her. 'They look good, your produce is proving very popular. Whatever you can give me, I can sell.'

She carried it over to the baskets set up for displaying the vegetables and unpacked the beans, peas, potatoes and carrots, arranging them in a pleasing array.

'Hettie said she'll bring in some butter for you on her way to the day club later.'

'Excellent, I've got a waiting list for it. Many of my customers would rather spend their ration on Hettie's homemade butter than the usual stuff. It's very tasty, so not surprising.' Grace paused for a moment. 'Have you heard anything from Anna?'

Thea shook her head. 'No, nothing since she was moved from Holloway.' She shrugged. 'At least when she was in there I knew where she was, but she could be anywhere now.'

Grace bit her bottom lip, looking uncomfortable. 'It might ... I hope this isn't anything to do with Anna ...' She went over to the counter and picked up a copy of today's *Eastern Daily Press* newspaper, which lay open where she'd been reading it. Handing it to Thea, she pointed at the large headline on the front.

INTERNMENT SHIP SUNK BY U BOAT.

Thea read the words in bold, black print and then carried on with the rest of the article, feeling as if an icy hand had gripped her heart. It described how German and Italian enemy aliens had fought for their lives after the liner *Arandora Star*, on which they were being taken to camps in Canada, was torpedoed in the Atlantic and sank with the loss of about a thousand lives.

Had Anna been sent on to Canada after she'd been moved from Holloway? She looked up at Grace, whose eyes were full of sympathy and concern.

'Could Anna have been on it?' Thea's voice was strained.

Grace touched her arm. 'I don't know, I hope not. It doesn't say who the passengers were other than Germans and Italians. I checked through the article over and over, but there's no mention if they were men or women.'

Thea read through the article again, the descriptions forming images in her mind of what had happened two days ago out on the Atlantic in the early hours of the morning, and how the detainees had been woken from their sleep as the torpedo hit and the ship began to sink. How they'd panicked and rushed for the lifeboats, how fights had broken out between the Germans and Italians in their desperation to survive. If Anna had been among them it would have been horrific for her.

Thea closed her eyes, hoping that Anna hadn't been on the *Arandora Star*, but there was simply no way of knowing. She *had* been moved from Holloway at the right time to have sailed on the ship.

'Are you all right?' Grace's voice was full of concern. 'I know it's easy to think the worst, but she might not have been on the ship, and if she was then she may have survived. It says there were a thousand survivors. We have to hope for the best.'

And a thousand drowned as well, Thea thought. 'Can I buy a copy of this? I need to show it to Hettie and Marianne so they can read it for themselves.'

'Take this one, there's no need to buy another.'

'Thank you.' Thea stowed it in her empty basket. 'I'd better get back.'

Grace opened the door for her. 'Don't give up hope, and let me know if you hear anything, won't you?'

'I will.'

Outside, Thea strapped the basket on to the back of her bicycle, doing her best to fight back tears; every day of this horrible war seemed to bring yet more waste of life. Even if Anna hadn't been on the *Arandora Star*, other people had, and they were all members of somebody's family and were loved and missed, their only apparent crime to have been born in a country that now considered them an enemy.

Chapter 41

The squawking of the seagulls woke Anna, as they did every morning. The sound of the large birds was a constant background noise from sunrise to sunset over the small town of Port St Mary, and although some of the other women complained about them, Anna rather liked them. She loved to watch them flying, sweeping and circling, landing on the rooftops, bobbing up and down, beaks open as they made their distinctive cries. She'd come to associate the sound with the sea, the sky and the deep joy of being out of prison.

Although strictly speaking she was still very much an internee, the women's camp here on the Isle of Man was a world away from the confining walls and cells of Holloway. Here, they were staying in hotels and the area assigned for the women's camp was a massive fifteen square miles, including Port Erin as well as Port St Mary. It felt like a whole new world, one in which she wasn't limited to a single hour's exercise in a small yard every day, but instead had a wide vista of sea and sky to enjoy.

Throwing back the covers, Anna padded softly over to the window, taking care not to wake Eva who was still asleep, her breathing soft and regular. The two of them were sharing a room on the top floor of a small hotel, which had fine views out to the sea. She pulled the blackout away from the window at one side and looked out, drinking in another beautiful summer's day, the sun glinting diamonds on the sea.

It was a week today since they'd arrived on the Isle of Man, brought here by steamer from Liverpool. It had taken all day to get to Liverpool after they'd left London, and they'd stayed a night in a seamen's hostel in the city before being taken to the docks the next morning. They weren't the only ones taken to the port that day either; they'd seen men being led to a large ship, the *Arandora Star*, which they'd passed on the quayside on their way to their much smaller steamer. Word went around amongst the women that they were Italian and German internees who were being sent to a camp overseas, and Anna had been worried that that was going to happen to them too, but fortunately in their case they'd only been brought as far as the Isle of Man.

She was relieved to have been sent here. The island was beautiful and Port St Mary was on the southern tip, with a glorious curved bay where she and many of the women now enjoyed spending time on the beach, paddling, swimming and relaxing on the sand, something they would never have imagined they'd be doing when they'd been behind bars.

Of course, she could never forget that she was still a prisoner, subjected to rules like the nine o'clock curfew each night and daily roll calls, but this was no ordinary prison and if she had to be interned, then this was a good place to be and hugely better than Holloway.

Eva stirred in her bed and sat up. 'What are you doing?'

'Good morning!' Anna smiled at the older woman. 'I am just enjoying the view, it is another beautiful day.'

'I'm pleased to hear it.' Eva got out of bed and came over to the window and looked out. 'I have decided to go to the Marine Biological Research Station today to see if I can do something there. I cannot sit here and do nothing, and since we have no idea how long we'll be on this island I want to do something useful.' They'd discovered the station the previous day on one of their long walks exploring their camp and Eva had been very interested to see it. 'Do you want to come with me?'

Anna shook her head. 'No, I am not a scientist like you, I would not be any use to them.'

Eva raised her eyebrows. 'They might not want me. But I have to ask, and if there is the smallest chance they might be able to find me something to do, then it's worth a try.'

Anna glanced at her watch. 'I am on the rota for setting the breakfast tables this morning, I must get dressed.' Every one of the internees staying here had jobs to do to help with the running of the hotel. They took it in turns to wash up in the kitchen, set up or clear the dining room, and they were all responsible for keeping the communal areas and their own rooms clean.

'You should be thinking about what you can do to

occupy yourself, Anna. It is important to keep busy, just like we did in Holloway.'

'I know, but I am enjoying the freedom of just being allowed outside for now,' she said, buttoning up the front of her blouse. 'Taking long walks, watching the sea and swimming. It feels such a relief after being trapped behind walls in Holloway . . . but I will think about what I can do.'

'You should use your skills and talents like I intend to.'

'I hope the research station will be very pleased to have someone like you come and work with them. It's not every day they have a scientist from a London university turn up on their doorstep and offer to work for them.'

Eva raised her eyebrows. 'I hope you are right.'

Once Anna had finished clearing up after breakfast, she headed out for a walk, passing by the shops. Some of the internees were enjoying spending their money here, those who had any to spare. Anna didn't have much and was being careful with hers, because without a job she had no more coming in. Fortunately, her board and lodgings were paid for, so she'd only spent money on some stamps. She'd written to Thea the day after they'd arrived, telling her where she was, but how long the letter would take to reach Rookery House she didn't know, as they'd been warned that their letters would have to be censored before they were sent on. If it was anything like in Holloway, then it might be several weeks before Thea learned where she was.

Anna sighed. It was no use dwelling on things that were out of her control. She might still be a prisoner, but at least her prison was this beautiful place. She twirled around taking in the green hills, the neat houses by the bay and the wide sweep of sand fringing the sea, which was a deep shade of blue and sparkled with diamonds of light. One thing that being interned had taught her, especially in Holloway, was to appreciate the small things, enjoy the moment and try not to dwell too much on what she couldn't change.

The beach looked so inviting this morning, so she headed down onto the sand, kicking off her shoes and making her way across to the sea, her feet sinking into the soft sand that grew firmer as she reached the water.

She gasped as an exhilarating rush of foaming wave broke over her toes and rushed past her further up the beach until her legs were submerged in cold seawater up to the calves. She threw back her head, closed her eyes and took a deep breath of clean salty air. This was the closest to freedom she'd felt in months. She was still very much a prisoner, but now in a gilded cage.

Chapter 42

Prue turned this way and that, checking her reflection in the dressing table mirror, and was satisfied with what she saw. Her neatly pressed WVS green summer dress looked smart but was also practical and comfortable to wear for whatever task lay ahead of her, and today's was an important one.

When the call had gone out from the Ministry of Aircraft Production for the collection of aluminium to make more planes to help defend the country, the WVS had taken heed, and today it was her responsibility to gather Great Plumstead's contribution. She hoped that all the posters she'd put up around the village and the announcement at the last WI meeting would have encouraged housewives to sort through their homes to find aluminium pots and pans that could be spared and donated.

She smoothed down her hair, which she'd pinned into a bun at the nape of her neck, and then headed downstairs to get breakfast over and done with so that she could get out and collecting.

Prue was halfway down the stairs when there was a knock at the front door which sent her hurrying down to open it, her chest tightening. Visitors didn't usually come at seven o'clock in the morning – something must be wrong. She flung open the door and saw her brother, Reuben, standing there dressed in his denim overalls, which he wore when he was out on duty with the Local Defence Volunteers as their proper uniform still hadn't been given out.

'Reuben! What's wrong? Has something happened to Thea or Hettie? Marianne or the baby?'

'No, they're fine as far as I know. I've just come off duty and heard from our platoon captain that Norwich was bombed yesterday evening; several people were killed.'

Prue gasped, putting her hand to her mouth, her thoughts immediately going to her sister Lizzie, who lived in the city. Had she been hurt ... or worse? 'Do you know where? Was it near Lizzie's house in College Road?'

'No, the planes were targeting factories, Boulton and Paul, Barnard's Ironworks and Colman's. Some of those killed had just left work.'

Prue sighed. The bombs had thankfully landed nowhere near where Lizzie worked in the centre of Norwich or where she lived, the planes having clearly picked out factories that were involved with manufacturing things for the war. But nevertheless innocent people had been killed either at work or on their way home, only a few miles from here. It was shocking.

An icy shiver went through her as it hit her how far the fingers of war were stretching these days. Now *nowhere* was safe. The bombers could come back any time and industrial cities were a very real target. Next time the bombs might reach further into the city, into the centre . . .

Lizzie was at risk living in Norwich. She should get out of there, leave while she had the chance, Prue thought. She could come here, they had the space.

'Do you think the bombers will come back?'

Reuben shrugged. 'Possibly. They know there are factories there, so no doubt they will sometime.'

'I'm going to ask Lizzie if she'll come and live here. She'd be safer if and when they do come back.'

'I doubt very much she'll agree to that.' Reuben raised his eyebrows, his eyes meeting hers. 'Thea has offered for her to live at Rookery House after she moved there but she said no. You know how independent Lizzie is.'

'I know, but I'm still going to ask. She can say no if she wants to, but at least I'll have offered.'

'Up to you.' Reuben smiled at her. 'I need to get home, I just thought you'd want to know.'

'Thank you for coming to tell me, I appreciate that.' She reached out and touched her brother's arm.

'Best to hear the truth from me, rather than what people will be gossiping about in the shop when word gets around. You know what it's like with them adding on bits that didn't happen.' He nodded and turned to go before pausing on the path to the front gate and looking back at her. 'You'd better tell Victor. He's been on duty at the furthest roadblock from here, so he won't have heard it before we stood down.'

Prue nodded. 'I'll tell him.'

Prue was busy making porridge, pondering the best way to ask Lizzie about coming to live with them, knowing how prickly her sister could be about her independence, when Victor arrived home. She heard him come in the front door and knew he'd follow the same routine as he always did, going upstairs for a wash and a shave and getting changed for work. She had about ten minutes of peace left before he arrived in the kitchen expecting his breakfast to be ready. His arrival home always set her on edge, so she tried to distract herself by mentally planning the route she and Alice, who'd now finished school, would take around the village as they collected the aluminium in the handcart this morning.

'Good morning,' Prue said when he came into the kitchen and plonked himself down at the table. Most wives would be pleased to see their husbands return safely from a night out on patrol; Prue wasn't, but for the sake of keeping a reasonably peaceful home she did her best to be polite.

Sadly, Victor didn't share her manners, merely grunting as she placed a bowl of porridge on the table in front of him.

'How was your patrol?'

'Fine.' Victor reached for the jar of honey made by Thea's bees and spooned a generous amount on top of his porridge. Mixing it in, he began to eat hurriedly.

She poured them both a cup of tea and put his in front of him. 'Reuben called in on his way home from night patrol.'

Victor narrowed his pale blue eyes as he glanced up at her. 'What did *he* want?'

'He came to tell me that Norwich was bombed yesterday evening; several people were killed. He knew I'd be worried about Lizzie.'

Victor dropped his full spoon onto the table with a clatter, blobs of porridge splashing onto the oilcloth. 'What?' His face had drained of colour and he grabbed hold of the table, his knuckles showing white.

Prue stared at him, taken aback by his reaction. He and Lizzie had never got on, so to see him so concerned about her was puzzling. But then perhaps it was just the fact that it was Norwich, and not so far away from where he sat right now, and a place he regularly went to for meetings. Norwich being attacked had brought the war closer to home and that was a most disturbing feeling.

'Don't worry, she's all right,' Prue said. 'Reuben knew I'd be worried about Lizzie if I heard that the city had been hit. He wanted to tell me where it was, and it wasn't anywhere near my sister's.'

'Where was it?' Victor's voice was shaky.

'At some factories – Boulton and Paul, Barnard's Ironworks and Colman's. Some of those killed had just left work.'

Victor let out a loud sigh of relief, picked up his spoon from the table and started to eat again, colour flooding back to his face. It seemed he was quite recovered from his odd reaction.

'I was thinking, now Norwich is clearly on Hitler's list of targets, that I should ask Lizzie to come and live here. We've got the room and she'd be safer here than in Norwich ... if and when the bombers come back.'

255

'No! Absolutely not!' Victor's eyes narrowed as he glared at her.

Prue grasped the back of the chair she was standing near. 'But next time the bombers might hit the centre of the city where she works or the area where she lives.'

'I'm not having *her* living here and that's the end of it.' He didn't wait for Prue to respond, but dropped his spoon into his bowl, got up and swiftly left the room. A few moments later she heard the bang of the front door closing behind him as he left for work.

Prue sighed. He'd behaved very oddly this morning, but in true Victor style he hadn't given her a chance to argue with him, he'd said what *he* wanted and that was that. If he wasn't willing to have Lizzie living here, then Thea probably would be. She'd ask her later when they went to Rookery House for the collection round. It didn't really matter where Lizzie lived as long as she was safe. Having her and Victor living in the same house would have been a volatile mixture anyway. Her younger sister wouldn't have tiptoed around him to keep the peace as Prue had done all these years.

Chapter 43

'The last time I pushed a pram it had a baby in it, not a sewing machine!' Anna joked, thinking she must write about this in her next letter to Thea and everyone at Rookery House.

'Do you have a baby?' Renate asked. She was a Jewish, German refugee like Anna. They lived in the same hotel and had got to know each other since they'd arrived.

'No, it was the baby of one of the women who lived in the house where I stayed in Norfolk. Her name is Marianne; she is a dressmaker like you. She designs and makes garments for people in the village.'

'You miss your home and the others, yes?'

Anna missed being at Rookery House and thought about it and everyone who lived there every day. She desperately longed to be free and back with them. As beautiful as it was here, there was no forgetting that she was still an internee, her life was governed by others with their rules. It might be bigger here than the cell and the limited areas of Holloway that she'd inhabited, but it was still a prison camp and she wasn't here of her own free will.

Renate and Anna had both talked about where they'd been before they were interned; Renate had been working as a domestic servant and had been glad to be removed from her job.

Anna looked at Renate and nodded. 'Yes, I do, but we are here now and have to make the best of things – and at least this place is so much better than Holloway!'

They were on their way back from Port Erin, where they'd gone to collect the sewing machine that Renate was hiring to use for the dressmaking business that she was setting up. She'd borrowed a pram to transport it back and Anna had gone along with her to help.

'Yes!' Renate laughed. 'I would not be doing this or have the chance to earn money doing what I love, and am good at. You should find job, too, Anna.'

'You sound like Eva.' She sighed. 'You are both right, I do need to do something to earn some money – and it would be nice to have a purpose again, and it would help pass the time.'

She'd enjoyed having a chance to experience the beauty of the place, the freedom to go on walks within their large camp area, but if she was honest with herself she was beginning to feel the need to do something more, to challenge herself; to use her mind and keep herself busier. She'd been trying to decide what would work for her. Having been snapped up at the Marine Biological Research Station, Eva had found a role perfectly suited to her. She was loving it, going off every morning happy to have something useful and interesting to occupy her time.

'Have you a plan?' Renate asked.

'Eva says we should use our skills and talents – like you and she are doing. So I should be teaching. I have noticed how poor some of the women's English is. If they want to stay here in England they need to get better. I could teach them, hold classes.'

'That is a good idea, you could charge for each lesson.' Renate smiled at her. 'How much?'

'I thought a penny a lesson and have classes with no more than six people in them, keep them small so it's easier for each of them to have my attention. If there are enough people who want lessons, I could hold more than one class.'

'You need to make posters, tell people what you offer.'

'I can put them up around Port St Mary and Port Erin,' Anna said. 'Do you think anyone would be interested?'

Renate shrugged. 'I think so. You can try.'

Anna nodded. 'I am going to. It would be good to have people to teach again, I miss it very much.'

Chapter 44

'Victor said no.'

Thea finished spooning fresh tea leaves into the teapot and looked at Prue. 'Did you *honestly* think he would say yes?' Her sister had told her about Reuben coming to see her after his LDV duty and giving her news of the Norwich bombings earlier this morning, and her idea for Lizzie to go and live with them. It was a worry that the enemy were getting closer to home, and naturally Thea and Prue were both worried for their youngest sister.

Prue shrugged. 'It wasn't a surprise, but I'm concerned about Lizzie. Could she come and live here?'

'Of course she could. But you know I've already asked her, not long after I moved in here, and she said no. I'll ask again, but honestly I very much doubt she'll agree, you know how Lizzie likes her independence.' Thea took the boiling kettle off the range and poured the hot water into the teapot.

Prue smiled at her. 'Thank you. I—' She paused at the

sound of the letterbox out in the hall opening and shutting with a metallic snap.

'That's this morning's post,' Thea said, wondering what news it would bring today.

'I'll go and get it.' Prue headed off into the hall while Thea refilled the kettle at the sink, pumping the hand pump to bring water up from the well.

She'd just put the kettle back on the top of the range for the water to heat up when Prue came back into the kitchen with a handful of letters.

'Who are they for?' Thea asked as she set out cups onto a tray ready to take outside for the mothers from the day club who were helping her in the garden this morning. They'd been coming most days for an hour or two since last week and had really made a difference with managing the workload.

'There's two for Marianne,' Prue said, placing two envelopes down on the kitchen table and holding the others out to her. 'And two for you.'

Thea took the envelopes and looked at the writing on the front. One was from Violet in London. And the other . . .

She looked up at Prue, her heart feeling like it had lodged itself in her throat. 'This is from Anna.'

Prue came over and stared at the envelope. 'The postmark's all smudged, I can't see where it's from. Open it then!'

Thea quickly tore the envelope open and took out a sheet of paper, her eyes immediately drawn to the address in the top right-hand corner.

'Look, she's on the Isle of Man!' She pointed at the address.

'It was written on the third of July, *after* the *Arandora Star* sank.' Prue grabbed hold of Thea's arm. 'She's safe.'

Thea's eyes filled with tears as an overwhelming sense of relief flooded through her.

'Go on, read it, see what's been happening. I'll finish getting the tea tray ready. I'll cut Hettie's Victoria sponge, shall I?'

Thea nodded and turned her attention to Anna's letter.

Dear Thea,

As you can see from the address I am now on the Isle of Man. We weren't told what was happening until the last minute so I'm sorry that I had no time to write and tell you I was leaving. We were taken by train to Liverpool, where we stayed for one night, and then we boarded the steamer to bring us here. It was such a joy to be out on the sea, to be able to look to the far horizon and feel the breeze on my face again after the confines of Holloway. I will never take for granted being out in fresh air again.

When we reached the island, we were taken by train to Port St Mary which is in the women's camp and where we are staying in hotels. I'm sharing a room with my friend Eva, who I told you about in previous letters, and we are lucky to have a sea view. Looking out the window at the sea each morning is such a pleasure and although we are interned and have to stay within the limits of the camp and not wander across to other parts of the island where there's a men's camp, we have plenty of space, fresh air and the chance to swim in the sea.

We have rules to stick to like the nine o'clock curfew at night and we all have jobs to do to help keep the hotels

running like the washing up or cleaning but it's not a
problem. If I must be interned, then this place is much,
much better than Holloway!

I hope everybody at Rookery House is well, I think of
you all often and miss being there with you. Your letters to
me are very much appreciated.

With all good wishes,
Anna

'You look like a weight's been lifted off your shoulders,'
Prue said. 'Is Anna all right?'

Thea nodded and smiled. 'Read it for yourself.' She
handed her sister the letter.

She was so relieved to know that Anna was alive and
well and making the most of where she now was. She'd
never imagined that Anna would have been taken to the
Isle of Man, but at least she was safe and in a nice place. No
wonder she was enjoying being able to see far off into the
distance and feel the wind on her face again.

'That's marvellous news, better than being shut away in
a prison,' Prue said when she'd finished reading. 'It won't
be as bad for her there.'

'No.' Thea picked up the teapot and poured tea out into
the waiting cups. 'Come on, let's go and tell everyone the
news while they have their tea break.'

'Anna's gone from one extreme to the other, it's bleedin'
marvellous!' Gloria declared as she settled herself down
on the grass in the back garden of Rookery House with a
cup of tea in one hand and a slice of Victoria sponge in the

other. 'Here's to Anna.' She held her cup aloft in a toast and everyone else joined in.

The news that Anna was alive and safe on the Isle of Man had been met with great joy by Gloria and the two other mothers who'd been helping with the hoeing this morning, and Alice, who'd come with Prue on their collections around the village, was equally pleased.

'How long do you think she'll be there?' Alice asked.

'I don't know,' Thea said. 'It's a much better place to be, but I still want to get her freed. And I'm sure that Anna wants her freedom again too.'

Chapter 45

There was an air of industriousness at the day club this afternoon, the gentle whirring of sewing machines combining with the chatter of the mothers as they worked. The open windows and front door of the hall brought in a welcome breeze to cool them as it was a warm August day.

Prue glanced up from hemming the bottom of a dress suitable for a toddler and smiled to herself, thinking how far they'd all come since that day last September, almost a year ago now, when – on the day war had been declared – the women had arrived unexpectedly at the station. With work and patience, the day club had become a real community hub in Great Plumstead and they were going from strength to strength.

This project developing the clothes depot was proving particularly popular. Many of the second-hand garments had already been loaned out to the mothers, whose ever-growing children needed bigger clothes, and they were

adding to the stockpile all the while, either through dona-
tions or, like now, by using the material that had been sent
over from Canada to make new garments.

Looking over at Marianne, who was patiently instruct-
ing one of the mothers how to sew neat buttonholes, she
thought how the young woman was proving to be an excellent teacher as well as a skilled dressmaker. She'd created
the patterns for the new clothes and under her guidance,
the women were becoming much more competent sewers
at their weekly sessions. They made the most of the time
when their children were asleep, babies napping in their
prams or toddlers lying side by side on makeshift beds on
the floor in the corner of the village hall.

Prue returned her attention to her sewing. She wanted
to finish the hem before she went to make tea for everyone.
She enjoyed being absorbed in her task, pushing the needle
in and out and drawing the thread through. It was a rare
chance to sit quietly for a while.

'Prue.'

She looked up and was surprised to see Thea and Lizzie
standing before her. What were they doing here? Her heart
began to race. Was something wrong? Why else would they
be here? Had something happened to her children?

'Has somebody been hurt? What's—' A sharp pain
stabbed her finger and she looked down to see a dark red
bead of blood blooming on it, threatening to run down
onto the pale blue of the dress she was working on. She
quickly pulled her clean handkerchief out of her pocket and
wrapped it around her finger.

'It's all right, nobody's been hurt,' Thea reassured her.

'Though a certain person might be after we tell her,' Lizzie muttered, exchanging a glance with Thea.

Prue was aware that the arrival of both her sisters in the hall had silenced the chatter of the mothers and everybody was looking at them. 'Let's go in the kitchen, I was going to make some tea soon anyway.'

She stood up and, smiling around at the rest of the mothers in an effort to reassure them that she was fine, led the way to the kitchen at the back of the hall. She closed the door firmly behind them once they were inside, switched on the hot water urn and then turned to face her sisters. 'What's this about then?'

Thea and Lizzie glanced at each other before Thea spoke. 'Lizzie's come to see you to tell you something that she's found out. She thought it would be best if I was here too.'

Prue frowned. What could Lizzie possibly have to tell her? They were sisters, but they weren't as close as she and Thea were. Her personality and Lizzie's tended to clash, though that didn't mean they didn't care and look out for each other. 'Go on, tell me.'

Lizzie cleared her throat and with another look at Thea, who nodded her encouragement, met Prue's eye. 'I've seen something that you really need to know about ...' She hesitated for a moment. 'Victor is messing around with another woman. I've seen them together in Norwich on Sundays, in fact I've followed them to make sure I hadn't made a mistake. He's being unfaithful to you ... I'm sorry.' Lizzie reached out and gently caught Prue's hand.

Victor being unfaithful to her with another woman. His dressing up smart, his eagerness to go to these so-called meetings every Sunday, his odd reaction to Norwich getting bombed. Everything slotted into place and Prue couldn't stop the sudden bubble of laughter that rose up in her throat; it spilled out, echoing around the kitchen. Her sisters looked at her in astonishment and she put a hand over her mouth until she managed to control herself again. 'Tell me everything, right from the start, including how you found out.'

'You're not angry with him?' Lizzie asked.

Prue considered for a moment. 'Of course I am, but only because he's a lying . . . ' She put a hand on her hip. 'Do you know he made me feel *guilty* about not having his best shirt ironed for him to go out to these so-called Sunday meetings, because I'd been busy helping out here and with the WVS, when all along he was going to see his *fancy* woman.' She threw both her arms wide. 'You know, I don't care that he's involved with someone else, and quite frankly she's welcome to him. Come on, tell me everything you know.'

'I first saw them together three weeks ago, quite by accident. They were coming out of a restaurant arm in arm, looking very cosy together.' Lizzie pulled a face. 'Victor looked more . . . umm . . . lovey-dovey than I've ever seen him before, so I was immediately suspicious.'

The fact that Victor had been in a restaurant was itself suspicious, Prue thought. He'd never taken her to one in all the years they'd been married and even before, his excuse being that you never knew what the kitchen was like, whether it was clean or not. And the cooking was far better at home – and cheaper. 'Did he see you?'

'No, he was completely focused on the woman. Anyway,

I followed them, and they went back to where she lives. It's not far from where we saw Victor that day after Edwin's tribunal, do you remember? We saw him coming down the street and you said how odd it was for him to be there in the week, as he usually had meetings in Norwich on Sunday.'

Prue nodded, recalling the look of shock on Victor's face when he'd seen them and how he'd said he'd had to come in for an emergency meeting. She remembered that she'd asked him about it when he got home that night, wondering how it went, and that he'd been very dismissive of her, getting annoyed with her and not answering her question. She hadn't thought any more of it at the time; her joy at Edwin's registration as a conscientious objector was more important than arguing with Victor.

'I knew something was up, but I didn't want to jump the gun and tell you without checking it again, so for the past two Sundays I've watched the woman's house.' Lizzie chuckled. 'Like some private eye! Sure enough Victor came back and they went out again to different restaurants and then went back to her house. That first time wasn't a one-off, I'm afraid. He's a regular visitor and he looks pretty smitten with her, though what she sees in him I—' Lizzie fell silent after Thea nudged her arm.

'Are you all right, Prue?' Thea asked gently.

Prue considered for a moment; how did she feel about this? Did she wish Victor would treat her that kindly, had he *ever* treated her like that? How he was behaving didn't sound like him at all, not the *real* Victor whom she lived with. Whoever this woman was, she wasn't seeing his true nature.

'I'm fine. This would have felt worse years ago, but I've lived with him long enough and put up with his ways and ... especially with what happened with Edwin, to not ever want *anything* of him again.'

'What are you going to do?' Lizzie asked.

'Nothing yet, so please don't tell anyone else about this. I need time to think.' Prue took a tray out of one of the cupboards and put it down on the table, adding cups to it. 'I'm going to get this tea organised. Do you both want a cup? There's some sewing you can join in with too if you'd like.'

'Yes, thank you,' Thea said.

'I'll say yes to the tea, but better not let me anywhere near your sewing if you want it done properly,' Lizzie warned her.

'Tea it is then. You both go through to the hall and see what the others are doing, I'll bring it through in a minute or two.' Prue wanted a moment on her own.

'You sure you're all right?' Thea asked, touching Prue's arm.

'Of course.' Prue smiled at her.

'I'm here to talk to anytime, you know that, don't you?' Thea said.

Prue nodded. 'Yes, thank you. Now, I must get this tea sorted or I'll have a rebellion starting in there.'

After her sisters had finally left the kitchen, Prue leaned against the sink and hung her head, needing to process what she'd just learned about the man she'd *sacrificed* ... the word popped into her mind ... sacrificed ... that was right ... years of her life to, putting up with his selfish, dominant ways for the sake of the children. How did she feel about him having a mistress? she thought. Shocked, amused and in a strange way relieved! The news would take a while to fully sink in and she needed time to decide what she was going to do about it, but one thing was certain. This was a turning point for her, one she welcomed with open arms.

Chapter 46

Over a week had passed since Lizzie broke the news to Prue about what Victor was really getting up to on his weekly trips into Norwich, but until today Thea hadn't had the chance to speak to her sister in private about how she was feeling and what she was going to do. Now, on their way in the WVS mobile canteen to provide refreshments at the station where troops from the local camp would be gathering, it was the perfect opportunity to ask, without the risk of anyone overhearing.

Thea glanced at Prue, who sat beside her looking out of the window at the passing countryside. The harvest was in full swing. The fields were busy with farmers and Land Girls stacking sheaves of cut corn into stooks dotted around the fields, everyone working hard to get the corn harvested while the good weather lasted. It was a glorious scene of golden fields under a summer's sky where small, flat-bottomed, puffy clouds sailed across the blue.

Her sister seemed quieter than usual and Thea was worried about her. What her plans were, she didn't know. Was the knowledge of Victor's unfaithfulness enough for her sister to end their marriage? If she were in Prue's place, she wouldn't put up with him any more, not after finding out what he was up to, but then she'd never have married Victor in the first place. Her sister had stuck with him for years, so would the knowledge that he had a mistress even change things?

Bringing the mobile canteen to a halt at a junction, she checked the road was clear and turned left, determined to find out. But before she could say anything she spotted a roadblock up ahead manned by a detachment of Home Guard, as the Local Defence Volunteers were now known, having been renamed by Churchill last month. Their new name, which she much preferred, seemed to have a certain ring of confidence about it, and that was badly needed at the moment. The news on the wireless and in the newspapers was full of how the RAF pilots were bravely battling against the Luftwaffe in the skies above southern Britain, and all the while the country was balanced on a knife edge, with roadblocks like this one becoming commonplace because of the threat of invasion.

As they approached, one of the Home Guard stood in the middle of the road facing them, his hand held palm outwards signalling them to stop. He looked very much the part, dressed in the khaki battledress uniform which was gradually being distributed to members.

Thea brought the mobile canteen to a halt a few yards in front of the roadblock and leaned out of the open window in the driver's door to speak to him.

'Afternoon, ladies,' the Home Guard nodded his head at them. 'Can I see your identity cards, please?'

Thea and Prue both obliged and handed them to him for inspection.

'Where are you off to?' he asked.

'To provide refreshments at a station,' Thea said, knowing that it wouldn't do to name the place or give details of who the refreshments were for, troop movements being potentially useful information for the enemy. The government were persistent in their message that nobody should be gossiping about details like that because of who might overhear them and use the information against the country.

The need for secrecy gave rise to an unpleasant feeling, a sense of suspicion in the community, but with invasion a strong possibility it was necessary for everybody to do their bit to protect the country.

'I'm sure it will be much appreciated.' The Home Guard handed their identity cards back and nodded to his colleagues, who raised the red and white painted bar that had been set up on crossed beams placed either side of the road. He stood back from the canteen and gave them a salute as Thea selected first gear and pulled away, passing through the opened roadblock with a wave to the other Home Guards.

Picking up speed again, Thea glanced at her sister, finally grabbing her chance to ask, 'Have you thought about what you're going to do . . . about Victor?'

Prue didn't answer for a few moments. 'I have . . . and I've decided to sit on that knowledge for a bit, watch and wait.'

'You mean see if he finishes his relationship with this woman?'

Prue snorted. 'No, she can keep him as far as I'm concerned. My concern is Alice and keeping the home going for her. Now that she's finished school and is spending more time helping you in the garden at Rookery House before she decides what she wants to do, I don't want to upset her by breaking up the home. Though it may be only a matter of time before she leaves anyway.'

'Have you told him that you know?' Thea dropped down a gear as they approached a sharp bend in the road.

'Absolutely not!' Prue exclaimed. 'I'll decide when I tell him and it will be when it's best for me, don't worry. One good thing about knowing what he's up to is that I no longer feel guilty about not having the housework done and everything up to scratch as it would have been before the war. I've got better things to be doing now, and making sure Victor's best shirt is ironed ready for him to go and see his lady love isn't one of them – he had to go in one of his everyday ones last Sunday.'

Thea laughed, delighted to see that for the first time in many years Prue seemed to have lost the haunted look which made her seem as if she was carrying a burden of unhappiness on her shoulders. The spark that she'd once had was coming back and Victor was going to have to look out when Prue told him that she knew about his affair. She'd love to be a fly on the wall when that happened.

'Do you hear that?' Prue swung around in her seat, looking out of her side window and scanning the sky.

'What's the matter?'

'It sounds like some planes.'

'They're probably heading back into RAF Coltishall.

We're not far away from it here, it's just over that way.' Thea nodded over to her right, where the aerodrome lay less than a couple of miles away.

'They're there, look!' Prue pointed out through the windscreen.

Thea braked, bringing the canteen to a crawl, while she glanced up through the windscreen to where three planes were silhouetted against the sky. They were coming in lower, growing bigger by the moment. A prickle of fear shivered across her skin. The sound of the engines wasn't right, they weren't our planes. As they drew nearer, she could see the black and white crosses standing out starkly on their sides.

'They're German planes!' she gasped, bringing the canteen to a halt. 'They're heading for the aerodrome . . . !'

'Oh my God!' Prue put her hands to her face. 'Do you think they're going to bomb them?'

Thea's stomach clenched. 'Looks like it.'

Thea jumped out of the mobile canteen and stood in the middle of the road watching. Prue quickly joined her, grabbing hold of Thea's arm as they watched and waited, time seeming to slow down.

Before the planes could drop their deadly load, a squadron of Hurricanes shot up into the air from the aerodrome, like hornets launching out from a disturbed nest, their engines roaring as they climbed into the air and banked around to face their foes. The alarm had clearly been raised, the enemy spotted and the pilots were taking off in a hurry to defend their base.

Thea watched, unable to tear her eyes away as the

Hurricanes headed straight towards the larger enemy planes, causing them to take evasive action, swerving off the course of what must have been a bombing run before they could discharge their weapons. They soared upwards, the Hurricanes on their tails, and a game of hide and seek began in the clouds above them, the vapour trails from the planes' engines painting white lines across the blue sky.

It was totally compelling to watch. Thea urged the RAF pilots on to repel the invaders, a mixture of terror, fascination and horror filling her as the planes swooped and dived, banked and climbed, the roar of their engines filling the air.

'One's been hit!' Prue shrieked as a black trail suddenly started to pour out the back of one of the planes as it plummeted towards the ground in a corkscrew motion. 'Is it one of ours or theirs?'

'I'm not sure, it's hard to tell from here.' Whoever it was, it wasn't a pleasant sight. Thea felt relieved to see several white parachutes suddenly bloom in the sky and float slowly down as the plane hit the ground in the distance, a black plume of smoke marking where it fell. 'There's only one pilot in a Hurricane, so it must have been one of theirs.'

The question of whether it was one of theirs or one of ours was definitively answered as a Hurricane came swooping down low over their heads with a rush of its engines, the pilot putting it into a full victory roll over the aerodrome before climbing steeply up again to join his comrades. They were now heading farther off in pursuit of the enemy planes, who'd clearly abandoned the idea of attacking RAF Coltishall and were fleeing into the distance.

'It was one of theirs,' Prue said. 'That's good, I think,

but I can't help feeling bad about it still. Whichever side those men are on, seeing them shot down . . . ' She sighed. 'They're all someone's sons or husbands, brothers, aren't they? Some women out there will be worrying about them just like I worry about Jack and Edwin.'

Thea squeezed Prue's arm. 'I know, but thankfully there were survivors this time and they'll be picked up. The war will be over for them now, they'll be POWs. It would have been worse if they'd dropped their bombs on the aerodrome, a lot more casualties.'

Prue frowned. 'War's a horrible beast.'

'It is,' Thea agreed. 'Come on, we need to get going again, there are people depending on us for their tea and sandwiches.'

Chapter 47

'Take it in turns, one to be the shopkeeper and the other the customer, then swap around when I tell you in a few minutes' time,' Anna instructed her pupils. 'Practise what we have learned today.' She watched her class as they did what she'd told them, gradually moving around the room and listening in on their conversations.

To her delight, her adverts to run classes had worked well and now she was teaching English lessons each morning during the week and on a couple of afternoons as well, the desire to improve their English proving popular with many of the internees. Anna was loving it. Being back teaching – although within the confines of a prison camp – was a delight. Her pupils were attentive and eager to learn and made good use of their time here, clearly recognising that improving their language skills would help them once they were released.

'Good morning, I would like to buy some sugar ...

flour ... butter ... ' one of the Austrian pupils said, her English heavily accented, as Anna listened in. She nodded at her encouragingly, pleased to hear how much she'd improved since she'd started her classes. What was particularly rewarding about teaching these women was how determined they were to learn, listening carefully to what she taught them and conscientiously practising. She'd even heard them outside of lessons working together. Her classes were focused on useful English to start with, so it would help the women in their everyday lives and their work, with the aim that they could live here as easily as they could in their home countries and not be hindered by being unable to understand or make themselves understood.

As usual, the hour flew by, and after giving the women some words and phrases to practise for their next lesson, Anna left them chatting amongst themselves. She'd promised Eva that she would help her with a new venture she'd been put in charge of at the Marine Biological Research Station this afternoon.

'Be very careful how you move around, the rocks are slippery. Keep an eye on the tide and listen for my whistle.' Eva regarded Anna and the six other women who were working on the seaweed collection today, her face serious. 'I'll blow it when the tide turns, and you will need to quickly work back towards the shore.' Her face broke into a smile. 'So, let's get to work!'

Anna picked up her basket and headed out with Eva and the women across the rocky shore to begin collecting, knowing that their work would be helping to fill the gap left by the halting of seaweed supplies that used to come in from Japan and America. Eva had explained to them how the seaweed was used to make agar plates for scientific purposes and how important that was. Everything they collected today would be dried and sent off to the mainland. With their help, the Marine Biological Research Station was helping the country to become more self-sufficient rather than depend on overseas supplies, just as farmers and householders who were now growing more food for themselves were doing. Eva had taken on her role in charge of the seaweed harvesting with great gusto, delighting in them being able to do their bit here by foraging for seaweed on the shoreline.

'I had a letter from Thea this morning,' Anna said, carefully negotiating the slippery bladder-wrack seaweed covering the rocks as they made their way down to the sea's edge. 'She is still writing letters to try and get me freed, but no luck so far.'

'Well if she keeps on long enough it might work,' Eva said, wading through a rock pool. 'What is it they say about the squeaky wheel and oil?'

'Ah, it's a squeaky wheel that gets the oil! If someone makes enough noise or fuss, then they get noticed.' Anna laughed.

They'd reached the water's edge and started picking, taking care not to remove all the seaweed so that there'd be more another time. Anna loved the colours and shapes of it and how the types changed as they went down the shore. Eva had taught her how the toughest seaweeds, which could survive being out of water for longest, grew at the top of the shore and the more delicate ones further down. It was interesting to see how beautiful each type was, how different in colour and form. Helping Eva had opened a whole new world for her, rather like working in the garden with Thea had. Anna enjoyed the afternoons she spent out on the shore picking seaweed.

Picking a handful, she gave the seaweed a firm shake to remove some of the seawater and then placed it in her basket.

'Look at this starfish.' Eva gently lifted it out of a rock pool and held it in her palm. 'It's a beauty.'

Anna reached out and touched it, surprised at its firmness. 'Can I hold it?'

'Of course.' Eva passed it to her.

Holding it in her palm she felt a funny sensation on her skin. 'It tickles.'

'That's all the feet moving. Turn it over and have a look.'

Anna carefully turned the starfish and saw there were lots of tiny sucker-like feet waving under each arm of the star.

'See, that's how it moves along, on all of them. This is its mouth.' Eva pointed to the middle of the underside.

'I love this about seaweed harvesting,' Anna said gently, feeling the tiny feet with the tip of her finger. 'I'm learning so much about the animals and plants here on the shore.'

Eva smiled at her and nodded. 'It's always good to learn. Put it back carefully in the pool. We need to get on and pick before the tide turns.'

Anna released the starfish back into the rock pool, thinking not for the first time how lucky she'd been to meet Eva on that first day in Holloway. The woman had made a huge difference to her time being interned, and without her positive influence, Anna knew that she'd have found things much harder. She had been very fortunate to have had some strong, kind women helping her since she came to England. First Julia, then Thea and now Eva – all of them had supported and encouraged her through difficult times.

The tide had turned and their party of pickers had almost reached the high shore again, their baskets full of salty-smelling seaweed, when one of the women, Inge, suddenly slipped on a rock and landed with a thump on her hands and knees.

'Oww!' Inge yelped.

Anna hurried over to her. 'Are you all right, are you hurt?'

Inge struggled to get to her feet again, turning over her hands, and Anna saw that her palms were grazed and bleeding.

'My knees.' Inge pulled up the bottom of her skirt and both her knees were cut, blood beginning to trickle down her legs.

'It's all right, I can help you.' Anna put her hand on Inge's arm. 'I did first-aid training before I was interned. I know what to do.'

'There is first-aid equipment at the station you can use,' Eva said, having come over to see what had happened.

Two of the other women took Inge's full basket of seaweed and carried it back to the marine biological station between them, while Anna took Inge's arm with her free hand and walked beside her as she limped the short distance to the station.

With Inge settled in a chair, Anna recalled the instructions that Nurse Williams had given them at the WI meeting and carefully put them into practice, first cleaning Inge's wounds and then covering them with bandages to keep them clean.

'Your hands and knees will probably sting for a few days and you need to keep them dry.'

'Thank you.' Inge smiled at her. 'Is good you know what to do.'

Anna returned her smile, glad that she'd been able to put what she'd learned to good use and in doing so, had felt that bit closer to the people she'd left behind in Great Plumstead. She might not be there at the moment, but what she'd learned alongside her friends, she had carried here with her, and that warmed her heart.

Chapter 48

Thea was tired and grumpy, and even the beautiful day, the blue sky overhead dotted with dappled clouds, did nothing to raise her mood as she pedalled her bicycle into the village this morning. She felt like she'd hardly slept last night; although she'd been tired after a busy day's work in the garden, her mind had refused to be quiet and allow her tired body to properly rest. She'd lain there listening to the sound of bombers' engines as they passed overhead on their way to attack Hitler's war-making forces or factories. The news was full of reports about what the RAF had been doing to fight back, targeting sites in Germany, Holland and France – even Berlin had been hit. Hearing the planes going out always sent a shiver down her spine knowing that they were heading for enemy territory, and that there was a good chance that not all of them would come back again. As the planes droned overhead she always wished them well.

Unsettling and worrying as it was, it wasn't the thought of what the young men in the bombers were heading into that had kept Thea awake, but her growing impatience and frustration. Despite writing numerous letters to get Anna released, she'd had no success. She'd received replies to some of her appeals, but none of them had hit the mark of reaching who could really help. Her letters had seemingly only got as far as various secretaries who, although they sympathised with Anna's situation, were unable to do anything about it themselves. They had suggested other places that she could write to – and she had. But nothing had worked, and her patience had grown thin. Now it was the first week of September and Anna was still a prisoner; she might be in a much nicer place but she did not have the freedom she deserved.

Thea glanced at her latest letter – which she'd written yesterday evening and was going to send this morning – in the basket at the front of her bicycle. Was it another waste of time?

Arriving in the village, Thea quickly delivered the fresh vegetables she'd picked in the garden this morning at Barker's, along with some of Hettie's butter and cheese, and then headed for the post office to buy some stamps.

There was no one else in the post office. Blanche Stimpson was serving behind the counter and greeted her warmly. 'Good morning, Thea. You're just the person I want to see, I was going to telephone you later ... I have some news for you.'

Thea frowned. 'Some news? What about?'

The bell above the shop door pinged as another

customer came in. It was Rosalind, closely followed by her friend Sylvia.

'Good morning,' they chorused.

'One moment, please.' Blanche went to the door behind the post office counter, opened it and called through to her husband to come and serve. He quickly appeared, putting on his spectacles, and took her place behind the counter. 'Thea, would you come through to the back, please. I need to discuss something with you.'

Puzzled at what was going on and amused by the looks of curiosity on Rosalind and Sylvia's faces, Thea followed Blanche through into the living quarters. 'What's this about, Blanche?'

'Take a seat.' Blanche indicated for her to sit down in one of the chairs at the kitchen table. 'Is Anna still on the Isle of Man?'

Thea nodded. 'Yes, unfortunately!'

'Have you had any positive response to your letters?'

'No. Nothing.' She waved the letter she held in her hand. 'I was about to send this off, but it's probably going to get exactly the same reply.' She sighed. 'I'm running out of patience, Blanche. I'm going to have to do something different to get Anna's case noticed and dealt with properly because letters don't work.' She'd often talked to the other woman about the letters when she'd gone in to the post office to send them off. Blanche always took a keen interest in how things were going and asked for news of Anna.

Blanche put her hand on Thea's arm. 'I think I might have something that will help.' She smiled. 'My niece,

Sarah, has recently started a new job in London, at the Home Office, and her boss is someone who could possibly help you. I took the liberty of writing to Sarah to enquire if she could help you, and she's willing to. If you could go down to London, she will make you an appointment with her boss so you can speak to him directly and put Anna's case. It would be so much better than writing letters.'

Thea stared at Blanche, lost for words for a few moments ... How far Blanche had come since her first unpleasant meeting with Anna. Now here she was offering a lifeline, possibly giving her a better chance by actually enabling her to speak to someone about Anna's unfair internment. It might have a far better chance of working than all her many letters had done.

'Would you be able to go to London for a meeting?'

'Yes, of course.' Thea blinked back sudden tears, taking hold of Blanche's hand. 'This is the best news, thank you so much.'

Blanche's cheeks grew pink. 'I hope you don't mind me making enquiries without talking to you first, only I didn't want to get your hopes up in case it came to nothing, I know how hard you've been trying to get Anna home again. My sister is full of Sarah getting a job in the Home Office and apparently her boss is a fair man, so she says. He just might be able to help get Anna out, or at the very least know who could.'

'When can I go?' Thea asked.

Blanche got up and took a piece of paper from the kitchen dresser, handing it to Thea. 'That's the telephone number for Sarah's office. If you call her directly there then you can arrange a date and time which is convenient for you . . . I know you have responsibilities with your garden, your animals and the WVS mobile canteen.'

Thea nodded, her mind rushing ahead thinking about what she'd need to organise so she could go. She'd need people to cover her work, particularly someone to milk Primrose, but that shouldn't be a problem; Marianne and Alice had learned to milk and both enjoyed it, and of course Reuben would also help. While she was in London she could make the most of the long journey and go and see Edwin. She knew that Prue worried about him, despite his letters reassuring her that he was fine and enjoying his work at the London Hospital in the East End. Violet had been asking her to visit again as she was keen to show her the ambulance station where she was station officer. A trip to London would hopefully let her achieve all of those things, and if she could get everything arranged and Sarah could make her an appointment, even possibly at the end of the week, she could go there on Friday and be back on Sunday, staying over at Violet's flat.

'I'll go home and telephone Sarah right away.' Thea stood up. 'I can't thank you enough for this, Blanche. You've made more progress than I have made in months of letter writing.'

'I'm glad I could do something to help. It would be lovely to have Anna back here in the village and free again. It wasn't right what happened to her.'

'I know, let's hope this finally works.'

'Let me know how you get on,' Blanche said, show-ing Thea out.

'I will.' Thea smiled at her, now feeling a great deal brighter and more optimistic than she had been when she'd arrived at the post office.

Chapter 49

Thea glanced at her watch; she should have been seen half an hour ago. Sitting here in a corridor deep inside the Home Office in London, she was finding it increasingly hard to remain patient. She'd turned up for her appointment, made for her by Blanche's niece, Sarah, determined to get Anna released. Sarah had welcomed her warmly and asked her to sit and wait for Mr Kershaw, her boss, to see her, warning her that he was running late because of an unexpected phone call he had to make.

Distracting herself from the slow drag of time by watching people hurrying along the corridor, hearing the clacking of typewriters from other rooms that led off it, Thea recalled how she'd felt like a fish out of water when she'd arrived at Liverpool Street station this afternoon much later than she'd planned. The train from Norwich had been delayed, its journey interrupted for the more important troop trains to travel. The noise, the smells, the hustle and bustle, the sense of people rushing this way and that, had hit her; she was so used to the peace and slower pace of life in the countryside now.

The city was on a war footing. At the heart of a country at war, one which was clinging on by its fingertips, waiting to be invaded, thankfully it hadn't yet come under heavy attack from the enemy bombers, unlike some places in the country. But it was a question of *if*, not *when*, because Hitler wouldn't be able to resist hitting at the capital eventually.

The war was changing so much about life, causing people to do things and make journeys that they'd never have done before. She would never have come here, to this grand building just off Whitehall. The interior, with its grand staircase, ornate decorations and marble pillars, had made her stop and stare when she'd arrived – yet, filled as it was with people rushing around going about their work, the inside of the building reflected the hustle and bustle of the city outside.

'Miss Thornton? Thea.'

Thea looked up to the sound of her name, to see Sarah standing in the office doorway across the corridor. 'Mr Kershaw can see you now, if you'd like to come in.'

Thea leapt to her feet. 'Thank you.'

Mr Kershaw stood up and came round his wide wooden desk with its inlaid green leather top, and held out his hand to Thea. 'I apologise for keeping you waiting.' Thea shook his hand. 'So let's get straight down to business, shall we?' He indicated for her to sit in the chair facing his desk and returned to his own behind it and sat down. 'I understand that you're here about an interned enemy alien?'

'That's right, Anna Weissenborn.' She nodded. 'She's a friend as well as my employee and I certainly don't think of her in those horrible terms; she's a young woman who had to flee her home because of the way she was being treated by the Nazis. That description is too harsh, and is definitely not the way Anna is. It's only by chance that she was born in Germany, and it doesn't mean she shares the same views or in any way supports the regime there – quite the opposite in fact!'

Mr Kershaw held up his hands to her. 'I'm sorry, we use that term as an official category; I mean no offence to you or your friend. So tell me why you think Anna should be released. Why were we wrong to intern her?'

Thea took a moment, gathering her thoughts, knowing that she needed to be concise and to present Anna's case clearly and quickly.

She cleared her throat and began. 'Anna is Jewish and came here from Berlin, where she was a teacher of languages until she was forced to give up her job because of the Nazis' rules. She came to this country on a domestic permit in early 1939. After she left, her father was taken by the Nazis and he died shortly after they finally released him in January. In March she came to work for me, in Norfolk, after her previous job came to a natural end and worked hard helping me grow food for our local community. She took part in village life, joined the WI and learned first aid. She even learned to knit so she could take part in the village's drive to make garments for servicemen, the scarf she made was lovely. Anna is well liked by everyone who knows her; she quickly became an asset to our village, doing her bit for the war effort, and is greatly missed. We want her to come back again so she can carry on as she was – she enjoyed what she did.'

Thea's voice cracked and she paused for a moment to compose herself. 'She was interned in May, even though she'd been given a category C status at her tribunal and so shouldn't have been. Category C means someone has been classed as being no threat to the country – and that was exactly right for Anna, because she isn't a threat! She was brought here to London and put in Holloway Prison and then moved to a camp on the Isle of Man.' Thea sighed. 'And she's still there ... but she shouldn't be, she's not a threat, or a Nazi sympathiser. She has more reason to want them stopped than many of us after what happened to her and her father. She's just a young woman who's been caught up in this and should never have been interned at all.'

Mr Kershaw nodded as he listened to her. 'And what do you want me to do?'

'Free her. Let her come home again, back to Norfolk where she lives at my house and has become an important member of our household and village.' Thea took a bundle of envelopes containing replies out of her bag and showed them to him. 'I've been writing letters to try to get her released since May, but I haven't succeeded, and that's why I've come here today, in person, hoping you can do something to help Anna. She doesn't deserve to be kept in a camp, because she's done *nothing* wrong apart from being born in Germany, a mere chance of fate.'

Mr Kershaw sat back in his chair. 'I can see that you

have been most dedicated in your quest to see Anna freed, it does you credit. You have to understand, though, that it was deemed necessary to take that action, although most unusual that a category C enemy ... ' he nodded his head in apology, 'that your friend should have been interned.'

'The policeman who came to get her thought it might have been to do with the fact that we live near the exclusion zone around the coast. I was with him when Anna was taken as I'm a member of the WVS, and was asked to accompany them. It was a big shock.'

'I can imagine.' Mr Kershaw glanced up at the clock on the mantelpiece. 'If you can give my secretary all of Anna's details: full name, address, et cetera, I will see what I can do to hasten her release.' He stood up, signalling that their meeting was over.

That was it, her time was up! It had flown by and Thea had no idea if it had done the trick or not. She held out her hand to him. 'Thank you very much, I appreciate your help.'

He gave her a firm handshake. 'I can't promise anything, you do realise that?'

'Yes.' She gave him a warm smile. 'But I do still hope you can get her freed.'

Back outside again, Thea headed towards St James's Park for a quick walk and dose of greenery to help calm her jangled nerves. Mr Kershaw had given her no guarantees, but at least she felt she'd got further with Anna's cause than with any of her letters. Knowing that he was going to investigate was a huge relief and well worth the long journey and the anxious wait. And if nothing happened, she could write to him now she knew his name and where to find him.

As she crossed over Horse Guards Road and into the park, the change in her surroundings from buildings to trees and plants felt wonderfully calming, and other people who were there seemed to have been affected in the same way; they strolled rather than hurried along as they would probably have done out in the busy streets. A gentle walk here was just what she needed before she headed to Violet's flat in Holborn. Her friend wouldn't be there as she was starting her shift at half past three this afternoon, but she'd arranged to leave the key for Thea with her neighbour and would see her in the morning. Tomorrow afternoon she'd promised to take her and show her around the ambulance station before Thea went on to meet Edwin in the East End.

'My headmistress friend, Louisa, tried to persuade me to go back to teaching again because they're short staffed, wanted me to join her school at their evacuated home at Longleat. She did her best to tempt me with the grandeur of it, but there's no way I'd give up my job – I love it,' Violet explained as they turned into the Minories on their way to Ambulance Station 75 the next afternoon.

The pair of them had been talking non-stop since they'd got up this morning, making the most of being together and catching up on each other's lives, and Thea was enjoying it very much.

'You'd be safer there if London gets bombed. And imagine living in a huge, grand house like Longleat.'

'I'll go back to teaching when all this is over. I think it's more important for me to be *here* than teaching history and English now.' Violet halted by a wide arched passageway. 'Here we are – Station 75's through there.'

'I'd never have known it was here,' Thea said as they walked under the archway and came out into a large cobbled courtyard with a crescent of grand terraced houses on one side and flat-topped mews garages on the other.

'We're in the garages, obviously, and we use the flats above for our common room, offices, the separate women's and men's rest rooms for catching up on some sleep . . .' Violet raised her eyebrows behind her round, horn-rimmed glasses. 'If we're on an overnight shift and it's quiet.'

The garage doors stood wide open, with ambulances and cars parked inside ready to go. Seeing them took Thea back to another time and place: France during the Great War when she'd been an ambulance driver along with Violet, when their vehicles – much earlier models than these – had stood waiting for the order to go.

'I'll need to go in and do the handover with the deputy who's in charge of this shift first. But once I've done that, I'll give you a tour and you can meet the crews on my shift. You can come up and wait in the common room if you like, or out here until the current crew have signed off and headed home. There are some deckchairs in the garage if you want to sit in the sun for a bit.'

'I think I'll wait out here, I won't get in the way then,' Thea said, 'and I can have a look at the ambulances, if that's all right?'

Violet nodded. 'Of course. The common room and my

office are up here.' She opened a door and gestured up the flight of stairs. 'Come up if you need to find me, if not I'll be down once I've done the handover.'

Thea smiled at her. 'I'll be fine.'

Left alone, she wandered into the garages and looked around at the ambulances, noting that they weren't all the same. Some were clearly proper ambulances, but others were converted vehicles with an ambulance back attached to a car's chassis. Needs must in wartime – the demand for ambulances outstripped the supply. But as long as they did the job and got casualties to hospital that was all that mattered.

'Hello, are you new?' a plummy voice asked, making Thea jump.

She turned around to see a tall, slender young woman, with honey-blonde hair and wearing cheerful pillarbox-red lipstick, smiling warmly at her as she wheeled her bicycle into the garage and leaned it against the wall.

'No, I'm a friend of Violet's – Station Officer Steele's. She's going to show me around after the handover.'

'Oh, you're Thea! You used to drive ambulances with the boss during the Great War.' The young woman held out her hand. 'Welcome to Station 75. I'm Margot Churchill, otherwise known as Winnie. She told us you were coming today.' She raised her eyebrows. 'Warned us to be on good behaviour!'

So, *this* was Winnie, Thea thought, shaking her hand, recalling how Violet had said how much the young woman reminded her of herself in their ambulance driving days, with her irreverent attitude to rules. 'Delighted to meet you.' Thea shook her hand. 'Violet's told me about the crew here and how good you are.'

Winnie's grey eyes widened. 'She did?'

Thea nodded.

'Hello.' Two more young women came into the garage, one with dark curly hair and warm brown eyes and the other with auburn hair. 'Bella, Frankie, this is Thea, the boss's friend who she drove ambulances with in France.' Winnie introduced them both.

'Hello.' Thea shook both of their hands. 'Pleased to meet you. Are you all ambulance drivers?'

'Not me!' Bella pulled a face. 'I'm Frankie's attendant, happy to help – but not do the driving.'

'But you will one day, it ain't because you *can't* drive,' Frankie said, her East End accent a contrast to Winnie's plummy voice.

Bella shrugged. 'I know what to do, how to change gear and steer and everything, it's just when I get out on the road it all seems to go wrong.'

Winnie put her arm around Bella's shoulders. 'You'll get there, you just have to keep on practising.'

The sound of more voices out in the courtyard heralded the departure of the previous shift's crew. Several of them came into the garage to collect their own bicycles and left with a cheery goodbye.

'We'd better go upstairs and sign in,' Frankie said. 'Do you want to come up and 'ave a cup of tea, Thea? We usually 'ave one while the boss goes through the shift's orders.'

'All right, thank you.'

Upstairs in the common room, Thea sipped at her cup

299

of tea, watching as Violet stood before her crew going through their duties on the shift. It reminded her so much of when they'd been working together in France, and of the camaraderie between the crew members. From what she'd seen here this morning, it looked like the crew of Station 75 were a close bunch, although very different in their backgrounds: some from the upper class, like Winnie, and others working class. But it didn't seem to matter here at all, they were all working together as a team.

'Right, let's get to work.' Violet ended her talk and the crew quickly left the common room and went down to the garages to carry out their essential checks and maintenance on the ambulances, making sure they were ready to go at a moment's notice.

'That took me back,' Thea said once she and Violet were left behind. 'How does it feel to be the one in charge instead of sitting here being told what needs to be done?'

'Rather odd to start with,' Violet admitted. 'But years of teaching was good training for telling people what to do and not taking any nonsense.' She sighed. 'It also feels like a lot more responsibility though, and that's a worry sometimes.'

'They all clearly have a great respect for you, you can see it.'

'Some of them don't always agree with the rules.'

'Sounds just like how you used to be.' Thea laughed.

'Come and watch what's going on from my lookout.' Violet led her over to the window looking down on the courtyard, where the ambulances had been brought out of the garages and were being checked over by the crews.

'I met some of them downstairs in the garage. Winnie,

Frankie and Bella all introduced themselves to me. They seem very nice young women.'

Violet smiled fondly. 'They are, although Winnie has a tendency to want to do things her own way, never mind the orders.' She glanced down to where Winnie was busy checking the oil level in her ambulance's engine, her blonde head under the raised bonnet. 'Poor Frankie got caught in the middle of a water fight on her first morning here, she'd barely set foot in Station 75 when Winnie squirted her with cold water, despite knowing full well that stirrup pumps are essential pieces of equipment and shouldn't be used for playing around with. I saw it happen from up here.' Her lips twitched and her face broke into a smile as she shook her head. 'She wasn't aiming to get Frankie; she was just an unfortunate victim of Winnie's determination to get back at Sparky for doing the same to her a few days previously. Anyway, I had to make it perfectly clear to her that water fights are strictly banned.'

'It's just the sort of thing you'd have loved to do though.' Thea caught her friend's eye.

Violet grinned. 'I know! And I would now, to be honest, but it wouldn't do for a station officer to be doing that, would it?'

After a guided tour of the station, during which Violet explained how it was run – from the different eight-hour shifts to the lack of uniform and the necessity to wear their own clothes – Thea joined the crew members, who were now sitting on deckchairs out in the courtyard enjoying the sunshine while they had a break and Violet dealt with some phone calls.

'What do you think of our station?' asked the man who'd been introduced to her as Sparky, rolling himself a cigarette from his tobacco tin.

'It's very impressive,' Thea said. 'Very organised, you're all ready to go at a moment's notice.'

Sparky nodded. 'We do our best.'

'Have you thought about driving ambulances again this time?' asked Mac, who Violet had told her was a conscientious objector. 'Or running a station like the boss?'

'If I'd still been living in London, I think I'd have been tempted, but I'm doing my bit out in the countryside and enjoy working for the WVS going around with the mobile canteen. If I was asked to drive ambulances as part of my WVS duties I'd say yes. You never know what you'll get asked to do as part of the WVS, and it isn't always pleasant. One of the jobs I was asked to do . . . and is the reason I'm here in London . . . was because of what's happened to my friend Anna. She works for me, she's a German refugee from Nazi oppression – she was interned in May and I had to accompany her for the WVS when they took her in. Only I didn't know what I was being sent to help with until the last minute, and it was a terrible shock.'

'What happened to her?' Frankie asked.

'She was brought here to Holloway Prison. I came with her and stayed with her as long as I could. I went back the next morning to try to get them to let her out because she shouldn't have been taken at all. She was given a Category C at her tribunal, so she was officially not a risk to the country.' She sighed. 'But they wouldn't let her out or even let me see her.'

'That's awful,' Bella said, her eyes wide in horror. 'Is she still there? Did you come down to see her?'

'No, she was moved to a camp on the Isle of Man. It's much better for her, but's she's still interned.' Thea sighed. 'I've been trying to get her freed for months, writing letter after letter, but with no success . . . so that's why I came to London. I went to the Home Office yesterday and spoke to someone who I hope will finally be able to do something.'

'What will you do if she isn't freed?' Winnie asked.

'I'll just come back again and keep trying,' Thea said. 'I won't give up.'

'That was delicious.' Thea put her knife and fork down on her empty plate, having finished her meal in one of the East End's finest pie and mash shops.

'Discovering pie, mash and parsley liquor has been one of the joys of coming to work here.' Edwin speared his last piece of pie and dipped it in the remains of the liquor before popping it into his mouth.

Thea smiled at her nephew, who she was glad to see was looking both well and happy. Today was his day off and she'd come to meet him after her visit to Station 75. When she'd suggested they get something to eat, he'd recommended this pie and mash shop, where she'd insisted on buying him a meal, knowing that he didn't get paid for his job as an orderly at the hospital. Members of the Friends Ambulance Unit, like Edwin, received their board and lodging and a small amount of pocket money, but he didn't have much to spare, so she was glad to be able to treat him.

'So how are you finding working at the hospital?'

'Good.' Edwin laid down his knife and fork. 'I enjoy it. It's hard work but it's worthwhile and I feel like I'm really doing something to help. I enjoy talking to the patients. I was taking an elderly man down to X-ray the other day and he was telling me about how he'd worked all his life on the docks. He said that you could tell where the ships had come from by the colours of their funnels: the ones from the West Indies are painted red with yellow and black bands and the letter W – they were the ones that brought the bananas in, he said. It's a very different life here to Great Plumstead . . . I miss it.' He paused, looking thoughtful. 'Anyway, how's Ma and Alice? Ma says she's fine in her letters, but I don't think she'd tell me even if she wasn't.'

'She's busy and happy to be that way, you know your mother.' Thea didn't mention Prue finding out about Victor's affair – it wasn't her place to tell Edwin. It would only upset him, and he'd be worried about his mother.

'She's doing wonders for the WVS's various campaigns in the village and all her usual jobs, with the day club and WI as well.'

'And Alice?'

'Now she's finished school she's been helping me a lot in the garden. I think she really enjoys it and she's a real help with Anna still gone.' She'd already told him about her visit to the Home Office.

'That's good.' Edwin drained the last of his cup of tea. 'I was wondering if you'd like to go for a stroll around Victoria Park. I like walking in there when I'm off duty, gives me a dose of greenery, reminds me of home.' He grinned.

'Yes, that would be nice.' Thea stood up. 'I know what

you mean about needing a dose of greenery. I felt just the same when I lived here and needed regular walks in the parks to keep me going. I think growing up in the countryside gives us a built-in need for green space around us, otherwise being surrounded by buildings and streets with hardly any plants and trees can really drain us.'

They'd not long left the pie and mash shop, a little after half past four, and were heading for the park to enjoy the warm September evening, when the rise and fall of the air-raid siren began to wail out across the rooftops.

'Not again!' Edwin gave a deep sigh. 'It's been going off a lot over the past few weeks. One of the patients on my ward calls it the Moaning Minnie. We'd better find shelter, though we'll probably just get in there and settled and the all-clear will go again. This way.' He touched Thea's arm and led them off in the opposite direction to which they'd been going.

'Has there been bombing?' Thea asked as they hurried along. 'I haven't heard anything on the news.'

'They were only nuisance raids, a plane or two coming over to cause disruption and send us all hurrying to shelters. That's all I—' He suddenly halted and stared up at the distant sky towards the east. 'Look!'

Thea followed his gaze and spotted in the clear blue many small, black specks, flying in formation like swarms of flies while smaller specks darted around them, sunlight glinting off their silver bodies. They were enemy planes. Bombers. And from the black smoke that curled and billowed up into the air in the distance towards the mouth of the River Thames, they had started to drop their deadly cargo.

She opened her mouth to speak but no sound came out.

Edwin grabbed hold of her arm. 'You need to get to the shelter, quick! It's down there at the end of that street. I must get to the hospital, they'll need as many staff on duty as possible – there'll be a lot of injuries.'

The sound of the planes' engines was growing steadily louder, a noise that seemed to penetrate the air all around her. It was one Thea had heard before back home in Norfolk when enemy planes had flown over, but this was much worse. The crash of exploding bombs added to the chorus of noise, as more explosives met their targets over the docks.

This wasn't good – London was under attack.

'Hurry up!' Edwin urged her. 'You need to go, now!'

Thea shook her head. 'No, I'm coming with you. I'd rather help than sit in some shelter. Put my experience to use.' *And keep an eye on you*, she added silently, thinking she couldn't stand the thought of Edwin going off to do his duty instead of seeking shelter. It might be what he was trained for, but she had a strong urge to protect him, to look out for him for the sake of both her sister and herself. It was a feeling too urgent to ignore.

Edwin frowned, his blue eyes anxious. 'The hospital could be bombed.'

'And so could the shelter. I'm coming with you,' she said, her eyes holding his. 'Let's not waste time here arguing over it. Lead the way.'

By the time they reached the casualty department of the hospital, the first ambulances were arriving. After a brief introduction to the nurse in charge of the waiting area – who gratefully accepted Thea's offer of help – she was kept busy.

As more and more casualties came in, Edwin was ordered through to assist in administering emergency treatment. Thea helped carry stretchers in from arriving ambulances, or supported walking wounded, finding them a seat in the waiting area until they could be treated.

Going out to meet another ambulance, she recognised Winnie from Station 75, her pillarbox-red lipstick bright beneath her steel helmet.

'What are you doing here?' Winnie asked, jumping out of the cab and hurrying around to the back doors. She opened them to reveal another crew member who Thea recognised from earlier today, who was inside looking after four casualties.

'I'm here to help, put my ambulance experience to good use.' She assisted as Winnie pulled a stretcher out from its runners and took hold of one end while the young woman took the other. 'My nephew came back when the siren went, and I couldn't just sit in a shelter and do nothing.'

'Any help we can get is jolly welcome,' Winnie said over her shoulder as she led the way inside the hospital.

A nurse hurried over quickly to assess the unconscious woman, checking the label tied to her. 'Take her through to the treatment rooms,' she instructed.

They did as she said. Edwin spotted them and waved them to an empty treatment table, helping them transfer the woman onto it.

'What's it like out there?' He directed his question at Winnie.

'Bad.' Winnie pulled a face. 'I've got three more casualties in my ambulance for you, and we'll be back with more in a while. It's going to be a very long shift.'

By the time Thea had helped Winnie unload the rest of her casualties and she'd driven off to rescue others, more ambulances were lining up to unload their injured. She was kept busy, which helped take her mind off the drone of the planes, the screaming and crumping of bombs, and the clanging of bells as fire engines raced to deal with the flames filling the air with the acrid smell of burning and fragments of ash that drifted down to the ground.

When the all-clear finally went at half past six, after an hour and three-quarters of bombing, the sense of relief was almost palpable. Casualties were still coming in, but at least the danger of being bombed had gone.

But that didn't last long.

Thea's heart plummeted when the air-raid siren went off again two hours later, just as she was thinking that perhaps she could make her way back to Violet's flat. The bombers had come back to have another go at an already reeling London.

Thea had to dig deep to keep on going, unloading more and more injured people from ambulances which continued to pour in as the night went on. All the while there was the background noise of the air raid – the planes, the hollow boom of the ack-ack guns firing back at them and the rapid staccato rattle of the Bofors. The blackout was completely useless tonight, broken by the raging fires in the docks which had turned the night sky into an odd luminous orangey-yellow and was drawing the bombers in to their targets as surely as moths to a flame.

The waiting area was packed with injured men and women, who sat huddled in blankets on the benches, many with shocked, filthy faces, blackened with soot or brick dust, temporary bandages covering their injuries. It was a scene from a nightmare that went on and on through the night, and Thea lost count of the stretchers she carried in, the injured that she helped. She just knew that she had to keep on going, like all those who were helping here tonight.

Chapter 50

It had been a glorious September day, one of those warm ones that felt like winter was still a long way off. And with it being a Saturday, Prue didn't have any commitments at the day club, or even the WVS, and had spent the day working in the garden tending her vegetable plot. She'd also ventured out for a walk, checking on how this year's blackberries were coming along in the hedgerows around the village as she'd organised another WI picking and jam-making session for Monday, as last year's had been so successful. It would hopefully be the first of several throughout the month for as long as their sugar supplies lasted.

Now, making her way up the stairs a little after nine o'clock, her body was pleasantly tired from all her activity and she was planning to have a bath, before relaxing in bed and enjoying a good read of her latest book from the library until she finally drifted off to sleep. A sudden, loud knocking on the front door made her jump, and she retraced her steps, hurrying to open it, wondering who it could be. From the way they were banging they sounded like they were in trouble.

Pulling the long blackout curtain to the side, she opened the door and was surprised to see it was one of the men from the village's Home Guard. 'I need to speak to Victor,' he said, looking worried, not bothering with the usual social greetings, as he stepped inside the door and she quickly closed it behind him.

Prue would normally have asked why, but from the look on the man's face, whatever he was here for was urgent. 'I'll just get him.' She turned to go to the sitting room where she'd left Victor a few minutes before, reading the newspaper, but having heard the loud knocking he was already on his way.

'What's the matter?' her husband asked, directing his question at his fellow Home Guard platoon member.

'Code word "Cromwell" has been issued. I've been sent to spread the word.'

Prue looked at Victor to see what his reaction was. She'd not heard mention of any code word before, but the look on his face told her it was serious.

'Can you let Reuben know. There's a telephone at Rookery House, it'll save me time if I don't have to go out there,' the guard added. 'The platoon's to meet at the guard hut as soon as possible.'

'Understood.' Victor nodded, and the guard quickly slipped out of the door and disappeared into the night.

'What's happening?' Prue asked.

Victor's eyes met hers. 'That was the code word warning us that invasion's imminent.'

She gasped, putting a hand to her mouth.

'I need to put my uniform on. Can you telephone Rookery House and tell them to get a message to Reuben immediately – tell them to say that "Cromwell" has been issued and to report to the Home Guard hut. He'll know what to do.'

Prue wanted to ask more but didn't get a chance as Victor hurried upstairs.

They were about to be invaded!

Everyone had known it was a strong possibility, but now it was about to happen.

Her hand shook as she picked up the telephone receiver from the table in the hall, and she took several calming breaths to steady her voice before the operator asked her what number she required.

She counted the number of times the telephone rang across the other side of the village, imagining Hettie or Marianne going to answer it as Thea was in London. Perhaps they were already in bed. It seemed to take ages before Hettie's voice came on the other end.

'Hello, Rookery House.'

'Hettie, it's Prue. Can you get a message to Reuben straight away, tell him "Cromwell" and to get to the Home Guard hut as soon as he can.'

'Of course, what's it about?' Hettie asked.

'No time to explain, but I'll come over. Just go and tell Reuben, he'll know what it's about. Go now, please! I'll see you soon.'

As she put the receiver down, Victor came hurrying down the stairs, his big Home Guard boots clumping loudly.

'Hettie's going to tell Reuben. Thea's in London, so I thought I'd go over there and take Alice with me.'

Victor nodded. 'Keep together and stay there. Remember what it said on that leaflet about when the invader comes.'

'What do you think will happen?' Prue asked.

'We'll put up a fight, that's what.' He looked at her briefly and then left.

As he closed the door behind him, the church bells in St Andrew's suddenly began to ring out across the village, a sound that hadn't been heard for some time and which had been designated as a sign of invasion. Prue usually loved hearing the bells, but now their pealing across the darkness made the hairs on the back of her neck stand up. Their freedom was in peril.

As she and Alice arrived at Rookery House a short while later, Prue was surprised to see Hettie and Marianne standing in the gateway, the pair of them looking ready to do battle, with Reuben's dog Bess sitting there watching what was going on. In the faint beam from her torch, Prue could see that Hettie was wielding her solid wooden rolling pin in one hand and a heavy iron frying pan in the other, while Marianne had a broom and the hook they used for chopping kindling.

'What's going on?' Prue asked.

'We're getting ready to do what Churchill said, fight them in the streets,' Hettie said. 'I've put some weapons out for you behind the gate if you want to join in.' Prue shone her torch to look and could see more improvised weapons propped up by the gate, including a mop, a small axe and a couple of heavy saucepans, along with some rope. 'We've got to use what we've got. A good whack around the head with this,' Hettie swung her rolling pin around, 'would put a Nazi paratrooper out of action for a bit, long enough to tie him up.'

'Reuben told you what "Cromwell" means, then?'

'Of course he did. We all need to be prepared, and anyway the church bells ringing out were enough to put the wind up us, we all know what they were signalling. If they're coming to try and take over our country I'm not going to stand back and just let them take it without a fight. Are you going to join us?' Hettie asked.

'Can we, Ma?' Alice asked.

Prue nodded. 'Of course we can't stand back and do nothing, but it's going to be a long night. Perhaps we should split into pairs and take shifts, say two hours on watch and two hours off, at least that way we can all get a bit of sleep. Who knows what tomorrow will bring, so we need to be ready, not exhausted because we've been awake all night.'

'Good idea,' Hettie agreed. 'You and I will take the first watch, while Alice and Marianne can go and get some sleep. Alice, you go in Thea's room, she won't mind.'

'But what if a load of paratroopers arrive while we're asleep and you're overrun?' Alice asked, looking worried.

'Then we'll shout and kick up a fuss, so you'll know. Keep your bedroom windows open and then you'll be able to hear,' Hettie said. 'Off you go, both of you.'

'I need to check on Emily, anyway,' Marianne said. 'Come on Alice, it'll be our turn soon enough.'

As the pair of them disappeared back to the house, quickly swallowed up into the darkness, Prue chose her weapons, taking the mop and the heavy saucepan. She didn't like the idea of using an axe on anyone, not even the enemy. If it came to it, she'd rather whack them with a frying pan.

'We don't know which way they'll come from,' Hettie said, positioning herself in the gateway so that she could see down the road away from the village. 'If I look this way, and you stand by me looking the other way, we've got each direction covered, and if either of us sees anything we can give the other a nudge. Best not to shout out and let the enemy know we're here, if we can surprise them then we'll have the advantage.'

'What about shouting to let Alice and Marianne know?'

'Do you want your daughter fighting the enemy, or Marianne with a young baby to care for?' Hettie's voice was serious.

'No.'

'Then that's only as a last resort. If anyone comes, *we'll* sort them out.' Hettie swung her rolling pin around in the air again, clearly prepared to do what she had to do despite her years and small stature. What she lacked physically, she certainly made up for in determination, Prue thought.

Standing in the darkness, under a clear sky, pin-pricked with thousands of bright stars as the quarter moon dipped down to the horizon, Prue was acutely aware of every sound, every rustling of small animals in the hedgerows, the pair of tawny owls in the woods further down the lane past the house. Every sound seemed intensified as her ears strained to listen for approaching enemy soldiers, her eyes struggling to see into the darkness, her hands grasping the wooden stick of her mop, the heavy frying pan propped against her leg ready to grab.

This listening on full alert reminded her of those long-ago childhood games of hide and seek that she'd loved to play with her brothers and sisters when, waiting in a good hiding place, she'd listen out for their footsteps, the blood thrumming around her body with anticipation of discovery. Now, she waited for a much more dangerous foe, the odds far greater. But she wouldn't back down, she would stand and fight for her family and her country.

Bess suddenly got to her feet and started to growl, a low grumbling. She'd heard something unusual.

'Shhh, Bess! Lie down!' Hettie hissed. 'Do you hear that?' she whispered. 'Something's coming this way.'

Prue's heart skipped. There was definitely something coming. It hummed along and was getting louder.

'Get ready.' Hettie positioned herself opposite Prue across the narrow lane.

With her heart banging hard in her chest, Prue raised her mop in the air ready to bring it down on whoever was coming, aware of the vague shadow of Hettie armed and ready opposite. And then out of the deeper darkness came a dark shape on a bicycle.

As one, Prue and Hettie launched their attack and brought him down, whoever it was crying out in alarm as he fell sideways, the bicycle landing on top of him, its wheels still spinning.

Bess launched herself at him, pinning him down with her paws on his chest, growling menacingly.

'Quick, Prue!' Hettie shouted.

Prue poked her mop head into the man's chest alongside Bess. 'Don't move, we're armed and dangerous!'

'What the blooming heck are you doing?' a man's English voice said.

'Stopping you from going any further. Your war is over!' Hettie said.

Prue took the torch out of her pocket and shone it in the man's eyes. Despite its soft beam he squinted and grimaced, shielding his face with his arm. 'Is that you, Mrs Wilson?'

'*Arthur?*' She recognised the butcher's sixteen-year-old son, who worked in the family shop in the village and was a member of the Home Guard – they'd only gone and attacked one of their own. 'I'm so sorry, we thought you were an enemy paratrooper.'

Sensing that this was no enemy, Bess started to lick Arthur's hand, her usual friendly self again.

'One that had stolen a bicycle,' Hettie added. 'I'm sorry, have we hurt you?' She picked the bicycle up and held it as Arthur got to his feet.

'Only my pride.' He laughed. 'I wouldn't have wanted to be a real enemy paratrooper meeting you two. Is that a rolling pin you've got there?'

Hettie waved it around in the air. 'Yes, needs must. We haven't got guns, so rolling pins, saucepans and mops will have to do instead. I think we owe you a cup of tea and a slice of cake. I'll go and get you one if you stay here on guard with Prue.'

'Very kind of you to offer, but I need to get back to the platoon. I had to go and deliver a message and I'm due back, but I'll be more careful as I go along – there might be more of you ladies out tonight.' Arthur took his bicycle from her.

'Churchill said we'll fight them on the streets, and that's what we're ready to do!' Hettie chuckled.

Chapter 51

The all-clear had eventually sounded a little after half past six that morning, after ten long hours of bombing. After a gruelling night, the steady note, so different from the rising and falling wail of the warning alarm, brought a huge sense of relief to those in the emergency department at the hospital, to both staff and casualties waiting to be seen.

Thea looked around at the casualties, who were covered in brick dust from exploded buildings and blood from their injuries, with temporary first aid having been applied before they were brought in. Many were wrapped in blankets to keep them warm, but nobody was complaining; all were stoic as they waited their turn to be seen, none minding as more urgent cases were rushed through to the treatment rooms. The ambulance crews had been back and forth all night long.

'You still here?' a voice asked.

Thea turned around to see Frankie and Bella carrying

another casualty in on a stretcher, this one unconscious. She'd seen them several times over the course of the night, as well as Winnie and her attendant, and every time she did it was a relief to find that they were still going, not injured or . . . She didn't want to think about that.

'Yes, still here.' Thea hurried along and opened the door to the treatment rooms for them. 'And you two keep turning up like bad pennies!'

Bella laughed as she passed her. 'This is our last, we'll be heading back to Station 75 and knocking off, and the next shift will take over so we can go home and get some sleep.'

'Is Violet . . . Station Officer Steele all right?' she asked.

'She's fine, she's been organisin' us all like clockwork,' Frankie said. 'Though must 'ave been a nightmare 'cos the telephone has 'ardly stopped ringing all night with calls for 'elp.'

'It's been quite a night all round.' Thea had been worried about her friend and all the lovely crew she'd met at Station 75, who like these two young women had been sent out under the paths of the bombers.

Stepping outside a short while later, after the staff on the next shift had arrived to relieve the weary nurses, doctors and support workers who'd battled through the night, Thea and Edwin stood staring around them in horror at what the raid had done.

'Look at it!' Edwin shook his head sadly.

Thea put her arm around him. This was the first time he'd witnessed the destruction war could bring and it was

320

a shock. She recalled that sickening feeling of horror and disgust at what man could do to man in the name of war, when she'd first arrived in France and seen the remains of shelled villages, the muddy wastelands that the men were fighting over. This was perhaps harder, because it was on home soil.

'It's hard to see, I know, but it's what war can do.'

'That's why we shouldn't have wars!' He turned to her, his tired eyes bright with unshed tears.

'I agree, but there's always been those who are willing to cause disagreements leading to fighting, it goes way back in history. Fighting is sadly nothing new, only the weapons used to do it get more sophisticated and cause more damage and are able to kill and injure more innocent people.' She sighed deeply.

The beautiful Sunday morning, which had dawned warm and sunny, was at odds with the damage inflicted on the battered East End from the air by modern weapons of war. Windows had been blown out and slithers of glass were strewn across the pavements; smashed roof slates crunched underfoot as they started to pick their way carefully along the street. It was a world away from a normal East End Sunday morning; today the gutters were running with water from shattered pipes and the air was ripe with the stench of burning warehouses, their contents fuelling the black smoke which billowed up into the blue sky from the infernos started by the bombs.

'You need sleep,' Thea said gently. 'Go back to your lodgings, have something to eat and then sleep. You'll feel better after that.'

Edwin yawned. 'I'm so tired ... The injuries on some people ...' He bit his bottom lip.

'It's what you've trained for. I know it's still a shock when you first see it for real, but it will get easier, I promise you.'

'Perhaps I'm no use to the Friends Ambulance Unit.'

Thea halted and turned him to face her. 'You're doing brilliantly, Edwin. It's natural to feel this way, you had quite a baptism last night.' She smiled at him. 'Don't be hard on yourself. You're tired, hungry and shocked, that's a potent combination.'

'Do you think they'll come back?'

Thea shrugged. 'Possibly. Probably. You just need to take it one day at a time.' She couldn't think beyond getting some sleep herself, though a niggling worry about Edwin staying here in London and the possibility that the enemy planes would return was worming its way into the back of her mind. But he was doing what he wanted to do, and if he was at risk then that was his choice. She needed to remember that she'd been at risk herself when she went to France. She'd known it, yet still gone.

Edwin yawned again. 'I'm sorry.' He closed his eyes. 'I could fall asleep right here.'

Thea pulled him into a tight hug. 'Off you go – get back to your lodgings and sleep. I'm heading back to Violet's and I'll get some sleep before I get the train home.' She reached up and touched his face. 'Take care of yourself. And be careful.'

He nodded. 'And you.' He smiled at her and headed off in the direction of his lodgings. She watched him go until he turned the corner and was gone. She wished him well and hoped that, if and when the bombers came back, he'd stay safe.

Back at Violet's flat, Thea had just washed quickly and was boiling the kettle to make some tea when her friend returned looking weary and pale.

'Thank goodness you're all right!' Thea rushed over and hugged her tightly. Stepping back, she searched Violet's face. 'Is everyone safe at Station 75?'

'Yes. I didn't leave until they'd all checked back in.' She sighed, her whole body sagging. 'It was a hell of a night. Caught us all out. We knew it could happen and we'd trained hard to prepare for it but ... ' She sniffed back the tears that were threatening behind her glasses. 'It was such a beautiful day yesterday – people would have been out enjoying themselves, and then look what happened. The docks are still burning ... '

'Come on, sit down.' Thea pulled out a kitchen chair and pushed her friend down onto it. 'Have you got any brandy or whisky to go in our tea? I think we could do with a nip.'

'There's some in the sitting room, in the cabinet.' Violet went to get up.

'Stay there, I'll get it.'

Sitting nursing tea laced with brandy a few minutes later, they recounted the night's events to each other.

'I never appreciated how hard it would be to send my crews out in the middle of an air raid,' Violet said, her voice trembling. 'I'd rather have gone out to each call myself ... Having to choose who went where, not knowing what they were heading into or if they'd come back in one piece

323

was . . . dreadful.' She shook her head. 'It was like sending them to their doom.'

Thea reached out and took hold of her friend's hand. 'Listen, they all signed up to do that job, just like we did, and going out in raids has now become part of it. It's good that you care, but you mustn't let it get to you. If there are more raids to come, you'll drive yourself crazy if you keep on like this.'

Violet nodded. 'I know but . . . it's hard. I feel responsible for them.' She stifled a yawn. 'I need to sleep.' She stood up. 'Are you still heading back today?'

'Yes, I have to, but I need some sleep first too.'

'If I'm not awake when you're ready to go, wake me up so I can say goodbye, won't you?'

Thea smiled at her friend. 'I promise.'

Chapter 52

Prue had watched the sun rise on what promised to be another beautiful late summer's day. Now, despite having had very little sleep, she felt on full alert as she stood in the road outside Rookery House watching out for Nazi paratroopers. So far there'd been none; the only person the women had attacked had been poor Arthur, the butcher's son, who she hoped wouldn't be any worse for taking a tumble off his bicycle. She'd go and see him to be sure once this was all sorted.

'They're taking a long time coming, I wish they'd just appear so we can get on with it.' Alice was on lookout facing the opposite direction.

'Hmm ... ' Prue made a noncommittal response. She'd rather her daughter wasn't involved in a skirmish with an enemy paratrooper, but she understood Alice's determination, because that same need to do something and stand up for their country was firing her up, keeping her alert despite the lack of sleep.

She'd hoped last night, when she sent Alice indoors with Marianne to get some rest while she and Hettie did the first shift, that her daughter would sleep on and not come back out again. But she'd set Thea's alarm and had appeared outside two hours later, insisting on doing her bit and that Prue and Hettie should get some sleep. Prue couldn't go inside and leave Alice and Marianne out alone, so she and Hettie had set up makeshift beds in the gateway of Rookery House in two deckchairs, with a pillow and blanket each, and had settled down on them for a couple of hours. Prue had dozed fitfully, frequently waking up to check what was happening, but nothing had occurred, just the sounds of night-time in the countryside.

Now it was not long after half past six in the morning and Hettie was asleep in her deckchair, snoring softly, while Marianne had gone inside to feed baby Emily. Prue was wondering what they should do, whether one of them should go into Great Plumstead to find out what was happening, when Bess suddenly let out a loud bark and took off in the direction of the village, her black and white tail held high, waving rapidly from side to side like a flag.

'Bess, come back! Bess . . .' Alice called after her. She stopped as Reuben came around the corner on his bicycle, with Bess bouncing along in delight at his side.

'We've been stood down,' he called as he braked. He dismounted, coming to a halt by them.

'What about the invasion?' Prue asked.

'Have the army arrived to deal with it?' Hettie heaved herself out of her deckchair having been woken by Bess's barking. 'What's going on?'

'It was a false alarm, there's been no invasion,' Reuben said. 'We haven't been told what triggered it though, something must have happened to issue "Cromwell". We'd better listen to the news.'

'Oh, thank God for that!' Hettie sighed. 'We were ready for them though, and will be again if they give the word.'

Reuben grinned. 'I heard what happened to young Arthur. He said you were quite a force to be reckoned with, wielding your rolling pin.'

Hettie nodded, smiling broadly. 'I might have a good few years on him, but I can still put up a fight.'

'There were other women out in the village as well. If the enemy had come they wouldn't have known what had hit them. They certainly wouldn't have been expecting to be met by women defending their country with kitchen utensils – you did a magnificent job.'

Prue's eyes met Hettie's, the older woman looking delighted at what Reuben had just said.

'Well, if we've been stood down, let's go and have some breakfast and listen to the news, see if they tell us what it was all about,' Prue said.

'I'd better go and see to Primrose,' said Alice. 'She'll be ready for milking.'

'There'll be some breakfast waiting for you when you're done,' Hettie said.

A short while later, the kitchen of Rookery House was filled with the smell of frying bacon and eggs. Hettie declared that they needed something like that after the night they'd all had, and it was worth using up their week's ration.

Prue set the table while Reuben turned on the wireless set to give it time for the valves to warm up before the news came on.

'What did you do last night?' Marianne asked him, as she rubbed Emily's back to wind her after her feed.

'We set up roadblocks to stop any enemy movements and there was a lookout on top of St Andrew's church tower as well,' Reuben explained as the wireless crackled into life and the seven o'clock Sunday morning prayers came on. 'If any enemy troops had come this way, we'd have blocked them and hampered their plans.' He frowned. 'It was a worrying night, though. We honestly thought that that was it . . . that they were coming.'

'Let's hope they never do,' Hettie said, dishing up the eggs and bacon onto plates.

'Well, if they do, we're prepared to act. Last night was a practice,' Prue said, slicing into the loaf of bread.

'Take a plate and sit yourselves down. I'll keep Alice's warm.' Hettie put Alice's breakfast in the slow oven ready for her when she came in after milking. 'We can listen to what's been going on while we eat.'

Prue was chewing on a mouthful of delicious bacon when the news began, and the serious tone of the news-reader instinctively told her that something was very wrong. Not that they ever sounded cheerful, but even his opening greeting felt full of sorrow.

'*The German air force has unleashed a wave of heavy bombing raids on London, killing hundreds of civilians and injuring many more.*'

Edwin and Thea were in London.

The bacon in her mouth suddenly tasted as if it were made of ashes. Prue forced herself to swallow it as she silently laid down her knife and fork as the newsreader went on.

'*The Ministry of Home Security said the scale of the attacks was the largest the Germans had yet attempted ...*'

Around the table, everyone had stopped eating, their faces shocked at the news.

'*The first raids came towards the end of the afternoon, and were concentrated on the densely populated East End, along the river by the docks.*'

Edwin was in the East End.

Prue squeezed her hands into tight fists, listening in horror as the newsreader spoke of how three hundred bombers had attacked the city for over an hour and a half and how the entire docklands area had seemed to be ablaze, hundreds of fires lighting up the sky, so fierce that once darkness fell, they could be seen more than ten miles away. Those fires had guided a second wave of bombers in at half past eight, and that raid had lasted for eight hours, shaking the city with deafening noise as the bombs rained down.

As the news moved on to other reports, Reuben got up and turned the wireless off, and no one protested. They'd all heard enough.

'Thea and Edwin are there!' Hettie's blue eyes were bright with tears behind her round glasses. 'What's happened to them?'

Prue didn't want to let herself imagine what fate might have befallen her son and sister. Edwin's work at the hospital put him right in the heart of the East End and in the target area of those bombers last night. They'd come not once but twice, and the bombing had gone on for eight hours. Could he have survived that?

And what about Thea? Where was she? Prue knew she'd been going to see Edwin; had she been caught up in the bombing too?

She stood up, the legs of her chair scraping on the tiled kitchen floor. She needed to get some fresh air.

'Prue?' Reuben's face was full of concern.

'I just need some air.' Before anyone could stop her she fled outside into the garden, where the sound of the birds singing, the gentle greenness and the colours of the flowers were just as they had been earlier before breakfast, oblivious to what had happened in London. Everything here was carrying on as normal. She had the urge to shout out at it, tell it to stop because of what had happened.

Gulping sobs welled up in her throat and she started to shake.

'Ma?' Alice's voice seemed to come from far off.

Prue wiped at the tears running down her face with the back of her hand and forced herself to calm down.

'Ma, what's the matter?' Alice put down the pail of milk, looking worried.

Prue sniffed. 'We just heard on the news ... London was bombed last night, the East End hit by three hundred bombers in a massive attack.'

Alice's face went pale. 'Edwin ... and Aunt Thea.'

Prue nodded and opened her arms. Alice hurried into them and they stood holding on to each other until a cough made Prue look up.

'Should we try and telephone someone to find out if Edwin and Thea are all right?' Reuben asked.

Prue shook her head. 'There's no telephone where Edwin lives. And I don't know about Thea's friend Violet, where she lives or if she even has a telephone.'

'There'd be one at the ambulance station where she works though. It's not far from the Tower of London, Thea told me,' Alice said.

'But that doesn't mean that she'd be there right now, or that she'd know where Thea is.' Prue sighed. 'We just have to wait and hope they're all right.' She looked at Reuben. 'Do you think the attack is what set off the invasion alert?'

He nodded. 'Must have been, probably thought they were attacking all over, not just London.'

Prue put her arm around Alice. 'Come and have some breakfast.'

Reuben picked up the pail of milk. 'You need to finish yours, Prue.'

She shook her head. 'I'm not hungry. You can have it.' Food was the last thing she wanted right now.

Chapter 53

It was a little after six o'clock that evening when Thea stepped off the train in Great Plumstead and stood staring around at the familiar station for a few moments. She was grateful to be back home, but her heart was heavy after the events of last night and having witnessed the state of the East End this morning.

As the train had carried her away from Liverpool Street station, she'd had a good view of the extent of the damage and had seen the fires still burning, the sky thick with smoke. The air raid had been horrific and there was a good chance, now Hitler had turned his sights on London, that the bombers would be back – maybe tonight. And all those there were like sitting ducks. She was scared for Edwin and Violet and the lovely crew that she'd met at Station 75. Each of them was in danger and she wished that they could have left with her, but she knew they wouldn't because they wanted to do their job. And she understood that: she'd gone to France and been in danger herself, narrowly missing being hit by stray shells while driving her ambulance on more than one occasion. The danger hadn't stopped her, just as it wouldn't stop Edwin, Violet and the others; in a way it had made her even more determined to stay and do everything she could to help the wounded. Now all she could do was hope that none of the bombs that might rain down on London had one of their names on it.

In the meantime she had to find Prue. She knew her sister would be frantic with worry about Edwin, no doubt having heard about the raid on the wireless, and would have been fretting all day. So she headed to her sister's house rather than returning straight home.

She knocked on the front door. As soon as her sister opened it, she could see Prue's feelings etched across her face, a tense nervousness to the set of her mouth, her eyes underlined with dark shadows.

'Thea!' Prue exclaimed, throwing her arms around her and hugging her tightly.

'Edwin is fine,' Thea said when her sister eventually let her go, knowing that it would be playing on her mind.

Prue sagged with relief, tears filling her blue eyes. 'Thank God! I've been so worried since we heard about the raids on the wireless this morning.'

'Can I come in?'

Prue nodded. 'Of course . . . ' She shook her head. 'Please do.' She stood to the side and ushered Thea in. 'Have you just got back? Do you want something to eat or drink?'

'Yes, I came straight here from the station, thought you'd

want to know that Edwin was safe.' She smiled at her sister. 'Some tea would be lovely, thanks.'

When they were settled at the kitchen table a few minutes later with a cup of tea each, Thea told her sister what had happened, how she and Edwin had been in the pie and mash shop just before the air-raid siren had begun to wail and what had happened from there.

'The first raid was bad enough, but then they came back again for another go at the docks and it went on and on. It felt like it was never going to end, we could hear the bombers droning overhead, wave after wave of them.' Thea paused, remembering the sound of those engines, which had played out like a backdrop to the noise of exploding bombs and the shrill clanging of fire engine bells. When it eventually stopped it had left an eerie quiet. 'The bombers knew what to target. Hitler's hit our vital supplies that were brought in from abroad and stored in the warehouses. You could smell what was burning in the smoke.'

'Do you think they'll come back?' Prue asked.

Thea shrugged. 'Probably. I know that's not what you want to hear, but realistically if they've bombed London once, then it's likely they'll come back to have another go at it.'

Prue nodded. 'I wish Edwin was somewhere else.'

Thea reached out and touched her sister's arm. 'I know, but he's not going to leave unless he's ordered to. It's what he's trained for, Prue. Just like my friend Violet and all the crew at her ambulance station. None of them are going to leave, they'll stay and do their duty.'

Prue took a sip of tea. 'We had a drama of our own

around here last night. The code word for an invasion was sent out, must have been triggered by the London air raid, and the church bells were rung and the Home Guard were out in force.' She smiled. 'And so were the women of the village.' She explained what had happened and how she, Hettie, Marianne and Alice had been on patrol outside Rookery House. 'Hettie was most determined. She's quite a force to be reckoned with, wielding her rolling pin.'

Thea laughed, imagining Hettie in action, knowing very well how she could react if someone upset her. It reminded her of an indignant mother hen, feathers ruffled and beak ready to peck. 'Is she all right now?'

'Yes. Alice has stayed there today to help with the jobs, she's getting a dab hand at milking now.' Prue took a sip of tea. 'How did you get on at the Home Office?'

Thea shrugged. 'I'm not sure. The man I spoke to was nice and said he'd do all that he could, but until Anna's actually free I can't know whether my visit has made any difference.'

After the events of last night, her visit to the Home Office seemed like a long time ago; she felt like she'd lived through a lot since then. In the space of a few short hours she'd experienced things she never thought she'd see in London, and parts of the city were irrevocably changed, people killed and injured simply because of where they lived.

'I hope it did work and she's freed soon,' Prue said. 'I . . .' She fell silent at the sound of the front door opening, and a look of alarm flashed across her face. 'Victor's back!' she hissed.

Thea had no wish to see him. And, knowing that Victor

wouldn't be pleased to see her here either, she didn't want to cause her sister any more upset today. She stood up. 'I'd better go, I'll nip out the back door.'

But she'd only made it as far as the door, and was reaching for the door handle, when Victor came into the kitchen, halting abruptly at the sight of her. He narrowed his ice-blue eyes, looking from her to Prue and back again.

'What's this? What's going on?' He glared at Thea. 'What are you doing here?'

'Thea was just . . . ' Prue began, her face pale.

Thea felt her temper flare, recalling one of her last encounters with Victor last autumn, when he'd demanded that she revoke the job and home that she'd given Edwin after he'd thrown him out because he'd registered as a conscientious objector. The months since then had done nothing to change her opinion of him, and the news that he was having an affair had lowered her opinion of him even more. She might be in his house, but Thea was not going to be intimidated by him.

'I came to see Prue.' She met his gaze firmly. 'To let her know that Edwin is safe. I was with him last night in London.'

Victor waved his hand as if batting away an angry wasp. 'I don't want any mention of that coward's name in this house!' he roared, his cheeks growing blotchy as his temper erupted.

Thea took a step towards him. 'Edwin is no coward. He showed great bravery last night, he didn't flee from his job despite the bombs raining down. And he's still there, prepared to do it all over again.' She narrowed

336

her eyes, putting one hand on her hip. 'You should be proud of him.'

Victor's eyes flashed. 'He's no son of mine,' he jabbed his finger at Thea, 'and you have no business telling me what I should do. Get out of my house!'

'Victor!' Prue gasped. 'Thea's my sister.'

'And this . . . is . . . my . . . house!' he roared, punctuating each word by thumping his fist on the kitchen table.

Thea looked at him, shaking her head slowly. 'You're right, it is your house, Victor. Sadly you place more importance and value on your possessions than people.' She touched Prue's shoulder. 'I'll see you soon.'

Prue forced a smile. 'Thanks for coming to tell me, I appreciate it.' She stood up. 'I'll see you out.'

Thea followed her sister out of the kitchen, ignoring Victor as she passed him. 'Will you be all right?' she whispered to Prue as they reached the front door.

Her sister nodded. 'Yes, don't worry about me.'

Thea touched her arm. 'But I *do* worry. Why don't you come back to Rookery House with me?'

'No, I'm fine here. I'll go to bed in a minute so I won't see him till tomorrow morning, and then he'll be focused on getting off to work . . .' Prue said in a low voice, 'and making more money.'

Thea frowned. 'But won't you have to see him in your bedroom?'

Prue's face flushed. 'We have separate rooms . . . Have done since Alice was born.'

'Oh! I see.' Her sister had never let on about this in all those years.

'I'll be fine.' Prue's eyes met hers. 'I'm used to handling Victor.'

'Have you changed your mind about the other thing . . . ?' Thea asked.

'No, I'm waiting for the right time. But don't worry, it's made a difference all right,' Prue reassured her. 'He might have blustered in there, but it doesn't affect me now the way it might once have.' She shrugged. 'Go on, get home. I'm sure you're exhausted, and Hettie and the others will be waiting to see that you're safe.'

Thea nodded. She put her arms around her sister and hugged her tightly.

'Just remember there's a home for you at Rookery House whenever you want it.'

'I know, thank you.' Prue stepped back. 'Now, off you go. I'll see you tomorrow. We've got a mobile canteen run to do so you need to get some rest.'

Chapter 54

Looking around at the other women's faces as they sat listening to the news on the wireless in the sitting room, Anna could see they were all feeling as she did: sickened, saddened and worried. The newsreader continued describing how London had been attacked last night, injuring and killing people and causing massive fires in the docks.

Eva, who was sitting next to her on the sofa, put her hand on Anna's arm. As Anna turned to look at her friend, she saw that her face was pale and drawn.

No one spoke until the newsreader had finished and then the room erupted with the sound of people talking all at once. The news had shaken them all. They'd become secure on this island, and discovering that London had been attacked had slammed the war right back into their lives.

'Are you all right?' Anna asked, leaning closer to Eva to make herself heard.

Eva shook her head. 'No, not really.' She closed her

eyes for a few moments and when she opened them, they were bright with tears. 'I suppose we knew it was likely to happen at some point, but still it is a shock that it has ...' She shook her head. 'And the ferocity of it — so many bombers ... for hours and hours. I have relations living in the East End. What has happened to them?'

Anna thought of Violet Steele, who'd come to visit her in Holloway and who ran an ambulance station not far from the docks. Was she safe?

'How can I find out? I feel helpless here.' Eva threw her arms wide. 'Living on this island has distanced us from what is going on and suddenly this hits us. We hear about it, but cannot do anything to see if our friends and family are alive and well.'

'You can write to them, but it will take time to get there because of the censor ...' Anna said.

'Will they come back?' someone asked in a loud voice.

'What if it is a start to the invasion?' another woman asked, looking worried. 'What will happen to us?'

The room fell silent. No one wanted the Nazis here in Britain, bringing with them their poisonous beliefs and rules. Anna shuddered at the thought that the place she'd fled to might be overrun by those who'd forced her and many of these women to leave their homes and families. It was a real worry that it could happen here.

'They have not come yet!' Eva's voice was loud. 'The British will fight back! It will not be so easy to invade here — not like Holland and Belgium.' She looked around the women. 'Do not despair!'

She stood up, and with a nod at Anna stalked out of

the room. Knowing Eva well, Anna could see that despite her fierce words, her friend was worried, both for what was happening in London and what might happen to the country as a whole if Hitler decided it was time to send his troops across the Channel.

The other women started to talk again, their voices anxious. Anna wished that she could go out and walk by the sea for a while, to give herself time to think, but with the nine o'clock curfew in place she could not. It reminded her again that she was still very much a prisoner in this beautiful place. Instead she picked up her book and headed out of the room and into the quiet of the dining room to read. She needed to escape for a while and stop thinking about what had happened, or what might happen.

Chapter 55

'Hello, any news from Edwin?' Thea asked, going into the kitchen of the village hall. Prue was washing up the teacups used by the mothers at the day club, which was in full swing in the main room.

Her sister turned to look at her, and Thea was shocked at how strained she looked, the dark shadows under her eyes standing out starkly, her skin much paler than usual. Prue's anxiety over Edwin was clearly taking its toll.

A week had passed since the first air raid on London, a night which had become known in the newspapers as Black Saturday, and the bombers had returned to the city every night since. News of the nightly attacks were plastered over the front of the newspapers and reported on the wireless, making anyone with family or friends in London worried over their safety.

'I had a letter from him this morning,' Prue said as Thea went to stand beside her near the sink. 'He's been moved from the hospital and is now either working in rest centres, where people go after they've been bombed, or . . . is being sent out in the middle of air raids to give first aid to people in shelters.'

Prue slapped her hand into the washing-up bowl, sending a wave of soapy water sloshing out into the sink. 'He could be hit at any time. Who'd send people out in the middle of an air raid?' Her voice grew increasingly hoarse as she battled to hold back tears.

Thea put her arm around her sister's shoulders. 'It's what's happening, I'm afraid. People are sent where they're needed – ambulance crews, firemen, FAU first aiders. It's their job.'

Prue shrugged Thea's arm away and took a step back, turning to glare at her. 'But he could get *killed*!' Tears spilled over and slid down her cheeks and she grabbed hold of the edge of the sink, bracing herself as she leaned forwards, her head hanging down.

'I know,' Thea said gently, putting her hand on Prue's shoulder. This time she didn't shrug it off. 'I'm not going to lie to you and say he'll be all right. We both know his job puts him at risk, but so do many other people's. Jack was in danger when he was with the British Expeditionary Force. My friend Violet and all her ambulance crew could be injured or killed while doing their job . . . They know it, but it doesn't stop them. It didn't stop me when I went driving ambulances in France, either, did it? You always hope you won't be injured or killed, but you know it could happen. So you make the most of every day. Even we're not immune from danger here, are we? It's far less likely, of course . . . but nowhere is completely safe now.'

Prue pulled a handkerchief out of her pocket with her wet hand and dabbed at her eyes with it. 'I know, but it's been going on night after night . . . How much longer?'

'I don't know.'

'It was bad enough worrying about Jack, but now he's safe up in Scotland training. It's Edwin who's in danger.'

'How did he sound in his letter?' Thea asked.

'Fine!' Prue frowned. 'That's the thing, he sounds very upbeat, saying he's really enjoying helping people. Told me about the families who're pouring into the rest centres who've lost everything apart from what they're standing in – their homes and belongings all gone, destroyed by the bombs.'

'That's what he wanted to do, Prue – to help people. He's making a difference and that's good. You should be proud of him.'

'I am!' Prue snapped. 'I just don't want him to bloody well get killed doing it, that's all.'

'I know.' Thea nodded sympathetically. 'There's no simple fix to this, you just have to accept it and carry on. Try not to let the worry take its toll on you.'

Prue spun round to face her again. 'You haven't got children. You don't understand!' Her face puckered and tears were threatening again.

Thea took a steadying breath before replying. Prue's words had stung her like a slap to the face.

'You're right, I don't have children, I've not had the chance . . . But I do very much care for Edwin. And I have friends who are as good as family to me there, and I'm scared for them all. I need to keep going though, carry on, because there are things I need to do here, responsibilities I need to honour. I must stay strong, I can't crumble, and neither must you, Prue.' She reached out and touched her sister's arm. 'A lot of people rely on you – all those women and children out there.' She nodded towards the main hall. 'The WI, the WVS, all the things you do. And of course Alice. You're a strong, capable woman, Prue. Edwin would hate to see you torturing yourself over him and what might or might not happen.'

Prue stared at her, her blue eyes wide, as Thea's words hit home. She took a shuddering breath, her tense shoulders dropping. 'I know what you say is right.' She blinked away more tears. 'I need to pull myself together.'

'Yes, you do.' Thea smiled at her. 'It doesn't mean you won't worry, or that you don't care, but you can't let it beat you down. No one knows how long this is all going to go on for, so you need to protect yourself, or it'll drive you under.' She put her arms around Prue and hugged her tightly.

Stepping back, she met her sister's gaze again. 'I'm always here to help you and for you to talk to. Remember, it's better to let it out than bottle it up. A worry shared is a worry halved, as they say.'

'Thank you.' Some colour was coming back into Prue's cheeks again. She managed to smile. 'I'm sorry about what I said about you not being a mother . . . you would have made a lovely one if you'd had the chance. You've been a marvellous aunt to Jack, Edwin and Alice. They all adore you.'

'It's all right, I forgive you!' Thea smiled at her.

'Thank you. You can start helping me by drying those cups if you like.'

Thea laughed as she grabbed a tea towel, relieved to see a spark returning to Prue's eyes. 'Edwin's no fool, you know, he will be careful.'

Prue nodded. 'I know. It's just worrying goes with the territory of motherhood.' She scrubbed at a cup to remove some red lipstick from the rim. 'But it's what he wants to do and I'm so proud of him.' She pulled a face. 'His father isn't though, but then he's a fool!'

'Indeed he is! I presume Victor's still doing his so-called Sunday meetings?' Thea raised her eyebrows.

'Oh yes, but strangely I haven't had time to iron his best shirt since Lizzie told us about his fancy woman.'

Thea laughed. 'Good for you!'

Chapter 56

What had she done? Anna had turned over and over in her mind what she might have done wrong to deserve being summoned here, to the camp commandant's office, but she couldn't think what it might be. She'd never broken the nine o'clock curfew or failed to do her share of work in the hotel. Her classes were going well and were popular, perhaps that was the problem. Had somebody complained? But surely teaching people how to improve their English, preparing them for their lives once they got out of here, was a good thing, wasn't it?

She sighed. Whatever it was she'd find out soon enough. Anna leaned back in her chair outside the office of the women's camp commandant. Dame Joanna Cruickshank was a woman she'd only seen briefly, but she was aware of how firmly she ran the camp. She was known for being well organised and doing her job efficiently, and wasn't afraid to pull up those who failed to do what they should. Was that about to be her?

The summons had come as a shock. She'd been in the middle of a class when one of the staff who worked with Dame Joanna had arrived to tell her that she wanted to see her and to go with her right away. Anna had quickly instructed her pupils to carry on practising what she'd just taught them and had come here.

'Miss Weissenborn.' Anna looked up to see Dame Joanna. 'Would you like to come in, please?'

Anna nodded, stood up and followed her inside. The older woman closed the door firmly behind them.

'This is Mr Charlton, a local magistrate.' Dame Joanna introduced a grey-haired man who sat on the far side of a wide desk, on the left-hand side of a row of three chairs. 'And Sergeant Miller,' she indicated the policeman who sat on the far right.

Both men nodded their heads at her and chorused, 'Good afternoon.'

'Good afternoon,' Anna managed. Dame Joanna indicated for her to sit down on the single chair placed in front of the desk, before going round behind it and seating herself in the middle chair between the two men.

Anna clasped her hands together tightly, her heart beating fast as she waited to hear what she'd done wrong. It must be something bad to have a magistrate and the policeman here.

Dame Joanna smiled at her. 'I expect you're wondering why I sent for you here today.' She raised her eyebrows, looking Anna directly in the eye.

Anna nodded, her mouth feeling as dry as the baked sand of Port St Mary's bay on a hot summer day.

'We wish to talk to you about your life here in England. I understand you came here in early 1939 to work as a domestic servant?'

'Yes.'

'And then worked as a governess and more recently as a gardener?'

'Yes.'

'But prior to coming to England you were a teacher?' Dame Joanna paused for a moment, waiting for Anna to nod her agreement, and then went on. 'And you came to England as a refugee from Nazi oppression.'

'Yes.' Anna was painfully aware of both the magistrate's and the policeman's eyes on her as she answered the older woman's questions.

'And at your tribunal you were given a category C as you were deemed to pose no risk to the security of the nation. Has that changed in any way?'

'Absolutely not.' Anna's cheeks grew warm. 'I now have even more dislike of the Nazis and all they stand for. They caused the death of my father earlier this year in Berlin. I would *never* do anything to help them.'

'I'm sorry to hear about your father,' Dame Joanna said sympathetically. 'It was exceptional that you, as a category C enemy alien, were interned, and I believe that only happened as a result of where you were living at the time. However, the reason for bringing you here today is to inform you that you are to be released.' She smiled at Anna. 'As of tomorrow morning, you will be a free woman again and can return to your home in Norfolk, assuming that it is still there for you?'

Anna gasped, putting her hand to her face. 'I can go home?'

Dame Joanna smiled. 'Yes, you can go home again. You'll be free.'

Tears filled Anna's eyes; she had never expected this. 'Thank you.' Her voice came out in a croak.

'Is a home still there for you in Norfolk?' the magistrate asked.

Anna nodded. 'Yes, Thea, who I work for and whose house I live in, has told me that it is there waiting for me when I get back.'

'Excellent.' The magistrate smiled at her. 'I'm sure they will be pleased to see you return.'

'So, tomorrow you will take the steamer from Douglas to Liverpool and you'll be given a travel warrant to get you home again,' Dame Joanna explained. 'We wish you well with your future.' She stood up, signalling that the meeting was over, and came around from behind her desk, holding out her hand to Anna. 'Good luck.'

'Thank you.' Anna shook her hand, her mind still taking in the news that she was being freed. She'd never considered that as an option when she'd been summoned here. It was astonishing . . . and utterly marvellous.

Eva stared at her for a few moments, and then her face broke into a wide beaming smile. She threw her arms around Anna and hugged her tightly. 'That is the most excellent news!' She stepped back and looked at Anna, nodding her head. 'Truly wonderful. I am so happy for you.'

Anna smiled at her friend. 'Thank you. I could not believe it when Dame Joanna told me, it felt like a dream . . .

I wish that you were being freed too.' Anna had come straight from Dame Joanna's office to the Marine Biological Research Station, wanting Eva to be the first to know.

Eva batted away the comment with her hand. 'I will be one day, and in the meantime, I need to be here to do all this. It's important work.' She gestured at the dried seaweed which she'd been packing into boxes ready to send to the mainland.

'I will miss you.'

'And I will miss you, but it is great that you will be free again and that gives me much joy. We will write to each other, yes?'

Anna nodded. 'Of course, I think we'll be friends for life. I don't think I could have got through any of this without you, Eva.'

'You would have, but perhaps you would not have volunteered for those jobs in Holloway. They kept us busy, did they not?'

'Yes, I will never forget what it was like in there.'

Eva put her arm around Anna's shoulders. 'It has taught us to appreciate many things, though. Being able to go outside when we wish, fresh air, sunshine, rain, wind on our faces ...' She laughed. 'Nothing in our life is wasted, remember that, even the bad times teach us things. Now, are you busy? Because if you're not, I would be glad of some help packing the seaweed.'

Anna stood on the deck of the steamer as it left Douglas behind, looking back at the island that had been her home for the past few months. The sense of freedom was both exhilarating and terrifying after her internment, and stepping back into the real world seemed strange. She'd become used to knowing that her life was controlled by others, that there were rules to follow; suddenly here she was out with no curfew, no limit to the places she could go, no one to censor her letters. It was what she'd dreamed of, the same as every woman she'd left behind, but the reality was going to take some getting used to.

It was hard to comprehend that, hopefully within the day – depending on the trains – she'd be back at Rookery House and could pick up her life again. Her return there would be a surprise to Thea. She hadn't written to tell her, as letters took so long to arrive that she'd be certain to beat it home. It would be wonderful to be back there again among the friends who'd done so much for her, and who even during her internment had kept on doing all they could to get her out. Had her release been a result of Thea's letters, she wondered. Had they finally had an effect?

She breathed in the salty air and watched the Isle of Man gradually grow smaller as the steamer headed south-east to Liverpool. She would never forget her time there, but she was so grateful that it was over.

Chapter 57

Having finally arrived back in Great Plumstead, just over twenty-four hours after she'd left the Isle of Man, it had taken Anna much longer to get to Rookery House from the station than she'd expected. She'd been stopped in the village by several people she'd known from the day club or the WI who'd been pleased to see her. It had been heartening to be welcomed back; it felt like a homecoming.

Now, nearing the house, she was filled with excitement, her limbs fizzing with anticipation.

She halted in the gateway, looking up at the house that she'd pictured so often in her mind since she'd been taken away in the back of the police car early that May morning. Since then, the seasons had shifted from spring into early autumn, and the leaves of the oak tree in the front garden were a dark, leathery green, the field opposite the house packed with large, leafy sugar beet which had been just small plants when she'd left. Time had moved on here, things had changed, but so had she. She'd never have wanted to be interned, but hard as it had been, it had brought her friends, given her experiences and taken her to places she'd never have gone otherwise. All of those had shaped her, and it wasn't wasted time – it had taught her so much.

A shriek from one of the upstairs windows caught her attention, and she looked up to see a shocked-looking Hettie waving a feather duster wildly at her out of the open window. Anna beamed at the sight of the older woman, waving at her in return, delighted to see her.

Hettie gestured for her to come in and disappeared from the window, no doubt making her way downstairs. Anna hurried round to the back door, but before she could open it a breathless, flushed Hettie threw it wide open and grabbed hold of her, pulling her into a tight hug.

Finally letting Anna go, Hettie stepped back and looked up to her, searching her face. 'You should have let us know you were coming, we would've come to the station to meet you.'

'There wasn't time. I only found out that I was to be released the day before yesterday, and even if I'd written to tell you, I'd have been here before you got the letter. I thought it might be a nice surprise.'

'Oh, it is! The best sort. Leave your suitcase here, we'll go and find the others. They're in the orchard picking plums.'

Leaving her suitcase in the kitchen, Anna followed Hettie outside, the older woman linking her arm through hers. 'When did you leave the Isle of Man?'

'Yesterday morning. I had hoped to be able to get back

here last night, but trains were delayed so I had to spend several hours overnight in the ladies' waiting room at Peterborough station. I managed to get a few hours' sleep luckily, and then carried on my journey here as soon as I could.'

'Well, you're here now, that's all that matters. It's good to have you back, Anna, it really is. We've missed you and it's been awful thinking of you in that prison and then the camp. Thea's never given up trying to get you out, and it looks like her trip to the Home Office finally worked. It's been hard for her not having you working alongside her too, she's missed your help badly. Luckily some of the evacuee mothers have been helping her out in the garden. And Alice, too.'

Anna frowned. 'When did Thea go to the Home Office?'

Hettie quickly explained how Blanche had helped Thea get an appointment at the Home Office through her niece working there. 'She wrote and told you about it.' Anna was surprised that it was Blanche who had helped and seemingly made all the difference to getting her freed. She would be sure to thank her when she saw her.

'While Thea was in London she got caught up in that first big air raid,' Hettie added.

Anna stopped, shocked at the thought of Thea being in London as it was battered by the bombers, having gone there to try and secure her release. 'I did not know, I did not get her letter before I left . . . We heard about the raid on the wireless though. Was she hurt?'

Hettie shook her head. 'No, she ended up helping out at the hospital where Prue's son was working.' She suddenly smiled. 'She's going to be so pleased to see you. And Marianne too. She's down at the day club now, she'll be home later this afternoon.'

Thea must have heard their voices, for she turned and spotted them as they walked towards her. Dropping her basket, plums falling to the ground unheeded, she let out a shriek and launched herself towards them, running full pelt. Catching hold of Anna, she squeezed her in a tight hug, lifting her off her feet and swinging her around.

Putting her down again, Thea kept her hands on Anna's arms and looked at her, tears running down her face. 'You're free! You've come home!'

Anna nodded, unable to speak. Her throat was thick with emotion.

'When did you get out? How are you?' Thea's eyes searched her face, looking for clues.

'Yesterday. And I am fine.' Anna explained again what had happened and how there'd been no time to write and tell them she was coming home. 'I am so pleased to be back here and see you all again.'

'It doesn't matter about not writing, the important thing is that you're free and you're here now.'

'Welcome home!' said Alice shyly, coming up to them.

'Thank you.' Anna smiled at Alice, who she hadn't had a chance to get to know very well before she'd been interned.

'I can hardly believe it.' Thea cupped her own face with her purple-stained hands. 'Have they let everyone go?'

'No, no one else that I know. Others may have gone from Port Erin, but not from where I was. I wish they were all free now too – it was hard to leave them behind.'

'It must have been you going to the Home Office that did it, Thea. It finally worked after all them letters,' Hettie said.

Thea gave a shrug. 'Perhaps. It doesn't matter, the important thing is that you're out. This calls for a celebration!' She looked at Hettie, who nodded in agreement. 'We'll have a special welcome home meal tonight. Alice, you must stay, and I'll ask Prue and Reuben to come as well.'

Sitting around the table in the kitchen of Rookery House after they'd finished a delicious meal, Anna felt as if she'd never been away. It was warm and comforting to be back here amongst people who, in the short time she'd known them, she'd come to like and care for very much. Being back with them felt right.

'Thank you very much, Hettie. That was delicious.' Anna smiled at the older woman, who had cooked a meal bursting with flavour: a cheese and egg flan, seasoned with herbs from the garden, alongside fresh homegrown vegetables, and finished off with a plum cake. Most of the ingredients for the meal had been home produced from Primrose, the chickens and the garden, which was reflected in the fine taste.

'My pleasure.' Hettie beamed at her. 'You know I like to feed people, and I daresay where you've been you wouldn't have got such good home-cooked food.'

'No, especially not in Holloway.' Anna pulled a face. 'I'll never forget that porridge on my first morning in there. It was like eating glue, nothing like what we have here.'

'What was it like in there?' Marianne asked. She'd been thrilled to see that Anna had come back when she'd come home from the day club with baby Emily, who'd grown so much in the months that Anna had been away.

'It was difficult to begin with, but I got used to it.' Anna was aware that everyone around the table was listening to her, their kind faces full of sympathy. 'Luckily, I met Eva, who became a good friend and had the cell next to me. She encouraged me to volunteer for jobs and that was good advice and made all the difference. It was not anything exciting, just sweeping up and getting meals from the kitchen, clearing up the dishes afterwards and taking them back, but then we did not have to stay in our cells most of the time and it kept us busy.'

'What about exercise? Did they let you outside?' Reuben asked.

'Just for one hour a day in a small yard with high walls. We could only see a patch of sky and I missed seeing green plants around me, so when we moved to the Isle of Man it was wonderful to have so much space, light, sky and green around us again.' She smiled at the memory. 'I know I was still interned there, but it was a beautiful place to be.'

'We didn't know where you'd been sent to. We were worried that you'd been on that ship that was sunk, the *Arandora Star*,' Hettie said.

Anna nodded. 'We heard about that; it was awful.'

They fell silent for a moment, before Prue asked, 'What did you do to pass the time there?'

Anna told them about the walks she had taken with Eva, setting up her English classes and helping with the seaweed collection, going into more depth than she'd been able to in her letters. Some of those, she expected, were still sitting on a desk on the Isle of Man waiting to be censored.

After they'd finished and had cleared the table, washed and dried the dishes, Prue and Alice had headed off home, and Reuben back to his railway carriage house. Anna went outside with Thea to shut the chickens safely in their coop for the night and check on Primrose.

Now, leaning over the gate of the meadow to watch Primrose grazing in the mellow evening light as the last of the swallows flitted over the grass, Anna turned to face Thea. 'Thank you for everything you did to get me freed. I appreciate it so much that you didn't give up and I am sure that you going to the Home Office made the difference.'

Thea's bright blue eyes met hers. 'You should never have been interned . . . ' She put her hand on Anna's arm. 'And I was determined to get you out again, no matter how long it took. I only wish it had happened sooner, not taken over three months.'

'Please do not be cross about it, because it was not all bad. I made good friends and will keep in touch with them, and I have learned from my experiences and had the opportunity to spend time in a lovely place.'

Thea smiled. 'Your positivity does you credit.'

Anna glanced out across the meadow where Primrose's tail was swishing away the flies, her toffee-coloured coat glowing warmly in the rays of the sun which was making its way down to the horizon. 'There are people back in Germany who are being treated far worse than I was. I may have had my freedom taken away for a while, but I was never badly treated.' She turned to face Thea again. 'Thinking about what's happening out there puts what happened to me in perspective.' She smiled. 'I am back now and I want to put it behind me and get on with my life. I am looking forward to working in the garden again, as long as you still have work for me to do.'

Thea laughed. 'There's *always* work to do here, and it's going to be so lovely to have you back here helping me again.'

Chapter 58

Prue reached for a cluster of plump blackberries, taking care not to catch the nearby web in which a garden spider sat patiently waiting for a meal. She, and other members of Great Plumstead's WI and mothers from the day club, were out on another blackberrying expedition making the most of a bumper crop. Like last year, the WI had been able to buy in extra sugar specifically in order to turn the abundance of fruit ripening in the hedgerows around the village into jam. With rationing biting hard, food was at a premium, so they couldn't waste any of the free fruit. The jam they'd made last year had been very popular, and had sold well on the WI's weekly stall at Wykeham market and in the village's grocery shops. The jars of jam they'd already made this autumn were selling well on the stall.

Adding the berries to her basket, Prue glanced at Anna, who was picking nearby. It was five days since she'd been freed and had settled back into life at Rookery House, and she'd come to the WI meeting earlier in the week.

'Have you heard from any of your friends who're still on the Isle of Man?' Prue asked.

Anna turned and looked at her, shaking her head. 'Not yet. I have written to Eva a couple of times, but letters going in and out of there are censored, so it takes longer for them to get to her. I miss her.'

'It must have been hard to leave her and the others behind. Do you think she'll be released soon?'

'I hope so.' Anna reached for some berries just above her head. 'She keeps herself busy with her work at the Marine Biological Research Station, running the seaweed collection and doing other jobs there, too. She ran her own laboratory at a London university before she was interned, so I think the research station was very glad of her offer to help.'

'I'm sure they were.' Prue had been interested to hear about the seaweed collection, which Anna had told them about on her first night back. Like their blackberry picking, it was an example of people making the most of what they had on their doorstep, rather than relying on imports from other countries.

'Eva encouraged me to work there as well, doing something that I was good at and loved.'

'Your teaching?'

'Yes.' Anna smiled. 'I did not know if anyone would be interested, but there were many women who wanted to learn and improve their English, and it was very enjoyable to help them, they made excellent progress.'

Prue watched the young woman's face as she spoke,

seeing how her eyes were lit with enthusiasm. 'You must miss that.'

'Yes, I do, but it is even better to be free.'

They fell silent for a while, while the other women chattered in the background, with the occasional chortle or squeak from some of the babies who were in their prams parked nearby. Some of them were sitting up watching what was going on, safely secured by their baby reins, while others were napping.

'It would be lovely if you could combine the two again, being free and teaching, wouldn't it?' Prue asked. She was thinking that Anna's talents were rather wasted tending vegetables. 'Couldn't you do some around here?'

Anna frowned. 'But I do not know any women around here who would need to improve their English, and ...' She glanced at the women working at intervals along the hedgerow around the field. 'You all speak English far better than me, it is your native language.' She smiled. 'So none of you need lessons from me!'

Prue shrugged. 'It was just a thought. You clearly love to teach.'

Anna nodded. 'I do, and I will be able to do it again one day, but for now I am happy to work in the garden at Rookery House. It is a lovely place and I owe much to Thea for not giving up on trying to get me freed. I know she found it hard having to manage on her own, Hettie told me. I could not betray her loyalty. My work is at Rookery House for the moment. I can return to teaching in the future because Thea needs my help now.'

'It was hard for Thea after you were interned, but it's been much better since she's had some help from the

363

evacuee mothers and Alice,' Prue said. 'She's delighted you're back, but not because of you working in the garden. You being free was the most important thing to her.'

'Anna! I heard you were home, it's so wonderful to see you.'

Prue turned around to see Blanche hurrying towards them, having just arrived to help with the picking.

'Hello, Blanche.' Anna smiled warmly at the older woman. 'I have much to thank you for. You helped Thea get her appointment at the Home Office.'

Blanche's cheeks grew pink. 'I was glad to help. I only wish my niece had started working there a few months earlier so we could have got Thea down there quicker.' She reached out and touched Anna's arm. 'How are you?'

'I am fine, happy to be here again. I missed Great Plumstead and everyone very much,' Anna said. 'But I made some friends in prison too!'

'I was glad to hear you were moved to the Isle of Man, that must have been much better than Holloway,' Blanche said.

'Yes, it was, but still a prison camp . . .'

Prue quietly slipped away, leaving the two of them to talk, glad to see that Blanche's former animosity towards Anna had gone for ever. Her genuine interest in Anna now, and her help to get Thea an appointment at the Home Office was gratifying to see. Anna's arrival in Great Plumstead had brought changes not just to her, but to others. She'd not only gained from coming here but had also brought a much-needed change and clarity to the community.

*

A little while later, when the blackberrying party had moved on to the hedgerow bordering a lane in the village, Prue went to work near Thea. She'd been thinking about her conversation with Anna and couldn't let go of the niggling thought that the young woman's skills could be better used. It might not strictly be any of her business, but she had to say something.

'How are you getting on?' Prue asked her sister.

'Good.' Thea popped a plump blackberry into her mouth and chewed.

'It's a good crop again this year and we'll have plenty of jam to sell.' Prue added another handful of berries to her basket. 'Thea, I was talking to Anna earlier about her teaching on the Isle of Man and how much she enjoyed it. She's clearly a passionate teacher.'

Thea glanced at her and nodded. 'I know.'

'Well, don't you think that's what she should be doing . . . using her experience, skills and talent to teach, rather than working as a gardener?'

Thea didn't say anything, just carried on picking.

'What do you think?' Prue urged her, wondering if she'd gone too far. Her sister had put a huge amount of effort into getting Anna freed, and having her back working alongside her would take the weight off her shoulders.

'I happen to agree with you.' Thea turned to face her. 'But it's not my decision to make, is it? Anna could teach around here if she found a job, and still live at Rookery House if she could find work near enough. I would never tie her into working in the garden.' She frowned. 'Is that what she thinks?'

'No! Rather the opposite, she feels loyal to you and wants to honour her work at Rookery House, especially after all you did to get her freed.'

Thea bit her bottom lip. 'But I didn't do that to have her come back to work for me ... It was about her being *free*. That was what drove me on.' She rubbed her purple-stained fingers over her forehead, leaving a streak of blackberry juice on her skin. 'I know for a fact that there's a shortage of teachers in some schools – Violet was telling me that a headteacher friend of hers had tried to persuade her to go back and take up a vacant post at her school. I wonder if ...' She paused. 'It might mean Anna having to go away again though.'

'What are you thinking?' Prue asked.

'Leave it with me. I've got an idea and I'll look into it. Don't say anything to Anna about it, will you?'

'Of course not. Let me know what you find out, won't you?'

Thea nodded. 'It might come to nothing, but it's worth a try.'

Chapter 59

The letter Thea had been waiting for all week had finally arrived in the afternoon post. She picked it up off the mat inside the front door and quickly slit the envelope open, eager to discover what it had to say. She skimmed through the letter, pleased to see what her friend had found out. Now she could approach Anna with her suggestion.

Tucking the letter back into the envelope, she went through to the kitchen where Anna was making some tea. The pair of them had just come in for their tea break, but Hettie and Marianne were out at the day club, so it was just the two of them when they sat down at the table with steaming cups of tea in front of them.

'I've just heard from Violet.' Thea nodded at the envelope she'd placed on the table.

'How is she?' Anna asked. 'I hope she's all right, still keeping safe in the air raids.'

'She's fine. Very busy at Station 75.' The raids were still

continuing in London, without a single night's break since Black Saturday. 'One of the reasons she's written to me is because of an idea I had, and which Violet has helped me with.' Thea smiled at Anna. 'It's something we were wondering if you'd like to do.'

Anna's brown eyes widened. 'What do you mean?'

Thea took a sip of her tea while she decided the best way to put her suggestion to Anna. In the end she chose to say it straight out. 'How would you like to go back to teaching?'

'I would of course, and I *will* when the war is over.' Anna gave a shrug. 'But for now, I'm very happy working here for you – I enjoy it very much.'

Thea nodded. 'But wouldn't it be better to use your talents *now*? There's a shortage of teachers and Violet has a friend, Miss Louisa Gray, who's a headmistress at a school which has a vacancy for a languages teacher. She's very interested in interviewing you for the job.'

Anna stared at her, clearly shocked. 'But I am *needed* here, Thea. The garden is a lot of work and I know it was hard for you managing alone while I was interned.'

'Yes, it was,' Thea agreed. 'But I found help, and I could do so again if you were to take this teaching job. Though I must warn you that it's not here in Norfolk, but in Wiltshire, at Longleat, where the school has been evacuated to – it's a grand house rather like Great Plumstead Hall.'

Anna sighed. 'I will not leave you again to struggle . . . You helped get me free and I owe you my loyalty.'

'I appreciate that, but honestly, Anna, you don't owe me anything. I would be delighted to see you using your skills, if that's what you want to do, and I think it would be as great a contribution to the country as growing vegetables. Most people can help in a garden, but not many can teach well. I would hate to see your talents being wasted here when there is a real need for them elsewhere.'

Anna took a slow sip of tea, a pensive expression clouding her face. 'If I got the job I would have to leave here *again*.'

'I know, but you can always come back in the holidays. This will always be your home, for as long as you want it to be.' Thea reached out and touched Anna's arm. 'It wouldn't be the end of anything. You'd just be going off to do your work somewhere else like so many are doing now.'

A smile tugged at the corners of Anna's mouth. 'It would be good to be teaching again ... Are you sure you'd find someone else to replace me?'

Thea nodded. 'I have someone in mind who might like to – Alice. She worked here a lot while you were away and seemed to enjoy it.'

'Like her brother did.' Anna smiled. 'Would I have to go for an interview? What did Violet say?'

'The headmistress – Miss Gray – said that if you're interested in the post then you should write to her telling her about your experience and send any references you have, and then she will arrange to interview you by telephone.'

Anna frowned. 'I only have one reference, from Mr Jeffries, my last employer. I have nothing from the schools that I taught at in Berlin.'

'Doesn't matter. I will write you one. And Violet has met you and has already given Miss Gray her glowing recommendation of your character. So ... what do you think? Do you want to apply for the job?'

Anna's face broke into a wide smile. 'Yes, I do, as long as you are happy for me to do so. I will be sad to leave here, but if I can come back again it will not be so bad.'

'I'm delighted you're going to apply.' Thea smiled at her. 'And you can always come back, Anna. My home is your home, you have my word on that.'

Chapter 60

Anna paced up and down the hallway of Rookery House, frequently glancing at her watch, willing the hands to move faster around to three o'clock, the time that had been arranged for Miss Gray to telephone her for her interview.

What if she couldn't answer any questions, Anna thought. Or if she forgot what made a good lesson. Imagine if she became too tongue-tied and couldn't say anything sensible at all. Who would want to employ her then? Miss Gray was the head of a school where parents paid a lot of money to send their daughters – she wouldn't want anyone in her school who couldn't even hold a sensible conversation, let alone convince her that she knew how to teach.

Anna stopped, staring down at the coloured smudges of light on the tiled floor where the sunlight was streaming through the stained glass in the front door . . . If she failed to impress her and wasn't offered the job, then she'd be happy to stay here working at Rookery House. But though instantly made her feel better, and her shoulders relaxed. If this came to nothing she'd still be in a very good place.

The telephone suddenly started to ring, making her jump and her heart race. She checked her watch and it was three o'clock exactly. Hand hovering over the telephone receiver for a moment, she took a deep breath and then picked it up.

'Hello, Rookery House.'

'Good afternoon. This is Miss Gray. Am I speaking to Miss Anna Weissenborn?' The headmistress's voice was clear, no-nonsense, but also had a touch of warmth to it.

'Yes, good afternoon, Miss Gray.'

'I read your letter carefully, and your references, and was impressed with your experience and how well you are regarded by those that know you and have employed you.' Anna had explained in the letter she'd sent with the references from Mr Jeffries and Thea, about her previous teaching work back in Berlin, her job with Thomas and her classes on the Isle of Man. 'Now,' Miss Gray continued, 'I'd like you to tell me about how you teach, what you think is important and how you get the best from your pupils.'

Anna's thoughts skittered off in many directions as she tried to think how best to reply. How *did* she teach and get the best from her students? Teaching was so natural to her – it was her vocation. It was hard to pin down what she instinctively did, like trying to catch the mist in your hand on a foggy morning.

'I, umm . . .' she began haltingly. She took a steadying breath and went on, 'I know from my own learning experience that if I am enjoying something as I am being taught, then it is so much easier to learn. My aim is always to make lessons as enjoyable as possible for my pupils. I am clear about the point of what they are learning and how it will help them, so that they understand why they are being taught. Languages can be tricky to learn, so I encourage my pupils to practise often and I share with them useful skills that would help them if they had to speak that language outside the classroom. I do not want to just teach from a textbook, I want to teach them real-life, everyday language – the women I taught on the Isle of Man needed to learn how to communicate when they went shopping with employers . . . ' Anna found her passion for teaching taking over and she carried on expressing it to Miss Gray, giving her examples of what she'd done from her time in Berlin and with Thomas. 'I love what I do,' she finally added.

'It certainly sounds like it!' Miss Gray chuckled. 'I can feel your enthusiasm coming down the telephone wires, Anna. It's jolly good to hear.'

'Thank you.' Anna's cheeks grew warm. She hoped she hadn't talked too much.

'As our school is boarding, staff are expected to assist with extracurricular activities, not just their own lessons, such as covering evening prep and helping with Wednesday after-noon games and Saturday afternoon activities such as walks, games, crafts, drama, et cetera, depending on weather and season. I hope that is something you would be prepared to do. You would of course live here at Longleat with all your meals and accommodation provided, but you won't have holidays free to go home if you wish. I checked with the authorities and they are happy for you to move jobs to work

373

here.' She paused for a moment. 'How does that sound? I'd like to offer you the position of languages teacher for a trial of one term, and if we're both happy with how things have gone after that make it permanent.'

Tears filled Anna's eyes, and she swallowed the lump that had risen in her throat. 'That sounds wonderful. Thank you. I would like to accept your offer.'

'Excellent!' Miss Gray's voice was hearty. 'I will send a letter of confirmation of your job offer today, if you can sign a copy and return it to me, and I'd like you to start as soon as possible. We're only a few weeks into term here, so if you can be in position quickly the girls won't have to put up with my rather poor French lessons for much longer.'

'I will be there as soon as I can,' Anna said, wondering if Thea would have expected her to be going so soon.

'Of course. Let me know when you're arriving, I'll arrange for you to be met at the station. I look forward to meeting you soon, Anna, and I'm sure you will be a tre- mendous asset to our school. Goodbye then.' She rang off.

Anna replaced the receiver, smiling happily. She had a teaching job again! She'd be imparting her love of lan- guages to pupils, and the thought was like a warm hug as a tide of excitement welled up in her. The only problem was she had to leave here to do it, but Thea had encouraged her and said that this would always be her home to return to – she could have her teaching job, Rookery House and all who lived here in her life. The best of both worlds.

'That's wonderful news. Congratulations!' Thea jumped down from the ladder where she was picking apples in the orchard, beaming at Anna, and threw her arms around her, hugging her tightly.

'Thank you.' Anna hugged her back. 'Are you sure you are happy about me going away to teach?' she asked as they loosened hold of each other and stepped back.

'Absolutely. I will miss you, but I'm thrilled that you'll be doing what you're passionate about. That's so important in life.'

'Have you asked Alice if she would like to work for you?'

'Not yet, I was waiting until you'd had your interview with Miss Gray, but I'll ask her later. Do you know when you're starting?'

'As soon as possible. Miss Gray's teaching French at the moment and is keen for me to take over.'

'If you left on Friday, it would give you the weekend to settle in and you'd be ready to start teaching on Monday,' Thea suggested.

That would give her just another three days here, Anna thought. Three days to get herself organised and prepare herself to start again in a new place.

She nodded. 'I think that is a good idea.' She looked around the orchard and over towards the garden, and then back at Rookery House. 'I will miss everything and everybody here, though.'

'I know, but it will still be here for you when you come back in the holidays. If you want to, that is.'

'Oh, I will, absolutely. Rookery House is my home now. I might not always be here, but it will always be in my heart.'

Chapter 61

'What did you say?' Prue asked, putting the last items of cutlery into place on the kitchen table ready for tea. Thea had already asked her whether she'd mind if she offered Alice a full-time job at Rookery House when Anna left, only she hadn't let on to Alice that she knew about the job offer.

'Yes!' Alice beamed at her. 'I'm so happy to have a proper job there. It's been fun working there this summer, and so much better than getting a job in an office like some of my friends have done. I like being outside and Thea's good fun.'

'I'm delighted for you. I've seen how much you enjoyed working there while Anna was interned.'

But not everyone will be so happy for her, Prue thought.

Victor wouldn't. Alice helping out over the summer had been one thing, but a regular job working as a gardener wasn't what he'd deem good enough for his daughter. He'd had higher hopes for her, ultimately including marriage to someone he approved of. However, Alice had ideas of her own and wasn't afraid to stand up for them.

'You'll have to tell your father when he gets home.' Prue glanced at her watch. It was nearly a quarter past five; he'd be back soon, ready for his tea. 'Just be prepared for him not to like it,' she warned her.

Alice frowned. 'Edwin worked there and Father didn't mind that.'

'He did actually. He told Thea that she shouldn't employ him, but she said she'd do what she wanted.' Prue couldn't help smiling. 'Anyway, Edwin's situation was different from yours, with your father sacking him and throwing him out because he was a conscientious objector.'

'Do you think he'll throw me out? I could just go and live at Thea's – she'll have room for me with Anna leaving.'

Prue's stomach clenched. The thought of Alice moving out, leaving just her and Victor living here, was horrifying. She knew her daughter would go one day, but at just sixteen years old she hoped that she wouldn't leave just yet.

'I hope not. Let's just play it by ear and see how he takes it. You can always say you'll move out before he has the chance to say you *should*. Call his bluff on it – he might not like the idea of you leaving,' Prue suggested, knowing that Alice was one of Victor's few weaknesses; he did love his daughter and she suspected he would hate the idea of her going to live at Rookery House. He would even tolerate her working there as long as she still lived at home.

Alice nodded. 'Do you think it's best I play down how much I want this job? Say it's just a stopgap until I decide what I want to do?'

'Absolutely!' Prue laughed. 'You've clearly learned a lot over the years living with him.'

'You taught me well, Ma.' Alice grinned at her. 'I know Father's not an easy man. I've watched how you handle him.'

'You know, not all men are like him, Alice. They're not all so . . . ' Prue's heart ached at the thought of her daughter having had to grow up observing how she was always so careful around Victor, judging when to say something and when it was best not to. Knowing that the safest way to get certain things done was to gently sow the seed of an idea in him, so that when it came to it Victor would think it was his idea and be more likely to agree to it. It had been like living with a wildfire, never quite knowing which way the wind would blow it next. She hoped her daughter would never get involved with a man like him.

'I know that, Ma. Don't worry. I know enough kind, level-headed men to know that Father's a hot-headed tyrant at times. Uncle Reuben, Edwin and Jack aren't like that.' Alice gave a sigh. 'It's taught me to be careful when it comes to choosing a potential husband, though that's a very long way off yet!'

'I'm glad to hear it. You've got plenty of time yet and should enjoy yourself,' Prue said, straining the carrots out of the saucepan in which they'd been cooking.

'Why *did* you marry him, Ma?' Alice's blue eyes held Prue's.

Prue's cheeks grew warm. 'If I hadn't done then you wouldn't be here,' she said, avoiding Alice's question.

'I know, but he's not the type of man I would ever have thought someone like you would love.' Alice put her hand over her mouth. 'I'm sorry, Ma, I shouldn't have said that . . . it's not my business and, like you said, if you hadn't married him then I wouldn't exist – so I'm glad you did.'

Prue put her hand on her daughter's shoulder. 'Let's just say I was a lot younger and naive in those days, and besides, there weren't so many men around to marry. Many of the lads I'd known growing up were killed during the Great War, leaving more women than men of my generation. Look at Aunt Thea. She's never married since her fiancé was killed in France.'

'So, Father was one of the few left . . .' Alice frowned. 'But he'd already been married, and Jack and Edwin's mother died.'

Prue nodded. 'Yes, and he was left with two small boys to care for.'

'I bet they were pleased you married him.'

'I was very happy to become a mother to them, too.' Prue quickly turned around and busied herself taking the casserole out of the oven, not wanting to discuss this any further. She'd feel uncomfortable talking about it with anyone, but especially her daughter. She didn't want to admit that it was the chance to become a mother to those two dear little boys that had been her reason for marrying Victor.

The opening of the front door heralded Victor's return, and for once Prue was glad he was back. It would prevent Alice from asking any more awkward questions.

Alice had the sense to wait until Victor had eaten his tea, stuffing the food in and clearing first his plate and then his pudding bowl, before she told him about her job. She'd seen Prue do it often enough, knowing that his temper was always better when he had a full stomach.

'I was offered a temporary job today, Father,' Alice said, smiling at him sweetly. 'Just something to tide me over until I find something better.'

Victor looked at his daughter, his ice-blue eyes instantly alert. 'What's that?'

'Just taking over from Anna, working in the garden at Rookery House. You know I've been helping out over the summer, and so it's an easy job for me to do for a little while before I go off and join one of the women's services.'

Prue bit on her bottom lip to stop herself smiling at Alice slipping in the bit about joining one of the women's services. That would undoubtedly take her away from home, which Victor wouldn't like. Compared to that, her continuing to help out at Rookery House was nothing to complain about; she'd still be living here and working in the village.

'You're too young to do any of that service nonsense,' Victor said, fiddling with the spoon in his empty bowl.

'That's what I thought, Father,' Alice agreed. 'So, a job here in the village, where I can stay living at home with you and Ma, and still be contributing to the war effort by growing food, is perfect for now. Don't you think?'

Victor flicked a glance at Prue, who forced her expression to remain neutral. He was like a fish on a hook about to be reeled in, and she was enjoying the spectacle very much.

Returning his gaze to Alice, he nodded. 'Good idea.' With that he stood up and went off to his study as he always did.

Alice and Prue waited until he'd gone before they dared

look at each other. But once the kitchen door shut behind him and they'd heard the opening and closing of his study door, they both broke into beaming smiles.

'That was very well played,' Prue said. 'Not a peep of resistance from him. You should watch out, the government will be snapping you up to handle important negotiations with tricky individuals.'

Alice pulled a face. 'Not yet, though. I'm going to enjoy myself working for Thea for a while.' Her face grew suddenly serious. 'I do want to go off and do something in the women's services sometime, Ma. I'm not sure what yet, if it would be the WAAFs, Wrens or whatever, but I want to get out there and see some more of the world like Jack and Edwin are doing. You never know, they might bring in conscription for women as well and I'll be made to go.'

Prue nodded and forced a smile. 'Of course, but until you do decide, we need to make the most of you being here.' She reached out and squeezed her daughter's hand, fighting back the gut-wrenching feeling that this awful war was going to end up carrying all of her children off to distant places before it was done. But not for a while yet, she hoped.

Chapter 62

Anna looked out of her bedroom window over the back garden of Rookery House, drinking in the view. She'd already been around saying a private farewell to everything this morning after an early breakfast; enjoying letting the chickens out of their coop and watching them wander off around the orchard to forage. She'd taken Primrose out to the meadow after Thea had milked her, saying goodbye to the gentle cow before touring the garden and meeting Reuben and Bess on their way to work. He'd wished her well and said he'd see her in the holidays. This slow, methodical farewell was important to her; last time she'd left she'd been snatched away without warning, with no chance to imprint everything on her mind to remember while she was gone.

Now, with her suitcases packed and ready on her bed, it was almost time to leave for the station. She was excited to be starting a new teaching job, but also felt a tinge of sadness at having to leave here and all those whom she lived with. They'd become like family to her. A teaching job nearby that would have allowed her to still live here would have been perfect, but as life had shown her, things rarely worked out exactly as you'd like them to. She might be going away but she'd have Rookery House to come home to in the holidays, so she should look on it as having the best of both worlds.

A gentle knock at the door brought her attention back to the present. 'Come in,' she called.

The door opened and Thea stepped inside. 'Are you ready? Only we need to get going, you mustn't miss your train.'

Anna nodded and smiled. 'Yes I am.'

Thea picked up her cases and started towards the door.

'Wait!' Anna hurried over to her. 'Thank you for all you've done for me, Thea. I cannot ever hope to repay you for your kindness.'

Thea put the cases down. 'There's no debt, Anna. As long as you're safe, well and happy, that's all that matters to me. You're just going away for work and will come home again.'

'Thank you. This does feel like home. And you, Hettie, Reuben, Marianne and Emily are like my family now.' She threw her arms around Thea and hugged her tightly.

'And you're part of our family too,' Thea said as she loosened her arms around Anna. 'I love that about this house, it gathers people and they become part of our family – blood ties don't matter here, it's friendship, caring and sharing that do.' She smiled, her bright blue eyes warm. 'Come on, the others are waiting downstairs to escort you to the station – you're getting quite a send-off!'

Anna was pleased to see Prue and Alice waiting for them at the station, joining Thea, Hettie, Marianne and baby Emily to wave her off.

'The school is very lucky to have you join them,' Prue said, walking beside her on to the platform after Anna had bought her ticket.

'I'm lucky to be going there,' Anna said, smiling at her. 'I'm glad Alice is taking over from me, I was worried about leaving Thea without help again. Can I ask you something?' She put her arm on Prue's to hold her back so that the others walked on ahead of them out of earshot. 'Was it you who suggested to Thea that I should be teaching? Remember our talk when we were blackberrying?'

Prue's eyes, which were the same bright shade of blue as Thea's, met hers. She nodded. 'Yes. I hope you don't mind, but I hate to see talent go to waste, and as it turned out Thea was thinking along the same lines as well.'

'Thank you. I would never have had this chance without you nudging us into action. Though I would also have been happy to stay and work at Rookery House.'

'I know, but if teaching is your vocation then it's what you should be doing.'

'What are you two chatting about?' Thea said, coming over to them. 'The train will be here soon.'

Anna glanced at Prue, who smiled back at her.

'Nothing for you to worry about,' Prue said, putting her arm through Anna's and leading her over to the others.

'There's plenty of food and a bottle of cold tea and

another of water in here,' Hettie said, indicating the packed basket she'd brought for Anna to take with her. 'You can't rely on being able to get anything on the train and if you get delayed, I don't want you going hungry or thirsty. There's a couple of jars of honey to go on your porridge as well.'

'Thank you. I am going to miss your lovely cooking, Hettie.' Anna put her arms around the older woman and hugged her tightly. 'I promise I will write and tell you all about how I am getting on.'

'I'll be waiting for your letters.' Hettie's eyes were bright with tears behind her glasses as she let Anna go and stepped back.

Anna had received hugs and good wishes from all of them by the time the train steamed into the station. Her heart beating fast, she opened the door and climbed aboard with her luggage, quickly finding a seat by a window so she could see them. She slid open the window so she could carry on talking to them until the last moment.

'Write and let us know that you've got there all right,' Hettie said.

'I will.'

The guard blew his whistle, and the engine at the head of the train responded with chuffs of smoke as the driver prepared to leave.

Anna's eyes filled with tears and she put her hand out of the window. 'Goodbye. Look after yourselves until we meet again.'

Reaching up, Thea took hold of Anna's hand and squeezed it. 'Go and enjoy yourself. We'll be waiting for you when you come home.'

The train began to move, and Thea had to let go. Anna waved out of the window and continued to look back as long as she could. They were her family now and she'd come back again. Leaving them was hard, but knowing they were here to return to made this parting easier. It wasn't goodbye, just farewell for a while.

Thea waited until the train rounded the bend and disappeared from sight, a mixture of gladness and sadness in her heart.

'We spend far too much time waving people off these days.' Prue linked her arm through Thea's. 'I always try to remember that though the trains have taken them away, they can and will bring them back again.'

Thea smiled at her sister. 'I know. We just need to keep carrying on in the meantime.'

'Anna's been very much a success story, you know,' Prue said. 'She's gone through a lot and is still positive, happy and has a great deal to offer. And she's had a lasting effect on people in this village. Those girls she's going to teach are jolly lucky to be having her.'

They made their way out through the booking office and into the station yard. The stationmaster was talking to Hettie, Marianne and Alice, his voice animated.

Seeing them, he stopped and directed a question to them. 'Have you heard the news?'

Thea frowned. 'No, what's happened?' Her immediate thought was that something terrible had happened with the war. An invasion wasn't under way, was it? If so, the church bells would have been ringing out across the village, but they'd remained silent since the night of the false alarm several weeks ago.

'They've only gone and requisitioned Great Plumstead Hall. It's going to be turned into a convalescent hospital again, like it was in the Great War,' he said.

'That'll bring a few more changes around here then,' Prue said. 'I remember what it was like last time. I used to help out there.'

'I was a kitchen maid there,' Hettie said.

Thea listened as the conversation turned to reminiscing about the Hall's past as a hospital, her thoughts drifting to the changes it would bring to the village. There would be an influx of staff, as well as patients and visitors. Nothing stayed the same for long in this war. Changes came along all the time and they'd just have to roll with them, doing what they could to get through it.

Acknowledgements

With all my books, I would be lost without the wonderful archives where I can research the lives of those who lived through the war years, and discover gems that inspire my stories. Thank you to the Imperial War Museum and the Royal Voluntary Service, formerly the WVS. Thank you to Norfolk library service for supplying many research books and for access to local newspapers from the 1940s.

The team at Sphere have done a magnificent job in bringing the book together. Thank you to my editor Rebecca Farrell, Tamsyn Berryman, Francesca Banks and Steve Gove.

Thank you to my fabulous agent, Felicity Trew, who supports me through the ups and downs of a writer's life.

A big thank you to all the bloggers and readers who give their time to read and share their thoughts and reviews on my books.

My fellow writers are a great support and I appreciate

their friendship, company, wise words and listening ears. Thank you especially to Pam Brooks, Victoria Connelly, Elaine Everest, Fiona Ford, Jean Fullerton, Jenni Keer, Lizzie Lamb, Clare Marchant, Heidi-Jo Swain, Claire Wade and Ian Wilfred. Belonging to the RNA's Norfolk and Suffolk chapter and the Strictly Saga Group is a great joy – thank you all.

Finally, thank you to David, who listens and supports me in all I do.